"Kali. Durga. The Bl
drinker of blood."

Her mouth gaped and clashed shut, the bloodstained tusks champing. That ghoulish face recalled the horrors I had witnessed since the case began – the crimson leech and the poisonous lizard, Hope dead, and Master Caradoc, and little Sarah. There was an aura of obscene flirtatiousness in her dance. A girdle of skulls clocked out chalky cadences with each sway, each spin, each undulation. Blood dripped from a fowl she held, blood spattered the Queen's body, blood filmed the room with a scarlet haze so thick I felt the salty tang of it on my tongue and fought back the sickness in my throat. The Queen gave a smothered cry and flung Lady Byron aside. Her sword came up and across with the practised slash of a battle-tried fighter. She severed one of the many writhing arms. It fell to the floor and wriggled like a snake while the black blood wrapped itself in a cloak around the dancing goddess.

"Kali, who drinks blood."

Also by Esther M. Friesner

New York by Knight
Elf Defence

Druid's Blood

Esther M. Friesner

Published by arrangement with
NAL PENGUIN INC. NEW YORK

First published in Great Britain in 1989
by HEADLINE BOOK PUBLISHING PLC

ISBN 0 7472 3312 8

Printed and bound in Great Britain by
Collins, Glasgow

HEADLINE BOOK PUBLISHING PLC
Headline House
79 Great Titchfield Street
London W1P 7FN

For my husband, W.J.
Who gets to compose the music
(With a little help from Vaughn Williams)
When they make this one into a movie
If I have anything to say about it.

CONTENTS

PROLOGUE

His Last Curtain Call

"*Porca Madonna!* Where in the name of all holy is he?"

Maestro Bertoldi drew back the heavy burlap curtain to steal a peek at the house. A cold sweat spangled his brow. Only once before in his long career as a travelling theatrical entrepreneur had it been necessary to tell an American audience that the show would not go on. The scars from that last announcement's aftermath still twitched and smarted when the weather was about to change, a dearly purchased barometer. No matter their many different races and governments, the Americans all took their theatre seriously.

The divine Sarah studied herself in a hand mirror, oblivious to her employer's distress. She made a minor correction in the line of her lip rouge, but remained dissatisfied. She never was completely content with her appearance or her performance. That was the secret to remaining a great actress with a living Art, so far as she was concerned.

"I said, 'Where is he?' " Maestro Bertoldi grabbed her elbow, forcing her to face him. "Damn the man, I should have known better than to hire a Briton into my troupe, even one so talented. They are a mysterious people, as unreachable as that spell-shrouded isle of theirs. They only let you in when *they* choose. Ah, if only he had not proved himself to be such a great talent . . ." Maestro Bertoldi's balding head shook slowly from side to side, his rotund body steeped in regret. "He is not in his dressing room, he is nowhere backstage, he is not even with one of the upstairs whores—"

"Surprising." Sarah made a small moue of amusement. Like all her actions, it was meticulously controlled. Control: that too was the secret. Passion was only an appendage of control. Alas, it was something the elusive British actor had never learned. For him, passion was all, and all was a passionate self-immersion in the role to be played.

Maestro Bertoldi's glare was meant to be piercing and deadly as a Shakesperean poignard. It came up blunt against

Sarah's cool disdain. "What is so funny about this? Perhaps you would like it, *Madame,* were I to send you before the footlights to announce that the play is cancelled? Have you seen the house? Dons from the great western outposts, *Mynheers* from the eastern trading centers, *voyageurs* from the south, redmen of the Seven Nations, and a sprinkling of joy-seeking Turks and Venetians from Florida thrown in, just to make our doom assured! These are not the sort of people who accept apologies."

Sarah shrugged with Gallic fatalism. "I never did like playing Peoria. You get such a rough element. Never mind. Tell them the bill has been changed. We can do *The Shame of Maudie Jones* without him."

Maestro Bertoldi clapped a hand to his brow. "You would give these ruffians a moral tale when they are expecting a play of murder, intrigue, deception, masterful deduction? Oh, I curse the day I ever chanced upon that copy of the *Strand* magazine!"

"No one obliged you to steal that story and turn it into a play," Sarah observed.

Maestro Bertoldi shook his head again, wondering at the predicament into which his own ambition had led him. "It was such a fine tale, such a rivetting character! Who would ever think that a simple British doctor could create such unnatural life on paper? I swear there must be some of their dark magic in him."

"He was not identified as one of the Golden Brotherhood in the magazine. The editors would not overlook such an important fact about one of their contributors. He is simply a talented writer."

"If he is so talented, why has he written no further adventures of the great detective? Surely the man has not ceased his consultations. There must have been other cases after 'The Crimson Cryptogram'!"

Sarah gave the little Italian a look of disgust. "Why should he write more tales? So you can steal them for the stage? You sound as if that doctor wrote about a real person! He is only a character in a story, this great detective of yours. The author tired of him and turned to other topics, if he has continued his writing career at all. Why should a physician waste time on such sensational trip-trap?"

"A *British* physician has time aplenty on his hands, what with the network of the Golden Brotherhood. I hear that their healing spells are near miracles!" Maestro Bertoldi sounded obnoxiously knowledgeable. Stroking his thin moustache he said, "And if this great detective is just a character, as you claim, why did the doctor speak of sharing lodgings with him?"

Sarah sighed. "For the same reason our leading man chose to sleep with me when we first played *Romeo and Juliet*. It made it more real for him!" Her lips twisted, recalling old times. "*Dieu*, it got crowded in that damned coffin."

A rising sound of feet stamping, hands clapping, assorted war-whoops, and shouts in many tongues made itself an undeniable presence on the far side of the curtain. Maestro Bertoldi began to shake. "I would give my soul to have that British jackass back in your coffin right now."

"So would I," Sarah murmured demurely.

The theatrical entrepreneur twisted the huge beryl ring from his left forefinger. "Here, Sarah. This is yours if you go out front now and explain things to our customers."

Sarah examined the ring coolly while the hubbub out front grew louder. Finally she accepted it and parted the curtains.

"Gentlemen, gentlemen, your attention please," Maestro Bertoldi heard her say in that clear, carrying voice of hers. She spoke the polyglot patois familiar to all who frequented the great American trade routes and commerce centers. "Gentlemen, we regret to inform you that due to the tragic loss of our leading man, we are unable to present *The Crimson Cryptogram* for you this evening."

The Italian flinched at the howls of rage that went up from the frustrated theatregoers.

Sarah sounded as if she were a trifle shaken herself, for she hastily added, "Instead, I will perform for you the famous soliloquy from *Hamlet*—"

The audience underscored their displeasure with a sound of smashing chairs.

"—in the nude."

While Maestro Bertoldi mopped his brow and waited for his heart to slow to normal, a small sector of the great American smorgasbord learned why they called the lady the divine Sarah.

On a train bound for Nieuw Amsterdam, a slim, ascetic-looking young man settled his Inverness more comfortably on his shoulders and tamped more shag into his pipe. His keen eyes were fixed on a goal only he could see, lying far beyond the eastern horizon, across the ocean sea.

When his train reached the port city after many days travel, he spared not a glance on the clean, trim streets with their flower-hung canals and prosperous, ruddy-faced burghers. He made straight for the docks, all his possessions in the modest handgrip he carried.

An Indonesian slave in the third shipping office he tried flashed him a remarkably white smile. "You are in luck, *Mynheer,*" he said in lightly accented Trade. "We have a ship cleared for access to Britain scheduled to leave within two days. I can give you a third-class berth on her very cheap."

"How much for a private cabin?" The young man spoke flawless New Dutch.

"Mynheer?" The slave was equally taken aback by the man's linguistic facility and his spendthrift request. Most speakers of New Dutch he knew were not so profligate with their funds.

"A private cabin, I said. I know what these wooden sailing ships can be like in rough weather. I have no desire to experience anyone's seasickness but my own."

The slave frowned. "If you prefer, Mynheer, you can take a regular steamer to Iceland and transfer there to a Britain-bound sailer."

"And wait for that transfer for how long?" He opened his grip and dropped a handful of gold catamounts on the counter. "Will that be enough for the private cabin?"

The Indonesian slave gaped at the fabulous coins. Born and bred in Nieuw Amsterdam, there to die unless he bought his freedom, he had only heard legends of the gold catamount, sole legal tender of inter-American trade.

"Yes, yes, Mynheer, assuredly; the finest. Too much by half—"

"Then take it, book my passage, arrange for the proper documents, and find me a suitable hotel room in which to pass the interval until the ship departs. Keep the change."

At this, the slave fell into a frenzy of gratitude. He only calmed himself with some effort and tried to resume the proper air of efficiency and service.

"It is done at once, Mynheer. I shall see to your every comfort. And how shall you have your name on the necessary documents?"

"Sherbourne Rath. You shan't need to procure me an entry visa. I am British-born."

"Just so, just so." The slave seized the telephone, made a couple of calls, then beamed at his client. "Your conveyance will be waiting outside within the quarter hour, Mynheer Rath. Another will bring you to your ship this Thursday, in plenty of time to settle into your cabin. If I may serve you in any other way . . ."

"None."

"And rest assured, you shall have complete privacy in your hotel as on the ship. No one will know a word of who you are or where you are bound, not even my owners. I will . . . adapt the office records."

Sherbourne Rath gazed down his aquiline nose at the slave, a freezing glance of contempt. "Not everyone who desires privacy needs secrecy. I am avoiding no one and nothing, and you would be making a grave error to assume so; a graver one if you nourish hopes of extorting further funds from me as the price of your silence. Even if I did need to purchase your complicity, you might not live long enough to enjoy your wages. Statistics show that a clear majority of murders are committed by blackmail victims against their tormentors. Of course this does not even take into account those unsolved murders whose motive might likewise be the termination of blackmailers. As they are unsolved, we shall never know, shall we?" He smiled briefly, without warmth, at the stunned slave. "Good day."

In the motorcab that took him to his hotel, he had leisure to review his performance. He found it wanting. "He would never have gone on at such length. No, not in that situation." He steepled his long fingers, tapped his lips gently. "I must learn to be what I know I am."

One week later, in the middle of the Atlantic Ocean, a most resourceful and dedicated young man found a way to alter both the ship's register and his own travel documents. In essence, Sherbourne Rath, late of Maestro Bertoldi's travelling American theatrical company, stepped over the rail, plunged into the sea, and was never seen again. A different gentleman entirely occupied Rath's cabin for the remainder of the voyage. No one noticed the exchange except the gentleman himself.

Several weeks after the death of Sherbourne Rath, a very bemused John H. Weston, M.D., moved into new lodgings with a man whose name, face, character, and profession he knew well, although he had never met the gentleman before in his life.

The life of Dr. John H. Weston was such that this miraculous coincidence of Nature and Art did not overawe him for too long. Besides, it was wonderful to be able to exercise his creative faculties again without the need to await fickle inspiration. He took his transformation from Boccaccio to Boswell right in stride. Nor did he mind the more frequent cheques from the *Strand* magazine.

Often, in the long winter evenings, Dr. Weston would look up from his desk to stare at the long-limbed figure stretched out upon the divan, feet to the fire, a pipe of aromatic shag in his mouth or the precious Stradivarius in his hands. The music he drew from the old violin was sweet enough to overcome the most intrusive London noises wafting up from Baker Street below. Not even the annual ruckus of the Blessing of the Mistletoe parade could quench the master's music.

Dr. Weston rested his chin on his hand and sighed happily. It was just as he had imagined it would be when he wrote "The Crimson Cryptogram," and it did much to ease the pain of his former loneliness.

For his part, though he said nothing, Maestro Bertoldi's former leading man felt the same. He had left Britain because he could not bear to live magicless in a land where magic reigned. He had sought magic of his own, following tales of the marvels to be found in the still uncivilized lands oversea. He had been forced to compromise, to accept the minor magic of an actor's life, but that had not been enough for him. He wanted to be the one to work wonders.

Then Maestro Bertoldi had given him that role. He read it, went back and read the story from which it was stolen, steeped himself in the character of a man whose simplest deductions appeared to arrive through stronger sorcery than anything the Golden Brotherhood could command.

The magic of the unaided human mind opened before him. In that moment, he knew there was one place on earth where he truly belonged.

Brihtric Donne, consulting detective, had come home.

CHAPTER ONE

George of the Clubfoot and His Abominable Wife

I am John H. Weston, M.D., and there is more to me than you might expect if our acquaintance is limited to those few modest adventures I have published in the *Strand* magazine to the greater glory of my good friend Mr. Brihtric Donne. This adventure, however, is my own, and more by way of testimony than glorification. Faith knows, I would have had some distinctly different tales to tell of the great detective had I approached his own exploits half so honestly as I shall here unveil mine.

(Indeed, I have within these pages revealed much of Donne's character that does not appear elsewhere in my reminiscences. And if some of these incidents here set down are not so flattering as Donne or his admirers would prefer, at least they have Truth to support them. Although why Truth should be so highly prized a virtue in a world that has also produced cosmetics, politics, and magic, I have not the meagrest idea.)

But enough. I suppose the beginning of the affair that was to shake Britain to her foundations was purely my fault. I could have stayed in bed. (Not that I did not wind up there, ultimately; but this I shall speak in its proper place.) Ah, but it was Beltaine eve! The bonfires were bright, the street revels loud, and my good friend Mr. Brihtric Donne was being an even greater pain in the arse than usual. National holidays always brought out the worst in him.

"Pagans," I heard him mutter, his hawklike profile darkly outlined in the glow from the blaze in Baker Street. "And like all pagans, they lack method. Method, Weston! A logical mind in place of some overbearing wizard's mumbo-jumbo! *That's* what will save Britain someday."

I shrugged. The sounds of revelry were enticing, more so than Donne's company. While I do admire the man, and will always be grateful to whatever caprice of Fate threw us together, there are moments I've been tempted to give him the needle where he'd long remember it.

I reached for my jacket. The May night was cool, but surely not cool enough for a man of my hardy constitution to don an overcoat or cape. "I'm just popping out for a bit, Donne." I tried to keep it casual. "Get a bit of fresh air."

Donne snorted. "Fresh air? Save your explanations for your credulous readers. We both know what you're going out for. Thank God you're a medical man. So much easier to obtain the cure for whatever 'fresh air' you'll pick up tonight."

"Now see here, Donne—"

"It's no use lying to me, Weston," he said, and sank moodily into his favorite chair while his long, slender fingers groped for the meerschaum and shag. And the worst of it was, I damned well could *not* lie to him. I'd tried it, and he'd only met my poor excuses with supercilious disdain as he coolly rattled off the height, weight, nationality, and special skills of my companion. Her profession was beneath mention.

I slammed the door as I left, and nearly bowled over poor Mrs. Hendrik on my way down the stairs. Our worthy landlady was ascending with the tea tray. There are times I think she was born clutching a painted tin tray and a half-dozen leaden scones.

"Whoops, sir, but you gave me a start!" she exclaimed, balancing the tray on her amply upholstered bosom. Then she added slyly, "Out for a bit of Beltaine fun, are we?"

I tried to emulate Donne's hauteur, and failed. The man has the advantage of a physiognomy that radiates contempt automatically. I, on the other hand, give the sorry first impression of a forty-year-old puppy. Well, so I am. Imposing? Hardly. Not even Mrs. Hendrik took me seriously.

"Run along now, dearie," she burbled. "You'll find good times aplenty. Oh, that I was young again!" She sighed—a seismic maneuver that almost upset the tea things—and gazed longingly up the stairs to the closed door of our rooms. I bid her a curt good night and elbowed past, cursing privately. Just like all the rest of them, the old biddy! Enamored of Donne up to the eyeballs, and he not giving half a twopenny damn for any of them. While as for me— Ah, but that was what Beltaine eve was for; good hunting for those of us who needs must hunt.

The Baker Street bonfire was a modest one. I watched

the younger sprigs cavorting around it for a while. I felt curiously old. I spotted the boy Jones, one of Donne's famed "Irregulars," behaving regularly enough with Mildred from the bun shop down the street. The *boy* Jones! He'd told me he and the other Irregulars would soon be setting off on a Northern cattle raid. *Boy*, forsooth. Was he old enough for stealing kine and molesting bun-shop girls? Was I that much older myself?

" 'Elloo, guv. Gawds syve th' Queen an' all. What're yew doin' 'ere on yer lownsome, eh? Fancy some comp'ny?"

A slender arm linked itself through mine. By the firelight I saw her face, enthusiastically if not artfully painted. She could not have been more than seventeen. I disengaged myself.

"Thank you, my dear, but not tonight. I am merely contemplating the—ah—holiness of the rituals." That, and doing my damnedest to come up with a way to have my "bit of Beltaine fun" while putting Donne off the scent. This trollop wore enough cheap Calais water for even Lestrasse to trace my activities should I go with her.

The lady took umbrage. " 'Ere! Yew ain't one o' them as fancies boys, are yew?" she sniffed. I indicated not. This intrigued her. "Wot, then? Bit o' spankin' when we're naughty? Daisy 'ere'll oblige," she offered eagerly.

"Madam, the last woman who so used me was my dear governess, Ruth Bowyer, and I was six years old at the time. I have no desire to renew such customs, even for old times' sake."

Now she was really interested. "No girls an' no boys an' no spankin's?" Her mental exertions were almost visible.

"Correct. Nor do I intend viewing the Ascot races with more than a sportsman's interest," I informed her. "The rites of Epona—"

The girl Daisy snorted rather like a horse. "Didn't think yew was one for the 'orses. Taykes a *real* man t' serve the Goddess. But *yew?* Yer little better'n th' toffs wot's plyin' about 'Er Majesty's own Beltaine foire this night." Her scornful laughter was harsh. "Friend o' mine, Lucy, she once tried workin' th' Queen's bash. Not a sausage! They all goes there fancyin' they'll be good enough fer 'Er Majesty t' choose. But it's always th' syme. Off she goes with tha' poet chappie an' leaves th' rest t' ply king with th' one true sceptre as they're ever loikly t' 'andle." She roared with merriment, then slipped me a familiar squeeze. Most disturbing. "Sure y' down't want t' come with Daisy, guv?"

I have performed surgery on the battlefield. I have removed spearheads, blades, arrows, and occasional run-of-the-mill impotence spells. I assure you, these are nothing next to the difficulty of removing a determined London prostitute from her quarry. Daisy clung like a limpet to a pier piling, and so strategically that I hesitated to put her off with an insult. She was admirably placed for taking instant, painful vengeance.

"Uh . . . my dear young woman," I managed as she gave me yet another tantalizing sample of her handcraft skills. "My dear girl, you've hit on it exactly."

"Down't I know it!" chortled Daisy.

"No, I mean that is precisely where I am bound at present—Her Majesty's Beltaine festivities. Indeed, if I am not there within the quarter-hour—"

The girl sprang back, mercifully loosing me. She squinted at me suspiciously. "Yew one of *them?*" she demanded.

"Them?" I echoed weakly. Daisy was young, but I had the feeling we'd hear more of her. Even her first faint tries at arousing my commercial interest had been fearsomely successful. I struggled to regain some Donnesian calm.

"*Yew* know," she insisted. "*Them.* Th' woise. Th' bleedin' Brother'ood. 'Ere, where's yer sickle, then?" Her hands darted for me a second time. I danced away.

"Ah, ah, ah! Mustn't touch. Instant death if you're not an initiate, you know. Must run. Regrets." I fear my dignified retreat would have taken the palm in any sprinting contest. I lost sight of her as I plunged into the darkened streets.

Panting, I leaned against a shuttered haberdashery. Not every street in London could afford Beltaine fires. The lowing of the cattle sounded far away, but the honest reek of them permeated the city. I debated returning to Baker Street or seeking my fun elsewhere. The prospect was depressing. I'd only meet another of Daisy's guildmates and Donne would have the last laugh. Only he wouldn't laugh. He'd chuckle, dryly.

Then it struck me. Eureka! What had I just told Daisy? By all gods, save the Queen! And why not John H. Weston, M.D.? I was as fine a man as any I'd encountered round Her Majesty's bonfire. And surely—though I'd never be chosen for Queen's Consort this night—I'd find some lady suitable and agreeable. I'd only known of the Queen's

Beltaine Festival by hearsay. And that, as Donne would concur, is no substitute for first hand observation. Why, I might even get a monograph out of this! *On Sexual Response in the Wealthy Woman.* It had promise.

I mused as I made my way through streets bright and dark. How long had it been since I'd seen our dear Lady? Once, years and years back, I'd caught a glimpse of her soon after her Accession, but such times are never apt for seeing the new British sovereign at his or her best. For one thing, there were all the dead bodies to be cleared away, and a little matter of a leftover hellhound molesting strollers in the Strand. As a medical man, I was too busy binding wounds to get more than a quick impression of a small woman, delicate yet plump, with fair hair and bright blue eyes. I also recall several subsequent impure nightly reveries in which my imagination cast her in the leading role.

I heard the Queen's Beltaine Festival long before I saw it, though the bonfires were certainly the largest in the isle. Swarms of young men pressed shoulder to shoulder ahead of me, their holiday finery rumpled and torn from much jostling. Here and there I heard a hasty curse, and saw the imprudent, unprotected recipient go down, stunned or dead.

There are times other than the purely professional when a doctor's knowledge of physiology proves useful. I cleared a path for myself through the throng of hopeful young things by a bit of judicious nerve-pinching here, a smattering of pressure manipulation there, and one good boot in the cobblers for a difficult subject. Ere long I was in sight of the fire, and if not for the sheer force of people around me, I'd have collapsed in awe.

It blazed gorgeously, a wild scarlet horse leaping and curvetting, straining against its tethers. Branches of pine spat up fountains of sparks, dry brambles crackled, and at the heart of the fire the sacred oak burned with a fierce, steady light. Above all, Magister Nelson gazed down from the summit of his monolith and allowed the stone Dragon of France to continue feasting on his granite arm.

The Brotherhood ringed the flames with the white of their woollen robes, their snowy beards and hair turning them to walking ghosts. Golden sickles glinted. Acolytes and apprentices scurried between their masters, and blue-marked priestesses cavorted naked, driving the royal herd around and around the sacred fire. Druid or not, what man could witness such a spectacle and remain unmoved?

"If they don't get on with the choosing soon," said a languid voice in my ear, "I shall go home, get drunk, and abuse my page. Or else I shall write another canto or two of *Don Juan* and abuse my publisher."

The speaker was sharply hissed down for his insolence. Public censure only made him laugh and add, "On second thought, why don't the rest of you go home? I'm to be her chosen one this year. Again." He gave a heavy-hearted sigh. "Why was I cursed with such a perfect lover's reputation? I know it goes well with my face, but—"

"How would you like me to alter your face for you, Bucky?" came the challenge.

A circle began to form. I'd have thought it impossible, but room was made for them to have it out. Now I could see the face of the man who'd been so eager to go home and indiscriminately abuse pages or publishers. One look, and I knew I was wasting my time. The man had only spoken the plain truth; Her Majesty would choose him.

Some things are self-evident. Just as women seem unable to resist the unapproachable Donne, so too do the ladies perversely flutter around men whose soft good looks and melting eyes make them supremely approachable. Up for grabs, in fact. This gentleman seemed to have been grabbed more than once in his lifetime. His features were clean Greek beauty, his eyes were large and brimming with either intense sentimentality or advanced hay fever, and the whole was capped by a cluster of grape-black curls. Damn him to the pits!

My sympathies were therefore with the challenger. This was a lusty young man, broad-chested as a draft horse. The Queen's Beltaine Festival was not supposed to include commoners, but it looked as if a listless countess or marchioness somewhere in this fellow's ancestry had gladly included one of the field hands in her personal calendar. The chap had the ham fists of a ploughman and the morals of a trueborn British peer. Our beautiful, jaded friend was doomed.

"Hey, leave off that! The Brotherhood'll see," came an urgent whisper.

"They'll see nothing. This won't take long." The challenger snickered. He handed his jacket to me and stuck out his fists. "Ready?" he demanded.

"If I must," sighed the other, "I must." And without troubling to remove his own cape and coat, he converted the challenger's face to haggis in short order.

I can scarcely describe it as a fight. One moment I'd been

holding the jacket of a pawing bull, and the next I was being asked by the winner whether I knew any safe and sure method for removing bloodstains from broadcloth. "I'd best see to that man," I said.

"Oh, don't bother," my new friend remarked lightly. He fingered his fallen adversary's jacket, which I still stupidly held in my hands. "A poor bit of goods; last year's cut. No style. As in all things. Your face, sir, is familiar. I have seen you before, and not playing seconds in a street brawl. Come with me. My eyes are a bit weak. I want to get you more into the light. Accompany me and I'll get us both inside Her Majesty's front rank of candidates. She *will* be looking for me, after all, and it's not kind to make a lady search too far afield."

He flung the jacket aside and propelled me through the press. Young braves who had seen his recent exhibition of fighting skill melted away before us like snow. As we shoved them aside, I became aware of a slight irregularity in his gait. I looked down and saw that this pretty boy-god was not entirely unflawed after all. He had a perceptible limp, the inevitable result of a clubfoot. If I felt any pity for him, I had not the time to express it. I felt the heat of the gargantuan fire stronger on my face. Nelson's monument was no longer visible above us, long since lost in the billowing smoke. A naked priestess writhed past, her thighs a welter of blue tattoos, her stone knife flashing. My mind was so turned about by the many surprises of the night that I hardly noticed when I stumbled and fell against a figure robed in white.

"Pardon," I mumbled. Looking back, it was one of several things I might have said. All would have been wrong.

"Oh I say. You've done it now," said my companion. Whether his subsequent vanishment was done through spells or simply fancy footwork—well, I never did think to ask. I was left confronting a very, very angry Druid. Alone.

I have seen full many a horror since my association with Donne. The glare of a snake's icy eyes, the bulbous stare of a tarantula, the smoky yellow regard of a hungry panther; all, all as nothing next to the piercing glower of the Druid lord I'd had the ill luck to jostle.

"You . . ." It was a hiss. "You *dare* to address me thus?"

"Ah. Yes? I mean, I said I was sorry." Glancing down, I saw that my misstep had been squarely on the hem of his white robes, leaving a distinct footprint. What with all the cattle about for Beltaine, it was not the most wholesome of footprints, either. "If you'll only have your—um—acolyte send that round to number 221 B Baker Street, I'll be more than happy to have it cleaned for—"

"Get this fool away." From hiss to growl it went. "Now. Before I mar the rituals."

"Better do as he says, old chap." My friend was back again, and he yanked me away by the elbow. "Doesn't do to twit the Iron Duke." He hustled me into the relative shelter of the crowd nearest the bonfire. On the other side of the flames I could see the triple row of Druids ranged to await the coming of the Queen. They drifted back and forth in the shadows like seafoam.

"The Iron Duke? You mean I stepped on *Wellington's* robe?" That gave me the shakes. High out of sight I could feel Magister Nelson smiling down coldly. The Iron Duke was not only the Archdruid of all Britain, but a man to be reckoned with even if stripped of all his magics. Nelson had possessed greater spells and more recondite knowledge of dark things, but it was Wellington who had survived every clash of sorcery in the late wars, Wellington who had led our forces into the very belly of France, Wellington who had lived to depose the Corsican mage from his obsidian throne in the fastness of the Carnutes' Forest.

"Don't let it trouble you. He's got more than a few to spare at home. Offering to have his robe cleaned for him! My good fellow, I really must insist on shaking your hand and having you call me by my given name. George, if you please. George Noel Gordon, Lord Byron; Geordie to my friends, of whom I have none."

His smile was quite disarming. I took his hand warmly. "One at least, I hope. I am John H. Weston, M.D."

"Devil you are!" He looked at me hard, as if imprinting my unfortunate face on his brain. "So that's how I know you! I've read your stories time and again. Tell me, is he *really* such a bear for deduction? Strikes me that when you write about how deuced brilliant Donne is in every case he takes, you might be like the farmer's lad who threw the spear first and drew the target round it after."

"I assure you, m'lord—"

"Geordie." He was quite firm about it.

"Geordie. I assure you, Donne is all I write of him. If anything, I've suppressed more than I've written. It doesn't do to tell the public too much."

Geordie gave me a canny look. "Keeping the good parts for your private papers, eh? Good for—"

"*Byron.*"

The black robe wavered like a living piece of the darkness. I never saw the face of the acolyte who wore it, but that voice—! That voice might have belonged to one young in years, but old in living. Lord Byron turned and tried to see who summoned him. He saw what I could not, and his face went pale in the firelight.

"What are you doing here?" He spoke in a croaking whisper. "Don't you know what time it—?"

"*He* knows. He has sent me for you. Will you come? Or will I have to send one of his other servants after you?"

Poor Byron! Only minutes since he had faced a man twice his size in combat with enough *sang froid* to discountenance the devil. Now he confronted a mere youth whose hands—soft and dainty things that rested on his lordship's shoulder—had never formed fists even in dreams; and he was afraid.

"No, no; don't do that. I'll come." He gave me a weak smile. "Sorry, John, but you understand. Only—will she? Poor dear Lady. It's not done to disappoint the Queen. I only wish—" An idea struck him. Snakes are also said to strike. He pulled away from the waiting acolyte, mumbling a hasty excuse, and pressed his lips to my ear. "John, whatever this business is, I'll be shut of it quickly. I *must* be with the Queen tonight. I'll very likely be back before the choosing, but in case I'm not—here, take my cape. Yes, the collar stands up—so! She'll know it. She's a lovely lass, but a bit nearsighted and too proud to utter the sharpening spells. Yes, yes, perfect; we're of a height and both with dark hair, curly. Ha! And once she's chosen you, old chap, you wait until you're well inside the Palace before you let on. Then you tell her I'll be along directly. Thanks, thanks. You'll never regret this."

Never.

Then he was gone, swept up in the acolyte's black wake, and I stood wrapped in his cape as close to the bonfires as the heat would allow.

I had not much time to reflect on this strange newfound friend's comings and goings, for just then a shout went up from the fires. Shielding my eyes from the glare, I joined my gaze to that of the massed mob of noble young bloods gathered at Nelson's feet and beheld the swollen silver belly of the moon gleaming in full splendor behind the fallen mage's statue. The clouds of smoke had been swallowed up in that lambent white light as if by magic. The Dragon of France shivered in fear, its stone tail writhing, alive for a moment and then still for another year's time.

A second shout went up and cut itself off into a shock of perfect silence. Not even the royal herd lowed, held enrapt by the spells of their attendant priestesses. And now a deep humming sound began to swell—the hum of the untouched forest's heart, the hum of mighty rivers dreaming, the sounding of the earth's own harpstrings, tightly tuned and calling male to female, woman to man. It grew the way a living watercourse grows, went to the flood, and then settled over us all like the wings of an unseen presence. My own body grew taut with the yearning magic even as my heart settled sweetly in my breast, content.

She came. The whitecapped Druid sea parted to let her come. She was clad in foaming white robes, and the horse she rode was white also. Slowly, slowly she came, and when I saw her, I suddenly knew the true meaning of majesty. The content of my heart broke in that moment, and the yearning for her—for her!—leapt up and took full possession of my soul.

She reined in her horse by its mane. I felt her eyes on me. "That one," she said, and rode on.

Two acolytes had me by the arms before I could fully know what had occurred. "Come on," said one, tugging me after the retreating white rump of the Queen's steed. "And for Epona's sake, watch where you st— Oh, bloody damn!"

"Calm down, Kevin; easy does it," the other counselled. "He can wipe his feet before he goes up to her."

Kevin put his nose dangerously close to mine. "This one doesn't look like he's got the brains to wipe his nose."

"You little bastard! I'll wipe the ground with you, and see if you've the brains to stop me!" I jerked free of his odious grasp and squared off. Kevin only spat neatly between my feet.

"Right. A live one." So saying, he did a complicated wiggle of the fingers in my face and that was all I saw of the Beltaine fires before I hit the pavement.

No; Donne would deplore such inaccuracy. I merely *assume* I hit the pavement. I awoke with enough of a pain in the back and head to make such a deduction the only possible one. A pain, by the bye, which further allowed me to infer that Kevin's companion hadn't thought it worth while to bother catching me after Kevin's stunning spell took hold. I opened my eyes and all I saw was stars.

When I say I saw stars, I mean it literally. They were embroidered in silver thread on the blue damask canopy hanging above me. I traced the outlines of the Great Wagon and the Three Sisters before I felt something cool and wet on my brow.

"I see you're yourself again," said the Queen. Despite the pain in my neck, I turned my face towards her. She was smiling as she smoothed the damp cloth on my forehead. "I really must speak to those boys. They seem to think that their job begins and ends with getting my chosen consort into my bed. They'll never earn the white robe this way; no sense of style."

"Geordie said the same thing," I mumbled. "About style. You see, a man challenged him to a fight, and I was holding his coat—the man's, I mean—and when it was all over, Geordie said—" I had regained my tongue about five minutes before I regained full consciousness, it seemed. I had no idea of what I was saying, though as I rambled on a warning siren went off in my head with the cheery message, *John, you sound like runner-up in the village-idiot contest!*

"Hang Geordie, whoever he is," said the Queen. Her blue eyes smiled warmly into mine. She removed the wet cloth and laid her tender hand on my forehead instead. Her gentle touch jangled my nerves so badly that I recommenced babbling. I heard my village-idiot warning shrieking itself hoarse, but I was having none of it.

"You don't know Geordie? But he said you always choose him on Beltaine eve! He's about my height, same hair color—wait, wait, maybe you only know his proper name, George? George Gordon, Lord Byron? The poet fellow, y'know. Your Majesty, he gave me his cape and asked me to tell you—"

She laughed. I never heard a sweeter sound issue from a woman's throat. "I seem to have chosen a coat rack for a consort. You really must calm yourself, my dear. You won't enjoy it at all if you're so nervous."

Nervous? I? I am a medical man. The human body has shown itself willingly to me in all its manifold shapes, some not far removed from the orangutans, some a step below the angels. I had seen women in my consulting room who were perhaps not so plump as the Queen, perhaps a shade closer to perfection in the female form. By classic standards, Her

Majesty's looks were ordinary. Even Daisy's body had been younger, fresher. Then why was I lying there gibbering? When she finally tossed the wet cloth aside and climbed into the bed beside me, why did I feel the overwhelming urge to flee?

Donne would have shrugged it off as beyond the pale of logic. I only knew that I was afraid.

The Queen knelt on the bed, her limbs still shrouded in the soft, clinging white wool robe. Her fair hair was knotted up high on her head, but now she released the knot and let it cascade round her shoulders. I lay frozen, arms at my sides, stiffer than any of Her Majesty's palace guards.

"Oh my," said the Queen, clapping her hands together with delight. "So shy. We are *most* amused!"

She swung her legs around and sat beside me tailor-fashion. "What's your name, dear? When you're not a coat rack."

"I—I—Geordie said that he'd be along to see you as soon as he took care of some business he—"

She stretched out full-length and rested one hand on my chest, where it idly began to pluck open my waistcoat buttons one by one, as if it were an independent being. "Whoever you are, you are not a very obedient British subject. I distinctly asked you to let Geordie go hang and then I asked you your name. *Are* you British? Or have I picked out a damn foreigner this time?"

You may insult my intelligence. My looks are open to criticism. But by all the gods of wind and water, let no man question my loyalty as a true born Briton! Truer-born than Her Majesty herself, if truth be told. Enraged, I sat bolt upright in the bed just as the last of the waistcoat buttons yielded itself to the Queen's attentions.

"Madam, I am your loyal subject. But my loyalty extends beyond this room. I was entrusted by Lord Byron with—ah—holding his place in your—your affections, and it would be a stroke of gross disloyalty to betray that trust."

"Oh," said Her Majesty, and began on my shirt buttons.

I inchwormed backwards; a bit too far, as it happened. Really, you'd think a Queen's bed would be wider. My shirt tore open as she futilely tried to reel me in by hanging on to the fragile cloth. Her lovely face peered down at me where I lay on the floor and creased with badly contained mirth. Sullenly I regained my feet.

"Come back to bed and lose that scowl. It makes your

moustache quite too fierce for me." She patted the coverlet invitingly.

"Your Majesty, I prefer to stand."

"And I prefer not. Come to bed."

"Madam, my friend will be here at any moment."

"And your friend shall be turned aside at the bedchamber door. Do you think I am a fool, sir? My eyes may be weak, but for Beltaine eve alone I take the trouble to anoint them with the moonwaters. It would not do to find my bed occupied by a sorry specimen. I did not choose dear Geordie's cape, thinking it held Geordie. I chose you. It was time for a change."

I made a small sound of amazement. The Queen's smile broadened, showing off two delicious dimples. Wordlessly I sank back to the bed, and in my bewildered state I did not notice as she swiftly undid what was left of my wardrobe.

No matter what Donne claims, damn it!

But alas, the hour makes the man. Unmakes him, rather. The fear that had been rising in my throat abruptly plunged downwards to affect more sensitive regions. Her Majesty was extending her pleasure in my supposed shyness by taking her time about slipping off her robes. Her shoulders were pearly, suffused with a radiance made even more tempting by the glow of the tapers lighting her bedchamber. The robe made a milky pool around her thighs as she knelt on the bed, then slipped soundlessly to the floor when she nudged it aside.

And I, in agony, unmanned.

"My dear, you really are taking timidity a bit too far," said the Queen. She studied the situation. "I have a spell that might serve. Would you mind?"

I drew up my knees and gazed at her miserably. "Madam, there is nothing I would not do to content you. But in this case, I fear a spell will do no good. I am—" Here I paused, wondering how much of the truth I dared tell her. "I am proof against medical magics."

The Queen arranged herself directly opposite me, her fair brows knitted in concentration. "I have heard of such things. You poor fellow! How you must suffer when you fall ill."

"Not a bit. I am Dr. John H. Weston, at Your Majesty's service." I bowed as well as my position allowed.

"Not very much at my service. However, I should like you to leave off calling me '*Madam*' and '*Your Majesty*.' My name is Victoria Alexandrina, and I am well pleased to meet you, Dr. Weston. May I call you John?"

A formal introduction! Ludicrous, on the face of it. Naked as our mothers bore us, we clung to the niceties of etiquette. It was all I had to cling to. I told her that I would be terribly injured if she did *not* call me John, she replied with some scrap of tea-chat, and before long we were conversing in earnest, as eager to know each other's loves and hates as if we were children newly acquainted.

Of course she told me far more than I could ever hope to risk telling her—then. I heard all about her sad, solitary childhood: the long hours of study; the time spent honing the powers handed down to her through the royal bloodline; the friendships she could never dare to make for fear that one day, when King George should abdicate or die, she would have to face a friend in the battle for the throne and slay him.

"Yes, John," she said, resting her dear head on my shoulder, "I do believe that what I missed most in all the years of my reign—of my life—has been a friend."

Words, words, words. Oh, the strengthening power of words! She was no longer my Queen, I was no longer the subject chosen to play the god's part in her bed that night. No, we were friends, and if a gentle word led to a gentler touch, if that touch led to warmer caresses and these in turn to the heat of full passion—friendship is a wonderful thing, is it not?

My sleep, when at last it came, was exhausted and deep. I awoke, I know not how much later, to my own chuckling. I had been dreaming of Victoria, kittenish and tempting, counselling me before our first embrace to "close your eyes, grit your teeth, and think of Britain, John." My eyes flew wide, and I thought the dream had turned into a nightmare.

There stood the Iron Duke. The bedcurtains were only partially drawn, and through the narrow gap at the foot of the bed I could see his flowing beard and thundercloud face. Victoria was facing him, and her own face looked equally stormy. I checked my breath and feigned continued sleep.

"And I say I *will* have him!" Victoria's look was one of defiance. "It's time, it's past time that I gave Britain her heirs, and I tell you that never, in all the years of my reign, have I had a consort who pleased me half as much as he."

The Iron Duke was unmoved by the little Queen's insistence. "He! A nobody with not the barest touch of Bran's blood in his veins! Don't look at me that way, girl, you know I wouldn't lie about such things. You can read his blood as well as I; do so. You'll see that I'm right. If you're bound to take your consort, wait until next Beltaine and take one of your own kind, from the blood royal. The Rules most clearly state that none of Bran's direct and true line shall wed a commoner and keep the crown." He twitched the bedcurtains aside and roasted me with his eyes while I shammed on. "A common herbalist, what's worse!"

Tchah! That cut me. If old Wellington could read blood half as well as he pretended, he'd have sung another tune. But there would be no music lessons that night. He slammed out of the Queen's chamber and left her trembling with fury.

"I *will* have him. I *will*!" She tore the curtains wide. From under judiciously lowered lids I could see everything. The look she gave me was a sore test of my acting abilities, for when I saw that loving look I wanted only to spring up and take her into my arms again. My willpower held, and she turned from me none the wiser.

She flung herself across the room to where the oil portrait of her predecessor, Uncle George, beamed with alcoholic benevolence, piggy eyes sunk into rolls of pink fat, chins piled on chins. Victoria scowled and shaped her rage into a blade of bilious green fire that arced across the chamber and pierced the painted heart.

"Ouch!" howled King George. The beady eyes shifted uneasily. "Oh. Oh, it's you. What do you want, eh? What's all this? Not got a kinder way to call on me? Not nice to abuse your old uncle, y'know. Not done in the best circles. At Bath we never—" A Canton vase smashed against the portrait's gilded frame. The former monarch nearly jumped out of his varnish. "Why, child!" he exclaimed tenderly. "What's wrong?"

"I've chosen the man I want for my consort and Wellington claims I can't have him!" cried Victoria. I felt my heart beat faster. "*He* says that the Rules won't allow one of Bran's line to wed a commoner."

"And what *do* the Rules say?" King George wagged one finger. Solemnity did not become him.

"You pompous ass, I didn't summon you here to play schoolmaster! I want you to tell me whether Wellington's right!"

"My dear niece, I haven't an inkling."

Lightning blanched the room. The ormolu curls wreathing George's frame hissed to life as king serpents that darted at the late monarch's horrified eyes. Behind Victoria's tiny form a phantom began taking shape—a red-haired witch with a ruff of snowflake lace ringing her hawk-nosed face and a royal crown nestled among fiery curls.

"*Men!*" railed the apparition. "I've seen them lose hair, teeth, and virility, but never once lose the slightest measure of ignorance. Witlings, every one!"

"Ah, hulloa, Lizzie," said the portrait affably. "Vicky summon you too?"

"When I need a summons to come where I like, I'll kiss a pig's arse first," stated Elizabeth. "Care to volunteer, George?" She tossed her head back and laughed.

"Sounds just like her old man," commented King George. "Which ain't meant as a compliment, don't y'know." To the former Queen he added, "Since you've been so good as to stick that letter-opener nose of yours in where it's not wanted, perhaps you'd be good enough to help the gel out. Wants to know something about the Rules, she does."

"God's death!" roared Elizabeth. She drifted through Victoria and squinted up at the portrait. "And hadn't I enough to do in my reign? Do you expect I've memorized the Rules? What's the roil about, ha?"

My sweetest Queen explained her problem to her venerable ancestress, even pulling back the bedcurtains to allow Queen Elizabeth a good long look at me. I felt her small green eyes dancing the length of my nakedness. Belatedly I wished I'd climbed under the coverlet. Eliza's snicker was most perturbing.

"Not a bad stallion you've picked for your paddock, girl. I've seen better, but too much of a good thing spoils a woman for marriage. Settle down now, before you know what you're missing; or what he's missing." Elizabeth returned her attention to George's portrait. "Well, *I* vote she should fight to hold this one, and the Golden Brotherhood be damned. Recall *anything* pertinent in the Rules, Georgie?"

"Not a demmed thing. *Will* you remove these serpents now?" As he spoke, one especially determined snakelet struck, lodging its fangs in his plumply jeweled hand. With a high-pitched whinny he exploded from his frame in a shower of perfumed sparks.

"Fat lot of help he was," said the Queen.

Eliza agreed. "Dear niece, it would seem you've no other choice. You must consult the Rules yourself."

Victoria brightened. "Of course! It's ever so obvious, really. I've that right; no other in all Britain may do so. Dear Bess, you have such a good head on your shoulders!"

"I suppose I do. I never did take after Mother," said Elizabeth; then she was gone.

Victoria stood beneath the empty picture frame for a moment, hands clasped. Then she returned to the bed and tugged all the curtains back. I remained as I was, too inexperienced an actor to feign slow waking. I admit to some curiosity as well, and all of it self-serving. What Rules were these that held my fate contained in their lines? Consort of all Britain—I, John H. Weston! Was it hunger for a crown matrimonial that made me lie there, waiting to see what she would do next? No, not that; I had more than enough experience of crowns.

The candle by our bedside was guttering. I surreptitiously watched her light another from it, a fat yellow one which she rammed onto a spiked holder. Bearing this, she hastened to the wall where her uncle's deserted frame hung. Her slender fingers fumbled over the carvings of horned gods and horses, cauldrons and swords, until she found a catch. The panel slid back silently. She slipped into the hidden warren like a ghost.

Could I do less than follow? There was no time for me to struggle into my many layers of street clothes, so I shielded my nakedness with only Geordie's borrowed cloak. This was hooded, and I do not know what instinct compelled me to raise the hood until it entirely concealed my features. Then I too entered the world beyond the bedroom wall.

The maze ran out and down, through corridors of wood and stone, through halls where ancient oaks, still rooted and thriving, had been built whole into the winding passages. Dead leaves brushed my face, crackled underfoot. I kept back those small cries of pain and surprise when my bare feet trod on fallen twigs and keen pebbles. White berries shone pearly-pale from the overhanging branches in the dappled half-light.

Lower and lower went the maze. Soon there was only dead grey stone to either side of me, the rough-hewn roots of timeless monoliths that plumbed the heart of London-town. My cape rasped against them as the walls seemed to lean in closer. The jagged ceiling dipped so low that I was forced to stoop and feel my way, having long since lost sight of Victoria's vagrant candle flame.

At last I felt a moist, cool stirring of the air. Watery light beckoned me forward, but I hung back. It would not do to have her discover my unbidden presence. I went cautiously as far as the place where the narrow stone corridor ended in a frieze-draped archway, and from there I clung to the shadows and watched.

The Queen stood in the center of a square-cut chamber. At the far end of this, an altar waited, empty, the shiny red streaks dripping from the top slab too bright to be more than simulacra of recent sacrifice. From the altar, the face of a bull glowered at her, hollow eyes filled with fire burning from within the altar stone. My beloved Queen approached, set her candle down beside the fane, and with one touch of her hand tilted back the slab. I came perilously close to rushing from hiding with a loud protest when I saw her plunge her hands into the midst of the hungrily leaping flames.

"You waste your time, Your Majesty. It isn't there."

Victoria whirled, and I hugged the shadows even more tightly. A crack in the wall behind the altar widened as I watched, and disgorged three hooded figures clad in white, in black, in scarlet.

"She speaks the truth, Your Majesty," said the one in white. His voice was dry, drawling, and when he pulled back his hood I saw wolvish teeth gleam against skin burned black by a stronger sun than shines on Britain.

His was a face suitable for smiling when other folk spoke of drowning puppies. From what I could deduce of his build from the all-shrouding Druid's robes, he was a strong, well-set-up man of about my years; and yet I flattered myself that in a fair fight I could easily take him down. Even from a distance, his eyes shone with the inner fire common to the great jungle cats of which I had only read. Somehow, with his sleek jet hair and his thick moustache, he gave me the hideous feeling that he also shared with those terrible and beautiful beasts a fine thirst for blood.

I recognized the voice of the creature in black who now hung in the shadow of this malevolent man like a bat haunting a ruined tower. It was the selfsame acolyte whose coming had so frightened poor Geordie. Only now did I realize that the supposed acolyte's voice was so high and musical not because of tender years, but because the speaker was a woman. She leaned close to the dark man, laughing. The third one—the one in scarlet—hung back.

Victoria gasped, then plunged her hands into the fire a second time. The flames left her untouched as she rummaged through their blaze easily as a parlor maid might search for a teaspoon in a drawer. But her hands emerged empty.

"You see?" The man in white yawned.

"But how—? How could you touch them?" the Queen demanded. They were coming closer, white robe and black. Victoria thrust out her hands in a warding spell, but the brilliance of her conjuring dimmed to a feeble glow around her, then went out. The woman in black seized her by the wrists. Her hood fell away from her face.

"Lady Byron," Victoria breathed.

"Your Majesty," the woman replied, her words as twisted as her smile.

I meant to reveal my presence then. Hearing the name of Byron—knowing now the true identity of the "acolyte" who had whisked Geordie away and left the field to me—I paused for perhaps ten heartbeats; ten too long.

Victoria's small body tensed like a longbow, and the spell left her lips in a bolt of sheerest power. She meant killing magic—I did not then know why—but the dark man caught it with a word and hurled it back again. It burst into coruscating waves of light that froze whatever human they touched. The Queen stood transfixed—and so did I. Only the tingle that ran through my blood told me that I, in my hiding place, had been the unguessed victim of a holding spell. I was flesh turned to stone, unable to help, able only to play the hapless witness.

Lady Byron's face was chalky. I could see she had imagined the Queen's spell to be unstoppable. The dark man read her look of slowly subsiding terror and coolly jerked her chin up, forcing her to meet his eyes.

"Afraid, my dear? You ought never have thrown in your lot with me if you mistrust my powers."

"It—it wasn't that," Lady Byron lied miserably. The man's eyes glittered. He stroked her cheek gently, and four tracks of blood followed his caress. She whimpered with pain while the figure in scarlet stood sentinel, like myself a wordless watcher.

Lady Byron sank to the stone floor, dabbing at her ruined cheek with the drooping sleeve of her black robe. The man in white ignored her. "You don't do much credit to the idea of marital chivalry, George. But then, you do little credit to any enterprise that takes you out of the bedroom."

"It's not my place to question you in matters of—of discipline, m'lord." Geordie spoke from the shelter of his scarlet hood. Never have I heard a man so drained of spirit.

"Indeed," said the dark one. "You have less ambition than your wife, but you sometimes surprise me with your intelligence. You have outlived your usefulness to me"— Poor Geordie shuddered—"and yet I think you will serve some further purpose in my plans."

"But—but as the Queen's Beltaine consort—"

The man in white brushed aside Geordie's hasty self-justifications. "That stage is done with; ended. You ended it yourself tonight when you allowed her to find a substitute for her royal bed."

"It was you who summoned me away!"

The dark man raised his brows slowly, his face a mockery of innocent surprise. "Do you question me, George? I ask so little of my people, and still they manage to fulfill all my biddings. I summoned you, true. But I did not instruct you to dawdle after I released you. There was time to return to the fire, time to be chosen. Ah, but never mind. We do not need time any longer. My humble thanks to you for all the years you've kept Her Majesty harmlessly occupied. Had she found a man both suitable and eligible—as you never were, being married—she might have come seeking to consult the Rules that much sooner."

"*Where are they, damn you? Where are the Rules Britannia?*"

She spoke. Her own magic, deflected back upon her, still knew its mistress and could not hold her speechless the way it held me. Her cry of anger did not seem to discomfit the dark one. He regarded her the way I have seen small boys study captive butterflies.

"You will learn that in good time, Your Majesty. How much time is up to you. I was considering returning them to you as a gift—a wedding gift."

"Wedding?" Geordie's head came up abruptly. "But after all these years preventing her from choosing a mate, you mean to— "

"Shut up, George. Ask your lady wife to explain my intentions to you over tea sometime—my more than honorable intentions towards Her Majesty. She has lost the right to rule by allowing the Rules Britannia to slip from her grasp, but that shall be our little courtship secret. And when we have married and the crown matrimonial is mine—when Britain herself opens to me—then my dear wife shall also open the secrets of the Rules and I shall hold more power than the Golden Brotherhood ever dreamed."

Victoria's laughter sounded high and brittle in the stone chamber. "By the Horned One, I like your talk of dreams! I don't know how you managed to make away with the Rules, but you've a piper's chance of using them! Not a drop of Druid's blood in you, is there? No, I guessed not, or you wouldn't need me to open the Rules for you."

"Her Majesty is most perceptive." The dark man cut a low bow. "Even Lord Byron's much-diluted line carries more Druid's blood than my poor common veins."

"And so you make those with little magic serve you, who must have none. Oh, that *is* good! Do you think I haven't dealt with treacherous alliances like this before? Your ambitions are nothing new to me, or to the Brotherhood. You'll make roast meat in the wicker man before they'll allow you to wed me. The Rules Britannia can only answer the commands of those descended from the Wise. They'll stay sealed from you, I promise."

He shrugged off the white robe he wore and I saw the scarlet coat of a military man, the row on row of service decorations. "I hate inaccuracy almost as much as I hate the injustice of this miserable island. And did you think I had no power at my own command when I turned your own spell back against you? Do you think the only magics in the world spring from your precious Druids? You are like all of the purblind Brotherhood; your vision ends where the ocean laps our shores. But there will be plenty of opportunities for me to instruct you. Annabella!"

Despite the pain that still made her moan softly, Lady Byron hurried to her master's side. He whispered a few words; she disappeared into the fissure behind the altar, and returned bearing a bronze tripod of a design I had never seen before. She kindled a pastille of charcoal in the shallow basin and sprinkled yellow powder over it from a leather pouch at her belt. At once a pungent, overwhelmingly sweet smoke began to send its tendrils up and across the rough stone ceiling.

"Farewell, Your Majesty," said the dark man. His words shot bursts of red fire across my eyes, already blurring and fighting off encroaching blackness. I felt the holding spell weaken as my knees gave way, but before I lost all touch with my senses I heard him add, "You will take her back to her bedchamber, George. Oh, don't give me that lamb's look! She'll remember nothing of this. Your wife has just seen to that. She and I shall depart the way we came. Go and—"

Nothing more.

I awoke fully clothed on the Embankment with the first streaks of morning rose and yellow in the sky. A sickly-sweet odor clung to me, though I hadn't the foggiest notion of where or how I'd come by it. Aching in every bone, my joints chilled through, I dragged home to Baker Street.

I had no reason to disbelieve Donne's gleeful deductions once he got his first whiff of me—no remembered reason at all.

Not then.

CHAPTER TWO

Vittoria the Circus Dancer

It was a week after Beltaine, and the headaches that had plagued me since that forgotten night had only just subsided. This time likewise coincided with the arrest and conviction of Vincent Lynch, the forger, whose apprehension left my good friend Mr. Brihtric Donne to sink once more into one of those idle periods he so detested. I returned from a dawnlight walk down the Strand to find him sprawled listlessly upon the divan. His pipe rested at his elbow, freshly tamped yet unlit. At first I was deeply concerned, afraid that he had reverted to the use of cocaine as a distraction from his enforced unemployment.

"No need to examine me so closely, Weston," he said. "I know how you deplore my harmless hobby."

"I should hardly call it harmless, Donne."

"You are entitled to your opinions, Weston, although you might do better to study facts about the drug, not prejudices." Then with a twinkle he added, "In view of the hour, you should know I'd be more likely to be taking breakfast than cocaine. It would never do to upset Mrs. Hendrik by having her come in and find me under the influence of anything more unnatural than her grilled kippers." He rubbed his long, white hands together in anticipation.

Just then there came a knock at the door. "That must be Mrs. Hendrik," I ventured.

"Must? Never say *must*, Weston. In fact, I should say that you will find a female caller considerably Mrs. Hendrik's junior." At this he opened the door.

My long association with Donne has taught me many things, chief among these his almost preternatural ability to pinpoint the origin and occupation of his client at first glance. Therefore I ought not to have been surprised when he likewise foretold the age and sex of this visitor, sight unseen. Our caller was indeed a lady, and one I found mysteriously and immediately charming.

"Mr. Donne?" Her face was lightly veiled in black, but a

gaudy satin gown in a patchwork of colors peeped out from beneath the sober, ashen redingote. Her voice—very warm and musical—had the unmistakable accents of Italy.

"Won't you come in?" invited Donne. "No, no, don't sit in that chair. Weston here will be the first to complain of my slovenly habits, but those papers form an important part of my files. On no account must they be disturbed."

"Donne claims to know where everything is," I put in. My voice was rough as a schoolboy's. She had lifted the black veil, exposing a delicate beauty not often seen. Both Donne and the lady ignored my sally.

"Mr. Donne, my name is Vittoria Pitti. Your name came to me— " She hesitated.

"That doesn't matter." He had perched himself on the edge of the table and was studying her avidly, his sharp eyes missing nothing. "The important thing is that you have need of my services. How can I help you, Signorina Pitti?"

The vision lowered her eyes. Blond curls framed her moon-shaped face prettily. "I am—how do you British say it?—a woman wronged."

"Wronged how, Signorina? Affairs of the heart do not fall within the usual purlieu of a consulting detective."

"I realize that, Mr. Donne." Her small, round chin lifted defiantly. "The wrong done to me has more to do with larceny than love. I have been robbed."

"Indeed? And what was taken?"

"A parchment, Mr. Donne. A relic kept in my poor Florentine family for generations, and said to be a grant of nobility from one of the Medici princes to his peasant mistress." She kept her head bent and her eyes averted. I imagined she must have been a rope-dancer, or some such other sort of performer whose chief stock-in-trade is grace and beauty. "My grandmother often told me that the patent was never claimed for fear of the prince's wife, a lady said to be jealous and well experienced in the elimination of her rivals. The scroll itself is worthless to anyone but myself, yet the box in which I kept it was of great value. I—I have not been without gifts from wealthy admirers, and so I caused my family's one claim to better blood to be enshrined in a kind of reliquary. It is of beaten silver and filigree work, set with cabochon pigeon's-blood rubies. I fear that if it is not recovered, the thief will destroy or discard the scroll when he disposes of the box. You must help me recover it, Mr. Donne; you must!"

For a moment, Donne did not respond. Then he vaulted from his table-perch and strode to the door. Flinging it open he said coldly, "A most interesting history, Signorina Pitti. I suggest you write it up in serial form for the papers. I shall be sure to follow it faithfully to its denouement, as soon as I have finished consulting the agony columns."

I drew in my breath sharply. The stricken look on Miss Pitti's adorable face wounded me, but had no effect on Donne. Ever the master of icy reason, his expression never altered.

"You think I am lying," Miss Pitti managed at last.

"I know you are," answered Donne. "Much as I admit a case would be welcome, I had rather spend my time in idleness than waste it on the track of lies."

Miss Pitti made no move to rise from her chair. I saw the tears begin to trickle down her cheeks. "Really, Donne," I admonished.

"Yes *really*, Weston!" he came back at me. "What is *really* at bottom here? We have all the elements of a cheap romance. Not one is missing! The beautiful damsel in distress, the purloined document, the added attraction of circus intrigue—for I perceive that you are a circus *artiste*, Signorina—all topped by the melodramatic black veil. All that is lacking is a fresh corpse and perhaps the hint of Borgia poison! But you prefer to set this little charade in Florence rather than Rome." He slammed the door in a rage and lifted Miss Pitti to face him standing.

"Madam, I am a consulting detective. That is all I am and all I claim to be. There is not a single drop of Druid blood in my body, nor is every drop there purely British! A lost item, no matter how valuable, might be found for you more easily were you to go to one of the Golden Brotherhood. Even their apprentices have mastered simple finding spells. *Why have you come to me?*"

In answer, Miss Pitti gave way to wild sobs, pressing herself close against Donne. I confess to a pang of envy to see him so burdened, but his own sentiments in the situation were merely impatience mixed with exasperation. He pried her away and sat back in the chair. Turning his back on her, he walked to the front window and surveyed what he could of Baker Street.

Miss Pitti soon recovered control of herself. "Very well, Mr. Donne." She dabbed at her eyes with a handkerchief extracted from beneath her redingote. "I will be truthful.

You say that the Brotherhood could find any item, *no matter how valuable.* Ah, but can they be trusted to return what they find? How easy to inform the seeker that their spells have not worked! How easy to keep what they have found for themselves! And even if I were to catch them at it, what could I do to force them to return my possessions to me? *Giuro,* they frighten me too much, these British magicians!"

"Go on," directed Donne. "I did not think a circus performer would care twopence for aged parchments and such claptrap devices. We are speaking of something so valuable that even a Druid would be tempted?"

Miss Pitti leaned forward, her blue eyes shining. "*Precisamente!* The box—the reliquary—is just as I described it, but instead of parchment it contains a collar of emeralds. Priceless! The circus was in Bohemia. There was a certain nobleman—"

"And of course such a rich gift would tempt any man, even a Druid. Thank you, Signorina Pitti. I appreciate the trust you place in me. At least if I become corrupt enough to keep the necklace, once located, you will only have to call upon the powers of civil law rather than sorcery to make me yield it up. Can you describe the necklace more fully?"

"Yes, certainly. Fifteen square-cut emeralds, the largest big as the first joint of my thumb, all set in gold, the clasp in the shape of a mermaid with diamond eyes. It was kept in the reliquary, but that in turn was hidden in a silk-lined box, polished oak with—with a border of carved grapes. It has been stolen, box and all, and the box—the box is also worth much to me. You see, hidden behind the lining of the lid is a photograph which—"

"My dear Signorina." Donne helped her up and smoothly began edging her towards the door. "You may rest assured that I will not deliver the necklace without both the silver reliquary and the outer oak box. It is my pleasure to serve you. If you will come back at this time next week, I shall have news for you."

"So soon?" The blue eyes flew wide. "Ah, you are truly what they say, Mr. Donne!" To this Donne smiled and raised her ungloved hand to his lips. I goggled. Such a courtly gesture was nothing like my friend. Had he at last succumbed to the charms that had so quickly enslaved me?

My fantasies lasted only as long as it took for Donne to close the door after our fair visitor, throw himself into the chair, and give a bark of laughter. "By heaven, Weston, I did enjoy that!"

"Enjoy it?" I repeated. "It's not like you to rejoice in another's misfortune, Donne."

Donne only laughed again, louder. "Good old Weston. Can it be that all these years as my Boswell have done nothing to sharpen your powers of observation? Or is it just further proof of what I've always said, that women destroy a man's powers of logical deduction?"

Lighting the pipe that had awaited him throughout the interview, he went on to ask, "Did you notice *nothing* amiss in the lady's story, Weston? Not one inconsistency?"

"Hmph, well . . . I thought her too fine a girl to be the sort to accept such expensive—ah—tokens of affection as that necklace."

"There is no necklace," said Donne.

"What? But you agreed to take Miss Pitti's case. If there is no necklace, there is no case."

"Neither is there a Miss Pitti," Donne continued.

"No—no Miss Pitti? But she was sitting right where you—"

"*Someone* was sitting here. Someone who has lost something valuable. Someone who must conceal the true nature of the lost article from many people, but especially from the Druid brethren."

"Yes, I gathered as much," I said. "A costly gift—"

"Someone" —Donne ignored me—"who is a most execrable liar and a worse actress. I am an excellent judge of such. Her theories of disguise and mendacity are childishly romantic. If the lady does not cherish a complete leather-bound set of Byron's works, I'm a Turk. And yet, Weston, inspite of it all, the lady is my client, and there is not a force on earth that will sway me from serving her to the utmost in the resolution of her case."

"Donne," I murmured, "you are in love with her."

Donne favored me with a revolted look. "Hardly. Unless you are referring to the love all trueborn Britons must cherish for their rightful Queen. Gods save her," he tacked on as an afterthought.

Before I could demand an explanation he had seized his Inverness and deerstalker and was at the door. "Come, Weston, the game's afoot!" He was exultant.

I was only able to overtake him several blocks later. When so caught up in a case, his long-legged stride invariably left me far behind. "What's all this about the Queen?

What's she got to do with that poor child's case? Is this another of your crack-brained theories?"

Donne stopped dead, an impressive figure whether glimpsed against the dramatic backdrop of a moorland mist or in full summer sunlight, as now. "At it again, eh, Weston? Sometimes I think you write up those absurd tales about me just to make yourself look more the martyr. Poor old Weston, forever being treated to the great detective's subtle scorn. What a condescending bastard you paint me! And what a humble, long-suffering disciple you make of yourself."

"That's small enough pay for all the wild goose chases you've dragged me along on. And for what? You love to see your name in print, Donne, admit it!"

Brihtric Donne sighed. "I am only human—as I've pointed out to you a score of times. However, if I like to see my name in print, confess that you're not averse to seeing your name across the 'payable' line of those cheques from the *Strand* magazine. Rather enlivens exile for you, I'd imagine."

I dug my chin into my collar. "Checkmate," I grumbled. "Meanwhile we're standing here like rabbits. Where the devil are we headed?"

"To pay a call on an old friend."

"At this hour of the morning?" Donne and I were early risers, nor had the mysterious Miss Pitti been a slugabed, but for the most part the Londoners were only just beginning to emerge from their homes or to make their sleepy way to their places of employment.

"For some, this isn't the hour to be quitting their beds. You shall see." So saying, he plunged into the London byways, and I had to redouble my pace. I could not dare risk losing sight of him, having no idea of where he was going.

Street signs became fewer, but Donne, with his precise recall of every city cowpath and barrow, had no need to consult them. I had lost all sense of place and direction by the time he finally stopped and rapped imperiously at a certain battered green door.

The door was one of a row in a shabby stable-turned-mews that had seen far better times. The overhanging buildings shut off much of the sunlight, giving the impression of perpetual dusk. We waited in the shadows for about three minutes. Then, with a rust-strangled creak, the door swung back a crack, and a single dark eye regarded us. " 'Oo's there?" came the hoarse question.

"Open up, Toddy, it's me," Donne directed.

The door opened six inches farther and a gnome with steely grey hair, bristly as a badger, peered at us. "Why, so 'tis you, Mr. Donne. Me an' th' girls was just about t' call it all in, in keepin' with th' hower an' th' hunlikelihood of 'avin' any further customers. But yer most welcome, sir, always most welcome. Come in! Come in!"

I gave Donne an incredulous look as we followed Rumpelstiltskin inside. "*Girls,* Donne? What kind of girls, damn it?"

Donne smiled and let the question pass.

"Ow, look 'oo's 'ere, me dears!" bellowed our guide. We were standing in a room whose walls were heavily hung with velvet draperies and furnished solely with thick, embroidered cushions. On these sprawled women of every race, coloring, and nationality save one. Even I was quick to notice the absence of any British roses in this unique and delicious bouquet.

The ladies—many sleepy-eyed and sullen—looked up and let out squeals of rapture. Donne acknowledged these with a bow. "Sheer business today, my dear young women. Only business, I fear. A case, you understand." A few groans answered this announcement, and Donne assumed a helpless look for my benefit.

"*Illic et Venus et leves Amores atque ipsa in medio sedet Voluptas,*" he quoted. I frowned. "Oh, hang the dog and be done with it, Weston! Go back to disapproving of my cocaine habit instead. Prudery does not suit a man who can't even recall where he spent Beltaine night."

"Is this what you've dragged me along with you for, Donne? To visit a—a *house?*"

"Dear me, what an idea, Weston," mused Donne. "I might consider it sometime. No, no, this call is strictly professional. Friedrich, if you'd be so good as to see us in your office?" This last addressed to the gnome.

"Just as you like, sir! This way!" Friedrich rubbed his gnarly hands together, all obsequiousness. We picked our way through the reclining ladies to a door in far better condition than its mate giving on the street. Beyond it I gasped at the luxurious appointments of the mannikin's office. I lowered myself slowly into the plush comfort of a large tobacco-colored settee beside Donne while tiny Friedrich plumped himself into a veritable throne at a mahogany desk suitable for a prime minister. On the wall behind him a naked odalisque stared at me with amorous eyes.

"Now, Donne, what can I do for you?" I started. The gnome had produced a large bandanna and passed it over his face a few times, and instead of the wrinkled, ancient creature who had first admitted us there sat a young red-haired man with Adonis' face atop a child's body. His speech was purest Oxonian.

"You see, Weston?" remarked Donne. "Now *that* is what I mean by good disguise. Friedrich can do nothing about his height, but he rises above such limitations. I trust you still maintain a well-stocked wardrobe, Friedrich?"

The little man grinned. "Best you'll see outside of Drury Lane, my friend. Sometimes the clients like a bit of fantasy when they visit our gentle hostesses. But you haven't come here at this beastly hour of the morning to discuss costuming."

"On the contrary, that is my purpose exactly. I apologize for disturbing your establishment so late after regular business hours, but my own poor selection of fancy dress lacks the attire that I feel would best serve for what I have to hand presently. You must furnish Weston and me with something appropriate at once. We have a most pressing appointment."

"The devil you do!" whistled Friedrich. "I'd dearly love to know what that might be."

"Perhaps your curiosity will abate when you learn that it has to do with the Brotherhood."

"Not them?" Friedrich shuddered. "You can keep your secret with your Druids. One of our clients last night was telling Nadja about some of your pretty festivals—Sammain, for one—and how a man's life's good as cut off if he falls into Druid hands on *that* night."

Donne showed his teeth. "If you were a trueborn Briton like myself, Friedrich, instead of a bloody foreigner, you'd know that it isn't a man's life that the Druids cut off if they catch him out on Sammain."

"Brr! Sometimes I wonder whatever made me leave Hamburg to settle in this godforsaken land," said the dwarf.

"I don't suppose it could be the money?" suggested Donne. "An establishment like this, stocked with Continental girls, must clear a pretty penny."

"Some things are worth more than money. You won't catch me out when Sammain rolls around. Your ghoulish holidays mean nothing to me, but I've become very attached to my *Frater Franciscus*, as they say." Friedrich shook his head and slid out of his chair. "I keep my wardrobe through here. Makeup's in the armoire's top drawer. Take what you need and bring it back when you like."

I was closest to the door that Friedrich indicated. I opened it and walked into what could have been a small room in itself. A dim light was burning in a red glass globe overhead, and there was no other source of illumination. Suddenly, I felt myself seized about the legs. I fell forward, borne down by the weight of an unseen assailant. Lithe hands reached for my throat, and heavy breath came hot in my face. As the slavering jaws came closer, I thought I smelled the reek of exotic spices.

"Kwei-fei! For pity's sake, leave the man alone!" Friedrich raised the chamberstick high. By its light I saw my attacker, an amber-skinned beauty whose sashless silken robe concealed nothing but her intentions. Reluctantly—though she was not half so reluctant as I—she rolled away.

"A good girl, that Kwei-fei, but literal-minded. I made her wardrobe mistress, you see," Friedrich said.

"You might've explained her duties a shade more precisely," said Donne.

"Would *you?*" The little man smirked. Kwei-fei sat crosslegged in the corner, a red lacquered pipe in her teeth. Cloying sweet smoke spiralled up. Beside her, running the length of the wall, hung Friedrich's costumes. More reposed in tumbled splendor on chairs, and still others peeped from an open steamer trunk under the single high window in the room.

"I'll leave you to make your choice, but if I were you, I'd steer clear of any matter involving the Golden Brotherhood," said Friedrich. "The girls would miss you awfully. We've 'ad us some right good times, Mr. Donne," he added in that vulgar accent.

Donne's hand fell on Friedrich's shoulder. "You're a good friend, Friedrich; a good and loyal friend. But this case is still too far from resolution to allow for delay. Time is vital. If you knew what I do, you would agree."

"Have it your way, then." Friedrich glumly left us to our own devices in the wardrobe.

"I don't know, Donne," I said while he rummaged through the heaps of cotton, satin, velvet, and homely calico. "That Friedrich is a queer bird, but he's got good sense. What are we getting ourselves into? How has that circus girl's tale anything to do with the Druids—or the Queen?"

The detective's face was iron. "If you dislike my methods, remain here. Friedrich could use you. You might even pick up a little ready money curing his girls of their occupational afflictions. As for me—" He returned to his search. At last he straightened, triumphant. "Here we are, Weston. This should fit you, and I know this one will suit me."

I touched the black acolyte's robe he had flung out for my inspection, and a thrill of half-remembered horror ran down the length of my arm. "Donne, are you mad?" He was already swathed in a master Druid's white garment and now attacked the makeup drawer in a nearby armoire chockablock with false hair, glassless spectacles, and other stage properties.

"By no means. But are you fit?"

"Fit? What are you talking about?"

His eyes strayed up, up to where the lone window sent a shaft of sunlight into the closet-room. Kewi-fei watched impassively as we completed our toilet and made our unorthodox exit.

In the parlor, the black-haired Russian beauty Nadja tossed down a shot of vodka and immediately choked on it. The golden sickle circled her throat, its fine edge sharp against her ivory skin.

"Where are they?" the Druid's voice boomed.

The other girls screamed. Some ran, but Friedrich's office door was locked. Musette beat on it furiously. Jeanne huddled among the cushions, sobbing.

"Where?"

The street door had yielded silently. Donne had seized Nadja before anyone realized we had come in. Behind his white-robed splendor I waited, black as a battle-crow, holding an ash-wood staff. He stood among the women like a ghostly shark in the midst of a school of brilliant fish. *"Where is the apostate?* Where is the unbeliever? The gods demand sacrifice! The dead clamor for his blood!"

"In there!" squealed Nadja, pointing wildly at the office door. "They went in through there not an hour ago, and there's no way out. Take them! Take them and go!" She gasped with relief as the "Druid" removed that deadly golden necklace.

"Russian bitch!" shouted Musette. She had awakened from her terror of the Brotherhood's supposed invasion.

Now she sprang at Nadja and jerked her back by the hair. "Throw him to the wolves so easily, do you? How many times has he helped you, ha? How many times has he served every girl in this house?"

"Musette is right," rasped Emilia. "*Porca Madonna*, she is right!" A small knife flashed from her white kidskin boots. "Damned whitebeard, in Rome we know how to deal with your kind!" Catlike she leaped for him, shrieking like a Fury.

There was more passion than skill in her attack. Donne seized her wrist, bending it back until she was forced to drop the knife. Then with a chuckle he said, "Such devotion really does one good. Thank you, Emilia; Musette. But as for you, Nadja—" He clicked his tongue. "Your backbone could stand some strengthening."

"*Donne!*" The Russian's black eyes were huge with wonder.

"And Weston." He swept his arm back to include me.

"But we saw you go into the office, and there is no door—"

"Ladies, in your profession as in mine, it is never wise to overlook a window. But I am pleased that our disguises are satisfactory enough to deceive you. We shall not keep you from your well-earned sleep any longer. Good day."

"I feel like a fool," I said as we left Friedrich's bawdy house behind us and took to the London labyrinth again.

"Better a live dog than a dead lion, Weston. We're not playing dress-up here. This is serious business."

"I still want to know where we're going."

"Where?" Donne's eyebrows rose beneath the two thick tufts of bushy white false hair he had applied to them. "Why, to seek out our little circus dancer. You shall see."

CHAPTER THREE

The Mortal Terror of Old Isaacs

The narrow alleys through which we walked gave way to wider streets which in turn changed to broad, well-paved avenues. Stately groves of elm cast bosky shadows. I recognized the better section of London, but it was precisely in such well-to-do neighborhoods that one was more likely to encounter the highest-ranking Druids. What should become of us if our masquerade was discovered? It was not a pleasant thought.

Donne was in his element. He strolled past knots of holy men as if he truly were their brother, even going so far as to cuff a disciple, clad like myself in black, for stumbling against him at the kerb. He cursed fluently in the Old Tongue and the poor lad scampered off.

"You're out to get us both killed," I whispered.

"If that were my purpose, I would have let that brat get away with jostling me. Yes, that would have been as good as tearing off my robes here and now. You have some talent for deceit, Weston, but you lack the broad strokes of the art. Never mind. You are perfectly suited to play the humble disciple. Now close up ranks. We are approaching our goal."

I raised my eyes cautiously and bit my lip to keep from gasping. Donne had led me right up to the gilded gateway of Buckingham Palace itself. The Marlborough dolmen brooded in front of it, sheltering Boudicca's Well. Was it fancy, or could I truly hear the moans and cries of the Romans who had met a drowning death in its depths?

The royal guards of the Palace door took one look at our robes and made no attempt to question us. Donne did not bother to knock, but grabbed the polished brass ring on the right-hand portal and pulled back on it firmly. The weight of the door itself swung it wide and we were within the Palace.

A small, unexpected shriek made me jump as we crossed the deserted entrance hall. Donne glared at me, then quickly spied the source. An ancient porter, neatly dressed in the Queen's livery, cowered beneath a marble-topped sideboard.

"Get up." Trembling, the man obeyed Donne's command.

"Master—Master, we did not expect—expect one of your august Brotherhood to pay a call upon us today. Nothing is prepared." It was touching to see the old porter's fright. The Golden Brotherhood commanded an awe bordering on terror among the common folk. No doubt a keen-eyed servant had spied our approach from an upper window and spread the word. Small wonder we met with no one when we entered the Palace.

"Her Majesty expects us. She waits for us even now," said Donne. "Are you the only one here to conduct us to her?"

"I—I'm not supposed to leave the door, Master. I'm not but the porter."

"You refuse to serve *me?*" Donne's ferocity was convincing. The ancient porter shook hard enough to disjoint himself, but still he kept his spine inflexible, his thumbs immovably in line with the side seams of his blue silk knickers.

Donne pressed on. "We are not used to being kept waiting. I would suggest you not compound your offenses. Conduct us to the Queen!"

"At once, at once," chittered the porter. His powdered wig slipped slightly forward, giving him a drunken look, but he wasted no time readjusting it. He fairly leapt through an archway flanked by statues of impossible Nubians, silver torches in their hands.

For the second time that morning I found myself treading a maze, this one as rich and luxurious as the first had been shabby and dismal, especially in the streets immediately surrounding Friedrich's "house." The squalor of those streets might as well have been a million miles away. Here, where no daylight penetrated, all was cool splendor. The few windows in Buckingham Palace, as any schoolchild knew, were those huge floor-to-ceiling affairs in the official reception rooms. Otherwise a hermetically sealed darkness was more conducive to the spell-weaving used in the ruling of Britain.

I smelled the tantalizing hints of scented beeswax candles burning in sconces along the endless walls where portraits of the former rulers of our happy isle watched us pass; Aelin the Unlearned, Canute the Convert, many Henrys and a handsome handful of Edwards, William the Conjurer, and of course the father of Britain's line and Britain's power, Bran the Blessed. Underfoot, intricately laid parquetry gave way to silk rugs and pink marble stairways. We climbed several of these before the porter came to a halt before a white-and-gold oak door.

"Shall I announce you?" His voice was quavering.

"You had best return to your post." Donne's lip curled behind the false beard. "There may be others waiting for you *not* to admit them." The porter bowed once, sharply, and vanished. Donne could not suppress a chuckle. "Scared out of his wits, but proper to the last. There's the strength of Britain, Weston! Her true strength. What people, what nation dare stand against us when even the servile classes would sooner die than forget their training? And it was no Druid spell wrought that!" He turned his attention to the door. "We shall enter unannounced."

I tried the knob. "We shall have to knock. It's locked."

Donne looked thoroughly amused. "Weston, you lack imagination. What are locks to a member of our order? A wave of the hand opens them, or a few well-mumbled mysticisms. Observe my own peculiar brand of sorcery." So saying, he raised his robes and gave the lockplate a swift, savage kick. The door burst open with a report like thunder.

Three fair-faced young women wearing the currently fashionable and absurdly hooped skirts of the Continent stood frozen before a huge fireplace. In the depths of the twilit Palace, even fine summer days could prove chilly enough to warrant a fire. When they saw us, their initial surprise melted to horror. One gasped, too frightened to cry out. The second screamed and fainted into the arms of the third, who began weeping hysterically, without tears. Donne swept down on them, his long white sleeves describing fantastic arcs of sheet lightning.

The effect was beyond any I had ever read of in the herbalist journals. The lady in a faint revived immediately and fled squawking from the room. The hysteric was stricken dumb, and the dumbstruck young miss recovered the use of her vocal cords long enough to shriek *and* have hysterics *and* faint. Donne raised his shoulders slightly in a what-would-you-Weston gesture.

"*Rise!*" Donne's voice rolled. The one maid-in-waiting left in her senses only goggled at him, her ridiculous sausage-curls bobbing at her cheeks while she made helpless flutterings towards her unconscious companion. "Leave her. She will recover. We have business this day with Her Majesty. Where is she?"

The girl made a weak effort to approach us. The curtsy she dropped was nearly too much effort; she rose from it with difficulty. Compassion stirred me as I noticed the tears starting in her fine brown eyes. "You need not take us to her," I said gently. "Nor announce us. Is she in there?" I indicated the tall door leading from the anteroom.

The girl nodded, then forced herself to speak. "Her bed-chamber. Oh please, Master, I must announce you! Her Majesty left strict instructions that no one was to dis—"

"Lionors! Who's thrown poor Morgan into such a state? The chit's brainless enough normally, but— Ah!"

A woman had joined us; a tall, handsome woman whose strong, patrician features were marred only by a freshly healing wound across one cheek—four long gashes, like a perfectly plowed field. In a royal palace where the fashions of any age and nation might be spied, to say nothing of the austere garb of the Druid hierarchy, she wore a simply cut sheath of dead-white dimity in the style of the late George IV's reign, an ornate brooch prominent at the high neck. A narrow band of blue satin passed under her bodice and was echoed by a similar bit of ribbon tying up a thick spill of brilliant auburn curls. On another woman, such artless dress would have had great power to charm; on this one, it looked as sinister as an executioner's mask. The waiting-maid Lionors' fist went to her mouth and she shook, but the tall woman's attention had flown swiftly to Donne.

"Who are you? What is your business with the Queen?" She showed no fear of his Druid disguise at all, and scarcely even the shadow of respect for his supposed rank.

"My lady, my business is none of yours. See to the waiting-maids and remember your place." Donne delivered his lines with just the proper balance of icy menace and subtle venom. "Perhaps when I have concluded with Her Majesty, I will prescribe a poultice for your complexion."

Automatically the woman's fingers fanned out to hide the awful scars. "The day I need your stinking poultices— By the Morrigan, do you think me incapable of healing myself?"

"You are incapable of obedience, that much is plain. You wear a pretty badge to show what comes of not knowing how to conduct yourself with your betters in spell-weaving.

Now, unless you want a matching mark for your other cheek, you and this poor child will carry your fallen friend out of here and leave us in peace."

Already the woman was beginning to weaken, yet she swayed back and forth in the doorway until I was reminded of a snake calculating its strike. For some reason, then unknown to me, the sight of her made my blood stir with a weird revulsion, as if she were a childhood nightmare sprung to life. I breathed a deep sigh of relief when she finally knelt to help Lionors carry out the fainted girl.

"Let us make haste, Weston," said Donne. "Lady Byron is not one to take her dismissal lightly. She will be back, no doubt accompanied by a few allies. Close the door and move something heavy against it. I fear I've done for the more conventional lock."

"How did you know who she—?"

I was unable to finish my question. Behind me I heard a sweet voice say, "Thank you, Mr. Donne. I see that my faith in you was well placed," and I turned to see the Queen.

She was standing with one hand on her bedchamber door, which had opened without the smallest sound. She looked for all the world like those outlandishly beautiful creatures the Iberians call angels and worship among their other gods. A very filthy angel, whose clinging cream wool dressing-gown was thoroughly stained with flecks of grey. She closed the bedchamber door behind her and came forward, offering Donne both her hands.

A sour stabbing hit the pit of my stomach as I watched him raise them to his lips. "Your Majesty speaks of faith, but trust ought to accompany it. Why did you lie to me? Why that foolish posing as a circus dancer when your persona had as many holes in it as your story?"

She met his eyes unflinching. "I had to be sure. I have—great faith in Dr. Weston." Here she gave me the most ravishing smile, though I was damned if I could comprehend my good fortune. Beltaine remained a mysterious lacuna in my brain, apart from leaving our flat and awakening on the Embankment. "I did not connect his name with the stories written about you until recently. However, a certain amount of poetic license can appear in the writings of even the most admirable of men. I had to know that all he wrote of you was true."

"I see. Weston, you have done well. How many authors can say they have so impressed our Lady?" My head was humming. Victoria still smiled at me in a way that seemed to demand some sort of reply on my part, but I just stood there like an ox. At length the smile faded, replaced by a look of hurt puzzlement. Oh, to buy back those days of sorrow I caused her, at whatever price! Donne continued. "Now that I have presented my credentials, as it were, will Your Majesty confide in me?"

The Queen waved us to a brace of brown velvet armchairs comfortably placed beside the anteroom fire. Donne shook his head. "I think I should like to meet my assistant first, Your Majesty." He nodded towards the closed bedroom door.

Victoria was taken aback. "Your assistant?"

"Or whatever you choose to call him. A man who has the Queen and Mistress of all Britain down on her knees in the hearth ashes like a common scullery wench must be powerful indeed. I wonder that you called me in on the case, having him already at your call." He was across the room and into the royal bedchamber without a by-your-leave. He only paused on the threshold to remark, "Weston, the other door?" in a gently chiding manner.

I wrestled a heavy boule writing desk to barricade the anteroom before joining Donne and Victoria. I found her sitting on the edge of a bed whose midnight-blue hangings, embroidered with silver threads, echoed in my mind. Donne stood, arms folded, over the hunched figure of a footman in full Queen's livery who knelt among the ashes of an ages-dead fire on the bedroom hearth. Above them hung a curiously empty ormolu picture frame.

"Well, my good man, you don't look as if your sorceries are *too* powerful," Donne was saying with a good-natured smile. The footman remained silent, but his right hand strayed to his cheek and made a bizarre, stroking gesture running from the sideroll of his powdered wig down the length of his gaunt jaw and back again.

"Mr. Donne, Adams is merely a Palace servant. I summon twenty such each day," said the Queen.

Donne's face set hard. "Your Majesty is still testing me, I presume. By no stretch of the imagination could an even mildly competent observer mistake a Jewish scholar for a royal servant."

The man called Adams ceased his outlandish self-caress and tried to get to his feet, his face a mask of confusion behind pinchbeck-rimmed spectacles. As he rose, he scuffed insistently in the hearthside ashes until Donne shot out one foot to arrest this. He knelt in turn.

"Ah, now I *am* impressed," he said, holding his chin. "No mere Talmudic scholar, but a master of the Kabbalah, no less. I ask your pardon, sir. Pray go on with your work. We shall be more comfortable in the anteroom after all."

My back bristled at Donne's high-handed manner with the Queen, and yet in our brief Continental adventures I had seen him treat clients of Victoria's preeminence just as masterfully. I could not imagine why I now resented what was a typically Donnesian attitude—all earthly rank reduced to nothing when compared to the powers of his deductive mind.

He took over one of the armchairs and stretched his legs out at leisure. The Queen took the other, leaving me to hover nearby, an unasked ghost at their feast. The supposed footman closed the bedroom door after us with a timid glance at Donne.

"Your Majesty has some explaining to do," Donne said, tugging off his false beard. "Whatever it is that you have lost must be valuable indeed, yet you dare not use the powers of the Druids who must by bloodright obey you. So, you call in agents unconnected with the Golden Brotherhood. A Jew, for one; myself, whose contempt for Druidical magics Weston has well documented, for another."

"Mr. Donne, you have astonished me—no easy thing to do, in view of all I have experienced in the course of my short life." The Queen folded her hands in her lap and by her presence turned the bourgeois armchair into a dragon throne. "Your observations about Adams—Isaacs, rather—are such that now I doubt there is not some taint of Druid's blood in your lineage. I cannot be too careful."

Donne inclined his head. "None of us can. So, his name is Isaacs? Very well, Your Majesty, you must play Weston to me this time. He was astounded when I named Lady Byron correctly, never having met the woman. So long as your aristocracy delights in flaunting their coats of arms on personal jewelry, their identities are plain to see. Did you not observe the brooch at her neck? The Byron mermaid crest stands out even at a distance, and in this poor light. As for

Isaacs, it was evident that he was anything but a Palace servant. Your hall porter is a far older retainer than the supposed 'Adams,' yet he carried himself with well-trained rigidity despite his years. He might forget his training, but his spine recalled it for him. Not so 'Adams.' He remained bent in the ashes—a scholarly bent, if you will excuse some wordplay. A true servant would rise to his feet and snap to attention when his mistress entered with visitors."

"He was helping me lay a fire, Mr. Donne," said the Queen, entering into a kind of contest with him.

"A footman doing a chambermaid's chore? Your servants, Madam, guard their differing ranks more jealously than do your nobility. And the ashes on your own gown show you were kneeling beside him. Are you in the habit of helping your domestics? I doubt it. Furthermore, where were the makings of the new fire? No, no, your excuse won't wash, though I hope your gown will."

He sprang from the chair and tore off his Druid's regalia, bidding me do the same with my acolyte's garb. Our ordinary clothes were underneath. All Druids but the highest looked upon their white outer garments as purely ceremonial, the way a judge retains his own plain tweeds beneath his impressive robe of office. What the Archdruid wore under his robes was the subject of much conjecture and not a few dirty schoolboy jokes. Both of our robes and all their accoutrements save the golden sickle Donne now tossed into the hungry flames of the anteroom fire.

"We shall have visitors shortly, and it would not do to be caught impersonating members of the Brotherhood. Would Your Majesty be so good as to speed matters for us?"

The Queen nodded and crumpled the sickle to common dust in her hands. This she tossed onto the fire, which blazed up with supernatural ferocity and devoured our costumes in a fraction of ordinary time.

Donne took all this for granted as he spoke on, his hands busy with a pencil and pocket notebook he had drawn from his jacket. He thrust an open page under Victoria's nose. I peered at it over her shoulder and could make nothing of the scrawl.

"A far cry from schoolboy Greek, eh, Weston? Did you never delve into the Hebrew tongue? Letters like these formed part of Isaacs' business in the ashes, which I was able to stop him from erasing completely. They are the symbols of some Kabbalistic ritual—one for finding lost objects, I would hazard. They simply confirmed my deductions as to Isaacs' race."

"Yes," I said. "But how did you mark him for a Jew in the first place? A scholar, granted, but a Jewish one?"

"Elementary. To the close observer, that is. That idiosyncratic gesture of his—thus—" He stroked his own jaw in just Isaacs' manner. "Now why would a man do that? A clean-shaven man, I mean. It is a gesture more than common among bearded men, especially when thinking or at a loss. I noted that the skin along his jawline was considerably lighter than that of the rest of his face, as well. Something had shaded it from the sun until recently. A beard, shaved off to fit the footman disguise, but sorely missed. Weak eyes, but strengthened with spectacles rather than moonwater spells. Why would a man whose life is study reject a spell that would help make his examination of crabbed texts far easier? Only if he were also a man to whom magic, the Wise, and all their works are anathema. You will find severe penalties for witchcraft in the Jews' holy books, Weston. So, a scholarly man, *not* a Druid, who must have had much to gain to make him shave off such a beloved bit of facial hair. Your Majesty spoke so vehemently against calling in the Brotherhood that I had to conclude further that this man must belong to a race not native to these shores, to guarantee his total lack of Druid's blood. The Jews fit this requirement nicely, are noted for their love of knowledge and their lushly bearded scholars, and would benefit immeasurably from royal favor, as the Brotherhood allows them to take refuge in Britain purely on the sufferance of the moment. Have I hit it, Your Majesty?"

She matched his smile. "Joseph Isaacs works for me on the promise of my granting royal protection to his people. You are everything I hoped for, Mr. Donne."

"Hope for my survival, then," said Donne.

A horrid screeching came from the hall door. The boule desk shuddered like a skittish mare as its feet began to drag across the parquet. It gathered momentum and shot aside from the door, which now collapsed inward as Lady Byron took the royal suite by storm.

She had come well escorted. My memories of Beltaine had not all been blasted from my mind. Ghosts still lingered, and among these the shuddersome phantom of the Archdruid of all Britain, Wellington, glaring with disgust at what my misstep had done to his robes. Now the phantom was here, in the flesh, and his glare had lost nothing of its acid in the intervening weeks. Coward that I am, I rejoiced to see that Donne, not I, was the object of it this time.

Behind the Iron Duke came two other men, one with a too-perfect face and a sorry clubfooted limp, the other dark-skinned and sleek as an otter, but without that creature's charm. My skin crept when he came near me.

"They're still here, Master!" Lady Byron's accusation sounded victorious. "Their robes must be somewhere—they hadn't time to hide them—" She nosed avidly around the room like a fox terrier on the scent, but turned up only empty burrows.

"Robes? I assure you, Master, Dr. Weston and I did not spend the night here." Donne faced Wellington's blazing look with equanimity. They might have been fellow field hands meeting for a pint of bitter at harvest home.

"I know you, Donne," the Duke snarled, his white hair crackling with electric life. "Still the apostate. Still the doubter."

"Still the rational man. You can make me no greater compliment."

"I did not come to flatter you. What are you doing in Her Majesty's apartments?"

Victoria would have spoken, making some excuse for us, but Donne was enjoying the game. "Why don't you gaze into your cauldron and find the answers there, Master? Are any secrets safe from the Brotherhood?"

The Iron Duke wheeled from Donne as from a creature beneath his notice. To the dark man in an officer's tunic he said, "Deal with him, Kitchener. He has no magic; you can handle him with ease."

"Lord Kitchener, is it?" Donne would not allow himself to be excluded. "Ha! Can any man have travelled as widely as you—seen what other nations are capable of achieving—and still play the Brotherhood's faithful sheepdog? When you lead your men—magicless mortals like you and me—against the iron guns of the foe and see them cut to ribbons by a Druid letting his shielding spell slip, how does it feel? How, when your dead clutch bronze swords and ash long-bows suddenly free of enchantments—ordinary, pitiful, primitive arms like that against all the modern world can devise?"

What his lordship thought, we were not to learn then.

The air was rent by a scream of horror so chilling and dismal that even the Iron Duke's face went bloodless. A second shriek, louder than the first, reverberated from behind the closed door of the Queen's bedchamber. Donne seized the doorknob in a thought's time, but leapt back with a muffled curse, his hand a claw of pain.

"The knob, Weston!" he gasped. I seized his wrist and examined the clenched hand, fighting back the nausea that flooded me when I saw the livid skin, white as that of a man frozen to death on Snowdon's stony flanks. The bedchamber doorknob was incandescent with a fearsome blue-white glow. It throbbed and pulsed like a live thing. A third scream came, and the sound of something heavy falling. The Duke spoke a word of power, and the door opened.

Donne and I were the first ones through the door. We saw Isaacs lying on his back before the hearth, his eyes wide and glassy, his face distorted into the mask of a man who has gazed too long at his own death. Donne ignored his pain to crouch above the dead man. A cold, noxious reek escaped and permeated the royal suite, making nearly all of us cough and wipe our watering eyes.

"Your Majesty! Your Majesty, please—" I was doing my best to bar the Queen from that grisly sight. This sudden urge I had to shelter a woman who could raise the dead of half a hundred British barrows at a song was as illogical as it was irresistible.

"Stand aside," she said firmly.

"Yes, Weston, let her in. Whatever did this has gone." I fought to recover my place in the ring surrounding Isaacs. His poor spectacles lay smashed and twisted on the hearthstone, his powdered wig entirely askew revealing the small black skullcap pressed against the sparse badger-grey hair.

"Get out, Donne," snapped the Duke. His staff crashed to the stone, making further havoc of the old scholar's spectacles.

Donne smirked in a fashion calculated to annoy. He straightened and pushed his long, aquiline nose dangerously close to the Archdruid's face. "Use your magic wand, Magician. Make me disappear."

The Iron Duke let loose a roar of rage and slammed his staff brutally into Donne's shoulder. The detective went down in a tumble of limbs on top of Isaacs' corpse. He whimpered like a kicked cur, cradling his death-white hand against his battered shoulder with a great to-do as he got up again and fled the room without another word.

I stood dumbstruck, too many emotions battling each other for any one to emerge and be recognized. My mouth opened and closed like a fish's, my eyes darting from face to face in the Queen's bedchamber, finding only hostility. Victoria herself would not look at me.

"Come with me, old chap," said a welcome, kindly voice. It was the handsome clubfoot, his hand strong on my elbow. "Your friend will have need of your healing arts. I'll see you out."

Donne was not in the hall nor on the staircase we descended. "He must have gone home," I muttered. "You needn't follow me, my good man. I assure you I haven't the faintest desire to stay here."

"But I insist, I insist!" And the grip the fellow exerted on my elbow was quite insistent. He steered me down the flight, but even as I saw the great front doors of the Palace—our good friend the porter recomposed and at his post—my limping guide took an unexpected veer to the right and I found myself being hustled through a low door hidden behind the curve of the grand marble staircase.

At once I began to see Druidic plots against my life, or at least against my person. Lady Byron did not strike me as a woman to have only one plan for dealing with intruders, especially those who insulted her. Had Donne already been seized upon? Was I being hastened to a like fate? The finest palace in all the world may also have the most convenient places for the disposal of unwanted persons.

I pulled up short in the musty darkness under the staircase and yanked my arm from the clubfoot's clutch. "See here, what are you up to?" I sounded stuffy enough to be a banker.

"Ah, John, not here! Not here! She can still spy upon me at this distance, if she chooses. I can never be certain. . . . Come with me; please come."

My chosen name came easily to this man's lips. Were my tales of Donne's exploits so widely known? There was also such a look of anxiety on that smooth face of his that I followed, for my association with Donne had contaminated me beyond redemption with a love of mystery.

There was another door leading from the cramped understair room, this giving on a pantry where the royal pickles and preserves in their military rows were passing the inspection of a frail, fair-haired lass armed with a feather duster. She did not seem at all surprised to see us pop out among the chutneys, but curtsied awkwardly.

"He's the one, yer lordship?" she asked in an awed whisper. She pronounced her *h* with the self-conscious emphasis of a reformed Cockney.

My guide chucked her under the chin. "The very one, Sarah. Have you prepared the room?"

She stuck out her bony elbows in another curtsy and on the downward swoop dropped her duster to tug back a set of false floorboards concealing a heavy trapdoor. He raised this and started down the ladder into depths from which the warm glow of light rose.

"I'm not going down there!" I folded my arms. "What manner of fool do you take me for?"

"Damn it, *come!*" His fist struck the floor, for he was already half consumed by the trap. "I didn't save your life on Beltaine to have you plague me with idiot's questions. You come *now*, before *she* gets the wind up."

Beltaine! Oh, I followed after that. I'd have followed the Morrigan herself to regain some memory of that lost night. The hideous torture chamber I'd envisioned beneath the pantry turned out to be a disused well, run dry and paneled up to make quite a cozy hideaway if one did not suffer from fear of premature burial. A comfortable chair, a tottery wooden footstool, a small pine table, and a clay oil lamp furnished it, but neither he nor I sat down.

"I haven't much time," he said, both hands tight on my shoulders. "The gods alone know how long I'll have before he takes her into favor again. Listen, no matter what she does to me, you must save the Queen. I would do it if my powers were what they should be, but not even the Archdruid himself will be powerful enough to stop my wife and—*Ah!*" His head jerked back, his pale fingers dug into my flesh through the light tweed jacket I wore, and I felt his full weight suddenly drag against me, as if he'd lost command of his knees.

I supported him as well as I was able, but he moaned and went boneless as a ragdoll in my arms. A sharp hissing noise from above made me look up to see the girl Sarah frantically waving for me to drop him and climb out of the pit.

"Ow, get up here, do! *He'll* be all right. But it's *her* that's a-callin' him now, and when he don't answer smart, she sends this on him. Poor Lord Byron, and him such a gallant gentleman!" She made a wild grab for me and nearly toppled herself into the secret room. "Move it, guv! When she strikes him down, she comes after him soon enough. I'll get you out o' the Palace."

Rather than have the girl fall in on top of us, I got out of the pit, dragging Byron with me. Clearly he did not want his wife to learn of this hideaway, and Sarah could not be expected to hoist him to the surface herself. Still holding him semi-upright, I lowered the trapdoor and replaced the false flooring.

"Ain't you the strong one!" the girl murmured. She produced a half-empty brandy bottle from behind the pickles, opened it, and smeared some on his lordship's lips. From the same place she brought out a common water glass and with my help arranged Byron into the believable pose of a man doing a bit of private drinking on the sly. Finger to her lips, she led me by another route out of the pantry and out of the Palace via what must have been a root cellar.

We stood in a small, dark courtyard, its narrow access only wide enough for wagons making deliveries of produce and fuel to the royal kitchen. "I shall smell of turnips for a week," I said, trying to brush the earthly aroma from my clothes. Sarah laughed, but I was serious again. "So that was Lord Byron. Whatever message he meant to give me, I couldn't make much of it. You seem privy to his doings. What did he want of—?"

"Another of your lady friends, Weston?" It was as if the cobbles had spawned Donne then and there. For a man I'd last seen in agony, he was bearing up well. "A tweeny, I perceive."

"Sarah Giles, sir, at yer service." Sarah did not accompany this with a curtsy, but bent her eyes on Donne with the same hungry, admiring look that he always—Oh, damn the man! "Lord Byron said the Queen'd sent for someone to help her. I'm *ever* so glad she sent for *you*." As an afterthought she looked at me and said, "Ow, then you must be *that* Dr. Weston."

Voices wafted up the open cellar door behind her. She cast a nervous glance over her thin shoulder and said, "I'd best be back. Ow, but Mr. Donne, sir, you *must* help the Queen! Look, here's it all writ down." She pressed a folded paper into my hand. "I—I love Her Majesty, I do. It's not right what's going on abovestairs. Not half wicked, it's not! Ow, go, go!" The cellar door slammed.

"Donne, what an extraordinary experience I've just had," I began.

"You shall tell me all about it. But not now. We would be wise to take Sarah Giles' advice. Whatever has been stolen from the Queen, whatever is afoot in that Palace, has already claimed one man's life." I saw his brows draw together darkly, for nothing so angered Donne as the waste of human life.

Then like sunshine after a June shower, he was all jollity again. He whisked me from the Palace environs and into a little public house off Llyr Street, where we took a table in the back room. "Not what you're used to, Weston, but the perfect place to exchange confidences. Give me the paper."

I passed him Sarah's note. He studied it for a time and set it down with a little sound of disgust. "Another would-be romancer, this one a tweeny. She claims there is a foul plot intended against the Queen, then says nothing concrete about it. She does, however, wax specific when she asks to be considered for a more elevated station than that of tweeny, should her aid in this case prove valuable. Well, well! Perhaps Mrs. Hendrik would have a place for her. She might be passable once washed. The girl offers to be our eyes and ears within the Palace and to report a week hence at the Silver Hand Inn in Seven Dials." Donne's spidery fingers plucked the paper to shreds.

"You'll meet her there?" I asked.

"No." Donne took a deep draught of his bitter. "You shall."

"But this may be worthless, the imaginings of an overwrought young woman with a taste for melodrama!"

"Overlook nothing, Weston." He held his empty glass close to his chest, his hawk's eyes steady on me. "There are too many questions left unanswered for us to discard any clue, however improbable the source. Neither of us came away empty-handed this morning. That is some consolation."

I watched as he leaned back and reached into his vest. He extracted a handkerchief in which something was obviously wrapped and laid it on the table. When he unveiled it, it was with the grace and effect of a conjuring artist.

"A feather?" I picked it up gingerly, holding it at eye level between thumb and forefinger. It was black and glossy right down to the root of the shaft. Moreover as I held it, it seemed to grow heavier. I was forced to cup it in my palm, and even then the weight of it grew until my hand lowered to the tabletop.

"Exactly. A feather, such as any pigeon in Regent's Park might molt." Donne was toying with me.

"Hardly that. I've never seen the like! Where did you get it?"

He took it back and looked long and hard at the uncanny plume, consulting it as a seer would his crystal. "It was a parting gift from Joseph Isaacs." He caught my inquiring look. "This feather, Weston, was clutched in Isaacs' dead grasp. I had no chance to take it for examination at first. Too many eyes were upon me. Therefore I deliberately baited the Iron Duke into striking me with his staff so that I might fall upon the body and seize the feather in the hubbub."

"Poor Donne. First your hand and then your sh— Why, your shoulder's fine! That blow made you yelp loud enough for me to think he'd broken it for you."

He allowed me to examine the once-afflicted hand. No sign of the gruesomely frozen flesh remained. "It would seem my luck that the effects were not permanent. As for my shoulder, it's a poor actor who can't roll with a blow."

We paid our score and strolled home. Donne could speak of nothing but the feather. Amazed as I was by its strange qualities, I saw no significance in the object itself. Then again, it might be that the thought of Mrs. Hendrik's luncheon awaiting us in our rooms allowed space for no other thoughts in my hunger-clouded mind.

Mrs. Hendrik herself was waiting for us at the head of the stairs. "A caller's here for you, gentlemen," she said. "Would you know if he's staying for lunch?"

"I was expecting no caller, were you, Donne?" I asked.

"By all means, include him, Mrs. Hendrik. That is, if it will not be too great a bother?" Clearly Donne was not going to trouble himself answering me.

"A bother? Oh, never a bother for you, Mr. Donne!" our worthy landlady bubbled, and toddled off to "see to things."

"Another client?" I wondered aloud. What sort of an answer would Donne give, committed to Her Majesty as he was? I felt sorry for our unknown caller and already pictured a painful scene in which some poor wretch was turned helpless away from the great detective's door; painful for Donne as well, who loathed to deny his aid to any worthy cause.

The man awaiting us did not look as if his troubles weighed too heavily on his mind. He was tall and swarthy, able to look Donne in the eye with a black gaze full of sardonic penetration. He was a relic of a time antedating even the bibulous reign of George IV, and while those of Druid blood could turn their magic to extending their lives as long as their power endured, there were mighty few strong enough in spells to survive from the days when men affected the flamboyant silks, scarlet heeled boots, elaborately plumed hat, and elaborately curled periwig that this man wore.

This seldom-seen costume had no effect on Donne. He merely bowed and said with his usual composure, "Your Late Majesty, I presume?"

CHAPTER FOUR

The Accommodation for Lord Backwater

I am understandably unfamiliar with the British succession. Therefore I never had dinned into my head the popular quatrain gleefully chanted by every street urchin with the price of a wicker man come Noll Cromwell Day, viz.:

When Wizard Cromwell killed his Dad,
It made Old Rowley jolly mad,
So good King Charley took an axe
And gave the bugger forty whacks!

Donne made up for this woeful lack in my education by reciting it on the spot. "Then the little devils set fire to their wicker manikins, emulating their pious elders. At least they refrain from locking up human sacrifices in the ghastly apparatus, though the local populations of rats, mice, and chimney swifts are often sorely depleted after Noll Cromwell Day. For myself, I never have appreciated the gods' insistence on such gruesome pledges of faith. But I am remiss. Take off your hat, Weston. You are in the presence of royalty."

"Ods fish, Mr. Donne, you do not appear to be at all astonished to find me here. Do you entertain kings so often, then?" His Late Majesty's dark eyes were merry.

"You flatter me, sir," replied Donne. "Until quite, quite recently, I have only had the pleasure of dealing with foreign monarchs. The past few days, however, have brought their changes. I cannot say I expected you to be the one, although upon reflection, to whom else should she turn?"

"My niece? She's spoken to you, then?" The former ruler of Britain leaned forward in his chair, his plumed hat dropping from his knees to the floor unnoticed.

"Niece, is it? I would think the distance in the bloodline makes her somewhat farther kin to you than that. But you like the girl. Her favorite, her 'Uncle' Charles. The one person with a Master Druid's powers whom she can utterly trust at a time when she dares trust no other Druid. But of course—" Donne settled back in his armchair and began to tamp shag into his oily black clay pipe in an offhand manner. "To whom else could she entrust the news that she has been robbed of the Rules Britannia?"

King Charles leapt from his chair with such force that it tottered crazily before toppling over.

"Calm yourself, Your Majesty," Donne directed. "Her secret is safe. Not for the world would I do anything to endanger that woman."

"How could you know?" The former King sank back into his chair. "You have no magic in you—I can read that much. None but the Brotherhood know of the Rules!"

"An inaccurate observation, Your Majesty. Clearly I know; and now thanks to my indiscreet mention of the Rules Britannia, Weston knows too."

Recalling King Charles' violent reaction, I hastened to say, "I know nothing more of them than the name. Good gods, Donne, even when we were with the Queen, she hadn't the time to tell us what had been stolen from her! How on earth did you guess?"

"I never guess, Weston."

At this point we were interrupted by the entrance of Mrs. Hendrik, bearing the first of several luncheon trays. She did not know the regal identity of our new client, but one look at his attire had told her that here was no ordinary caller. She had outdone herself. Grimy pink paper frills had been jammed onto our chops, her "best" linens and silver graced the board, and for the *coup de grace* she toddled in with a big-bellied silver samovar full of tea. Nothing had been forgotten. Not even those wretched scones of hers, worse luck.

Donne attacked his meal with enthusiasm. I had seldom seen him so elated. He even managed to consume three of our landlady's unfortunate scones, slathered with a gooseberry conserve that would have made an ordinary man remember his mortality on the spot. Over these he said to me, "The Rules Britannia, Weston, are the volume of sorcerous lore which has done more to defend Britain from enemies and invasions than any weapon, any general, or any diplomat. There is a good deal of scandal attached to them—scandal involving royal names, is it not so, Your Majesty?"

Charles averred that it was. "I pray you, Mr. Donne, if you are bound to tell your friend here the history of the Rules, allow me to do so for you."

"Your Majesty is most kind. Your method of explanation will be far more dramatic than my own, I am sure. But you may trust Weston utterly. He is as devoted to the safety of our Queen as any man here."

"He'd better be, or I'll come round and skewer the black-faced bastard myself the same damn day I read anything about this case, my visit here, or the Rules Britannia in that poxy *Strand* magazine." He said this smiling. It was not a comforting smile.

"Your Majesty has no call to criticize Weston's looks. A man cannot help his complexion. You yourself are rather swarthy." Good old Donne had come to my defense. It made King Charles laugh.

"Dark as a double-damned Pict, he is! But so am I, so am I. Well, he'll find this all the more interesting, then." He brushed the glittering bulge of the samovar with his right hand, and darkness filled the room. Only the silvery mirror-like surface glowed with the rippling light of a moonlit pool. The ripples drifted outward. Circles within circles of luminous magic eddied out, an ever-widening halo, and in its shining heart, a vision began to form.

Whiteness filled the circles. I saw a man like a mountain of snow, bearded to the waist, his hair bound with an Archdruid's silver fillet. Watery blue stones sparkled around the band, and his eyes held the same sharp blue. He stood poised on the chalk cliffs of Britain's southeastern shore, watching the rough grey waves of the Channel breaking on the shingle below.

Gulls veered and dipped against a cloudless sky. Beyond the breakers, the water was calm where Roman warships rowed the waves, slaves belowdecks plying their oars with vigor. Claudius' men were eager for this crossing to end, eager to finish the work of conquest that Julius Caesar had only superficially begun. Britain was rich. Britain was weak. Britain beckoned.

The Archdruid never took his eyes from those approaching ships. Behind him rose the pleas, the cries, the screams for mercy as the last of the Roman colonists were put to the sword. They were the lucky ones. Sacred wells swallowed many; many more were given to the cauldron. The few who thought they were to be spared would learn differently when the wicker men were built and they were locked inside to await the torches. One by one other Druids joined the lone man at his vigil.

"When shall it be?" asked one. He was very young, his hair still dark, his beard only half-grown.

"The gods know." The master clutched his jewelled oaken staff more tightly. "You and the rest can go. I will do what is necessary when the hour comes."

"Alone?" The younger man looked doubtful; afraid.

"Alone." The Archdruid's eyes were serene. "I shall suffice. You will see, Llyr. Think. How long have I been gone? How long has it been since any of the Brotherhood saw me?"

"On Mona we often wondered where you were. We believed the chiefs were entertaining you, Bran."

Bran shook his head. "The chiefs are as they always will be. They war constantly, they steal each other's cattle, they take each other's severed heads to hang from the rafters of their halls. There are as many Britains as chiefs; too many Britains. No, Llyr, I kept far from them." His eyes were on the horizon again. "I have been among the Dark Ones."

Llyr shuddered. "I thought the Dark Ones were all dead."

"The Dark Ones will never die out entirely. From the fastness of their western mountains their blood will run down the ages alongside our own. The stream will be thin, but it will be there. It must never flow into ours; we must remain pure. Oh, we have swords that the Dark Ones never dreamed of—bronze is a miracle to them—but they have powers . . . fearful, wonderful powers."

"You dwelt among them?" The thought repelled the young Druid, to whom the western Dark Ones were no more than vague tales and whispered rumors.

"I did. I studied their lore. What they might do to us, if they chose! The power, Llyr! The raw, savage power of a newborn earth runs through their spells. Had there been time enough, I think I might have stayed with them forever, drinking secrets, never seeing the pool of wisdom run dry. But I saw the shadow coming from the east. My place is with my true people. I have returned from the west as a thief. I have stolen knowledge they gave freely, thinking I meant to keep my word and stay among them. There will be no going back there now. Because I loved this Britain more than my honor, I can never go back to where the Dark Ones dwell."

"Master, what is that?"

Bran looked where Llyr pointed, to the thick ivory parchment scrolled around his oaken rod of office. He had all but forgotten it was there. "A shield, Llyr; a most incredible shield. It is the shieldwall no Roman shall ever breach, nor any other people. We built it together, the Dark Ones and I, but I alone will set it round the shores of Britain. Go with the others. The hour is near."

Llyr departed from his master on the cliffs, herding the other Druids before him. The Archdruid faced the sea. By touch alone his hands unrolled the parchment. His staff leapt upwards in his hand against the limpid sky as the spell's black thunder resounded across the narrow sea.

Of all the Roman fleet, less than a tenth of ships and men straggled back to safe port in Gaul. The ships were hardly worth the salvaging, the men were all stark mad. The sky over Britain was still as clear and perfect as a polished mirror, but the Channel seethed for days after. On both sides the people whispered of Nodens' monstrous children who tossed and turned their scaly, salt-crusted limbs as they returned to their dreams, their massive stomachs gorged with the flesh of dead men.

Swords flashed across the scene, but not in battle. The many chiefs of Britain came to lay their weapons down at the foot of a stone altar—a bull-faced altar to Mithras lately taken from its Roman builders. Bran stood beside the flaming eyes of the bull, receiving the chiefs' homage and submission. The blood of one recalcitrant chief dripped from the slab; the black cauldron awaited further offerings.

"The strongest among us rules." Bran spoke these words as immutable law. "Britain stands saved by magic. Only where magic fills the blood can you seek your king, O chiefs! Magic alone in the hands of a single ruler will keep this island ours. May the gods preserve us." A low, reluctant cheer came from the disinherited chieftains as the seeing faded.

Centuries rolled across the silver belly of the samovar. Lord Bran's son received the scroll of stolen power from his father's hand and ruled Britain after him. Hand to hand, father to child, mother to child, the yellowing scroll went down the years. Who held the scroll held Britain; and if he was a man who did not love the land above himself, he held Britain hostage. It lay protected in a leather sheath, then in a box of carved oak, then in a bronze casket. German tribes massed their ships on the Gaulish shore, and Danish longboats, and Norman drakkars, and all met the same fate as Claudius' doomed legions. The few shipwrecked survivors tossed up on the British beach were given to the gods. Britain remained inviolate.

Sometimes the scroll paused, waiting. The Druid King had left too many children, all of them mighty, all skilled in magic. A battle of sorcery tore the land, the waters, and the sky until only one mage was left to take up Bran's legacy. Each ruled as long as his powers lasted, and his powers were the force of his life. Sometimes the King stepped down before all of his magic was drained out of him, bringing death. In retirement he could use the mana left in him to extend his life beyond the normal span.

I saw Uther's son command the contents of the tattered scroll be transcribed and bound into the pages of a book, the book placed in a beechwood coffer, the original scroll destroyed. I watched him steal away to Avalon while Modred and his other sons fought to the death for possession of the book.

The last of the vision vanished. King Charles wiped it away with a breath. "There you have it, Dr. Weston. The Rules Britannia, the foundation of the land."

"Not to mention an explanation of your own robust health, sir," Donne put in. "Small wonder you abdicated. You were not one to cling to a crown when life might be more enjoyable spent in a cozy backwater like Maidenhead."

King Charles roared. "Maidenhead! And how did you nose out that I dwell there, sir? I never said a word about it. Next you'll tell me who I slept with last, Mr. Donne!"

Donne did not bat an eye. "Madam Gwynne. I hesitate to address her as Nellie in your presence. No, you read my blood rightly. I am no Druid; I even boast of Continental bloodlines. The worst sort of mongrel, as the Duke of Wellington would be pleased to say. But so long as former orange-girls insist on favoring a strong patchouli scent no longer fashionable with women of this century"—the once King raised his broad lace collar to his nose and gave it a rueful sniff—"and while cobblers everywhere mark their customers' soles with an easily identifiable code, my work is elementary." Donne indicated the faint chalk rubric on the high instep of His Late Majesty's footgear. "You must read my monograph on the subject of regional and local variations in shoemakers' hieroglyphs some day."

"Maidenhead and Nellie. I'll be damned."

"Let us hope not. That was an excellent luncheon! Let us return to business. Since I am already serving your niece, how can I further serve you?"

"By serving her, Mr. Donne, and letting me know about it." The former monarch was no longer merry. "Victoria confided her trouble to me not long ago. Even then I felt that something was seriously wrong."

"I should call the loss of the Rules serious."

"This goes beyond that. She told me she was going to use as many avenues of search, barring the Brotherhood, as she could. She mentioned your name as one possible source of aid, among others. I applied my rusty skills to the broil at once, but came away empty-handed. Wherever the Rules are, whoever has taken them must be the most powerful Druid in this isle!"

"Or no Druid at all," Donne murmured. Charles did not hear him.

"That I could find no trace of the Rules is bad, but what is worse is that when I tried to contact my niece with this news, she behaved oddly. She seemed to have no recollection of ever asking my help in the first place, none at all! I'd call that deuced odd, wouldn't you?"

My friend gave no indication of his opinion one way or the other. "You reminded her of her request, of course." Charles nodded.

"That was when she said she was bound to call you in on it—making sure you could handle the job first."

Donne's pipe was empty. He rapped out the dottle on the arm of his chair. "You will be pleased to know that I have passed Signorina Pitti's scrutiny."

"Who? Oh, probably one of those maids of honor Vickie's got around her." The former King's heavy-lidded eyes half-closed and he stroked his thin black moustache. "Not bad, some of them." He shook off the happy dream and concluded, "I won't interfere with you, Mr. Donne, but the girl's special to me, and if I'm needed, I want to know. Can't depend on her summoning me, not if there's a chance she'll forget to do it!" He retrieved his plumed velvet hat from the carpet and took a strip of paper from the band. "Here's the name of my London banker. He knows me only as Lord Backwater. I have used him before in matters of confidence, and he knows where to reach me in London as well as Maidenhead. Whatever's afoot here means secrecy, and maybe danger. Let's deal through him, if that's agreeable, sir."

Donne took the paper. "Mr. Lucius Hope of Threadneedle Street. Entirely agreeable. The element of danger is no longer problematical, Your Majesty." I could tell from his frown that he was thinking of poor old Isaacs again. Abruptly, he changed the topic. "In your reign you were known for a lively interest in the natural sciences, beyond the narrow-minded confines of Druidical magics. Tell me what you make of this."

He placed the black feather on the small marble-topped table between them.

King Charles had huge hands, but even so they did not dwarf the feather. "No earthly bird molted this, Mr. Donne," he said at length. "And I who've seen the Morrigan face to face when our lads sank Van Tromp's men in the Wadden Zee know that this is none of Hers!" He shivered and made the warding sign against the Battle Raven, the Morrigan, and her shining black wings. "Where did it come from?"

"It was given to me by Joseph Isaacs, one of the other agents Her Majesty has called upon to help her." The frown returned, as it would whenever Donne thought of a mystery unresolved and a death unavenged. "At the moment, I have only a theory about this object. I seldom discuss my theories." He took it from Charles and passed it to me. I closed my hand rather too quickly and tightly around the feather.

"Ow!"

It fell to the floor while I nursed the row of multiple minuscule punctures the thing had made across the inner base of my fingers. Donne picked it up.

"No ordinary plume, as you see. Weston, on my desk you will find a small box, a note, and a label addressed to one of my old Cambridge dons. Pack up the feather nicely, include the note, and take it round to the post like a good fellow."

He made no further comment on my injury, but I expected none. When Donne had an audience, he was happy. I left him chatting intimately with the late King, discussing the comparative merits of the latter's actress mistresses. I always knew Donne had a love of the dramatic. Whether it was as pragmatic a love as King Charles' for Moll Davies and Madam Nellie, I did not know. Friedrich probably did.

The post office was only a few doors away from our Baker Street lodgings. I did not have long to wait, being the only client there at so late an hour in the afternoon. The acolyte behind the counter was a bored young man who sent the feather on its way with a cheap transport spell, then gave me incorrect change. The mastery of magic is one thing, of mathematics quite another.

"See here, my good man, just count that out again, will you?" I requested.

His sniffed loudly in my face and stared dully at the coins on the counter. "Whassamarrer, then? Any them been cut?" Even under the vigilance of the Brotherhood, counterfeiters might still debase the coinage. It was one of the few "magics" that commoners enjoyed practicing while the Wise napped.

"It's not the *coins* I'm questioning, it's the *amount.* I've two and six coming."

"Not here you ain't." He shoved them at me with a greasy paw. "Be off. I got other customers."

I scanned the small office and, sure enough, someone was standing right behind me—someone I knew. The clerk was all hearty greeting, eager to have his petty thievery swallowed up in the to-do of another customer's transaction. This was not to be.

"Weston!" Lord Byron's doom-haunted eyes looked at me out of a face too haggard to be called handsome anymore. His fine white hand shook as he tugged my sleeve. "I must speak with you." He hustled me into one corner of the dingy post office. The clerk's inquisitive look was cut short by the arrival of three ladies, each burdened with multiple parcels and letters. As the sounds of questions and arguments rose from the counter, the two of us spoke on undisturbed.

"Friends of mine," said Byron, with a curt nod towards the argumentative ladies. The clerk had his hands well and truly full. "I waited, watching your lodgings. I dared not go in. She is spying; she watches everyone who comes and goes from your door. Only doing *his* bidding, damn her."

Before he could say anything more, I burst out, "The last time I saw you, you said something of Beltaine, of saving my life. Tell me how! When! I remember nothing!"

He shook his head sadly. I noticed the unhealthy yellow tinge to the whites of his eyes. "You wouldn't. She recalls nothing of what happened in the vault either; only that *it* is gone. The fumes . . . the fumes . . . *her* doing; my wife's—"

He was rambling. I had seen drunken men behave so, or those we used to call moonstruck. The harried clerk was slowly but surely taking care of his "clients." The diversion would not last forever. To be so close to an answer to Beltaine's blank riddle maddened me. I seized Lord Byron by the shoulders and shook him, crying "Black Arawn take your wife! *What happened to me on Bel—"*

The small white packet fell between us. He pounced for it, but I was quicker. It had a familiar look, and the apothecary's careful hand left no doubt as to the contents.

"White arsenic." I gave Lord Byron a hard stare.

"For rats," he said miserably.

Donne is not the only one who likes an audience for his mental calisthenics. "A likely story! A man of your position, buying his own rat poison? Doing a job best left to one of your servants? Hardly. Really, your wife may not be the most endearing of women, but such radical measures are not worth the price."

"What business is it of yours?" His voice was as mournful as his face. "You wouldn't be so quick to talk me out of it if you knew." He made a fruitless grab for it.

"My good man—"

"Give it back to me! Please, please, it's the rats. Oh, terrible trouble, the rats are!" He clawed my hands for it, but I held fast. "There's big ones, huge ones, and I must rid myself of them. Listen! Listen to me if you want to know what befell you that night. Come to the Café Royale; come and I'll tell you everything. Meet me there, only give me that—that—" His eyes twitched towards the clerk, mine automatically followed, and he nipped the deadly packet from my fingers before running out the door.

I considered asking Donne to collaborate with me on a study of imbecility among the peerage.

On my way out of the post office, I noticed a small man watching me from the other side of the street. In spite of the heat, he was muffled up in a greatcoat, slouch hat, and long woollen scarf. Only his large, abnormally black eyes were visible above the bridge of the beakiest nose I'd yet seen. His somewhat olive complexion was a shade or two lighter than mine, a rare thing to see in Britain. I did not pursue these casual observations. I had met with so many uncanny sights during my years in London that I put this apparition down to yet another streetcorner zany.

I was wrong. I was most terribly wrong.

CHAPTER FIVE

The Ersatz Laundry Affair

I did not return to 221B directly after my encounter with Lord Byron. I had no desire to play the foil to my friend Donne in whatever dialogue was then going on between him and His Late Majesty. Donne's sterling qualities aside, there were times aplenty when I wished I had not stopped by the Criterion for that fateful drink, had thus avoided the accidental meeting with young Stratford, and had done without the subsequent introduction to Donne which Stratford arranged. But there! If we could unravel the threads of the past, we would make a pretty tangle of it when we tried reweaving them to our fancy.

From thoughts of my own past, my mind wandered to reviewing the vision that King Charles had unrolled for us across the belly of Mrs. Hendrik's pet samovar. Part of it haunted me, I could not say why. It was the scene at the altar, when Bran the Blessed took the kingship to himself and received the fealty of the tribal chiefs. One by one the actors in that scene dropped from sight until I saw only the altar itself, the altar in which a fire burned forever and flickered through the eyes of a stone-carved bull.

I knew Donne would call me a silly romantic—one of his favorite terms of derision—for dwelling so long on such a minor aspect of what we had seen. No, I definitely did not want to hurry back. One needs a little respite even from the most beloved of friends. To kill time, I browsed in the shops of the Baker Street bazaar, giving special attention to Mildred of the bun shop. I mentioned our mutual acquaintance, young Cuchulain Jones of the Irregulars, but a perfectly innocent pleasantry concerning buns and ovens was met with a curt slap in the face. The girl had no sense of harmless fun.

Spirits dampened, I headed back to our lodgings, where I found an unlooked-for drama unfolding on the steps. An old woman, tiny-boned and wrinkled as a monkey, sat rocking herself back and forth before our door while sending up a perfect banshee's keening between snaggle-toothed gums. A large, lumpish white canvas sack kept her company. Already a small crowd of idlers and curiosity-seekers was gathering round her.

"Here now! Be off with you!" I lacked a walking-stick to flourish, but the crowd broke up anyway. The old woman looked at me with all the gratitude of a rheum-eyed hound.

"Arh, thankee, thankee kindly, Dr. Westing, sarr. Glad, glad am I to see 'ee. Na, don't look so sidesy at Meg, don't 'ee now. I knows yeer name fer I knows yeer face! 'E's told me yeer looks well enough, sarr, that Mr. Donne 'as did." She patted the sack at her side. "Yeer new wash'ooman, I be. When a 'ooman sees a man's smallclothes, sarr, she knows 'im better nor 'is poor ol' mum ever did. Fresh done today, all proper clear-starched an' goffered where called fer, but it's a stickly crayture I be, an' that loutish nevvy o' mine, what's supposed to lug this sack up yeer stairs fer me, 'e's off at a cockfight! I'll give 'un a cockfight when I lays hands on 'im I will do! Wrassled this bloody great sack seven blocks, I did, but la! these stairs, sarr, proves too much."

My heart went out to the poor misshapen creature. She was crabbed as an old stump. "I can take it up for you, ma'am. Is there a bill to settle?"

"Why, bless the man! Na bill, na bill, 'tis al paid out beforehand, like. Bless 'ee, Dr. Westing, bless 'ee!" She bobbed a mangled curtsy and scurried away to whatever basement hovel housed her. I shouldered the sack.

Shouldered it and nearly fell against the door. It was abominably heavy. How had such a frail old soul carried this monstrous load seven steps, let alone seven blocks? I was staggering and panting badly when at last I entered our sitting room.

"Good gods, Weston, what have you got there?" The former King was gone. Donne sat contentedly smoking a long black cigar, his feet on the fender.

"Laundry." I swung the sack from my shoulder and knocked it lightly against the wall before letting it start to slide unceremoniously to the floor. "I met the new washerwoman down— "

"*Be careful with that sack, you fool!*"

He was up and across the room in an instant, the sack seized with alacrity and lowered tenderly to the carpet. His long fingers undid the strings closing the neck of the bag while his discarded cigar smouldered unnoticed and set fire to the seat of his chair.

"Donne! For pity's sake!" I swatted out the minor blaze with a pillow, then turned to take him to task for this bizarre and dangerous hunger for clean clothes. My sermon died unuttered. Donne had opened a common laundry sack and decanted a Druid.

"John H. Weston, M.D., allow me to present Cambridge's foremost don of supranatural sciences and my very good friend, Master Caradoc."

The venerable Druid freed his feet from the sack and gave me his hand. "I hope Dr. Weston will forgive me for not weighing less. Judging from the knockabout ride he gave me, I was too much for him. Now that dwarf friend of yours, Brihtric, that Friedrich fellow, he can lift a marvel of weight for his height. Perhaps it has something to do with the placement of the center of gravity? I must make a note of that. There could be a monograph . . ." He still held my right hand while patting his robes for paper and pencil with his left. I took advantage of this pause to vent my feelings.

"I hope you're satisfied, Donne! I've been turned into a donkey at last! Friedrich!" I disengaged my hand from Master Caradoc's while he still hunted writing materials. "That bandy little brothel-keeper done up like a laundress, and now he's off somewhere enjoying a laugh at my expense! There are times, Donne, when your love of the dramatic frays the bonds of our friendship."

"Never that, Weston." Donne looked chastened. "Never that, I hope. I suggested this method of getting Master Caradoc into our rooms because it was absolutely necessary. We are being watched."

Lord Byron's mention of his wife's spying came to mind. I told Donne all about what had happened in the post office, including the affair of the rat poison.

Donne waved the plotted murder aside. "He will never do it. His methods are too crude by half. When a man changes so radically in so short a time, he is firmly in the grasp of some superior foe. Both Lord Byron and his wife are of the Druid line, though a very weak branch. For him to resort to common toxins rather than magic means that he is grasping at straws. Unless she grows extremely careless, she will win in the end. But I have no time to waste over the petty marital spats of the aristocracy."

He unlocked the tantalus and poured us all a round of

French brandy, a rare and precious prize from our days on the Continent. Master Caradoc breathed in the bouquet and closed his small blue eyes in rapture.

"Even I and my fellows at Gwenhwyfar College can seldom procure such exquisite contraband," he said. "The Cambridge authorities think we should set a good example for our students and drink only what's brewed in Britain. Tchah! The Brotherhood lost a treasure in you, my good Brihtric. Would you had been born one of the Wise!"

"No man is, and I would not choose to be. Magic holds its perils as well as its rewards." He poured me an additional tot of brandy, as if to make up for my recent stint as a laundry porter. "You see, Weston, I knew that we would be watched. I knew it from the time we entered the Palace. Whether it is Lady Byron alone who is keeping vigil over the comings and goings at our doorway remains to be seen. Therefore, in the note wrapped inside the parcel you just despatched, I suggested certain precautions to Master Caradoc, should he wish to see me."

"And I did." The old Druid beamed. He had a childlike sweetness to him, the effect of ages spent within the stone cocoon of Cambridge. "I could have transported myself here directly, Dr. Weston, but I thought it would do no harm to humor the lad in his request. So, soon as I knew what we were dealing with—and I do assure you, young Brihtric, it's most horrible jeopardous stuff you're mixing with this time!—I did just as he asked and sent myself to that dwarf fellow's—ah—home—no—house—no—establishment?"

"How would any Druid who is a well-founded adept most conveniently enter or leave a place, Weston?" Donne drained his glass and set it down. "By magic. And who is to say that our spy—or spies—are not watching the portals of enchantment leading here as well as mere earthly doors?"

"Well, they can't watch *both,*" said Caradoc.

Donne's ears perked up. "Is that so?"

"Oh, yes." The don tangled his fingers in his short ash-grey beard. "The rawest acolyte knows that. One watching spell precludes another. It's either watch the gates of magic or your ordinary door, not both. From a distance, I mean. There's nothing to stop a man from watching your common door in the flesh, with his own two eyes, while spying on the magic passageways to your rooms with his spells."

"As I can't envision Lady Byron lounging around Baker

Street just to see who comes to call on us, I conclude she is merely watching via spell," said Donne.

Master Caradoc nodded. "If that, young Brihtric. Frankly, I think you're being rather overzealous in your caution. I'd be first to bet that the lady in question is only keeping a lookout on her husband. Lord Byron suffers from *such* a reputation! Well, and if she is watching you, at least no one else can. One spell precludes another, as I said. First come, first served. Anyone else wanting to peep at your keyholes will get—will get—a busy signal, as it were. Like on the telephone, you know."

"The *what?*" It was wonderful to hear Donne use that note of awed astonishment that I had been forced to adopt so often when he—superior being—tossed off yet another miracle of ratiocination.

"The *telephone,* Brihtric. Oh, my. Really, you oughtn't have neglected your studies of Continental history. Now *I* like to keep abreast of changes over there, beyond Bran's Wall. I'll tell you all about my most recent trip there sometime. Amazing what they've accomplished without spells."

"Amazing." Donne's lip curled bitterly.

"But that's none of our affair. Britain's a snug land, isn't she? And we'd best act if we're to keep her so." The Druid opened the soft doeskin pouch on his belt and I saw the fateful black feather again. "Your surmises were all correct, young Brihtric. A bird's feather consists of a series of paired barbs branching out from a central shaft, or rachis, forming a flattened, usually curved surface, the vane. These barbs in turn branch into smaller barbules which attach adjacent barbs one to another by tiny hooks, thus stiffening the vane." He ran his fingers cautiously through the feather. "No barbules. No attachment of adjacent barbs at all. This is more like a clutch of needles welded to a central stem than a bird's feather. Even the Morrigan wears a raven's true plumage when she flies. And the tips form a flexible edge that could slash like a razor if drawn across flesh at the proper angle. Oh, there's magic in this feather, but it's no magic any Druid knows."

"There are other magics in the world," said Donne coldly, "just as there are other ways of life. Neither idea goes down well with your Brotherhood." His mien softened as he added, "You have been the sole exception to their close-minded smugness, Master Caradoc. Were all the Wise like you— But say, to what manner of being does that feather belong?"

Caradoc clasped his hands together. "I could not say. That is another reason why I've come to London in person. I mean to study the sources in the British Museum Reading Room and find you your answer. They are terribly fussy about users transporting the materials out without notice and have posted impregnable vigilance barriers. The only way to learn anything is to consult the books in person. I'd best hurry. It's getting late." The old man muttered something and disappeared. Donne's curses were more audible.

"After I *told* him not to come and go by magic! Damned absent minded professorial types!"

"I'm sure he'll be all right, Donne. You know, it is possible that Master Caradoc had hit it about Lord Byron. Only this morning I saw her give his chain a jerk, so to speak. If you ask me, he was a damned sight too chummy with that little tweeny at the Palace. Can't blame his wife."

I saw Donne's hand hover near the tantalus, then withdraw. Instead, he strolled to our front windows and contemplated the unmatched beauty of a London twilight, all violet and gold.

"She is lovely," said Donne.

"Who is?" Inwardly I hoped he was speaking of anyone but the Queen. Her dear face—smiling even in the midst of her troubles—flashed before my eyes while a phantom Donne bent to kiss her hand. And was that smile for him? The muscles of my jaw tightened.

Donne regarded me languidly. "What, not who. And yet, we paint Britain as a lady, with London the gem of her crown. Can you recall Paris, Weston? Hamburg? Madrid? How long ago was it that we travelled abroad? Ah, then I dragged you after me to view the wondrous works of progress the Continentals had achieved, and all without magic. Yes, even in France, where the last of her great mages was only recently dead! The factories, Weston! The great machines that would transform the land! How many do you think have been constructed by now? What masterpieces of engineering are they producing while we wallow in the past?"

"I remember," I said. I joined him at the window. Through an accident of design, it was possible to peer between two buildings opposite and glimpse the emerald of a city park, smaller sister to the wide, fertile fields that lay just beyond the city's verge. I thought of those fields, their placid cattle, the limpid sky arching over them, the clean beauties of blossoming hedgerow and silver-gilt wheat less than an afternoon's stroll from the heart of the great city. Then I thought of the Continental cities and I sighed.

Donne understood me perfectly. "I know what you are remembering. The smoke. The smells. Well, I remember them, too; and the faces of the factory workers. Britain has denied the mind of man in favor of the works of sorcery. We are walled off from the world—except when our leaders allow the gate to open slightly for reasons of their own—and the world goes on without us. I've called the Brotherhood a community of ancient moles, refusing to see beyond Bran's Wall, refusing to let the man without Druidic arts exercise the full possibility of his brain . . ." He opened the window and took a deep breath of air, ripe with all the heady smells of nearby field and forest. "There are times like these when I believe it is I who am the mole, and the Druids who are truly the Wise."

He shook off this reflective mood and clapped me on the shoulder. "We must not waste our time while Master Caradoc pursues the elusive feather's origin. It may be that there are other trails to follow in the Queen's case. Ah, what a day this has been for me, Weston! What an enlivening day! If every day—or even every alternate one—were like this, you would never have to worry about my resorting to the needle again so long as I lived. The evening may turn cool. Put on a light overcoat."

He took his travelling cape from the rack as he spoke and jammed his double-brimmed cap on his head. "Why, where are we going?" I asked. After a day like this one, I was looking forward to a well-earned rest before the fire, a light supper, and a glance at a good book.

"Why, to the Café Royal! Royal, Weston, not *Royale* as our friend Byron would have it. Affected pronunciation, which goes so well with his whole affected style. He did say you were to meet him there tonight?"

I thought back to his exact words. "N- no. He mentioned neither date nor time."

"Typical! Typical!" Donne was delighted. "He must be an habitúe of the place. If he is not there this evening, we shall determine from the waiters when we might most likely expect him. It will give us something to do. I hate being at a loose end. Besides," he continued as he rushed me from the room and down the stairs to Baker Street, "it gives us a harmless excuse for taking a pleasant evening's stroll."

In the street we saw many of our neighbors sharing Donne's idea. It was closing time, and the small businessfolk were shuttering their shops for the night. Mildred of the bun shop saw us descending the steps and simpered when Donne looked her way. His lack of response afforded me some tardy satisfaction for her slap earlier on.

"Have you ever been to the Café Royal, Donne?" I asked.

"No, but I know it by reputation. This way." He steered me past the post office.

Just then a mad ululation shattered the twilight's calm. The muffled man I'd so nonchalantly discounted as just a part of the London scene leapt from the shadows of the post-office doorway, both hands clasped above his head, a long knife glinting. His scarf was gone, his hat had fallen away, and in the soft glow of departing day I saw him plunge it full into Donne's chest. My friend went down, and the murderer darted his wildly gyrating black eyes at me before baying his triumph like a beast and taking to his heels.

I gave chase at once. The idle evening strollers and shopkeepers threw themselves out of our path, hugging the walls or stepping into the gutter. The madman moved with the grace of a deer, slipping into the street, narrowly missing the flailing hooves of passing teams. Horses shied and reared, their drivers cursing. I pounded after him, as insanely heedless of my own safety as was my quarry. I would make him pay for Donne's blood when I caught him, and gods help any man who tried to stop me!

He looked over his shoulder in midflight and saw me. He never broke stride, but he tore open his cumbersome greatcoat and his skeletal brown hands pulled out something I could not see.

Nor could he see the kerbside. Directly before the elegant Portman Rooms it was built higher than usual. If you did not know the neighborhood, you would stumble. The lamps had not yet come on, all was growing darker, and unless some capricious god took pity on that killer, he would fall and be mine within moments. I urged myself to a new burst of speed, wanting that man's death as I'd never wanted anything. Ah gods, how I would relish dealing with him!

And then, just as his feet caught the kerb and he rolled onto the pavement, something flashed from his hand. A shock struck me in the right leg. I fell as a red wave of pain rose up before my eyes and crashed down blackness.

CHAPTER SIX

The Tracking and Arrest of Hamid, the Baker Street Assassin

The first thing I saw when I came to was Donne's worried face looking down at me. This sight filled me with such joy that I sat up too quickly and was punished by having the room whirl. I slumped back and felt Donne's hand under my shoulders, placing my head on the pillow with inordinate gentleness.

"I am glad to see you so keen to resume our investigations, Weston, but I think you should measure out your limits first. The healing was, unfortunately, incomplete."

"It is you I'm glad to see. I thought that lunatic had killed you! But what healing do you mean?" I sat up, more slowly this time, and found that I had been laid out upon the sitting-room divan. There was a frightful series of rips in my right trouser leg. It looked as if some huge, nameless beast had lately taken me in its jaws and worried me like a rat, but the skin seen through the holes was unmarked. Only when I swung my feet off the divan did a sharp pang tell me that anything had occurred.

Donne showed true compassion in his face when he saw me wince and heard my smothered exclamation. "Does it trouble you so badly, old friend? I am truly sorry."

"As am I." Master Caradoc's boyish voice sounded behind me. He stepped around into my line of sight wearing a downcast look. "Oh, were I only a few years younger, Dr. Weston, I might have healed the both of you completely in one session and never thought of it twice. But the years take their toll. The older one gets, the more of one's magic must be turned to personal use. I am fast approaching the end of my life, and my powers want in proportion. But no fear!" He brightened measurably. "You may suffer some pain for a time, but I'll have recouped my strength enough by this hour tomorrow to finish the job."

"Donne, what does this mean? I saw a madman stab

you—to death, I thought. Who was he? What spell did he use to bring me down?"

"I was fortunate, Weston. My tweeds turned the brunt of the blow aside. If I fell, it was only from the force of the man's attack, and because it seemed prudent to repeat my little performance of rolling with a blow, as I did with Wellington. It was best to let him think he had succeeded in killing me. Had I shown signs of life, he might have tried again, with better luck. As it was, I received a superficial wound which Master Caradoc was kind enough to heal before tending to your hurts. It was no spell that did for you."

My friend helped me to my feet and let me lean on him as we walked haltingly from the divan to the mantel. I steadied myself there while he took from the drawer of his desk a small leather instrument case such as flautists use. This he opened on the desk top and one by one exhibited for me the confounding assortment of objects it contained.

The first was a dagger. The blade was not our familiar bronze, neither was it stone, brass, basalt, nor the purely decorative and functionless electrum blades our nobles sometimes sported. It was a bluish-white metal, and I could not bring myself to admit that what I was studying could truly be—

"Steel, Weston. Yes, you are touching it and you are still alive, no matter what the Wise may say. And why should you not survive contact with steel? It was a Druid himself—Bessemer the Heretic—who first perfected it. Unthinkable, is it not? Iron has the power that no other metal possesses to cut the effectiveness of Druid spells by its mere proximity to the sorcerer. And steel—steel might be termed super-iron. The Brotherhood call it deathmetal. It was certainly the death of Bessemer."

"There is no proof of that, young Brihtric," Master Caradoc said meekly.

"I stand corrected. Let us instead say that soon after his discovery, Bessemer the Heretic vanished without a trace, and his secret with him. But knowledge dies harder than men. Steel exists in the world beyond Bran's Wall. How far beyond you may judge from this dagger."

"The design," I said, "is quite as outlandish as the substance."

"An Oriental design," said Donne with some satisfaction. He had made several mysterious forays to the East in the guise of a Norwegian wanderer named Sweynson. "What would appear at first glance to be some ornamental but otherwise meaningless curlicues etched on the blade are really Arabic script. My own grasp of the language is rusty, but these lines seem to be a prayer for a sure eye, a steady hand, and a quick kill. Appropriate for the chosen murder weapon of a hashashin."

"Hasha—what? Donne, you speak with one riddle inside another. Bran's Wall only parts to allow trade ships to visit British ports. By order of the Inner Temple, no object made of iron—let alone steel!—can be aboard. Even the ships must be of the old style, made without iron nails. How could such a weapon get into Britain? Any ship carrying it would have been sunk as soon as it crossed into our waters. How could this dagger be the chosen weapon of anybody in this isle?"

The detective did not answer, but took a second item from the flute case, a white handkerchief which he unfolded to reveal a tiny square of a black, gummy substance with a distinctive smell.

"Hashish, Weston. As an herbalist, you should appreciate this. The Indian hemp plant yields more than rope. When this stuff is smoked or eaten, the effects on the human mind are said to be most pleasant. That is, if you find illusion to be pleasurable." He forestalled my questions with an upraised finger. "Bran's Wall has parted many times over the centuries. Even the Brotherhood realized that Britain could not remain perfectly isolated from the world outside except to her detriment. No, fresh blood was needed, fresh trade goods, and to a lesser extent, fresh ideas. Unlike the unlucky lands where change is forced upon the native customs and language through invasion, Britain has been able to pick and choose. Am I correct, Master Caradoc?"

"Oh my, he's off again," sighed the old Druid. In a confidential manner he murmured in my ear, "Give that one an audience and he shows off abominably. Should've been an actor. Or a politician. Now he'll deliver himself of a lecture about foreign words in the British tongue when all he needs tell you is that the word *assassin* comes from the Arabic *hashashin*, which in turn comes from *hashish*. Perfectly awful fellows—hired murderers—who take heaps of that repulsive stuff to get their courage up before a kill."

"Thank you, Master," said Donne. He did not look especially grateful. I guffawed. "Oh, shut up, Weston."

"Get on with it, young Brihtric, do get on," the don directed. "No one meant to steal your thunder."

With a baleful glare at Caradoc, Donne went on to the next item, another handkerchief. This one, when unfolded, revealed a small mount of metal oddments, all tinged here and there with blots of blood. "There you have the spell the hashashin used on you, Weston," said Donne. "A very unmagical, solid spell. Had he not tripped when he did, it might have been sufficient magic to kill you."

I fingered the scraps gingerly. "But—how could these be thrown with enough force to—*agh!*" My leg protested under my weight. Donne pulled a chair closer to the hearth and made me sit down before revealing the final secret of the leather case. He placed the case itself in my lap and signed that I was to open it. I did so, and my breath froze on my lips.

"*A gun.*" The words were a whisper. I had seen these during our adventures on the Continent, but never before or since. The gun—a small and primitive model with a barrel like that of a baby musket—was even more unthinkable to find on this side of Bran's Wall than the dagger.

Donne drew his chair opposite mine and produced his faithful black clay pipe. Master Caradoc had been hovering far from the fireplace for most of our conversation. Now I understood why. I was no Druid, nor was Donne, but for Caradoc to risk contact with so much steel—dagger, gun, and projectiles—was contrary to reason. Small wonder he had been unable to complete my healing in one session! The presence of iron in the wound must have debilitated his powers terribly.

"We are faced," Donne was saying, "with a pretty problem here, Weston. Steel in its most killing form has somehow gotten into Britain. And yet we know that to be impossible." He filled his pipe with shag and searched his pockets and the table for a match. None was to be found, and as there was no fire on the hearth—what with the mildness of late springtime—Donne could not light it with a paper spill either. Quite out of temper he growled, "Of course if we were living in a *civilized* country, I might have a bit of flint and steel with which to light my pipe!"

Caradoc was examining the spines of Donne's scrapbooks. His back was towards us, and so, breathing the words into my palm, I summoned a tiny tongue of flame from earthsheart and lit Donne's pipe for him.

"Good old Weston," said Donne so that only I could hear him. "One atom of your people's magic is worth more than all the Druids' lumped together."

"Did you say something, young Brihtric?' Caradoc inquired, still keeping a safe distance.

"Only that in coming here you disregarded my directions for the *second* time and transported yourself. We might as well wave banners with your name on them from the windows to announce your presence."

"You *said* to come at once; it was urgent." Master Caradoc could show a child's petulance as well as his innocence. "A good thing I did! A fine picture you made, holding up your friend, blood all over, both of you looking as though you'd been rolling in the gutter."

"Which I had. The hashashin did not simply hand over his weapons. The dagger he lost when he attacked me, the gun when I tackled him on the pavement outside the Portman Rooms. But he was lithe as a ferret and left me holding that greatcoat of his, which is where I discovered the hashish. I thought it better to see to Weston than to run him down."

"And I thought it better to come to you the fastest way I could!" Master Caradoc was clearly miffed. I liked watching Donne get a dose of his own bad temper. "Should I have walked all the way from the Museum, at my age? He'd be bled white by then!"

"Ha! The Museum!" Donne swept gun, dagger, and all back into the flute case and pushed it to the farthest edge of his desk top. "We must get you back there at once. We need answers! Where's my coat? I'll come with you."

The Druid forestalled him. "No need. I have your answer. I was on the point of *walking* back here from the Museum when I sensed your summons." The black feather sprang to Caradoc's fingertips. The old man was suddenly somber. "It is magic, but not ours. It is the feather of an afrit."

"Of course! Of course!" Donne began to pace the room in long strides, leaving a criss-cross trail of smoke behind him. "The moment I saw the dagger, the face of the hashashin, I should have expected something like this! Ah, Weston, for your folk the mysteries of the Continent are the last word in exotica, but what of the vast world beyond that? The East, Weston! The East!"

He tugged a folio from the bookshelves and placed it in

my lap. It was a volume on the myths and beliefs of the Near and Far East.

"Look it up! Look it up! You will find it all there—afrit, afreet, ifrit. No matter how spelled, a monster. An ogre, an implacable enemy, a render of human flesh, a creature whose appearance is so appalling that—that if indeed we hold one of its feathers, it is easy to see why poor old Isaacs died unmarked but for the horror on his face."

"But such things don't exist!" I protested. "It says here, in plain print, that such monsters are only myths."

Donne's sharp eyes danced. "And what do you think they write of our beliefs over there? The feather is *here*, Weston. It is actual. It is evidence as hard and indisputable as Joseph Isaacs' corpse! I'll take that, if you please, Master."

Caradoc was only too willing to part with the black feather. "An afrit!" His voice was very small with apprehension. Donne was twirling the feather between thumb and forefinger. Caradoc's eyes fixed on the whirling plume and he began to speak as if remembering a dream.

"Once—once when I was younger, I joined an expedition beyond Bran's Wall. We wanted the adventure of it, the fame one gets from a good cattle raid, but magnified; something for the bards to sing of forever. We were young—so young!—and proud of our burgeoning powers. We thought no people on earth stood before us, the wielders of British magic. The Brotherhood opened the passage for us and we transported ourselves to a land where there was no fog, never, and it was hotter than a hundred Beltaine fires. There were many acolytes among us, and some fledgling adepts; we had no trouble defeating the brown-skinned men who came against us. They rode strange beasts with lumped backs that bawled and spit in a horrid manner when we captured them. But I recall one man—he was some sort of shaman, I think. He knew we were using magic against his men, and he summoned up magic of his own."

The old Druid covered his eyes with his white sleeve and began to weep. "Oh, Pwyll! Pwyll, my brother! We felt the desert air heave with the strength of the shaman's spell. We wrapped our own protective magics around us as the sands turned dark as a thundercloud's belly. Only Pwyll stood free of our circle! Pwyll, who laughed at the Eastern wizard and called his spells empty air! I saw the sands tear themselves apart like living flesh, and out of the chasm rose a being so dreadful—the claws—the yellow flames of its eyes—the livid mouth—Pwyll! Oh, Pwyll!"

Donne seized Master Caradoc's wrist and forced his hand to close around a newly filled glass of raw Northern whisky. The old man drank like one entranced, then coughed and was his calm-faced self again.

"So you see," he said, "I know how real the danger is to us all. They are real, Dr. Weston. I give you my word, they are real. Alas, there are many of the Golden Brotherhood who share your belief that any mention of magic existing beyond Bran's Wall must be nothing more than nursery tales to frighten bad children. Ordinarily, I would say to leave them to their prejudices."

"Ordinarily, yes," said Donne. "But now?"

Caradoc spread his hands. "Now, young Brihtric, you must do one of two things. I have asked no questions. I do not even know how you came into possession of this feather. All I know is that the Council must be warned, and the Queen must know. Either tell me everything, and I will go to them—"

Donne shook his head. "My trust in you is absolute, sir, but my word was given to a client. You must trust me now."

"Or," Caradoc went on, "*you* must see the Queen and Council."

"The Council? Master, you don't know how deeply I am despised by the Council. My contempt for what they have done to Britain is well publicized, and they hate me accordingly. They will never listen to anything I have to say. They will not even allow me past the gates of the Inner Temple."

"On the contrary, young Brihtric, for that very reason you *must* go before them! They hate you, yes, but they do not hate blindly. They know of your travels, of your knowledge, of your familiarity with the outer world. You must take the dagger, the gun, the feather—all!—and you must tell them to beware. They will listen; they will act!"

Donne did not look as if he shared Caradoc's faith, but he said, "Very well. We shall speak to the Council and the Queen. Weston, do you feel up to it?"

"The pain is largely gone, Donne. I feel remarkably rested." I suffered only a slight limp as I borrowed a stout blackthorn cane from Donne's doorside holder. It was heavier than the norm, and probably lead-weighted at the head, but I meant to use it for support only.

"You should feel rested. You were unconscious all night.

I don't know what's keeping me on my feet after watching over you all those hours." Donne tried to look grave, but he could not repress a slight smile. Yes, he had been worried about me. "As for you, Master Caradoc, I'll ask you to remain here. If you stay put there's little chance of your forgetting my instructions about leaving by the *earthly* door."

"I don't mind being a prisoner in your rooms, young Brihtric," said Caradoc, "so long as you leave me the tantalus key."

Donne laid it down on the mantel while I slipped into my bedroom and made a hasty toilette. Having slept in my clothes all night was becoming an unpleasant habit.

"You're quite smartly turned out, Weston," said Donne when I emerged washed, brushed, and shaved, in fresh clothes, leaning on the blackthorn. As we came onto the street, well out of Caradoc's earshot, he further said, "You shall be the one to contact Her Majesty. I shall do my best to inform the council, though I know I won't get any sort of a hearing."

"What shall I tell Her Majesty?"

"Tell her that there is hope. There *is* hope, Weston. I see many threads which seem to run in diverging directions. The Rules are missing. One agent hired to find them meets his death through a monster out of Eastern legend. You and I are attacked by a distinctly Eastern hired murderer while working on the same problem. The threads run long, but they will meet! And I will be the one to track them to their source."

I nodded at the leather flute case he carried under his arm. "When you show that to the Council, they will have to believe you."

"I am not that great a fool. If the Council hate me deeply enough, what an opportunity for them, to find me in possession of steel implements! A moment, Weston; I shall be back directly." I watched him duck into the bun shop, where I spied him in earnest conversation with our Venus of the Currants. Mildred was all but undone by this unexpected attention. The flute case slid across the counter and vanished beneath it. Donne came out a moment later, whistling, with only his walking stick.

"There are some places, Weston, even safer than the Bank of Britain." He consulted his pocket watch. "We must inform King Charles of what has happened. On the off chance that the Council *do* heed my warnings of foreign arms and foreign magic at large in Britain, they may demand that the Queen produce the infallible protection of the Rules Britannia. This will be impossible, and she will need someone strong at her side. Yes, we must contact His Late Majesty. Meet me at Hope's bank at three. The office will be on the point of closing and therefore free of unwanted witnesses, but a conscientious moneyman like Hope would linger a bit longer. You to the Queen, then, I to the Inner Temple." He was off without another word, his long legs devouring distance.

I made somewhat less swift progress. My imperfectly healed wound hampered me, but I was stubborn. I would not indulge in the invalid's luxury of a hired wagon. Besides, I was angry with myself for what I considered to be an inexcusable example of carelessness. The hashashin had been standing out like a black bull in a flock of white sheep, yet I had dismissed him. Nevermore, I vowed. Each passerby along my route from Baker Street to the Palace received an unnerving stare, and one lady had me detained for a short, painful explanation of my motives to a bored Acolyte of the Law.

A block from the Palace, I began to wonder how I was supposed to gain admittance. No longer was I disguised as a black-robed acolyte, nor was Donne with me to supply a plan. I decided to follow the straightforward method of presenting myself at the door as sent for by Her Majesty. When the porter went to check this, surely the Queen would recognize my name and bear me out. Boldly I marched—with a limp—past the guardsman on duty. He was decidedly shorter than the fellow I'd last seen occupying this post, with a more olive complexion.

The porter who answered my knock was the same one whom Donne had bullied into conducting us to the Queen. Hearing my name and business, he gave me surprisingly little trouble.

"Follow me, sir. I can take you as far as the first-floor landing, but past that, you'll have to heed my directions."

"Can't you take me all the way to the Queen's presence?"

"Wouldn't dare. My job's to mind the door; ushers take visitors up. If you please, sir."

I dreaded being left to my own devices. I was never one for following spoken directions well, although with map in hand I could manage. As we went up the stair, I asked the fellow, "Where are the ushers, then? If it's their job to guide folk, why aren't they at it?"

The porter, seeing me struggling to keep up with him on my bad leg, stopped to give me a rest and an answer. "Because, sir, *she's* given them their notice. Half of them yesterday afternoon, nigh all the rest this morning. And the creatures she's replaced them with—! Why, they don't fit the livery, they don't understand half of what they're told to do, and they're not at their posts most of the time."

"Then they ought to be dismissed in turn," I said. The porter shrugged and continued the climb. "Or someone should present a complaint to Her Majesty; ask her why she's dealt so summarily with faithful servants."

The porter halted without warning and peered at me. "When I said *she*, I didn't mean Her Majesty," he whispered. At the top of the stairs, as promised, he gave me directions and left me.

Wonderful to say, I found Her Majesty's quarters without too many wrong turnings. As I blundered through the royal maze, I came across several of the replacement servants of whom the porter had spoken. He was right as far as their appearance went. They did not look proper in the Queen's livery. Not even old Isaacs had looked so ill-fitted. Most of those I saw were smaller-built than typical British servants, and their livery hung loosely on their bodies. One man whom I encountered in the portrait gallery, his back to me, came closest to filling out his uniform. I tapped him on the shoulder to ask directions. He turned, and I saw the pale, almond-eyed face of a Cathayan. He shook his head violently at my questioning and slipped away from me.

I knocked at the Queen's door, and when I heard that sweet voice bid me enter, it made me forget all the sordid, nagging tangles of garrulous porters, Oriental daggers, and impossible black-winged monsters. I flung the door open eagerly, and I did not care for anything but the thought of seeing her again.

Whatever I intended to say to her died unspoken. He was there—Kitchener. Damn the man, what business had he here? She was sitting with him on a brocade settee before the fire, and he dared to hold her hands between his own. He stood up briskly when I came in, his scarlet tunic agleam with those confounded rows of decorations, and he smoothed his thick black moustache with the air of a man completely at home.

"Dr. Weston, is it?"

"Lord Kitchener." I acknowledged his condescending greeting with as chilly a demeanor as I could summon. Her Majesty remained silent. I tried to catch her eye, but she kept her head lowered, her newly freed hands folded demurely in her lap.

"To what do we owe the pleasure? I see you have come alone. Gad, no one will believe it when I tell them! Weston without Donne. Is it credible?"

"Fairly as credible as finding you in the royal boudoir rather than the royal barracks," I replied. "Or out of the shadow of the Iron Duke. Your reputation as the Archdruid's right-hand man is legendary. You really ought to write up some of your adventures at his side. I understand the *Strand* magazine is looking for new authors."

I could swear that his whiskers bristled at that sally, like a tomcat's tail. The two of us must have resembled a pair of backfence warriors, hissing and growling, each summing up his rival before the real fight commenced. But we were not to have the chance to unsheath our claws. Not then.

"Your lordship, please, it's urgent. The ships—" Lady Byron was with us, unannounced. She had not bothered knocking, nor did she seem to pay attention to the Queen's presence. Victoria did nothing to correct this blatant discourtesy in her waiting-lady. The gods knew why, but the Mistress of all Britain was beneath the notice of those two sprigs of the minor nobility.

I was not so lucky.

"What are you doing here?" Lady Byron's gimlet eye clapped onto me.

"I have business with the Queen." It wasn't easy keeping up my dignity under that acid gaze.

"Business? What sort of business?" She darted a suspicious look at Victoria, but the Queen kept her head down. "You've business on a dungheap, not here!"

Perhaps I had been too hasty in my last chat with Lord Byron. There is much to be said for arsenic.

"Lady Byron, please! If Dr. Weston claims he has legitimate business with the Queen, then we must leave the good doctor to it." I had not expected Lord Kitchener to interpose himself and rescue me from that knife-tongued dragon. I was almost thankful to him. "You have a message for me—urgent, you say. Well then, I should like to receive it." He took her arm and swept her from the room. I waited for the door to click shut behind them, then for the sound of their footsteps to fade well away before turning my attention to the Queen.

"John! Oh my dear, dear John!"

She was in my arms in a rush of tenderness. I confess myself ill prepared for such a ravishing onslaught. I fought to catch my breath, convinced that I was hallucinating. Her loving cry had burst from her lips the moment I took my eyes from the closed door. She set the latch with a gesture; I heard the bolt fly home. Now she drew me, with a gentle urgency, into the scented haven of her bedchamber. The rustling of her low samite gown, the color of the sea, whispered half-words that struck sparks in my memory.

Beside the bed she stopped and touched my face softly, cradling it between her hands. "You've come back to me, John. Thank all the gods! I didn't know what you meant, you acted so strangely the last time I saw you. But why did you take so long to return? The days! The days that have flown since Beltaine! Can you guess how I've longed for you? Oh my darling friend! It is as a friend I need you now. You, who are all things to me—friend, lover . . . and consort."

I could not protest. I could not question. Her arms slid up around my neck. She was altogether lovesome, her shoulders bare above the blue-green froth of silk, a sea-god's daughter rising from the waves. I burned for her at first touch and clasped her close to make her feel the fires burning me. The fires . . . the fires . . .

Fires behind the empty sockets of a stone bull's face. Fires and smoke rising laden with the drugged fumes of a brazier. The nightmare rose up, three hooded figures, my beloved Queen, the hoods fell back . . . Byron, his wife, and the one she bowed to as her master. Fires, and an empty altar, empty fires . . .

Empty fires where at last I found my memory.

She was staring up at me anxiously, her hand passing lightly across my brow as if she sought to pull aside the curtains of forgetfulness. The memories poured back, and she saw them come. Her smile was the first thing I was aware of when Lady Byron's enchantment broke and I recaptured all that had been taken from me on Beltaine night.

"Kitchener." I said the name like the curse it was.

Victoria nodded and leaned against me, resting her head

on my breast; a precious weight. "For days I could not remember either. By the time I did, it was too late. He holds the Rules; I still don't know how he got them. Nothing mortal could survive the touch of the altar fire. It has burned since Bran himself kindled it, and the only human being who can reach into those flames is the one fit to wield the Rules themselves."

"And he cannot?"

"He is no Druid. No matter how far back his bloodline flows, none of the Wise ever sprang from it. He holds the Rules, but cannot use them." She clung to me with a new desperation. "Only I can."

"You are afraid he will destroy them?"

She shook her head violently. "He has worse intentions. He means to use them the only way possible for a usurper—through me. Why so surprised? It is a perfect plan. I have wasted too many years and too much of my magic in frivolities. Britain needs an heir, and the Council presses me to marry. Lord Kitchener is no Druid, but his blood is noble, and he has the Iron Duke's favor. He has Wellington's permission to court me. That is why he was here."

"Wellington's permission?" My eyebrows went up. "And do your desires count for nothing?"

"You are all my desire," said the Queen, and for a few moments longer I allowed myself to savor sweet oblivion in her embrace. It was she who pulled away, facing our difficulty. "I dare not exclude him. He will go to the Iron Duke and somehow force the issue of the Rules. I will be asked to produce them, and if I am unable to do so—it is death."

I knew she spoke the truth. Death was the traitor's lot, and what higher treason than the loss of the grimoire that was Britain's very life? "But he is the thief! He would be endangering himself by accusing you!"

How sweet, how sad her look! "Who would believe a magicless man capable of such a theft? Oh, you and I know he is not magicless, but the Council won't believe that, and he won't undeceive them. It is impossible. No evidence condemns him."

I held her hands over my heart. "However he has managed to steal them, wherever he has hidden them, even in the lowest chasm of Annwn, we will find the Rules Britannia. I swear it."

"I believe you, John. If any man can save them, you are the one."

"I—and Donne."

"You must hurry. It amuses Lord Kitchener to play the suitor. He and Lady Byron have all but taken over the management of the Palace. I must be their prisoner and dare say nothing to the Council for fear of what Kitchener might tell them." Her eyes flashed with rage. There was nothing soft or yielding about her now. "I must stand by meekly while *she* dismisses my servants, replaces them with others of *his* choosing! Foreign faces, aliens who came gods know how to this land! Bran's Wall is breached, and I must keep silent! For how long? How long before Kitchener tires of courtship? Pryderi's curse strike him down!"

How long before her angry cries brought Lady Byron back? I silenced my Queen the most pleasurable way I knew, and when she was again calm in my arms I said, "Play him well, my lady. Put him off, call him back, keep the game interesting as long as you can. Play to gain time. He may have magic, but there are other forces that can prove more powerful. I have learned that much from Donne's teachings."

"Yes," she said. But I could see little faith in her eyes. It was hard for a woman whose whole way of life was rooted deep in enchantments to accept that there were other paths.

I kissed her with all the love I had ever felt for woman. "There is hope, Victoria. Donne has said it, and he's not the man to see light where none shines."

It was half after one by the time I extricated myself from the windings and blind alleyways of the Palace. Many was the time I shook my head in disgust at the laxness now flourishing within those historic walls. While Lord Kitchener and Lady Byron shuffled servants like cards, any man might creep into that warren and scurry from cellar to garret at his leisure. I was more annoyed than relieved to find my way back to the door I'd come in by, occupied as I was in conjuring up a host of satisfactorily painful ends for His Lordship. The great door was opened for me by the porter, and I was halfway out when I thought to thank him.

The old porter was not there. The visage of a Pharaoh quizzed me from beneath the absurd powdered wig before the man slammed the door in my face.

With an hour and a half of idleness on my hands before the agreed rendezvous with Donne at Hope's bank, I thought to exercise my game leg by a ramble through Mag Mell

Park, a pretty enclosure not far from the Palace. The guardian of the gate was one of those rare birds, an Acolyte of Orders Grey, who meant to remain content with the minor magics and never continue his studies.

"Nice day for a stroll, sir," he said to me, a broad grin creasing his freckled face.

"That it is."

"Have you a weapon of choice, then, or would you care to try our special of the day?" He daintily plucked aside the waterproof cloth shielding a fine array of short swords, longbows, laden quivers, and leaf-bladed daggers. "We're recommending these," he added, lifting a small wooden crate for my inspection. It contained rawhide slings and lead balls. "Most effective, yet a challenge."

"No thank you, my good man. I've no hunting in mind."

"Hunting or not, I'd advise you to select something. For your own sake, sir. No charge made for the loan of weapons, and you can return them at any of the gates. Do, please. It's not Sammain by a long shot, but there's rumors come down that the bogles what stick to the old Roman ruins are a wee mite restless." In my ear he added, "Hobyahs, mostly; stupid bastards, but dead vicious."

I showed him my blackthorn stick. "I'll find this sufficient, thank you."

"Just as you like it, sir." He unlocked the gate. Just as I was going in, another idler was coming out. He'd had a successful time of it. Five small blue pelts hung from his waist.

Mag Mell Park was thick with trees and dark with ever-changing shadows. A Roman villa had once encompassed these grounds—Romans from the time of Julius Caesar, not Claudius. When Bran the Blessed cleansed the land, only a single descendant of their house was left alive, a virgin named Drusilla who had dabbled extensively in the occult. When Bran's men came to fetch her, she was nowhere to be found. Searching spells uncovered no clues, so the old villa gained the reputation of being haunted. Bogles, banshees, clootie-men, hobyahs, and their like soon found this a congenial retreat, and any man with a mind to might play the hero's part for an empty hour, slaying as many imps and monsterlings as the conservation laws allowed.

Of course there was no limit on how many would-be heroes the bogles might bag.

I had not gone far along the beech-shaded path before I

became aware of the disquieting sensation that I was being followed. That was all it was—a sensation. If anything was on my trail, it was stealthy. I heard no breaking twig or rustling bush, yet from my childhood I had possessed an infallible awareness of uninvited pursuers. The weighted blackthorn staff suddenly became a comforting companion. I leaned on it more heavily and exaggerated my limp, hoping to lure my tracker into the open by a display of vulnerability.

The ruse worked. Scarcely a dozen steps on I heard a large body break from the covert. I wheeled on my good leg, the blackthorn turned to a quarterstaff, ready to smash the fanged face of whichever one of Drusilla's pets meant to dine on me.

My staff met a knifeblade, not a monster. The crazy eyes of the hashashin glared at me behind our crossed weapons. He jumped back and gave a sickening howl, then slashed at me again. Again I parried, and a large chip flew from the blackthorn. He tittered, juggling his weapon. The short dagger leapt from one hand to the other, sunlight picking golden flashes from it. He caught it by the point in midleap and threw it. Without waiting for it to find its target, he snatched a second knife from his black tunic and launched it like a thought.

Had I tried to avoid the first blade by a sidestep, the second would have had me. Luck counselled me, and instead I dropped to one knee and lunged for the hashashin's legs with my weighted stick. He was expecting retreat, not attack. The lead-filled stave made a solid cracking sound as it connected with bone. The assassin screamed and fell. I followed my advantage, and fetched him a stunning blow to the jaw with my fist.

"Oh, I say, sir!" remarked the Acolyte of Orders Grey when I presented myself at the gate with the hashashin slung across my shoulders. "I'll have to look that one up in the guidebook. Ugliest damn banshee I've ever seen! Might be one of the sorts that's protected; rare specimen, you know."

"Not so rare as all that. This is a common murderer—though not a successful one. Summon an Acolyte of the Law, if you don't mind." It was with incomparable gratification that I watched the hashashin taken into custody. I agreed to stop by the local Hand of Justice station later to swear out a complaint.

My exploit in Mag Mell Park was invigorating. Paying off

an old score promptly took most of the ache out of my half-healed leg wound. I could hardly wait to relay it to Donne, but it was not yet time for our meeting. In this lighthearted mood, I meandered down to the Thames-side via Billingsgate Market.

The river near Billingsgate becomes too fragrant for most folk. Billingsgate is London's premier fish market, and the gulls who feast on the guts and leavings of the day's catch love it not half so well as I. Here I could smell the river and imagine it was the distant sea I adored, the sea to which I might never return.

Billingsgate swarmed with all sorts of folk from the fishing trade. Seamen of every stripe jostled for place at the rickety tables where fishing-boat captains signed up their crews. Porters, their heads protected with rock-hard cowhide hats like upended bowls, hoisted crates and baskets full of small, silvery bodies. They balanced these on their heads and cleared themselves a path from the docks to the great warehouses by a stream of profanity unmatched in all London. A good Billingsgate porter could melt a cauldron with his tongue, they said, or embarrass a Druid's oaken staff back into the acorn. At the edges of the crowd, fishmongers haggled with wholesalers. They leaned on their seaweed-packed barrows and traded insults while a small army of foraging cats rubbed their battle-scarred ribs against the tradesmen's legs.

One of these animals detached himself from the rest and began attending to my legs, twining his thin body in and out between my ankles and the blackthorn cane, mewling piteously. All a well-rehearsed act; he was fat as a pudding under his matted fur.

"Poor puss," I said, bending to scratch him under the chin. He flattened his ears and closed his amber eyes in ecstasy, nostrils thrumming. "I've nothing for you. Good puss." He did not take the hint. He renewed his caresses and redoubled his purr. I knew when I was defeated. "Oh, all right. I'll *buy* you a herring. But any further attempts at extortion will be met with the full penalty of the law, me buck!"

The cat seemed to understand. He unwound himself from my legs to let me walk over to the closest barrow, one already groaning under a glittering blanket of sole, Spanish mackerel, smelts, and alewives. I picked out a fine, fat specimen, held it aloft for my blackmailer's examination and approval, then looked about for the proprietor of the barrow.

I could not see a soul. The barrow appeared to be ownerless, which I knew was impossible. Nothing would have been easier than dropping the fish to the cat and ambling on, but I had no need to cheat an honest, if absent, workingman. Besides, my poor furred friend might get more than a boot in the ribs if he was caught feasting on stolen goods when the fishmonger returned.

"It's to be aboveboard, Tom, so we must wait," I said.

"Aye, honesty's best, now ain't it, laddie?" said a cracked voice behind me. A grizzled man with a leathery face and hands shuffled forward to take possession of the barrow. " 'Twould nae do t' have the puir beastie tak' the blame fer theft, na would it? Och, a fine fish ye've chosen! Royal generosity, I calls it. Royal." He weighed the herring in his hand and gave me a canny look that was unnerving.

"It's only a fish," I said, breaking away from the old fishmonger's piercing gaze and fumbling for my coin purse.

"Nae, laddie. 'Tis more than that, I warrant! A man may hide himself from a' who know him, but bluid will tell, and princely bluid tells most of a'."

I stiffened. "What are you saying?"

"Nae, 'tis only Old Jim's way, laddie. An' what makes a bonny prince, when a's said? Be it crown or kingdom? Be it spells and magickings? I ken a prince what built his throne o' broken hearts an' herring bones. Riddle that, riddle that, fer 'tis a dark riddle, and 'twill take a dark one t' answer it fer ye, m'laird." He lifted the handles of his barrow and rumbled it away up the narrow cobbled street without waiting for payment. I was left holding the fish.

Tom—or Tess, for all I knew—soon reminded me of whose fish it was. An urgent pawing at my leg yanked me out of the qualms the old fishmonger's curious words had raised in me. I tossed the cat the fish and needlessly adjusted my cravat, every man's sure rite for exorcising malaise. Two tugs are sufficient to exorcise the worst of our secret demons. I did not waste any more time, but went directly to Threadneedle Street.

Donne was waiting for me on the steps of the Scryers' Guildhall, leaning jauntily on a malacca cane with an ivory hound's-head top. "You are in good time, Weston. It wants only ten minutes of three. How did you find the Queen?"

"Donne, the most extraordinary thing—! I remember,

Donne! I recall everything that happened to me on Beltaine night! The Queen is in greater peril than we suspected, and I know now who has the Ru—"

He pressed a finger to his lips, commanding me to keep silent, and gestured faintly towards the Guildhall portico with his cane. Outside the Scryers' was not the best place to exchange such information. All it wanted was a hint of some mystery, and those most specialized and talented members of the Golden Brotherhood would start applying their far-seeing arts to pry out the answer. I covered my words with a cough and prayed no one had overheard me.

"And—how did it go with you?" I asked.

"Oh, excellent well. No sooner did I present my message to the Iron Duke than tears rose to his eyes and he begged my forgiveness for any poor opinion he had previously had of me."

"Donne, you are being sarcastic."

"And you are being perceptive." Donne's looks grew stern. "The indignity, Weston! I might have spared myself that. I knew they would not listen; I suspected they might ridicule. Even had I brought the physical proof and laid it before them, they would have found excuses not to see. When their eyes finally open, I hope to heaven it will not be too late!"

So did I. "Do you think it safe to see Mr. Hope now?"

Donne shrugged. "It will have to be. King Charles must be informed."

We left the steps of the Scryers' Guildhall and walked about halfway down the block to Hope's bank. It was a moderate-sized establishment, and from the look of the large front window, they had decided to close up early today. It was barely three, yet already the green oilcloth shade was pulled down to meet the painted bottom half of the window where the firm's name was blazoned in gold letters on a green ground.

"They appear done with the public business of the day," I remarked.

"Successful banks often give that appearance, especially those catering to the gentry. It allows their nobler clients the convenience of doing their business in relative privacy. They have only to knock for admission. Incidentally, Weston, you may often judge the success of a London bank by the design of its doorknocker," said Donne. He raised the heavy ring held in the jaws of a brazen dragon and rapped the door smartly. "I should say that Mr. Hope has done well." We waited a few minutes, but no one answered.

"Well enough to take off ahead of his time, gentry or not," I said. "We shall have to learn where he lives and find him at home."

I started to go, but Donne detained me. "This is not right. A successful banker is a creature of hidebound tradition. He would not close his establishment early without due cause. Something is amiss." He tried the shining knob and found that it turned easily. The door was unlocked. A gust of moldery air blew dread into our faces as we slowly entered the silence within.

CHAPTER SEVEN

The Nasty Story of the Crimson Leech and the Revolting Death of Hope the Banker

"Desolate," I said in a hushed voice. All was dark inside Hope's, the only light coming from the narrow slit where blind met painted panel on the front window. This was just enough to let us see grey bulks and outlines in the dark, and was altogether so oppressive that I felt my voice crushed to a whisper. "And—Donne, that smell—like a newly opened tomb."

"Exactly what this is, Weston," said Donne. He had shut and secured the door behind us, and now made his way with preternatural sureness of step into the shadows. He seemed gifted with catlike vision. This was not one of the times I envied it him. I saw him go towards what was presumably the tellers' counter and open the low gate in the slatted wooden barricade. He stepped behind the counter and ducked down. Seconds later I heard his smothered curse.

"Donne, what is it?" I hurried towards him. At one step my foot dragged on a curiously damp swath in the carpeting, causing me to stumble, but beyond this my blackthorn guided me well through the dark. I swung the small gate wide and at once had to press my knuckles to my mouth to suppress the cry of horror and revulsion that rose from my heart.

Five young girls lay dead behind the counter. Donne was kneeling beside one of them. He held her head on his arm in an affecting attitude of pity and sorrow. She had the wholesome, nondescript face of a hundred British working girls, her mousy brown hair meticulously plaited and crisscrossed at the crown, her simple gingham dress plainly the worse for countless thorough washings and pressings. Her sightless eyes goggled up at me until Donne charitably closed them.

"See, Weston!" said Donne, trying to reassert his old, falsely clinical facade. He was not that good an actor. "This poor child was the first to die. I found her lying on her back, her hands at her sides. She made no effort to protect herself from the attack because it was unexpected. The next girl in line has her arms crossed before her face—a useless gesture. The other three lie prone, arms outstretched. They were trying to flee when they were struck down. They never had a chance. The gate by which we came back here is the only way out, short of vaulting the counter through the spaces between the brass grilles. And how could they do so, hampered as they were by their skirts?" He touched a cheap cameo brooch the first girl wore pinned to her bosom. "What a harmless bit of vanity! A lover's pledge, perhaps. Who would gain anything by the death of this unhappy woman?"

"But Donne, what could have killed them? How did they die?"

In the poor light it was impossible to see the expression on his face as he turned the dead girl's head a quarter to the right, revealing a huge, round, raw wound on the left side of her neck. A very little blood still oozed from it, but the collar of her dress was immaculate.

"What could do this, Weston? A good question. She is bloodless, a large area of her neck badly lacerated, but there is no sign of any blood having been spilled. The others will be the same, I would swear to it." He laid her down with care, took up his malacca cane, and added, "And what of Hope?"

What indeed. My eyes were growing used to the semi-darkness of the bank. At the far end of the room, the mahogany door of the banker's private office gave off the weak but distinctive radiance of well-polished hardwood. Its frosted glass panel with Hope's name limned in gold leaf shimmered, calling Donne's attention.

"I will investigate," he said. "You had better wait here. It may be that our killer is still in there, waiting to see if any other prey comes his way."

"Surely whoever did this must have fled ages ago!" I could not conceive of anyone willingly remaining long at a scene of such merciless slaughter, not even the murderer himself. Donne had other ideas.

"Man kills either out of motive or madness. No matter which reason, it is often the sad case that innocent souls accompany the original victim in death. Did you not notice the cash drawers beneath the tellers' counter? Nothing was disturbed; bank robbery was no motive here, and robbery would be the only direct reason for killing those unlucky women."

"Then you think the murderer meant only to kill Hope?"

Donne pressed his lips together. "You conclude that Hope has been murdered without having seen the body. But if he is still in that office, alive? As of this moment we cannot say whether Hope too is a victim . . . or no victim at all."

"I won't allow you to go in there alone, Donne! Suppose it's as you say? Suppose Hope himself's run mad and is waiting for other victims? Let's summon the Acolytes of the Law to back us up, for the gods' sake!"

"The day I cannot handle a lone man, Weston, will be the day I quit Baker Street for Sussex and keep bees."

I read that in his eyes which told me there would be no further argument. I leaned against the teller's counter while Donne entered the banker's private office. My leg gave me a twinge, and I bent over slightly to massage the knotting muscles. As I did so, I heard Donne exclaim, "Dead, too!" I saw a light flare on in the office, then Donne emerge, silhouetted in the yellow glow. I was still doubled up awkwardly when he said, "Hope is also— My God, Weston, look out!" Too late; the monster dropped full upon me.

It was like being flattened by a titanic pillow. An enormous weight crushed the breath from my body. A stench like that of the Druids' altars, piled high with the still-warm and bloody carcasses of slaughtered cattle, choked me. By luck alone I had not let go of my blackthorn staff. I struck out backwards with it, blindly. The weight shifted somewhat, and I was able to use the stick to lever myself onto my back and see what pressed me down. I wrenched my head and shoulders out from beneath that awful thing, but immediately wished I had died without knowing what had killed me.

No spell of any mage's forging shall ever be powerful enough to make me forget that sight. My lower body was still pinned, and I could see the abomination that held me. Faceless, featureless, the color of clotted blood and long as two tall men, the nameless thing writhed and pulsed, its sides heaving. Petrified, I watched the nightmare rise up and undulate above me, snakelike. Only then did I grasp the way I was to die; die the way the girls had died.

Row after row they gaped hungrily for me. Not mouths, but living openings the size of a baby's head, each lined with waving circles of barbs, each contracting constantly in a nauseating suckling movement. Five still were red with stolen blood. I screamed and flailed at the beast's belly. My cane struck dully and rebounded; the maws closed down upon me.

"Weston! Weston, shield your face!"

Before I could obey, I saw Donne burst from Hope's inner office. As time slowed around me, I fancied that my friend had turned mage and conjured earthsheart fires in his naked hands. Then he threw the ball of brilliance, which struck the monster and burst into a rising sheet of flame. The creature gave a horrendous shudder and reared back, but my legs were still held fast. Senselessly I clubbed my captor, struggling to get free, but all my efforts did was to tear a burning agony from my wounded leg. Tears blurred my eyes.

"Your face, damn it! Cover your face!" Donne roared the command. I could smell burnt flesh, and I saw him leap the tellers' counter, then loom up from behind it with a fat black bottle raised high. He flung it—I swear I thought he meant to give me a merciful death with it—and when it struck the monster it was like the explosion of a small sun. Fire engulfed my sight. I felt my hair singe and crackle, the acrid smell of it strong and everywhere. A weight rolled from my legs. I blinked away the tears of pain that had saved my vision and saw Donne draw a limber bronze blade form his malacca cane and with it slash to shreds the still-quivering, smouldering body of the beast.

I dragged myself back and pulled myself upright with my stick. Donne had cut the last life from that hideous thing. Three fire buckets full of sand stood in a neat row beside what was probably the desk of one of the bank's junior officers. I emptied two over spots in the carpet which had caught fire while Donne used the third to extinguish the last flames on the creature.

He wiped his face with a clean pocket kerchief, then wiped and resheathed his blade. "You're all right, Weston?"

"I—I believe so."

"Good man! Your eyebrows will grow back, never fear." I raised my hand to my face to confirm the loss. Donne smiled briefly, then glanced down at the dead thing. "So that is our killer." He nudged the unmoving red mass with the tip of his boot. I saw the broken fragments of the common table lamp that Donne had first thrown at the monster, and the shards of the oil jug that had nearly blown the worm in two. "Fascinating. The crimson leech is native to Egypt and the Sudan. In reality, it differs little from its British cousins, apart from the color."

"Great heavens, Donne, and the size of this thing—?"

Donne took a long breath. "Sorcery never creates substance out of nothingness. It can only alter what already exists. I had heard that Egyptian mages were capable of inducing monstrous growth in certain of the more primitive forms of life. The Golden Brotherhood lack this dubious skill. Egypt; again the East."

It was then I told him of my interview with the Queen and of Lord Kitchener's ambitions. Donne's eyes lit up brighter than any flame. He rubbed his hands together with obvious delight. "The final thread, Weston! The thread that will ultimately weave itself into a noose around Kitchener's neck! You have not followed your British military history any closer than your British succession, have you? Never mind. I shall make all clear to you later. For the moment, I must ask you to step into the late Mr. Hope's office. It is disagreeable, but you will find viewing his corpse to be most instructive."

Reluctantly I followed Donne. Hope was slumped back in his chair, hands still resting on his desk top, head lolling. That he was dead was clear, but something about the body puzzled me. I tilted my head to study it from all angles while Donne watched, amused.

"The leech did not kill this man," I said.

"Bravo, Weston! I shall train you to a new profession yet. You are quite correct; he died as Isaacs did, of fright."

"Seeing that monster nearly frightened me to death as well."

Donne shook his head. "The leech is a water-dweller, Weston. Magic enabled that one to survive on dry land, but even so, the animal needed to be shielded by some surface wetness. Its master accommodated his spells, and our crimson friend oozed about on a carpet of moisture, rather like a slug's trail. You will note some streaks in the outer room, where the leech slithered up the wall to hang from the ceiling until you presented such a tempting target directly beneath it. You did not touch the tellers' bodies as I did, so you would not possibly have felt the telltale wetness that remained on them from its earlier attack. Very light, really; scarcely perceptible. You will find not even a hint of moisture on Hope's skin, nor on any surface in this room."

I examined Hope and found it so. I also found an extraordinary object on the banker's blotter. "A lavender glove." I held it up for Donne to see. His smile told me that he had already noted it and was hoping I would do likewise.

"A lady's lavender glove; kidskin. The size is remarkably dainty. How many women in London would have such small hands as well as a taste for such an unusual color? What a shame that objects cannot speak. It would save me many an interview with the London glovers—to say nothing of the modistes and milliners. The owner of this glove was likely the last person to see Hope alive."

I pocketed the glove. Donne would want to add it to the other clues in the case. "I doubt the lady had a face repulsive enough to kill a man," I joked.

Donne did not reply. "We have much to do, Weston. Hope's death cuts us off from contact with King Charles. Her Majesty will need a strong ally if she is to stand up to Kitchener and reclaim the Rules, and later face the Brotherhood with this tale. Direct assault is unwise, but His Late Majesty might have some strategic suggestions for us all. He was always a brilliant tactician. Well!" He clapped his hands and took up his Malacca. "First we'd best bring the Acolytes of the Law to Hope's—indirectly—and then—"

"Then I'd best toddle 'round to the Hand of Justice station and press charges on that damned hashashasha—hired killer. Kitchener's hired killer, blast him."

"The hashashin's in custody?" Oh, I wish I could have stretched time, just a wee bit, and savored Donne's expression! But time belongs to the greater magics, so I had to end the moment by telling him what had happened in Mag Mell Park.

"Weston, you are a marvel!" He clapped me on the back, beaming. "There are always new aspects of you to amaze me."

He stepped behind Hope's chair, where a crack in the fumed-oak panelling indicated the presence of a door. "This might be a closet, but I am hoping—ah!" It was a closet, a deep one, really the size of a small room. "Dark, but not stale. I think what we seek might be at the far corner. Weston, might I trouble you? I have misplaced my matches again; lost them when I lit Hope's table lamp."

I called up the earthsheart fire to my fingertips willingly. The minor magics remained for me to use without penalty, so long as I did not abuse the privilege. By the firelight,

Donne and I entered the closet and soon found a second door in the rear wall. This was carefully bolted. A small breeze made my fires flicker; this door gave on the outside.

Hands sheathed in gloves, Donne undid the bolt and we found ourselves in a dingy alley behind Hope's. "Good. No one is about. Now we can stroll a few blocks away before calling the Law's attention to this bank."

We meandered back along Threadneedle in the general direction of the Hand of Justice station. As we went, a street urchin came racing past us, the leader of a swarm of such small fry. Donne intercepted the runt of the lot, a dirty-faced lad who protested vociferously until my friend held a few shillings under the boy's smutty nose.

"You look a trustworthy young sprout," Donne drawled in the exact accent of a bored town dandy. "Do you know this neighborhood well?"

"Should 'ope as Oy do," the boy returned boldly.

"Excellent. We are friends of Mr. Hope, of the bank. He is supposed to meet us for supper tonight at Simpson's, but we have been forced to change our arrangements and shall expect him at eight in the grill room of the Carlton. We haven't the time to tell him ourselves."

"Roight. Anyfing mo'?" Donne shook his head and flipped the coins to the boy's waiting hand. The boy snatched them in midair and took off like a streak—in the same direction as the pack. Donne snagged him before he made the corner.

"When I pay for a service, I expect it done," he snarled. He had him by his tattered shirt collar. The ragamuffin twisted and fought Donne's grip like a hooked salmon.

"Oy'll bloody well tyke yer bleedin' message t' yer myte, Oy will! Down't yew be cawlin' me nao fief, y' gryte hupsnickerty barstad!"

"Hope's," Donne said slowly, between his teeth, "is *that* way."

"Lor', 'oo said hit weren't?" The wretched child had begun to snivel. "But hit's bleedin' well naowheres near ayght neever, is hit? All Oy wanted was ter see th' big 'splosion, 'at's all, guv. 'Ow gawdam many toimes yer gonna see th' owle fuckin' 'And o' Justice stytion get whomped flatter'n a cow turd, hey? 'Ere, tyke yer filfy bobs an' stick 'em up yer arse!" He flung the coins in Donne's face, gave himself one impossible contortion, and hit the ground running. Donne and I ran after him, but with no intention of stopping him.

The Hand of Justice station! By all the gods, had any building ever stood there? Across the rubble you could see all the way to Mag Mell Park. Acolytes of the Law from neighboring stations were already searching the ruins for the dead and injured.

"Let us through! This man is a doctor!" Donne shoved me past a stand of gawking spectators and under the nose of the man who seemed to be directing the rescue operations. He was tall and broad as the slabs of Stonehenge, with the forearms of a roadman protruding from the sleeves of his acolyte's robe. Had he been born on the other side of Bran's Wall, he would have made a formidable blacksmith.

"Doctor?" He gave me a severe, searching look. "What we need's a resurrectionist."

"Are there no survivors, then?" asked Donne.

The fellow sighed and scratched his curly black hair. "A few, sir, a few. But they're all clear crazy. Babbling nonsense, they are, every time one of my boys tries to find out what happened here. You know how it is, sir. You have your building more'n three stories high, you need your binding spells to make sure it keeps standing upright, now don't you?"

"Or your steel girders," Donne said *sotto voce.*

"What's 'at, sir?"

"I was merely agreeing with you."

The acolyte was satisfied. "Well, there it is, then. Spells are like anything else; need looking at now and again. But it's easy enough to start taking 'em for granted. It doesn't do, sir; doesn't do at all."

"You are saying that the spells . . . wore out?" Donne lifted his eyebrows.

"I'm not saying anything. Leastways not until my master shows up, sir. If a binding spell breaks, it must be investigated; traced back to the man who cast it in the first place. A lot of shoddy sorcery's been perpetrated upon the good people of London in the name of economy. Shameful, that's what it is."

"Quite," said Donne, and sneezed.

"Battle Raven keep far from you, sir," the acolyte wished him politely. Donne fumbled for a handkerchief, gave his nose a trumpeting blow, and dropped the cloth into one of the many pools of water surrounding the site of the disaster. "Awww. Permit me, sir."

"Thank you, my good man." Donne pocketed the dripping handkerchief. "Are you certain there's nothing my friend here can do?"

The acolyte shrugged. "Have a look round, if you like; if you've the stomach for it. The survivors are all stark mad. Talking of dragons, they are, dragons rising out of the Thames to flatten this place!" He gave a short, barking laugh. "Last such beast in Britain was a poor old hen-dragon slain by Good Queen Bess. Everyone with half a decent public-school education knows that, but you'll find your full Acolytes of the Law gibbering *dragon-dragon-dragon* in your face for hours, if you don't get away. And as for them as didn't survive—" His shrug turned to a shudder. "We've been piling 'em over there, sir. Look if you must; there's naught to be done for 'em, and they're an ugly sight." He pointed to a score of sheeted figures laid out in a row on the eastern side of the ruined building.

Donne surveyed the bodies from where we stood, then gave the entire site a cursory look. "Your men have overlooked one victim." He gestured with his malacca to where the uncovered feet of a lone corpse lay just visible around the corner on the riverward side of the block.

The acolyte shook his huge head. "Didn't overlook a thing, sir. All's as it's meant to be."

"My error. Come, Weston. Let us see what help you can be to these good men." He slapped me on the back and set a brisk pace to the nearby shopfront which the other acolytes had appropriated as an aid station for the survivors.

It was a teashop. The proprietess might have been Mrs. Hendrik's fetch, but for the faded blue tattoos still adorning much of her exposed anatomy. She passed from table to table with a heavy tea tray, pressing cups of cheer on anyone to hand. I was assaulted with a scone. Donne got a cream bun. Such is the story of my life.

It did not take me long to see the truth of what our cooperative friend outside had told us. To a man, the acolytes who tended the wounded could but shake their heads hopelessly whenever they tried to elicit a sensible reply from their patients.

"—tell you I *saw* it! Oh, it was fearsome! Fearsome! Just looking out the window, I was, when there it loomed up, dripping slimy water from every scale. Then up it lifts one paw and—"

"—thought the sky had fallen on me. Oh yes, oh yes, just what we're told to fear! But then my eyes cleared and I saw it, thick around as all my body, and green as a dead man's teeth, the tail of the beast. Dragging through the ruins like—"

"—mother, mother, mother, mother, mother—"

These were all grown men, all Acolytes of the Law, all just as physically strong and impressive as the service of the Law demands. Yet there they huddled, pawing at their tea, rocking back and forth like old beldames, blinking and jumping and yipping aloud at any sudden movement. I had no herbs to draw upon that would help those poor lost souls.

"Let's go, Donne," I mumbled.

Donne was not there. I searched the crowded teashop in vain. How very like him to just wander off without a word. I went outside to where search and cleanup operations were still going on and found him kneeling over the solitary body he had remarked upon earlier. I tried to steal up behind him, but when I saw what he was looking at, I gasped.

He did not even bother to turn around. "Quite so, Weston. We have found our hashashin."

Found him! Found what was left, he meant. The hashashin lay upon his back, his eyes closed as if peacefully sleeping. My own sleep would be peaceful too were my chest carved open and my heart torn from my body. On the fellow's brow I traced a curlicued design.

"Arabic, Weston." It would be foolish to suppose Donne had not seen and analyzed it already. "Copy it for me, there's a good man. I must take it to the Museum to double-check what I believe this rather barbaric inscription means."

I did as I was told, rendering the bloody letters into more prosaic pencil scribblings in my pocket notebook. Donne rocked back on his heels, still examining the corpse with a ghoulish intensity.

"No wonder they laid this one aside from the rest," he said after a minute or so. "The other dead were obviously killed by the collapse of the building. The evidence is clear: broken bones, fractured skulls, plaster dust and crumbs of debris all over them. But this man did not share their deaths. He is in perfect condition—barring the small matter of a missing heart. Furthermore, he is as clean as if he had just stepped from the bath." He passed me his sopping handkerchief.

"Smell that."

I did. It had a distinct odor of bilge. I wrinkled my nose and gave it back hastily.

"Thames water, Weston. The river has inundated the entire Hand of Justice station site, but nowhere else. The same smell clings to this man's clothes."

Donne lifted the dead man's hand and motioned for me to pass him a sheet of paper from my book. This he ran under the victim's nails a few times, then folded and pocketed it.

"What do you expect to find there?" I asked, thoroughly disgusted. He gave me an arch look.

"A dragon's calling card."

"Donne, you are jesting."

"On the contrary, Weston, I am deadly serious. When I examine those scrapings under the microscope I should not be surprised to find a substance very like a snake's scales. There is magic afoot here, and doings such as not even the highest in the land can explain, let alone simple Acolytes of the Law. Among so many dead, one corpse stands out; one alone is clean, uncrushed! Yet here we have an undecipherable brand on the brow and—mark you, Weston!—the heart removed from his body by no human agency."

I brushed my moustache nervously with my forefinger. "I can scarcely believe my ears, Donne. You, who are so slow to admit the presence of things supernatural in any of your cases—"

"You mistake me!" Donne shot up and took my elbow, maneuvering me away from the dead hashashin. I wondered at his haste, but said nothing until we had put several blocks between ourselves and the fallen Hand of Justice station. We were proceeding back towards Baker Street and had just turned into Paddington Street before he spoke upon the subject again.

"We had to get out of there, Weston. Our friend the acolyte was beginning to look upon my fascination with the hashashin's corpse with real suspicion. It might never cross his mind to suspect anything supernatural in the death of a man whose heart was torn out, yet who had lost almost no blood—"

"Donne!"

The detective favored me with a tight-lipped smile. "I see that he was not alone in his inattentiveness."

I admitted not having paid particular attention to the condition of the dead man's body beyond being shocked and disgusted. Upon reflection I saw that Donne was right. There had been no pallor, no sinking in of the tissues, and not the smallest bloodstain upon the man's clothing.

"When the evidence indicates that the only possible agent in such a killing is a supernatural one, I willingly accept it. The Acolytes of the Law could not. As they dared not admit the truth of the survivors' tales of river dragons, they set the corpse that so disturbed their tidy universe well apart from the others."

"But—where could a river dragon have sprung from?" I was still more inclined to seek an alternate solution to the hashashin's death, and it showed in my voice and manner. "And why would it attack the Hand of Justice station?"

"Elementary. It did not attack the station *per se*; the station was merely in the unfortunate position of sheltering the beast's real prey. Dragons no longer dwell in Britain; river dragons never have. That is not to say that they might not dwell elsewhere and be summoned by the appropriate spells. The Chinese are very fond of dragons. A dragon is a melodramatic but effective way to punish an incompetent servant, *pour encourager les autres*."

"You mean the hashashin—?"

"Undeserving of the name, and certain not to be admitted to the paradise said to await his more skilled brethren. It is supposed to consist entirely of beautifully irrigated gardens and perpetually self-renewing virgins. A pity. But here we are!" He opened our door and preceded me up the stairs. "I shall ask Master Caradoc to accompany me to the Museum with that inscription you copied."

Master Caradoc would see the British Museum no more. He lay facedown in the doorway between Donne's bedroom and our sitting room. His head rested in a scarlet pool, and his white robes were deeply dyed with his own blood. Donne threw himself down beside the old don's body and gently raised the bloodstained head.

Had the ghastliness of what I saw not been so great as to numb me utterly, I believe I should have fainted. Master Caradoc's head had been nearly severed from his body. Only a thin hinge of tissue still held the two together. All color drained from Donne's face. For once the enormity of the crime was too much for him.

We had neither of us recovered sufficiently to be aware of the rumble of footsteps on the stairs below until our door swung wide and four black-robed and burly Acolytes of the

Law barged in. Two of them pounced upon Donne and pinioned his arms. He struggled briefly, a fighter by reflex, then subsided. The other pair made no move to accost me; they ignored me. Instead they struck a guardsmen's pose, flanking the door through which the Iron Duke in all his frosty majesty now entered.

Even Wellington's stony countenance blanched at the atrocity perpetrated in our rooms. He regained himself, fastened his cold eyes on Donne, and said, "He told me we should find you disregarding the commands of the Golden Brotherhood, but I never expected it to come to murder." He gave a sign to the acolytes, who marched Donne from the room.

"Wait! Wait! He has done nothing! Where are you taking him?" I latched onto the Iron Duke's flowing sleeve without thought or care of incurring the Archdruid's displeasure.

He glowered at me. "You." The simple word had the strength of a curse. "You may testify to your friend's innocence later. For now, Mr. Brihtric Donne shall reside in the Tower until such time as he stands trial."

"On what charge, damn it?"

"High treason, Dr. Weston; treason, murder, and trial for his life."

CHAPTER EIGHT

The Loss of the British Barque
Maura Oisin

I sat by the front window of my now-solitary lodgings and watched the subtle signs by which all city dwellers read the approach of autumn. The light cotton and silk dresses of the ladies gave way to heavier weaves. Pert confections of Italian straw tied with ribbon bows beneath a host of pretty chins turned to velvet and moire bonnets securely anchored to the hair with pins against the ever-chiller breezes. Summer had waned and September was already half gone, yet still my dear friend languished in the Tower. For all I knew, Sammain might yet find him there.

A familiar knock at the door took me from my reveries. Mrs. Hendrik bustled in. I do not believe the woman knew any other way of moving apart from bustling. She placed the tea things on the marble-topped table and poured out two cups, then bit her fist.

"Oh dear, Dr. Weston, there I go again! It's just that I do find it so hard to believe the poor dear man is really gone." A fat tear started in the corner of one eye, harbinger of the deluge to come.

"Mrs. Hendrik, you may take my word for it that Mr. Donne is not dead."

"Well, he might as well be, hadn't he?" She turned on me with remarkable ferocity. "For all anyone seems to care, he might as well be dead and buried, feeding the worms! *Some* people—and I'm mentioning no names now—but *some* people could stand a lesson or two on basic human gratitude, that's what *I* say!"

I picked up a scone and nibbled it, determined to keep the peace at all costs, no matter the degree of personal sacrifice involved. "Delightful, Mrs. Hendrik," I said, ignoring her opening salvo. I choked down the rest of it. "Truly a morsel for the gods."

"Bugger the gods!" snapped Mrs. Hendrik.

"My good woman—!"

Our landlady's pudgy hands flew to her lips. "Oh, *do* forgive me, Dr. Weston, sir. I'm half undone with worry over poor dear Mr. Donne. I don't know what I'm saying half the time." The tears began falling in earnest. She swabbed her ruddy cheeks with the hem of her apron. "*Dear* Dr. Weston, you're such a clever man. Why haven't you come up with some way to help Mr. Donne in his present difficulties?"

"Believe me, I have tried—"

"If you really *applied* yourself to the problem, I know you'd come up with something. I should be only too glad to offer you any small assistance required." She seized my hand and pressed it to her nankeen-bound bosom. "For *his* sake."

Oh, good gods.

"Mrs. Hendrik—" I removed my hand and clutched my teacup with both fists, in self-defense. "My dear Mrs. Hendrik, from the moment my friend was taken into custody until this, I have done all within my power to aid him. I have given more depositions, consulted more men of law, and trudged more weary miles between here and the Inner Temple than there are hairs on my head. Always I receive the same answers: Trial for high treason is at the Brotherhood's pleasure and can be conducted only by a panel of ranking Druids: likewise any other capital offense. I can do no more until the Golden Brotherhood see fit to bring Donne into the Star Chamber."

A war-horse would envy Mrs. Hendrik's ability to flare her nostrils and snort her disdain. "If it was you on the inside and him on the out, you can bet your last gold guinea he'd have found some way to free you, and the Brotherhood be damned! But you've other things on your mind, haven't you? Yes, don't think I haven't noticed. That little tow-headed slut you've been walking out with—nasty piece of business, she is, or I'm a troll. But waste your time on bits of fluff like that, oh, that's just *lovely*, that is, while Mr. Donne suffers behind those blood-reeking walls!"

The tow-headed slut in question was Sarah Giles of the Palace, but I saw no reason to apprise Mrs. Hendrik of this. Donne himself had encouraged me to keep up my contact with the little tweeny as our last thread of information leading to the Queen. Month by month there had been some odd and disturbing changes in the royal Palace, no less odd or disturbing than some I had noted in the London streets.

In point of fact, I had plans to go "walking out" with Sarah that very evening. I was not looking forward to it. Sarah's reports were too emotional, a few scraps of intelligence mixed with vast outpourings of indignation at the way she was being treated by the new Keeper of Her Majesty's Kitchen. Any attempt on my part to pin her down to specifics would only evoke a storm of tears as the girl moaned on and on about "our poor, unhappy Lady." Why poor? Why unhappy?

"It don't bear thinking on; no, it don't," Sarah had sobbed at our last meeting. "If only you could see her, sir, you'd know!"

"But I cannot see her, Sarah." I passed her my handkerchief. "The last time I sought admittance to the Queen's presence, I was turned away." The other patrons of the shabby café we frequented were starting to look at us rather too intently. You would think they would have grown used to our too-loud and teary tête-à-têtes by now. We were regulars. However, I suppose there are few sources of ready amusement in a hole like Seven Dials, if you discount the street murders.

"Well, you ought to! Oh, the poor, unhappy Lady!"

And that was most of what I got out of our meetings. Had Donne not insisted, I would have dispensed with seeing Sarah long ago. The little tweeny had an appetite for intrigue, but no head for it. At times I wondered whether my forced liaison with her was Donne's subtle method of revenge on me for having my freedom while he remained in the Tower.

Mrs. Hendrik was still berating me. I took a deep breath and counted nine. "I am well aware that Mr. Donne is a man of greater resource than myself. I cannot step into his shoes, nor would I flatter myself to try. I am doing what I can as well as I can, but you must take me at my word when I say that his continued incarceration hurts me more deeply than it can hurt any other creature living."

So melancholy did I look, so much quiet dignity did I summon up, that I completely overwhelmed Mrs. Hendrik. She emitted one loud bawl and ran from the room with her apron over her face. She was back within fifteen minutes bearing a cloth-covered basket and all contrition.

"Forgive me, Dr. Weston, for taking of the liberty."

"Not at all, Mrs. Hendrik."

"I've put up a nice basket for you to take to him the next time you go. Two bottles of lemon marmalade, one of my special chutney, and a dozen of scones. They do seem to improve with age."

So they did. Let them stand long enough and they were impossible to eat, a distinct improvement. Donne could use them to snipe at the Tower ravens, should the fancy seize him. I thanked her graciously and assumed the attitude of a man who wishes to be left alone with his thoughts. This worked for all of the five minutes between the time she left my rooms and returned with a copy of the *Morning Chronicle.*

"I thought a look at the news might divert you, Dr. Weston." She handed it over and departed.

Divert me! Yes, if one finds news of such a distressing nature diverting. The front page was fairly equally divided between two tragedies. Another young woman had fallen victim to the diabolical phantom of the night, a savage murderer that Fleet Street had dubbed the Ripper. Gad, how Donne must be pacing his lonely cell, gnawing the mouthpiece of his briar while he railed against the fate that had imprisoned him when he might be free to investigate and solve this horrible series of slayings! *Who is this maniac now making our fair London unsafe for the gentler sex?* the scribblers demanded. The Acolytes of the Law had spread their nets in vain; no spells seemed to uncover the Ripper's identity. The more direct methods of the Sisters of Boudicca Shield-Maidens' Guild found nothing untoward in any of the byways they patrolled nightly.

The second tragedy was less sensational, though greater in scope. The British barque *Maura Oisin*, while engaged in a routine patrol of Bran's Wall, had been lost with all hands off the Devon coast. The Queen's Council had put on mourning for the largely Druid crew, but apart from that could only bow their heads to the will of Nodens.

A rap sounded at the door. Mrs. Hendrik, looking like a rabbit with her tear-reddened eyes and sniffling nose, peeped in on me. "Begging your pardon, Dr. Weston, sir, but there are two extraordinary people asking to see you."

"Extraordinary, Mrs. Hendrik?"

"That, and not quite respectable, if you don't mind my saying so. The male person—I'm not free to call him a gentleman—sent up his card." She laid it before me on a small round silver tray.

FRIEDRICH GUTMANN
Hamburg, Eton, Oxon., Soho
Pander

"Send them up, Mrs. Hendrik." Our landlady pursed her lips, but complied. Friedrich Gutmann and a veiled, dark-haired beauty from his "stable" were admitted.

"So good to see you again, Dr. Weston," Friedrich said, shaking me warmly by the hand. His lady companion removed her veil and I saw the exotically lovely face of Kwei-fei, late of Friedrich's wardrobe. She shed her velours coat and took a comfortably crosslegged seat on the hearth rug, her exquisite limbs sheathed in the thinnest of red silk pajamas. More than my hand was warmly shaking when I finally pried my eyes away.

"And I—I am happy to see you, Mr. Gutmann. Will you join me for tea? I'll have Mrs. Hendrik bring up some more."

The angel-faced dwarf laughed. He was dressed to the nines, but with none of the cheap flash of his professional brothers. He resembled a miniature model of the most fastidious young man about town, all quiet good taste, yet the obvious possessor of a modest fortune.

"I'll thank you to exchange cups with me, then," he said. "Your landlady looked ready to dose mine with hemlock." He clambered into Donne's favorite chair and looked round him. "So this is where he lives! I've only seen it from the outside, you know."

I blushed. I did not like to recall my role in the means used to get the late Master Caradoc into our lodgings. I rang for Mrs. Hendrik, who promptly laid on additional tea things. By the time she brought them, Kwei-fei had produced an arm-long lacquer pipe and was puffing away serenely. Mrs. Hendrik left with her lips so firmly compressed that I despaired of ever seeing her open them again.

"You know, of course, why we've come, Dr. Weston," said Friedrich, sipping his tea. I admitted ignorance. He cocked his head as if not believing what he had heard. "No? I thought it plain. Three months and the better part of a fourth have gone by, and Donne still lingers in the Tower! Now, I know how close you two are—his Boswell and all that—but don't you think you've let this go on long enough? The original Boswell did more than merely chronicle the sayings and happenings of Dr. Johnson's life. He was a man of independent action as well." Kwei-fei giggled. "Action *apart* from after-dark doorway romps." He gave her a reproving look.

"What has that to do with—?"

"An example, Dr. Weston!" He pounded the table with a scone to emphasize his point. "You must emulate Boswell in more ways than one! But lest you fear to act alone, I have come to let you know that my girls and I will be behind you one hundred percent. We are a force with which to be reckoned, and our faith in you is at least as strong as our admiration for Donne."

I did not know how to respond. It was Mrs. Hendrik's charges against me all over again. It was Sarah's weepy accusations echoing in slightly altered form from the dwarf's lips. It was—worse—a repetition of the inner voice that gave me no rest by day or night, but wearily intoned, *You must do something. You must act. You must save your friend.*

Friedrich saw my silence as reluctance, which it was only in part. He cleared his throat. "I may be presumptuous in this, Dr. Weston, but the girls and I thought you might be galvanized into action were you presented with some slight token of our earnestness in this affair. I further thought that perhaps were that same token a memento especially dear to your absent friend, it might remind you of the many happy hours you two spent solving your cases together, and—ah—" He looked to me to rescue him.

"Stiffen my backbone?" I supplied.

"Pray don't take offense! Sometimes out best intentions remain mere intentions. I am forever meaning to open a branch office in Bath, but I lack the final spark to begin such an undertaking. Will you please look upon our little gift as only that final spark you lack?"

I had seldom been insulted so charmingly. "Thank you," I said. "I am certainly not offended, and I shall cherish your gift always, especially if it helps me find a way to free Donne."

"Excellent! Excellent!" Friedrich rubbed his hands together rapidly and slid out of his chair. "You must let me know immediately if you need any aid. Good afternoon!"

He was through the door and halfway down the steps when I caught him.

"I say! Your—friend's still on my rug."

"Kwei-fei? Well, of course she is."

"Uh—shall I put her in a chariot after she's finished her tea, then?"

"Whatever for? Her things will come round by wagon this afternoon. No need to trouble yourself."

"My dear man, you cannot possibly mean that *she* is the memento you intended?"

Friedrich winked. "Has it all over pressed flowers, eh what?"

Dearly as I would have liked to question the charming Kwei-fei upon some of my friend Donne's less rational pursuits, I prevailed upon Friedrich to depart with her. As Kwei-fei donned her concealing coat and veil, she began to cough violently.

"There! That's what comes of women smoking!" I said with all the self-righteousness of one who does not touch the filthy weed.

Kwei-fei seized a half-full cup of tea and gulped the remains, then dagged a fiery stare at me. Friedrich clicked his tongue. "Kwei-fei has never overindulged in the habit, sir. This cough has only struck her lately. A more observant man would swiftly diagnose the real cause."

"A man such as Donne," I stated, not without some bitterness.

"Look to the sunset some time soon, Dr. Weston. It takes no Brihtric Donne to perceive what is happening to our pretty land." They left without another word.

I wondered what he meant by such a cryptic utterance and followed Friedrich and Kwei-fei downstairs, intending to ask. I paused on the doorstep of our lodgings, thinking better of it. I had no wish to play Friedrich's fool a second time. Let his mysterious words keep their mystery; I had other fish to fry. I leaned nonchalantly against the outer doorframe to enjoy the sight of Kwei-fei's slowly undulating retreat. When I took my hand away I noticed a thin coating of grime.

Mrs. Hendrik came to join me. She saw the clean spot my hand had left and sniffed. "I don't know what it is, sir," she said. "I'll have the char wash down the door, but it's no use. It'll be filthy again before a day's out. I could swear things stayed cleaner longer when I was young."She looked up and down Baker Street. "Going to be another one of them yellow fogs tonight, they're saying. I don't know why the Brotherhood don't do something about them. We *never* had such fogs! Thick as pea soup! No wonder that awful Ripper fellow has such as easy time. Oh, there weren't such goings-on in my day, I assure you."

She shook her head sagely, the way you may see a yoked ox do, and pulled a tattered yellow envelope from her apron pocket. "This just came for you, Dr. Weston. It isn't from Mr. Donne."

"From whom *is* it?" If I wished to reduce her to shame for having pried, I had chosen the wrong party.

"How should I know? I don't read more than the direction on an envelope that doesn't come for me."

"Then *how* can you say it is not from Donne?" I held my upper lip rigid with icy scorn, but got a ticklish moustache hair in my nose and sneezed, ruining the effect.

"*Because*"—she mimicked my assumed dignity painfully well—"I wicker-well ought to know Mr. Donne's hand after all these years of collecting rent cheques with his signature on them, now hadn't I?" She flounced back into the house, then stuck her head out to sneer, "Elementary, my dear Dr. Weston."

Cruel; cruel and uncalled-for.

I remained where I was to read the letter. It would give Mrs. Hendrik time to clear the tea things from our rooms and hie herself back to perdition. I felt an annoying irritation in my throat and coughed to clear it. Could I be sickening for something? Now that I thought of it, a great many of my fellow Londoners had been exhibiting a marked increase in coughs, sneezes, and the like, yet it was too early in the year to attribute it to common colds, the grippe, bog fever, or the Sammain horrors.

I set the question aside. The letter was from Sarah. *I must see you tonight. Don't come the usual. I will be there early. I get off at seven, so half past or similar. This is important. Yours faithfully, &c.*

Her signature was affixed in a tight snarl of letters, the self-conscious hand of the lower-class girl surprised by literacy. Half-past seven was a good hour earlier than our normal meeting time. I wondered whether she actually had something of urgency to impart, or if this was only one more of Sarah Giles' pantomime dragons.

I took the letter upstairs and placed it in the center drawer of my desk. There too lay other relics of the case: the afrit's black feather and the lavender glove from Hope's. The colder bits of evidence still were guarded by Mildred, across the way, and a good thing. I felt chill fingers on my spine every time I contemplated what would have happened had the Iron Duke discovered true iron in Donne's possession. I shut the drawer again.

Mrs. Hendrik looked out of her apartment as I descended the stairs, a light tweed coat thrown on to baffle the evening cold. "Will you be wanting supper, Dr. Weston? I've a brace of lovely young lamb chops, fresh today from the butcher's."

"No thank you, Mrs. Hendrik. I couldn't say when I'll be in."

"I shouldn't be a bit surprised!" She slammed her door. Odd, I thought she had forgotten about my tryst. A good London landlady only forgets when you've already paid the rent.

The predicted fog was already sending tentative yellow swirls down Baker Street. I stood before my lodgings and sought the calming glimpse of greenery through the gap in the buildings opposite. The sunset was more vivid than any in memory—huge swathes of purple, scarlet, and blood orange—but it lacked the clear light it had once given so freely. There was no green to be seen through the buildings; only brown. How many times had I viewed the same scene since Donne's imprisonment and noticed nothing? Ah gods! Donne would have seen it in a moment.

What was happening to our sweet city? I wondered, and my mind echoed Friedrich's ominous words: *It takes no Brihtric Donne to perceive what is happening to our pretty land.*

My meeting place with Sarah lay on the Embankment, along that stretch of the river where a few foreign ships favored by the Brotherhood had secured permission to dock and unload their cargoes. All other merchant marine ships tied up farther downriver, at Tilbury. The easiest way from Baker Street to the docks lay through Billingsgate Market.

How different the great fish market looked in the encroaching night and fog. The huge warehouses loomed up deserted, but the silvery ghosts of unavenged herrings still made their presence known. A few lamps burned feebly on the street corners. Ordinarily lit by magic, they now used common oil to give their ineffective light. The Brotherhood could spare no Druid for such middling tasks as spell-lighting these days, and even the acolytes were needed more pressingly elsewhere. The thick yellow fog seemed to mock those pitifully illumined globes before smothering their weak shimmer in a heavy embrace.

"Och, why stare so at th' wee light, laddie? Can ye nae find the path that's set fer ye? Ye ken it well, but 'tis dark, 'tis fearsome dark where ye'll be treading anon!"

I whirled at the sound of another human voice, but saw no one. The fog had thickened, making the streetlamp's poor glow no better than the ember of a dying coal.

"Strike a light, laddie! Aye, ye've that much power she's left ye, but ye're sore afeard t' use it. Na can ye tell me how it is that a dead lass binds a man more canny than a living? A riddle most royal, and fit to keep a wandering prince company in the gloom."

I heard a heavy creaking sound, and through the fog a large, squat shape came towards me, rumbling over the cobbles. A lantern bobbed before it, casting more light than such a small tin candle burner ought. By this weird brilliance I recognized the outline of a Billingsgate fishmonger's cart. The lantern light caught and dazzled on the scales of a hundred fishes laid out on a seaweed bier. Perched atop the pile was the same plump cat I had befriended months ago, and pushing the cart was the man who'd called himself Old Jim.

"Oh, it's you," I said, feeling foolish for jumping at shadows. The fog had affected many in the same way. Yet I'd always considered myself proof against night terrors.

"Aye, and 'tis yerself as well." The ancient fishmonger set the cart down on its struts and leaned over to rub the tomcat's chin. The beast purred and the sound rumbled like the incoming western tides. " 'Tis a brave mon as cooms t' find himself alone and finds more that he bargained for beside. Few can stand without a second pair o' legs, laddie, and many's the mon marries 'em. But that wasn't t' yer taste, was it na? Na marriage, but over the hills and far, far ye'd go t' find the second half o' ye, Johnnie!"

"You're drunk, old man," I said curtly, folding my coat collar closer around my neck. The cat's purring ceased and it gave a warning yowl. Green sparks from its staring eyes cut the fog. It bristled, its neck ruff spread into an infant lion's mane, its ears flattened level to the snakelike skull.

"Och, there's ane beastie as knows truth from truth and drunk from dreaming. A regal beastie!" Old Jim roughly stroked the cat out of its rage. "Your Majesty would do weel t' favor such as Tam, here, when ye coom back into yer ane land."

My own land.

Oh gods, the silence then! The yellow fog softly cupped foul hands around us and blew a gentle breath that sent Old Jim's tiny lantern glowing even brighter. In the flare of light the cat's eyes grew impossibly huge and round, drawing me into the gaping darkness of the pupils. I allowed myself to be drawn deeper, deeper still into the yawning black beyond the gold-rimmed gates, and my ears began to fill with the song of a distant sea.

"Nay, laddie!" The fishmonger's sharp cry awoke me. I was leaning towards his barrow and was on the point of overbalancing myself. I stumbled and caught hold of the wooden rim to prevent a fall. A fat splinter rammed itself into my palm. I cursed thoroughly while the old man chuckled.

"Och, aye, the selfsame passion in th' bluid that's set ye here t' purge it free! 'Tis said a prince has temper enough t' dry the sea and teach the sky t' weep, but who'll be weepin' ere that? She was a bonnie lass, and right royal enough for any mon o' th' Council—save one. 'Tis said she wasn't all th' reason he fled, but gossip's like gin—th' stronger 'tis and th' more common t' coom by, th' better."

I forgot my injured hand for the moment. "What are you saying? Gods spare us all, who told you anything about her?" I reached for him, but the barrow's length lay between us, and the watchful Tam slashed at me with his claws, hissing.

"Tam, Tam me love, and would ye draw such bluid as his? No Druid's bluid, that; nae drap o' Druid's bluid at a'. Ye'll no be spilling common draps for a' that."

I never saw him move, and yet somehow before he'd finished speaking, he was nothing more than a swiftly retreating shape in the fog. A small shower of green sparks marked the place where Tam's eyes had hovered, then fell like snow into my outstretched hand. Where they touched the splinter, it melted to healthy flesh. I was left to wonder and to fear.

There was no time for me to waste searching the fog for a second sight of Old Jim's uncanny apparition. Flesh and blood, bad dream, or demon born and bred—whatever the fishmonger truly was would have to remain unsolved for the time being. Sarah was waiting.

I saw by my watch that I would be only a few minutes late if I doubled my pace. Really, I ought to have known better, but my recent meeting with Old Jim had rattled me badly. To race through such a fog was fool's haste. I took several wrong turnings that way and had to backtrack many times. The hour grew later. I was now well behind my time and completely turned around. I had managed to reach the Embankment, but could not for my life hit upon the proper street off it that would take me to my meeting.

"Concentrate, John, concentrate," I growled to myself, trying to conjure up the correct street by slapping my chilled hands against my equally cold thighs. It was an awkward maneuver, for I had to juggle my walking-stick back and forth from hand to hand all the while. There was something about the terrible yellow fog that made a man afraid to remain perfectly still for very long. It had the unhealthy quality of threatening to absorb you into itself if you lingered.

My gyrations must have done the charm. The fog shifted slightly and I glimpsed a riverside bench I had often passed on fogless nights. What distinguished it from the others along the same stretch of Thames was that some whimsical acolyte had given its wooden armrests the shape of ravens.

"*There!*" I gave the wooden ravens a jolly thump on the head with my stick, as pleased as if I'd carved the whole damned bench myself. "The street's exactly at right angles to you, my fine fellows. Who says I don't notice things?" Giving them one last rap, I cut a smart turn and strode merrily away, smiling like an idiot.

It is a wonder my fatuous grin did not freeze to my face. Gods know that the scream I heard was chilling enough. One scream, a long one, and then a series of short, sharp, horribly sobbing cries that rose into another long scream. " 'Elp me! Ow, sweet Lydy, *'elp me!*" Sarah. Her voice broke over me in a wave, and like a wave it died in a hideous bubbling swirl of sound.

The street where she lay was ironically free of fog. A single lamp cast adequate light, but Sarah was dead. Her arms and legs were splayed out and twisted, her body lay half on the walkway, half in the gutter, and her blood bathed the street.

"Save us," I whispered. It was all I could do to control the lurching of my stomach. Sarah Giles had been torn apart from throat to abdomen. While I had been congratulating myself on finding a stupid Embankment landmark, the unhappy little tweeny's game of Palace intrigue had turned to death. There was little doubt as to who was responsible.

"The Ripper!"

I did not say it. The Acolyte of the Law who seized my

arm and pinned it behind my back uttered those words, adding, "Got you at last, you bastard!"

"Now see here, my—ouch!—good man, I have nothing to do with—ow!—this. I am John H.—ah!—let go a bit, can't you?"

"You struggle some more and you'll get some more, you devil!" the acolyte snarled, giving my pinioned arm another wrench to show he meant business. "You can explain yourself at the Hand of Justice station." He raised his free hand and summoned a clean white beacon of light that pierced the fog and brought others of his calling at a run. They gabbled like schoolgirls when they saw the corpse.

"This him, then?" They shouldered each other aside to glower at me. It was impossible to make myself heard over their racket.

" 'Course it is! I heard the victim scream, right? So I nip here smart, and just in time to nab 'im proper. Now some of you take care of the poor girl, there's a good lot. I'm taking this one to the station."

One acolyte—a nasty large one with a lantern jaw—gave me a deeply meaningful stare. "Way the trials have been slowed up, nobbie, Epona knows when there'll be justice done to this 'un. Ever think we'd be doing the Masters a favor if we settle his case for them? All right and proper?"

To my horror, some of the Acolytes present approved of that chap's suggestion for summary justice against me. However, my original captor had other ideas.

"There'll be none of that! Make way, there; make way! It's the Hand of Justice for him and that's that. We've an oath to keep, even when it comes to scum like this. Make way, I said!"

Reluctantly they cleared a path for us. I was propelled forward, forced to step so close to Sarah's body that my shoes dabbled in her blood. I took my last anguished look at her as we passed—and stopped short in my tracks.

Clutched in her hand was the twin of Hope's lavender glove.

"Here! What's all this, then? Move along! Move along!"

I moved along.

CHAPTER NINE

The Astonishing Case of the Poisonous Lizard

Deirdre came to me that night, riding the back of a nightmare.

At first I imagined the dream was one of my own weaving, a pretty, bittersweet vision such as I'd often gently tormented myself with in exile. I was home again. Softly tanned doeskin trews and tunic were my second skin, and the blue stains of rank along my arms and across my brow were fresh and beautiful. It was full summer, and I stood proud on the Cornish sea-cliffs with my father's castle at my back and my ashwood bow in my hand.

Above me the seagulls mewed and soared, their white wings catching the hot light and burning silver. The moon's slim crescent joined their dance, defying the sun, and I could feel her bright powers pulsing up through my blood, winding spells around the sun's golden pillar. I thrust my bow against the sky and gave a hunting cry for the sheer joy of hearing my voice, and the salt air gave back the shout a hundredfold.

"I have ridden the sun in the moon's own hunt! I have brought down the stag who wears the stars for a crown! I have loosed the dark hound who sleeps beneath the earth! I have snared the white salmon of the world-waters!"

In my exultation, I nocked an arrow to the bow and loosed a wild shot at the sky. I watched the clean line of its flight and felt my soul ride the grey-fletched shaft. I drank the wind and held the world.

Abruptly it ended. My dream-eyes rode with the arrow, saw the moon's sliver rush headlong upon us, watched horrified as the stone tip buried itself in the white flesh of a goddess who cried out and bled down the bowl of the sky. On earth the roots of rock and soil shuddered. The ground heaved under me and I fell, snapping my bow. The wounded moon also plunged earthward, and the summer's vision dissolved into a shrieking vortex of madness. Earth herself was ripped apart, and demons streamed from her side. They rode steeds of bone and rock and blood, hungering for men. Their sweep devoured the land. I lay where I had fallen and saw my father's stronghold crumble while the sobs of the moon raked my ears.

Little by little, the vision dwindled until I was again aware of my prison cell in the Hand of Justice station. Only the sound of a woman's sobbing remained. I rubbed my eyes and saw the ghost of Deirdre.

She was beautiful. She had always been beautiful. No sighted man could deny it, and many would have been grateful to take such a woman to wife. She stood tall for one of our tiny race, nearly as tall as Victoria, and her blue-black braids trailed down her back to her heels. On her brow she wore the silver band that my father himself had bestowed in token of his approval of her as future daughter-in-law and lady of the realm. Her delicately embroidered tunic brushed the tops of her knees, hanging loose as a cloud.

"Deirdre . . ." I did not know whether this visitation was part of the dream or not. My voice sounded normal enough when I called her name, and she did not hesitate to answer.

"So, I am not forgotten yet? You thought it would be easy enough, I vow! Yes, turn aside from me and let my name be forgotten so that you might play the lord of all your desires." The ghost was no colorless phantom. I could see every detail of the living Deirdre, but slightly faded, like fine cloth left to soak overlong in water. She smiled, wolf-white teeth through pale lips, and spread her hands. Sea-weed dripped between her fingers.

"No, you will not forget me so easily, my lord! I could not marry you, so I took Nodens himself to my bed. I unbound my maiden tunic, I laid my sword, my bow, my hunter's belt on the grassy cliffs and called to the one lord who would have me."

"Deirdre, it was unnecessary! You had no cause to kill yourself. If I—didn't want to marry you, there were others."

"Others." Her voice sounded low and far away. Her long hands rose before her face to touch the silver circlet on her ebon hair. "But none like you. No prince of our people. Did you think I would take less than the man I deserved? My blood was as pure as yours! My powers were as great! Even beyond the grey sea-death, I command them!"

"I know." I sat up in my prison bunk and buried my face in my hands with a weary sigh. "I know."

Deirdre's laughter filled the cell. "John! Poor John! What

a name for a Pictish prince to bear! But what a perfectly common name for one of traitor Bran's sheep. The years of your exile are almost told, *John*. When they are done, you may return to our own land; our people miss their prince. But I will let no magician-prince return to them while I sleep with shells for bed and kraken for bedmates."

She raised her arms sharply, like swan's wings, and I saw her loosened tunic ripple around her. The plaits of her hair came undone, the blue-black glory floated upwards on unseen water. The sea's green secrets flooded my little prison cell. Deirdre's firm flesh bloated and whitened, swelling with long submersion. Her tunic drifted into tatters with the tides, and her dark, haunting eyes melted to the empty sockets of a clattering skull. Through lips now bone instead of flesh I heard her once again lay the *geasa* of my ruin upon me.

"No prince shall you be without your powers, and no powers save the smallest shall you command! What is yours is yours to use, but using it you shall lose the life of one dear to you! Summon the enchantments to serve you if you dare! Summon them, and witness death claim love!"

Her hands were bones, her body a sea-wracked skeleton wrapped in ancient finery. The black rag of her hair was bound to her shining skull by a silver circlet. She floated towards me, her chalky fingers dragging down my cheeks. Naked bone pressed itself into my arms while her hair twined itself around me in a thousand serpentine strands. My lips were forced to a grisly kiss. Mouth to mouth I stood with Deirdre's death, and a taunting hiss blew against my face with the clammy reek of a storm-troubled sea.

"And do you hope to wed the one you now love, John? The daughter of traitor Bran's line! He came among us and stole what little knowledge we were fool enough to share with him. We will never open the gates of the western mountain more to one of Druid's blood! How will the prince come back into his own with no powers to serve him and a traitor-queen? How will he tell his people he has chosen a bride of the weavers of cloth, the shunners of skins? Oh, sweet love, sweet John, I do not think that I shall sleep alone in Nodens' arms forever!"

The bones cackled and shook with wild laughter before a gust of freezing air burst between us and bore them away. I sank back onto my bunk and crossed my arms before my eyes, exhausted. Then I wept. I had never loved her, and I knew she loved only my crown, but Deirdre had been part of the earth's beauty and she had died because of me.

I think I slept. Deirdre's visitations liked to insulate themselves between layers of dream. This time my slumbering vision was a bland horror; Sarah's corpse and the lavender glove in its grip. Donne was with me, kneeling in the gore and saying that the evidence was conclusive; I was the Ripper. I was whisked to the Star Chamber, where Mrs. Hendrik sat in judgement. A panel of stone-faced Druids read the sentence of death and I was dragged out to the city walls beyond Cripples' Gate where Cuchulain Jones and the Baker Street Irregulars carried out the court's fearsome decree: death by pummeling with Mrs. Hendrik's scones everlasting. I gaped, and the first one went plumb into my mouth. It dripped Mrs. Hendrik's personal interpretation of lemon marmalade. That was too much! Even nightmares should have some sense of mitigating mercy.

"Get up! Stop your whimpering! I'm not paid enough to play nanny to a grown man. Get up, I said." The acolyte who had come into my cell while I slept shook me roughly until I came fully aware.

"Time—time for my trial?"

He gave a brief laugh. "For the likes of you? Not bloody likely! Trials in these times, he wants! The dungeons of the Palace and the Tower are packed with poor wretches waiting for a trial, and who's to give 'em one? No, you'd best make a full sacrifice of thanks that you've got no trial to get to. You're free. You've been cleared. Now off with you."

"Free?"

The acolyte shook his head. "Speak British or don't you? Free! Innocent! You never touched the girl! Is that clear enough?"

I finally gathered my sleep-drugged wits and sat up straight, tugging my crumpled jacket down smartly at the hem. "Of course it's clear enough, sir! If your brother Acolyte of the Law had possessed half an eye, he might have spared us both a wretched night. Did he think I'd carved up poor Sarah with my bare hands? Where was the knife used to do the deed? I'd no time to hide it, had I? A little basic observation and—"

"All right, all right, save your breath, mate." The acolyte lifted me by the elbow and steered me out of the cell.

We quick-stepped down a short hall and into the main room of the station. The sergeant on duty sat behind his tall clerk's desk and nodded beatifically when I appeared. "Ah, Dr. Weston! I hope we haven't discommoded you too much by detaining you?"

I grumphed through my moustache. He chose to ignore it. "That's fine, fine. I knew we could count on a man of your civic consciousness to understand our position. Justice must be served. I am sure you appreciate our recent difficulties."

"*Your* recent difficulties!" I put in every degree of frosty disdain I could manage. "You ought to spend a night in one of your own cells before you speak so glibly of *difficulties*, my good man. *Difficulties*, forsooth! My spine aches abominably, and I think I've picked up a touch of rheumatics sufficient to keep a trio of healers well employed for a week!"

The sergeant's benevolent glow dampened and went out. His brows drew together into a severe expression. He was unused to having former prisoners greet their impending release with anything but unbounded gratitude. "Cheeky sod," I heard him mutter. Aloud he said, "We have nothing to be ashamed of as regards our cells, sir. After all, we are not running a country inn for the gentry! In the best of times, we have received high praise for our facilities. The present crisis—"

"He had a visitant with 'im, Sergeant." The Acolyte who had released me spoke up just then. He did not appreciate my fractiousness either and was bound to take me down a peg or two for the honor of the station. His sergeant leaned forward and grabbed the edge of his desk like a parrot strangling its perch.

"A visitant?"

"Female, what's more." The two Acolytes of the Law exchanged smug nods. "I could smell her scent clear as any bell."

"Wonderful. A man who smells bells," I remarked to my collar.

"Well." The sergeant tapped his fingers on the desk top. "Well, well, well. *Strictly* against the rules, visitants. Having a bit of the old tickle-and-squeeze, were we, Dr. Weston? Very bad show. I shall have to report you."

By no stretch of the imagination could any man equate Deirdre's hauntings as the sensual ministrations of a typical visitant. However, to explain Deirdre's presence would entail explaining more facets of my life than I cared to reveal to a pair of punctilious acolytes. My inner demon was all for brazening the matter out—which might end by getting myself locked up in chokey on a true charge this time. I was saved from my own bravado by the intervention of an ordinary-looking man who had been sitting on a chair by the station door ever since I had been brought before the sergeant.

"Sergeant, *is* this Dr. John H. Weston?" he asked. He was a fairly big man, with a high brow, dark hair, and penetrating, intelligent eyes. His thick brown moustache was the twin of my own, and a medical man's leather bag leaned against the legs of his chair.

The sergeant consulted a yellow card on his desk. "John H. Weston, M.D., picked up on suspicion of being the Ripper. That's right."

"Well, in view of the shortage of qualified Druids, I was called in by the acolyte who manned your post before you came on duty. I performed the necessary forensic work and after close examination of this man's clothes under the microscope, I discovered not the veriest trace of the victim's blood on them. This, coupled with the fact that the murder weapon was missing and that it was patently impossible to kill a healthy young woman in such a barbarous manner without a struggle that would soak her assailant in the victim's blood, led me to recommend Dr. Weston's immediate release."

"And?" The sergeant was not impressed. He gazed at the doctor with a jaundiced eye.

"*And*, sir, I have been detained here ever since, while my own affairs go ha'penny mad. But I do not mind your lack of professional courtesy towards me so much as your obvious dearth of *reason* behind the accusations you are now levelling at this poor man. Visitants! The same card you so cavalierly consulted to affirm this man's identity as John H. Weston, M.D., also states that he is *no Druid*. It was there in black and white for me to read earlier, before I began my work, and unless some waggish acolyte has worked a spell of invisibility upon the ink, it should still be there."

The sergeant picked up the card again. "Not a Druid. Just so." He cleared his throat and saved face by turning viciously upon his subordinate. "Smelling visitants, were you, Cumhail? Smelling smuggled Gaulish brandy's more like it! Where'd this chap get him a visitant, and him without a spell to bless himself?" Cumhail quailed and the sergeant gave him a few more choice remarks on not judging every prisoner by his own randy tendencies. Now all unction, he turned to me.

"*Do* accept my apologies."

I damned well didn't.

Outside the Hand of Justice station, I took several deep breaths of free air. The doctor who had taken my part watched me now and smiled.

"It does feel good to be released, even if you know you were innocent to begin with, does it not, Dr. Weston?"

I returned his smile. "Your servant, sir. I am vastly indebted to you. I had no idea the Brotherhood was calling in ordinary medical men."

He shrugged. "They have no choice. Do you follow the papers? The ranks of the Golden Brotherhood are woefully thin of late. Bran's Wall must be constantly shored up with spells, or it crumbles, even though it is invisible. The patrol boats that see to its maintenance have been running into uniform bad luck recently."

I nodded. "Only yesterday I read about the fate of the *Maura Oisin*. A tragedy."

My new friend agreed silently. I cannot say what it was about the man that made me like him so well, so instantly. It was more than simple gratitude. It was more than our common callings as medical men of one stripe or another. Donne had been out of my life for too long, and I missed the comfort that conversation with a kindred soul can bring. I resolved to improve my acquaintance with the gentleman.

"I hope you won't think it rude of me, sir, but until this moment it simply has not crossed my mind to ask your name. You know mine already."

The doctor hid a smile by smoothing down his moustache. "I have had that pleasure for years, Dr. Weston. I am the slave of your wonderful tales in the *Strand* magazine."

I groaned.

"Have I said something to distress you?"

"No, no. My dear sir, not at all. But if you only knew what it is to be—to be *haunted*, as it were, by the creations of one's pen!"

The doctor pursed his lips. "I only wish I had the experience, Dr. Weston. My own few efforts beyond the medical journals have not met with the success of yours. But then, I do not share lodgings with such a colorful character as Brihtric Donne."

"There are times, my friend, when both Donne and I must share our lodgings with the Donne and Weston of my own making. It gets precious crowded at 221B with the four of us, I assure you."

"Well, two of you ought to take lodgings of your own, then." His grin was warm and sparkling. He offered me his hand. "Arthur Elric Boyle, M.D., at your service, should you ever decide to evict one or the other of your roommates. I could use the extra Dr. Weston to help me with my practice, although the extraneous Donne might be the more interesting of the pair."

"You may have the pick of the litter!" I shook his hand vigorously. "Will you allow me to treat you to some dinner? It is the very least I can do for the man who cleared my name—twice!"

Dr. Boyle proved to be a fascinating companion. His interests went beyond the narrow confines of the medical field. In exile, I had chosen to specialize in the curative powers of herbs and simples, lacking the time to achieve a true physician's degree. Dr. Boyle, on the other hand, was not only a fully licensed doctor but possessed thorough familiarity with herbalism, hermetics, hydrotherapeutics, and holistics.

"I also flatter myself to believe that I might have made a capable healer had my family been of the Brotherhood's bloodline," he confided. "The powers which healers tap to effect their cures belong to the 'other' world; the 'unseen' world, if you prefer. Druidic healers can contact and control such forces, but they are not the only ones permitted to study them. Ah! Here is that nice little eatery which was recommended to me by one of my patients."

We abandoned our conversation for the moment to enter the modest Soho establishment he had been seeking. Black-and-gold lettering on the front window welcomed us to Renfield's. Like many similar restaurants in that most esoteric section of London, Renfield's boasted an exotic menu whose elaborate dishes were served in an atmosphere of the utmost Spartan austerity. White oilcloths covered the twenty-odd deal tables without even a sprig of greenery in an empty wine bottle to relieve the stark decor. My chair had a game leg and tottered back and forth through the course of our astoundingly excellent meal.

We dined on rack of lamb so pink and tender that my heart filled with pity for the creature noble-souled enough to taste so succulent, and I was thereupon moved to resolve to become a strict vegetarian—later. We did not speak at all during the main course, but when the last morsel had been cleaned from the bones, Dr. Boyle resumed his dissertation on the healing arts.

"To cure the body is in some respect to cure the soul, Dr. Weston, and to cure the soul implies reaching it on its own plane. How are we to do this? You, through the more evanescent qualities of herbal vapors, perhaps. But how am I to penetrate the grossness of the fleshly envelope to reach the spirit within? No class I ever took in medical school offered me the answer. I have had to seek it on my own. Fortunately, there are some avenues open to those of us who are not of Druidic family. Spiritualism is one—the best one."

I swatted at a late, fat summer fly who had come seeking an open avenue to the leftovers on my plate. "I admit to knowing nothing about spiritualism, Dr. Boyle."

The fly evaded me and sent a mystic summons to several of his brethren, who swarmed over from a neighboring table. Boyle waved at them, doing no good. "That is a great pity, Dr. Weston. Your friend Mr. Donne would no doubt scoff at the seances I attend regularly, putting it all down to sleight-of-hand and humbug."

"Mumbo-jumbo," I muttered. The flies were now issuing blanket invitations to distant cousins and far-flung dependents. I whisked my napkin, but as it was the small tissue-paper sort favored in such places, it was like shooing the insects with a Continental postage stamp.

"Well, if your stories are not altogether fabricated, I would guess that Mr. Donne is not entirely closed-minded. I would like to invite him and you to join me at a seance some time. I am going to one tomorrow, as a matter of fact. May I count on your presence?"

Perhaps it was Boyle's sincerity, or the earnest desire to share his delight in occultism with us, and any cutting remarks Donne might have made be damned. His faith was so absolute, his intelligence so appealing, his attachment to his beliefs so unshakable that in a way he reminded me painfully of my imprisoned friend. The short brush I had just experienced with durance vile had been telling. I thought of Donne, pent in a far less casual prison than the local Hand of Justice station cell, and before the inner voice of reason could dissuade me, I was pouring out for Dr. Boyle's benefit all the guilt and melancholy and helplessness plaguing me with regard to the captive Brihtric Donne.

He heard me out without saying a word. When it became apparent that I had finished, he remarked, "And the girl—the Ripper's victim—she was not merely a bystander?"

"Poor Sarah! No, I was supposed to meet with her. Had I been closer to my time . . ."

He touched my shoulder. "You must not blame yourself. You do that too much. Even in the short time since we have made each other's acquaintance, I have noticed this tendency on your part. You cannot take the ills of the world onto your shoulders alone. The girl might have died anyway. Console yourself with the knowledge that you are not quite so helpless as you believe. You are the right hand of Mr. Brihtric Donne. He will not allow this matter to go unquestioned or Sarah's death to remain unavenged."

"Donne himself has little chance of acting. He is imprisoned." I clapped my hands together, trying to terminate the airborne careers of several flies, but they scattered. The noise attracted the attention of a scrawny fellow with sparse sandy hair. He was in shirt sleeves and manned the cash box. Now he sidled up to our table, rubbing his flabby hands together and looking at me in a disconcerting sideways manner.

"Is there any problem, sir?" he rasped.

"You are not our waiter, are you?" said Dr. Boyle. The whey-faced specimen emitted a thin, false laugh.

"Heavens, no, not I. I am the proprietor, sir." He left off rubbing his hands and pointed to the reversed *Renfield's* on the window, then to his own hollow chest. "Might I ask if everything was satisfactory?"

"The food—gods, yes, the cuisine was superb," I told him.

"Oh thank you, sir, thank you. This humble eatery is my first essay into commercial life after a long and most unfortunately unwilling absence. However, one benefit of my tenure . . . elsewhere was an education in the field of cookery and nutrition. I am glad you enjoyed yourselves."

"Yes, but—" I gestured impotently. "You *really* must do something about all these flies."

Renfield's rabbity eyes followed the offenders in their flight. His plump white tongue passed quickly over his lipless mouth. "I shall endeavor to do something about them, sir, I assure you." With a bob and a shuffle he was back behind the cash-box counter.

"A remarkable man," I said. "Remind me never to eat here again."

"Gladly, if you will do the same for me," said Dr. Boyle. "I wonder if Mr. Stoker had met *that* fellow when he recommended this place to me? Well, perhaps. My patients can be a most peculiar lot at times." While he picked up his medical bag, I settled our bill. Outside Renfield's, he and I exchanged addresses. Rather, I took his card. Any close follower of my *Strand* stories had the number 221B indelibly impressed on his waking mind.

"If Donne is imprisoned, you have only two possible ways open to you," he said before we parted. "Either you must free him, or you must act without him."

"Without Donne?" The thought was a cold one. "But how? I don't know where to begin. Dr. Boyle, you were instrumental in freeing me. Perhaps if we were to work together—"

He would have none of that. "Why do you fear striking out on your own, Dr. Weston? You are a capable man. Will you torment yourself with guilt for Sarah's death instead of doing something about it? Will you suffer vicariously for your captive friend when you might be the means of freeing him?"

"You don't understand!" I cried. "It's not that easy."

"You mean," said Dr. Boyle, "you will not make it that easy for yourself. Feel free to call upon me at any time, Dr. Weston. I will give you what help I can, but the field of using ratiocination in the solution of crime is not my especial department. You know Donne's methods; apply them." With this departing bit of advice, he was gone.

Mrs. Hendrik greeted me with raptures. "Oh, and here I thought that wretched little slut had turned out no better than she should be and murdered you for your purse, sure!"

"Mrs. Hendrik, that 'wretched little slut' presently reposes on a slab in the morgue. She was set upon and killed by the Ripper himself."

(*And what sort of Ripper wears ladies' lavender gloves?* asked a small voice in my ear.)

"Nooo!" Mrs. Hendrik's eyes grew round as saucers. She clasped her bosom as if in fear it might fall off. "Oh, the poor, sweet, precious girl! The dear heart of her!" She commenced snuffling into her apron hem. "And you, dear Dr. Weston, to lose the chosen of your heart in such a vile manner!"

By the time Mrs. Hendrik was through worrying the subject, Sarah Giles had been summarily promoted from the basest of London streetwalkers to the most virginal of a mysterious duke's younger daughters.

I took to my bed gratefully and was not troubled by any dreams or sendings. The following morning was one of those clear, crisp autumn days when the soul poises itself upon the lips and urges the body to grow impossible wings. Mrs. Hendrik came in with the breakfast things, singing.

"Mrs. Hendrik," I interrupted her in mid-warble. "Mrs. Hendrik, I'd appreciate it if you would make up a hamper for me. I am going to see Donne today." I had to inform him of Sarah's fate. I wondered what he would make of it all, though I knew he would berate me for having left the telltale lavender glove in the corpse's hand. No doubt Donne would have come up with an impromtu scheme for appropriating that tempting bit of evidence out from under the noses of the Acolytes of the Law.

I was not mistaken. When I finally gained admittance to his Tower cell he embraced my heartily, lifted the cloths of the two baskets I'd brought him, made a grimace of resignation at Mrs. Hendrik's offerings, heard me out as I recounted my adventures, and calmly tore me to shreds.

"Bravo, Weston, bravo. You mistake ratiocination for fictionalization, as always. You assume that the glove poor Sarah clutched so desperately belonged to her killer. Might it not have been her own? Did you see whether it came near to being her size?"

"What would a tweeny be doing with such fancy gloves?" I tried to defend myself.

"A tweeny is far more likely to covet showy but useless finery, Weston. Sarah enjoyed the trappings of high drama. Poor girl, she discovered too late the difference between play and reality. You did wrong to assume out of hand that the glove she held was not her own, and yet, Weston, I am led to share your assumptions."

"Ah-*ha!*"

"Do not"—he frowned severely—"take this as license to manufacture results where none exist. Sarah, like Hope, was a link we had with the royal family. The more of our links eliminated by the enemy, the more helpless we become, and the more isolated the Queen. Cut off your adversary's lines of supply and communication and you shall have his surrender all the more swiftly. That is classic military tactics, and just what one ought expect from a man like Lord Kitchener. First you are denied access to the Queen—and why should Her Majesty care to admit a common herbalist to her presence, one might ask?—then the one contact with the Palace left us is dispatched. We cannot know what machinations his lordship is up to now."

"Good gods, Donne, this is terrible! Sarah claimed she had something truly important to tell me the night she was murdered. Now I believe she actually did, or else why would Kitchener's minion pick that very night to kill her?"

"Excellent, Weston! I see I have not wasted my time on your education. 'Kitchener's minion,' you say, rather than 'the Ripper.' What makes you so sure?"

"Well . . . Well . . ." I fumbled for words. "The glove, you know, and—and all these headlines about the Ripper seem like such a perfect blind for anyone bent on mischief. You've only to ape the Ripper's style and any murder will be laid to his door."

"Or hers. Do not discount the possibility of a female Ripper, Weston." Donne smiled wryly. My answering look showed immediate disbelief. "And why not?" he countered. "If our worthy foe Lord Kitchener is tapping Eastern magics to his own purpose, that body of arcane knowledge is full of female spirits. They are at least as powerful and vicious as their male counterparts, although fairer to behold. Have you never heard of peris, Weston? Exquisite winged spirits whose beauty seduces a man moments before their delicate fingers tear him limb from limb, alive."

"But Donne, whatever Kitchener's called up to serve him, how are we to know? What are we to do?"

"We, Weston?" He closed his eyes and leaned back on the rough wooden bench that was the only seat to be had in that dank room. They had lodged Donne high in the White Tower, in what had once been a guard post. The narrow windows were meant for archers' convenience. They let in small light and great gusts of damp air from the Thames. The thick, curved walls seemed to drip moisture constantly, and the small brazier that provided a paltry amount of heat did little more than smoulder glumly. When winter came, Donne would be in sorry plight. Even when I had come visiting him during the summer months, this wretched cell was chill and dreary.

"They can't hold you forever," I said.

Donne rubbed his arms. They had grown thinner with captivity until my friend looked all bones and sharp angles. "Weston," he said mildly, "they can."

I felt a great rage rise within me, and in Donne's eyes I saw all the faces that had confronted me time and again with the stern demands of duty. *You must marry Deirdre. You must save your friend. You must help the Queen, whom you love. You must strike against Kitchener. Must* and *must* and *must*, yet I could do nothing. I was afraid. The only thing in all my life that I had ever done alone was to run away from a marriage that I knew I could not live with. And what had been the result? A girl had died and her dying curse had set a wall between me and the magic that was by rights mine to command.

"You are thinking of her again, Weston," said Donne.

"Her?"

He drew a long breath. "Amazing. Little wonder that I have avoided the close company of women—beyond the necessary. When we two first met, I perceived the mark of invisible female claws on your spirit."

I remembered that first meeting well. It had not taken Donne more than the space of five minutes to take me aside and inform me that he had seen through my herbalist's disguise to the truth.

"You have been in Aberystwyth, I perceive. You are one of the so-called Dark Ones, sir, and exiled for some offense against your race. There is a woman in the case as well. A match gone sour, or never sweet to begin with; and who but royalty still arrange marriages? No, no, do not look at me that way, my dear Dr. Weston—if that is what you would rather be called. I am no Druid wizard. I am an ordinary man."

Ordinary? That was Donne's little joke, the first of many. He promised to guard faithfully all he had learned of me by mere observation and deduction. I believed him, and he never betrayed my trust in all our years together. I revealed what few details he could not provide for himself—Deirdre's name, for one—and my confession linked to his sworn confidence formed the unbreakable lock upon our friendship.

"You are thinking of Deirdre," Donne said.

"Not only Deirdre."

"The Queen as well, of course. Weston, clear your mind of every thought but the Queen if you mean to save her. Don't worry about me; forget me, if need be. At the moment there are so few of the ranking Golden Brotherhood left in London that not enough can be spared to make up a jury to try me. I am safe from the traitor's death for a while. But the Queen! She has been without the Rules for a long time. How has that affected her power? Has she weakened?

That can only be to Lord Kitchener's advantage, and he will press it hard. You must concentrate your efforts where they are most needed, Weston; the Queen needs you."

"But what can I do? What should I do? You must have some idea—some suggestion—some direction to give me, Donne!"

He looked up at the rough-hewn ceiling beams, his lips pursing around an invisible pipestem. How much he must have missed the pleasures of tobacco in captivity! "What would I have you do? I would have you lay down your crutch and walk like a man."

I stared at him.

"Come, Weston, I have never seen you without a support of some sort. Long before you acquired that limp, you refused to walk unassisted. First your magic was what held you upright. When Deirdre cut you off from it, I took its place. Donne and Weston, Donne and Weston; never Weston alone. But the time has finally come and will not be put off, not if Her Majesty is to be saved. What would I have you do, you ask? I would have you act as if there had never been a Brihtric Donne."

His words haunted me as I retraced the spiralling steps down from his cell under the watchful eye of the guards. My heart was heavy. In the Tower courtyard a sudden breeze cut through me with a cold made more penetrating by my new, forced independence. I lingered in the shadow of the main gate, rubbing my hands to warm them before braving the streets.

Two guards shared my temporary shelter. They wore the blood-red robes of the Battle Raven's Children—a nearly extinct branch of the Brotherhood now sustained purely for the fine show they made upon ceremonial occasions. A brace of tame ravens perched on the shoulders of one of the guards and took tidbits of raw flesh from his fingers. The guards paid me no more heed than the birds, but kept up their conversation so that I could hear it perfectly.

I wished I could not.

"—yet another's gone."

"Aye, the fourth this month alone." The red-robed Child fed another gobbet to his pets. "And a crew of good men gone down with her." He stroked the glossy feathers of the raven on his right shoulder. "We had best brush up our strengthening spells, you and I, Iolo. They'll be scouting the ranks of the Children for men to ride Bran's Wall before Sammain comes round."

"Sammain!" His friend hunched up as if a slice of winter air had slipped down his neck. "I swear we'll see things this Sammain that all Britain's not seen for centuries."

"What?" A shred of flesh disappeared down a raven's eager gullet. "You going to wake to watch the dead ride?"

"It's no joking matter! The land's sick, I tell you, lying under a wasting that's sucked the blood from the furrow."

The Child who fed the ravens paused, deaf to his charges' importunate cries. The birds did an impatient jig from foot to foot, but no meat was forthcoming. "That's treason against the Queen you're speaking, Iolo."

"Treason! Treason or truth, and you'll see which when Sammain comes. If the Brotherhood's got eyes, they've seen what's become of the land, and they know how to read the workings of a curse; any novice could read this one!" Iolo's eyes slewed around to light on me. "You! You there!" He drew his gilded wand of office from his white leather belt and tapped me with it, making it impossible for me to slip away. Defiance of a Child could only bring a confrontation I ill desired.

"Master?" I rubbed my frozen hands more rapidly together, but the cold was spreading.

"Are you of the blood of the Wise?"

"Not a drop, Master; not one."

"Good. Then answer me this: When the land's blood runs dry, what does that mean?" I felt my mouth growing pasty. Every child knew the answer to that question. Every child dreaded the day of its asking.

"Speak up," said the Child who harbored the black birds of death. "It's a serious question."

"When the land's blood runs dry," I duly recited the proper answer, "then dragons battle beneath the earth—green to sere, blood to bone, full to famine, and life to death." I uttered the words in a monotone, a grey litany.

The two Battle Raven's Children nodded. "And what," said Iolo, "is all that will fill the furrow with life again?"

I knew the answer. I would never say it. "The—lifting of the curse, Master?"

Iolo was not satisfied. "Yes, but *how*? Surely you know *how*!" He spat his disgust when I shook my head. "No wonder the land's sick! She's let the people grow fat as milk-kine and neglected the ancient teachings. Didn't Cumhail say how she only rides at Beltaine for the bedsport? When's the last time since then that any's seen her making the proper sacrifices? She took the throne only because she was all that was left of that branch of Bran's line, and now all Britain's sure to pay for it! But she carries the price to save us, and that's what she'll pay out this Sammain, mark my words."

"Chhht. The man's not deaf." The raven-feeder bobbed his head at me. I affected a look of bland ignorance.

Iolo managed a smile. "He doesn't understand the half of what we're saying. He's a good, honest Briton, aren't you?"

"I hope so, Master. I'm not one of the Wise, to be sure, and I keep myself to myself with matters beyond me."

Iolo's friend laughed. "A comfortable philosophy. Look, fellow, I'm making this sacrifice to the Morrigan in your name." He tossed a fat chunk of beef high overhead. The twin ravens mounted the sky and collided in a burst of ebony feathers, fighting for the prize. The smaller was the quicker and more cunning, and he got it. "A good omen," said their keeper as the birds settled down to his shoulders again.

"For whom?" I heard Iolo mutter as I hurried away.

What is all that will fill the furrow with life again? Blood.

When the land cries out and seems to be cursed, it is read as a sign that the ruler has grown too weak to command. The liege-ruler of Britain *is* Britain, and when Britain suffers, her sovereign has failed. Blood is the price, and the ruler's life must be yielded up. The choking airs, the strange fogs, the brown blight on fields that once were green—all these were signs that the remaining Wise might easily read as cries for the Queen's final sacrifice. And Victoria would not be able to defend herself against their concerted power—not without the Rules.

Victoria would die. The Wise would demand it. Britain would demand it. She herself would realize that her rule had failed, and she would not even try to save herself from death.

I knew then that there was too much at stake for me to risk acting alone. If I miscalculated, if I failed, it would mean her death. How could I live then, bearing the full blame for it? No, the Rules must be recovered—I took an oath that they *would* be recovered from Kitchener's possession—but I would not go after him alone.

My thoughts turned to the one man who had impressed me as strongly and favorably as Donne and in as short a time. I pulled his pasteboard card from my wallet. Hailing a passing chariot, I was soon rumbling over the cobbles to the home of Dr. Arthur Elric Boyle.

The bell was answered by a thin, pleasant woman. "May I help you, sir? Doctor's hours aren't until nine tomorrow morning, unless it's an emergency."

"This is purely a social call, but it is rather important," I told her.

"Well, in that case I would advise you to return tomorrow. The doctor has gone to one of his meetings."

"Meetings . . . ah, the seance?" I recalled his having mentioned it, and inviting me to join him.

The lady in the doorway—wife or housekeeper, I could not tell which—allowed that I was right. "Are you a Spiritualist too, sir?"

"Yes!" When I lie, I begin to speak more rapidly. "Yes, of course, I am a fellow seeker after truth, a brother of Dr. Boyle in more respects than one, as it were, being a doctor myself, don't y'know, but I am originally from Manchester and our little group up there suggested I speak to Dr. Boyle when I came down to London, since I could not possibly do with missing too many sessions, especially because I have made *such* progress, a veritable breakthrough to the 'other side', or the 'unseen world,' if you know what I mean, and it would be terrible if it all went to waste for lack of a proper group to—"

She slipped a square of paper into my wildly gesticulating hands. Her expression of strained politeness led me to believe that she would have relished stuffing it into my mouth. "You'll find him at this address. Good day, sir." The door slammed, but genteelly.

The charioteer who conveyed me to the address on the paper was one of London's more garrulous types. I was tense as a drawn bowstring and not very receptive to his friendly overtures, which did not discourage him in the slightest. While my head spun with all the possible endings my coming interview with Dr. Boyle might have, he bantered on about every subject under the sun.

"—Course what with the dry spells we've been having, it won't do to expect too much in the way of crops this year, sir. A lean winter, maybe, and a hungry spring. My wife says it's all the Queen's fault—gods save her—but I say wait and see. Wait and see, don't you agree, sir?"

"Yes."

"Because after all, what's Her Majesty got to do with the weather? Now if we'd have had us fine growing weather and the crops *still* didn't come up, why then I'd be the first to call for the Queen to do something about it or step down. *Here* we are, sir. Eight-oh-two. Mind your step. Can't say as I care much for this part of London. Too damn many foreigners congregating here. Now I *know* none of 'em can be wizards, but don't it seem downright magical how they multiply? Why, I go home and tell my wife that I'm starting to see more foreign faces than I'd care for lounging around the better parts of London; even near the Palace, gods save us all! But she says it's my imagination—"

"What do I owe you?"

"Two and seven. Why, thank you, sir, much obliged."

I was glad to be rid of the charioteer and his wife. The day was waning, and in this part of London the buildings were all crushed together on either side of a narrow, crooked street that was nearly an alleyway. The taller houses leaned forward to meet each other across the street, keeping the lower reaches in artificial twilight. I struck a light—a common matchstick this time—to find the house bell.

My ring brought a frowzy servant girl, but her attitude was warmer and jollier than Dr. Boyle's more fastidious woman. " 'Ello, lovey, 'oo you want t' see?"

"I am looking for Madame Marushka, please."

"Naow! Oy should've guessed. 'Arf th' toime this 'owl's filled wif daycent payple it's 'coz she's 'avin' one of 'er see-antses. Just you follow me, ducks, and Oy'll tyke you roight hup." Her hips swayed entrancingly as she mounted the dark stair. A Venus in tattered petticoats, a Rhiannon of the backstairs, a goddess beneath the grime.

I pinched her bottom and she smacked my face.

"None o' that, ducks. Oy'm a good gel, Oy am. 'Ere's Madame Marushka's door. You jest keep your moind on them gaosts an' leave an honest workin' gel be."

I did as I was told. She sailed back down the stairs, and I rapped loudly at the door. It was answered by a wispy middle-aged man who looked like a vole in a business suit.

"Have you come seeking Truth?" he asked—using what he no doubt hoped was a ponderous and impressive voice.

"I have," I replied humbly.

"Pass, brother."

"*Pass, brother*. Oh, really, Harry! You'd think we were a clutch of barrow-robbers." The room I entered was not much lighter than the hall, but the woman who chided poor Harry carried her own radiance. She swept towards me in a whisper of wide rose-silk skirts and took both my hands.

"You're a new one, aren't you?" she asked, her dark owl-eyes alive with enthusiasm. "Madame Marushka will be so pleased. We'll be starting directly. Would you care for a cup of tea? Madame is Russian, but it's still drinkable about half the time."

"That would be perfect, Miss—?"

The young woman laughed, a rich sound. She threw her head back so that her thick curls of blue-black hair danced about her milky shoulders. "I honestly don't know how to introduce myself, sir. If I ask you to call me by my given name, would you consider me forward? But if I give you my full name, title and all, will that frighten you? I know it set poor Harry all agog for weeks. He wouldn't say boo to me without ten minutes' preliminary bow and scrape."

"I hope I am made of sterner stuff than Harry," I said softly. That made her laugh again.

"Very well. Ada Augusta, Countess of Lovelace." She made me a pretty curtsy. "And I assure you, I am not here merely to be slumming. I am as serious a seeker as yourself."

I raised her hand to my lips. "Then I am afraid you are terribly frivolous, my lady. I have only come here looking for a friend: Dr. Boyle."

"Who, Arthur? He's there, by the samovar." She linked her slender arm through mine and conveyed me across the shabbily furnished room. The walls were covered with a melange of thick sienna draperies, particolored scarves, and gilt-framed prints of simpering children or depressing historical prospects. A monstrous round table and its attendant chairs took up most of the available floor space. A scattering of abandoned teacups lay on the much-darned ecru lace tablecloth covering it. In some places the cloth was so hopelessly torn that it was easy to see the cheap green baize throw beneath.

Dr. Boyle was still drinking his tea and chatting with a plump, dowdy blonde in widow's weeds. She was pointing to this and that part of her anatomy and grimacing. He was merely grimacing.

"Dr. Boyle?"

"Ah, Dr. Weston!" He flew to my arms. "I am *so* glad to see you. But—" He looked over my shoulder. "Your friend—?"

"Still imprisoned. I have come alone."

"Alone? Good! That is a first step, at least."

"I have come to ask your help."

His smile dwindled. "I will hear you out, of course, but I believe you already know my thoughts. I will hear you out"—he raised a hand to forestall me—"after this session. That lady, from whose clutches you so felicitously rescued me, is a recently bereaved widow. Personally I think her husband caught hypochondria from her and perished of it. But even so, she has what we like to call a 'fresh' contact with the other side. Unless one is dealing with a particularly favored medium, the more fresh contacts present, the better."

I wondered what Dr. Boyle would make of Deirdre. My contact with the other side was constantly, painfully fresh.

"Then this session will be an education for me," I said, hoping to cajole him into reconsidering.

"Oh, undoubtedly. As a matter of fact, Lady Lovelace and I were among the first to arrive this evening and Madame informed us that we shall have the added pleasure of another widow among us."

"The pleasure of two widows; fancy!" My false enthusiasm was little better than a single coat of cheap varnish. It did not wear well, and it showed cracks readily. I shall never be the thespian that Donne is. There was an unfortunate silence. Dr. Boyle was no one's fool, nor was the adorable Countess of Lovelace. Her shapely hand had been resting on my arm; now she pointedly withdrew it and began to speak to Dr. Boyle in a manner that was obviously geared to exclude me.

Dr. Boyle did nothing to heal the breach. I had shown myself a scoffer in the temple. I was cast out. Not all the hangdog looks in the world would buy me absolution. I tried to speak up, to explain the stress under which I had been living, but Ada steered the doctor away from my contaminating presence. The little blond widow, having heard Dr. Boyle address me by my title, closed in to continue her recitation of ailments.

I was saved from this fate by the sudden clitter-clack of a fat, beshawled old dame, with a face like the scarlet harvest moon, thrusting her way through the thick bead curtains veiling the doorway leading to the rest of the flat. In her wake came a far smaller woman, brown-skinned and graceful as a candle flame. She was wrapped from head to toe in an exotic, diaphanous garment the color of grape hyacinths. On her brow, just between her large, umber eyes, was a small red mark. I could not help staring. True, I had been on the Continent with Donne a time or two, but I had not seen this lady's like there.

For that matter, I had not seen anything to approach Madame Marushka either—for it was Madame Marushka under all those shawls. Her British was thick with a Muscovy accent, and she made as if to embrace every soul in the room and enfold us en masse to her monumental bosom.

"Children! Children, let us sit down! Let the mystic circle be formed, my loves, and let us welcome our wanderers home again!"

"Oh my!" gasped my little widow, and she scuttled into one of the chairs set at the lace-covered table. I too moved quickly—quickly enough to take a seat as far from her as possible. As it happened, I found Madame Marushka herself seated directly on my right. She squinted at me, then pronounced, "A good aura! Who are you?"

"Dr. John H. Weston, Madame. I am new here, but I hope not unwelcome."

"Unwelcome? What is this talk of unwelcome? Dear child, as Father Svarog—whom you call the sky—covers the evil as well as the good, so do we welcome all who come here. What do you seek?"

I did not know quite what to say. Madame Marushka's sharp blue eyes unnerved me. There are some people one cannot lie to, unless one is an adept at the dubious art.

"There, there, good man. Never mind." Madame patted my hands briskly. "Can it be you do not even know what it is you are seeking? Never mind! We will help you. And now let us join." She placed her hands flat on the cloth, thumbs touching.

To Madame's right sat a prissy-mouthed man with thin steel-grey hair, and to his right sat the outlandish beauty, her kohl-rimmed eyes bright, filled with the single candle that burned in the center of the table. The Countess of Lovelace had the place beside her, then Dr. Boyle. I hoped he and she had softened towards me, after hearing Madame Marushka address me so kindly, but when I tried to catch his eye I failed. I believed I saw the Countess return my imploring look, but then Madame Marushka directed someone to turn out the other lights and Ada rose from her place to oblige. Beside Dr. Boyle sat the blond widow, followed by a brittle spinster, a beefy old gentleman of the breed that writes memoirs no one reads, and Harry to my left.

"We shall begin." Madame Marushka's words were uttered in a voice like a sunken ship's bell. To me she added, "My dear new son, you will have heard many strange things of our fellowship, but this is no charlatan's game. I am not a market-fair medium who pushes a button or twitches a string to raise ghosts. Any of our circle may open himself to the voice of the unseen. We wait, we meditate, we let the ageless rhythms of the sacred words convey us to the other plane. And then, whichever one of us the spirits deign to use as vessel and steed, we all profit by it."

A low, undulating sound was coming from the lips of every person around that table—everyone but myself and, I noticed, the dark woman. It was hardly possible to understand the words they intoned, or even to know whether they were words or gibberish. Suddenly Dr. Boyle stiffened in his seat.

"I am through!" he exclaimed. The chanting ceased. He leaned across the table; he stared at me. "By all the gods that ever lived, man," he said slowly, "*what have you done?*"

I shrank back into my chair. His face was alien, his eyes uncanny. "What crime could demand such a hideous punishment?" His voice rose until it thinned into an eerie whisper, and still he stared at me. "To be cut off, to be left so alone, so alone! Ah, friend, forgive me for ever having thought less of you! If I had to bear what you must, I think that I should rather—"

His lips snapped shut. His head swerved sharply to the left, then wavered. "What has come among us? What is here?" Fascinated, I watched him quest, like a trained hound, until his look settled on the impassive face of the dark-skinned woman.

"*Ah, gods!*" It came as a scream, then a wordless scream tore from his throat and he arched back so violently that he upset his chair with a resounding crash. "*Gods, the evil of it! The evil!*"

I rose from my seat—so did we all—but before I could scramble around the table to reach Dr. Boyle, a gust of wind extinguished the lone candle.

In the ensuing dark, I tangled with my unseen companions. Indignant demands for light mixed with frightened cries and muffled grunts as we all milled about, bumping into one another. I could hear Dr. Boyle thrashing about on the floor, and I persevered in my efforts to get to him. Madame's bulky furniture proved almost as much of an obstacle as her clients.

"Hang on, old man! I'm here!" It was Harry's voice. Slimmer than I, he had managed to slither free of the general melee.

"Go—go back!" Dr. Boyle gasped. "It is here, waiting to strike again! Harry, for the love of—"

Then Harry screamed, and I do not think I ever heard a sound more driving. *Deirdre be damned. I've this much left to use!* I thought, and summoned up earthfire to rekindle Madame Marushka's lamps.

Light flared. I was standing not three feet from Harry, but Harry was dead. His body lay with hands clenched, holding Dr. Boyle by the leg. Boyle himself still lived, but for how much longer? For there I saw, huddled on his chest, a hideous reptile whose like no sane man would describe outside the visions of drink. Stark white as a bone it was, but for a blood-red smear on the back on its head, which weaved back and forth, holding the doctor with the fascination of its black, ophidian eye. He moved, and the creature hissed, digging in with four-clawed feet to his shirt-front. Twin wings of feather-shaped flesh spread wide half-way down the creature's neck, and a scarlet tongue touched the doctor's face as gently as a lover's hand.

I lunged across Harry's corpse and seized the wretched thing just behind the head. Gods alone know what made me take such a chance. I acted without thinking, and felt the lizard's double crest slash my hand.

"Oh you would, would you?" I shook it angrily. A thick, noxious substance dripped from its mouth as it regarded me with almost human defiance. But the game was all up. I broke its back with a twist of my hands.

"Damn you! Damn you all for cowards! For Epona's sake, help me!" cried the Countess of Lovelace. I dropped the lizard's body and knelt beside Dr. Boyle, who held up a bitten hand and moaned. I looked up and saw her wrestling with the mysterious dark widow while all around her the others stood gawping mindlessly.

Saw! And who will believe what I saw? For as I watched Ada hold the woman's hands immobile, against all her efforts to get away, I saw the edges of her veiling lift and a third arm emerge, sinuous as a serpent. A third arm! Yes, and a fourth, and then a fifth and sixth until even the gallant Countess cried out in fear at the human Arachne she now held. Brave woman! Even then, she did not let go.

Not so the others. The spell of terror holding them broke in a wave of panic. They trampled each other trying to get through the door and away. Madame Marushka herself was gone. I stumbled over Dr. Boyle—if the creature's venom had not killed him yet, there might be time left him—and seized two of the monster's extra arms from behind.

Her head dipped, then turned completely around—completely! Human necks with mortal bones cannot do that without snapping. Her face never lost its look of demure calm, never lost an iota of its foreign beauty; never, not even when she opened her mouth in a wild laugh and a tongue dripping blood flicked out at me through a double row of razored yellow fangs.

The one I sought! The words exploded inside my head. It was like being trapped inside a belltower when the full peal rings out. My hands lost their strength, released her, clutched my reeling head. *Ahh! He will be pleased!*

Her four free arms windmilled out, striking Ada away like a fly. She came towards me, and I backed off until I felt the wall behind me and could go no farther. There were weapons in her hands now—sword, dagger, trident, drawn bow and shaft . . . and in one a human skull. The drift of gauzy silk she wore licked up around her in violet flames, and beneath its hem her tiny feet were lightly dancing.

"Spawn of Chernobog, by Dazhbog's power, begone! Byelobog destroy thee, Svarog turn his face from thee, Dazhbog's arrows slay thee!" Madame Marushka, a silver-bound book in one hand, a tufted horsetail in the other, loomed between us and the light. She whipped the horsetail forward, like a lash, and I felt cool droplets fall on my skin, soothing as spring rain.

Not so soothing for the fiend-woman attacking me. She wailed as if the water were everlasting flame, and whirled her flying veils close around her before vanishing.

"Dr. Weston!" The Countess of Lovelace's summons gave me no time to question or thank Madame Marushka. "Please come here at once. Dr. Boyle is dying!"

Dying? No, we were spared that much. The odious reptile had bitten him only once, in the hand. I lanced the swelling wounds and drew off the venom, then checked his heart and breathing. Both were only slightly more rapid than normal, and while his skin was damp with sweat, it was not dangerously clammy or discolored.

There was not a mark on poor Harry's body.

"A . . . weak heart," Dr. Boyle managed to say. "Harry was one of my patients."

The sight of that unnatural reptile would have given a healthy man palpitations. Madame Marushka lowered her bulk to the floor, released Harry's deathgrip on Boyle's leg, turned the unfortunate man over, and closed his eyes.

"May Father Svarog forgive me for ever having allowed that ogress to enter this house. I only saw what she wished me to see of her. She said she came from a distant land, that her people believe, as we do, that the soul does not wander forever but seeks another life in another body. She only wanted to speak to her husband's shade, to ask him where the wheel of life and death had spun him." The old Russian woman sighed and scrubbed a stray tear from her ruddy cheek.

"Dear Madame—" Ada embraced her. "You must not blame yourself. My blood carries some magic in it, but I could not see through her disguise until she struck. I saw her hand dart out and seize a drip of warm wax from the candle, then give it monstrous life! Look now. Where is the poisonous lizard?"

She spoke the truth. I had dropped the creature's body in plain view, yet now there was only a long thread of candlewax, snapped neatly in two, on Madame's well-worn rug.

"We must take you to a healer's croft," I said, helping Dr. Boyle to his feet. He was a formidable man, and his weight on my shoulder made my game leg throb abominably, but I refused to let on.

"And what of him?" Dr. Boyle indicated the corpse.

Ada slipped Boyle's other arm around her slender neck, taking most of the burden off me. I wondered if she had seen me wince. "Harry is beyond help, Arthur. Dr. Weston and I shall come back and do what must be done after we have settled you. Madame, will you be all right—?"

"All right?" The Russian woman's eyes sparkled. "Ha! Never will I be righter! Oh my beloved children, take good care of your friend and hasten back. Never in my wildest dreams have I had the opportunity for a contact half so fresh as this!" She scooped Harry up and gave him a warm hug that would have smothered him were he not . . .

Bearing Dr. Boyle between us, Ada and I had to walk about a block before we came to a street travelled enough for public chariots to frequent. Fortunately, once we hailed one, it was not a long or especially bumpy ride to the nearest healer's croft. Novices need practice, and the poorer sections of London provide full many an interesting case, especially in the wake of Beltaine, Imbolc, and the October brewings.

"You see, Dr. Weston," said Dr. Boyle as two strong-armed young novices tucked him snugly into a half-litter, "I would not have been able to help you, no matter what my own desires."

"Don't mind, sir." I squeezed his unwounded hand firmly. "Rest and be healed. We shall meet again, and I hope not to show myself such a charlatan then."

His smile was weak. "Nor I to show myself such a bigot. God be with you."

Outside the croft, I offered to put the Countess of Lovelace into a chariot that would convey her home.

"But Dr. Weston, are you not going back to Madame's?"

"And interrupt her conversation with Harry? I would rather die, which would give her *two* fresh contacts."

"You are incorrigible!" But she looked at me kindly. "Arthur is correct. We treated you shabbily. It takes time to convince the casual seeker. I am going back to Madame's, but not to hear Harry's shade. I have simply forgotten my shawl." Her bare shoulders trembled. I whisked off my jacket and draped it about them, then felt the autumn chill myself.

"By all means, let us go back."

In the chariot that took us there, Ada said, "So you are Dr. John H. Weston. Surely not the same—?"

I slammed my fist down on the chariot rail and almost lost my grip with the other hand, a maneuver that would have pitched me out the back of the vehicle onto my thick skull. Meantime she was saying, "Then if you are, I *must* talk to you at once, privately. After we leave Madame's—"

We were there.

So were the Druids.

"Ill met, Dr. Weston," said the Iron Duke. He was in an even fouler temper than I remembered him. It might have been brought on by a telling blow to his pride. Many a ship riding Bran's Wall had followed the *Maura Oisin* to a watery grave, all of them manned for the most part by Druid crews. So many of the Brotherhood had vanished without a trace that the Duke of Wellington had had to summon his brothers down from the wild Northern provinces to help him mind the workings of the British capital. Even the holy isle of Mona looked deserted. All this, coupled with the fact that he was now reduced to an escort of one very raw-looking novice, must have rankled him terribly.

"Well met, I should say, Master. I have been trying for weeks on end to lay a petition before y—"

"Enough!" He raised his staff, which crackled livid white with his displeasure. "You may save your breath and your parchment. Brihtric Donne will be dealt with, as shall all who violate the laws of Britain." He looked meaningly at Madame Marushka. His novice guard-of-honor held the old Russian woman by the arm, nervously. She was an imposing female who might have killed him in any of a number of ways while never meaning him a bit of harm.

"Oh, for pity's sake!" Ada found her scarf in a corner of the room and wrapped it round her shoulders with a flourish, then handed me back my jacket. She marched up to the Iron Duke and matched his gimlet gaze masterfully. "What are you going on about? Haven't you enough prisoners to play with that you must go arresting more? Not that you've got enough Brethren to give them a fair trial and release them, oh no! What awful transgression is Madame Marushka guilty of, pray?" As an afterthought she added, "Master."

"Your worthless father's daughter," the Archdruid mumbled. "If this book is hers, you ought to know of what crime she stands accused." He took the silver-bound tome with which Madame had overcome the ogress and pushed it rudely into Ada's hands.

She gave it a thorough examination. "I don't understand a word of it. It's in Cyrillic."

"A book of foreign magics, girl!" The Duke's white hair stood out from his head like the mane of a goaded lion. "Is that not crime enough?"

"Piffle," said Ada. "How could you have any such thing in Britain? Bran's Wall would stop it."

"Bran's Wall is breached! Breached or weakened. You! When did you come to Britain?"

Madame Marushka flung her arms wide, perhaps intending to embrace her new land symbolically. It floored the novice, who scrabbled up the tablecloth and squeaked, "None o' that, marm! None o' that!" He was ignored.

"To Britain! Ah! I came here only this summer, and already I feel that I am mother to all wandering souls of this isle! I cannot tell you, dear sir—Master, is it?—how I am anticipating your festival of Sammain, when I shall leave my doors and windows as open as my heart to any of the dead who need me."

I think I was the only one to hear Wellington mutter, "Crazy bitch." He then addressed Ada. "There you have it. The Wall was already giving way. How else could she have brought in that book undeterred? Her ship would have frozen once it touched the Wall. But the Wall is no longer enough. We have found other evidence of it—evidence whose exact nature does not concern you."

"Evidence that Donne brought before you months ago!" I cried out. "If you had listened to what he had to say then, there would be more of your Brethren alive this day, and no breach in Bran's Wall."

The Iron Duke drew close until he and I could have shared a breath. His eyes were dangerous. "Brihtric Donne is a traitor to Britain."

"The Golden Brotherhood is not Britain," I returned. "No matter how much you would like it to be so, it is not. Nor has Donne ever betrayed any of you. Master Caradoc was his beloved friend. When Donne is brought to fair trial, he will be found innocent by your peers, and you will look all the more the fool for accusing him. This much I can tell you of the man: He loves Britain better than any other man ever has or ever shall."

"Then he shall love Britain at the end of the hangman's rope. For I swear to you by Esus, I shall bring him to dance on air. I have wasted too long with him. Now I shall do what was suggested to me by one near the Queen. I shall bring him to trial before a jury of nobles—Druids or not."

"Yes, and break the very laws of Britain you claim to defend! No man may be tried for his life unless before a jury of the Wise."

"No . . . unless the Queen's Consent is given. And it will be given, Dr. Weston. I suggest you visit your friend in prison tomorrow, and every day thereafter. You may comfort yourself in future years by writing *The Final Days of Brihtric Donne*."

I would have said more, but Ada took my arm and urgently pulled me from Madame Marushka's flat. Wellington sneered and put me from his mind. My forced departure was a joy to him. I protested; Ada continued to drag me away. It was not until we were both in the street that she released me.

I rubbed my arm. It was frightfully sore. The lady had a good grip; I recalled her adamant hold on the ogress.

"Oh! Have I injured you? Forgive me, but Wellington's like a blind bull-mastiff these days. He'll snap at anything he can and destroy it if he's able. One more word from you, and I could see he meant to have you also placed under arrest on whatever charge was handiest."

"You speak of him so familiarly, my lady." An inquiring note crept into my words. Familiarly, and often downright rudely, I thought. Not that he didn't fully deserve it.

"Him? Father used to take me to see him when he still had a sense of humor. Even my slight trace of the blood entitled me to certain liberties when speaking with the old man, and I refused to abandon them just because they made him Archdruid and he turned into a pompous bore. Father often spoke of . . ." Her voice died. We had come to the same thoroughfare where we had summoned a chariot earlier, and by the lamplight I saw that there were tears in her eyes.

"My lady, what is it?"

The tears spilled over. "Ada. Please call me Ada. And please—please, Dr. Weston—you must help my father. You must not neglect him any longer! He is in desperate need of your help, and of Mr. Donne's."

"Your father? How can I neglect a man I've never—?"

Her face, even tear-wet, was as perfect as an Italian cameo. I had only beheld such perfection of feature once before, and not on a woman's face. Her next words confirmed my suspicions. "You know him. And only you know how greatly he needs you. For weeks he haunted the Café Royal, hoping you would come. Even now he returns there every fifth night, faithfully. He has left Mother—that much he has told me—but he will not say where he lives now, or how, or even upon what business he seeks you. Oh, Dr. Weston, I am so afraid!"

Lord Byron's daughter.

CHAPTER TEN

The Case of the Most Fetching Lady Donne Ever Knew

"Lord Byron's daughter," said Donne. "I think there is somewhat more to you than that, Lady Lovelace." He dove into the hamper I had brought along and flicked the covering cloth from a plate of cream buns. This time I had decided not to inflict Mrs. Hendrik's brutal idea of cuisine on a man already sore troubled. When Ada had come calling for me in her private Gaulish coach that morning, I had insisted on a short stop at Mildred's establishment.

"Mr. Donne," she replied, "what more could there be?" She accepted a bun from the plate and set it down primly beside her on the bench. The moment she had entered Donne's miserable cell, it was as if the spring solstice had occurred and the dead sun were reborn. He had ceded her the only decent seat at once.

"Either you are modest or you are toying with me, my lady. Your estimable colleague, Mr. Babbage, would not think well of that. He is reputed to have a high dislike for chicanery in any form."

Ada gave him one of her ravishing smiles and removed the cover from the hamper she had brought independent of my own. It was large and unwieldy, yet all efforts on my part to relieve her of it had been met with soft, determined resistance. From within she produced a gleaming bronze jug, cunningly sealed and outwardly insulated with cordovan leather, and three meticulously wrapped porcelain cups and matching saucers. She passed these, poured tea from the bronze jug, and offered cream and sugar before replying.

"I admit to testing your powers, Mr. Donne. But you ought to be used to that by now. To meet the great Brihtric Donne and *not* keep back something of oneself—waiting to see whether he can deduce it solely from observation—has become as British a pastime as cattle raids. It would be like a North Country visitor to London who does not stare at the sights, then swears he has better things to see back home."

I could not tell whether or not her excuses mollified Donne. As always, when involved in a case, his features betrayed nothing of the inner workings of the man's mind. Instead, he chose to speak to me.

"I mentioned the name Babbage just now, Weston. Does it mean anything to you? No. Why should it? Yet I tell you frankly that were this land different, ruled by men and not by magic, the name of Charles Babbage and his Analytical Engine would be graven upon the heart of every British schoolchild."

"I should hardly go that far, Mr. Donne," Ada put in. "The Analytical Engine never went beyond the design stage. Mr. Babbage lacked the money to continue."

"Money which would have come with government interest. But why should the Brotherhood back a machine that would lift many of mankind's burdens when they could continue to maintain their monopoly on providing solutions, and at a monopolistic price? But here! Weston is confused. Will you enlighten him, my lady?"

Ada poured me a fresh cup and prepared it to my taste. "Charles Babbage is a brilliant man, Dr. Weston. Using certain mathematical principles, he designed what he called the Analytical Engine. It was to be a machine that could perform complicated calculations in a fraction of the time a human being would require. Of course, the Engine would have to be given its problems in its own—how shall I call it?—Enginese?"

"A mathematically based calculator able to understand a mathematically based language," said Donne. I thought I detected the hint of a smile behind his tilted teacup. "And Lady Lovelace was the mathematician who devised the code through which we mortals might approach the Engine. She has also published a monograph called *Equations Relevant to the Use and Conservation of Magic*. She is acknowledged to be quite gifted."

"Gifted! You slight the lady, Donne. I should go farther."

"No doubt you would. But Babbage's astonishing device does not here concern us, Weston. You were telling me about her ladyship's father."

So I was. Donne listened to the whole story of last night's seance, his lank stride devouring the tiny cell in three paces each way. When I detailed the threats that Wellington had levelled against him, he said, "The Duke is within the law. It is allowable for a man to be tried for a capital offense without a Druid jury, if the Queen's consent be obtained that a panel of nobles may sit upon the case. Surely you realize from what source such a suggestion came?"

"Kitchener," I said.

"What, Lord Brass-Bottom?" exclaimed Ada. "What's he got to do with you being here, Mr. Donne? Epona knows, he's got his mucky fingers in enough pies at the Palace. Mamma likes him; reason enough to dislike him right there. I do visit her on occasion, when she is in attendance on Her Majesty. She has been promoted to Mother of the Maids, though why Her Majesty should so suddenly favor her, I can't say. More of Kitchener's doing. Every time I visit, he is with the Queen. They claim he is courting her, and that she is hearing out his suit with some favor. Preposterous!"

"Ha!" Donne stopped in midstride. "And why do you say that, Lady Lovelace? Feminine intuition?"

"Mr. Donne"—her tone was frigid—"don't be ridiculous. It does not suit your reputation. Druids manage the Palace workings at the executive level. These days, there are fewer Druids, and they are needed elsewhere. On my last visit to Mamma, I took the liberty of seeking out the Palace Secretary, also one of the Wise, with a question about whether private persons might purchase the sort of tea biscuits Her Majesty prefers. He was not in, but I took presumption a step further by glancing over the Household Accounts—looking for some mention of the biscuits, you understand—while I waited for his return. Mr. Donne, I there saw, in black and white, proof that with the exception of a number of servants I could sum up on the fingers of one hand, every former member of the Palace staff has been replaced by one of Lord Kitchener's recommendation. His lordship's name was given in the space reserved for comments—and in his lordship's own handwriting."

"And not the Secretary's? That sounds a worse imposition than your trespass, Lady Lovelace," said Donne.

"Trespass? Mr. Donne, you are a gentleman. You have not pointed out my other faults: picking the lock of the Secretary's office, for one."

"Lying to me, for another. Biscuits. Really."

"I told you no lies. I merely colored the truth. I knew you would see through to the heart of it. Yes, the Palace Secretary is also gone from his post, and yes, I went to his office with the intention of investigating the records, and no lock in Britain can stop me when I am set on something. You have been terribly idle during your confinement, Mr. Donne. All prisoners need exercise, but in your case I assumed that you would be more grateful for a puzzle with some pieces deliberately missing than for any amount of strolling time in the yard."

This time, Donne did smile.

"You are a resourceful young woman, my lady. I pledge everything in my power to aiding your father. Weston has admitted to me time and again that he feels unequal to handling our present case without my help. Therefore, it seems that I must escape. Yes, before the Duke of Wellington can make me do a decidedly unpleasant jig *en pleine air.*"

"The Iron Duke is stubborn and narrow-minded, but he would die for Her Majesty," said Ada. "He only works for your execution because he thinks the Queen wants it so, and the Queen's voice is in reality Kitchener's. Gods, how I wish I knew *why* that awful man exerts such influence over Her Majesty! What is his hold? I have sensed her hatred and fear of the man whenever I see them together in the Palace and he is not looking at her. Mamma sees it too, and revels in it."

Donne gave her a long look. Finally he said, "Lady Lovelace, I think that you might be the one soul other than Weston and myself who might be trusted with that information. First, though, I must find a way to escape from the Tower."

Escape from the Tower of London! How many had tried, how many had failed? Their bones lay unburied and unmourned in the shallow moat surrounding the great stone edifice. The Tower ravens had long since picked them bare and dry. The Morrigan's Children made a splendid appearance as Tower guards, but when an escape threatened, they were there for more than show. Thick bars of enchantment ringed the Queen's Tower, where those prisoners of Druid's blood were kept, but when ordinary men were locked away in the White Tower, it only took an offhand spell of enhancement and enlargement cast on a very hungry raven to bring any escape attempt to a bloody end.

"Can you not use your magic to free Donne, Lady Lovelace?" I asked.

"My spells are few, and my blood very dilute. I am even less of a mage than my poor dear father. The Byrons have been marrying money rather than power for too long. Soon our descendants will be hardly more than mortal. They may make extraordinarily good cooks, that being the last bit of mana to desert one. It will take more than I can offer to spirit Mr. Donne to freedom."

"Do not trouble yourself, my lady," said Donne. "I will hit upon a plan. Ah! But here I see that I shall have to summon the guards. We are about to be besieged by a pair of Britain's most ruthless and cunning warriors."

"Who?" said the northern curve of the cell wall. "Us?"

"Shut up, Diccon! You've given the trick away again," snarled the south.

Lady Lovelace and I watched in amazement as the two opposing points in the wall rippled and from each a young, fox-haired boy emerged. The features of their faces were so alike that they had to be close kin. The smaller and younger of the two was already snivelling pitifully when he stepped out of the stones. Donne scooped him up and edged Lady Lovelace aside on the bench so that he might hold the child on his lap and cheer him.

"Tears, your grace? That won't do at all!"

"I can't help it." Diccon took Ada's lace handkerchief gratefully and wiped his nose. "Ned's always so beastly to me, for no reason! You already *knew* we were there. I didn't give us away."

"If the truth be told, I heard His Majesty's stomach rumbling," said Donne. "Even through solid rock, it can be a sound with which to reckon. Had the hamper containing the cream buns been placed farther from the wall, your surprise would have worked. But not even royalty can resist cream buns. Will Your Majesty do us the honor?" He waved one hand towards the freighted hamper.

"*Your Majesty?*" I only saw two boys—boys with extraordinary powers, to be sure—sitting beside the hamper and happily stuffing their mouths with pastry. Diccon had slipped lightly from Donne's lap as soon as the invitation was uttered.

"Edward the Outplayed, briefly King of Britain," said Donne. "And his brother Richard, Duke of York. Now I *know* you have heard of them."

"Who has not heard of the Little Princes in the Tower?" I replied. "But I thought they were dead." Remembering their disembodied entrance, I added, "Are they?"

"I'm as alive as you are!" said His Majesty around a mouthful of cream.

"An unfortunate tendency of most historians is to romanticize facts," said Donne. "Two young princes, done to death under suspicious circumstances, reads far better than accounts of how King Henry the Usurper confined his kin to this Tower by devious means, where they remain to this day. I deplore their captivity, but I must admit their visits have lightened my own empty hours considerably." He rumpled the Duke of York's curls and a wistful look lingered on his face for about half a breath. I would never truly know all there was to know about my friend.

"Historians are either dustmops or failed dramatists." Ada spoke as if she were dead sure of the facts, and no exceptions admitted. "What I do not understand is why two of the strongest line of Bran's blood have been kept in the White Tower all these years. Magic does not guard the White Tower. What keeps them here?"

The boys shrugged. The young erstwhile King of Britain looked shamefaced.

"Do not take it to heart, Your Majesty," said Donne. "Henry the Usurper was a sly manipulator. Observe how cunningly he managed to gloss over all blame for the deed that might be laid at his door and instead damn your blameless uncle Richard with full responsibility."

"What? Not Uncle Diccon!" Both lads were loud in their protests. "I thought you only told us that for a jest," added King Edward.

"A jest with teeth in it, I fear. No, all I told you was true. Beyond these walls, the world believes that Richard, Duke of Gloucester, imprisoned you and later had you murdered."

"Enter the valiant Henry," Ada joined in. "He slew the evil hunchbacked toad, the unnatural uncle, the—I prefer not to go on mouthing such trash. Then, as a personal favor to the realm, he assumed the British throne and married your sister."

"No one tells us anything." The King was sullen.

"And Uncle Diccon wasn't anything like you've been saying," little Diccon sniffled, starting to weep afresh. "We adored Uncle Diccon!" Ada helped him to blow his nose.

"Your uncle's name is clear among respectable scholars," said Donne. "The public, however, would rather believe the more sensational versions. There are times I wish that I had Druid's blood within me, that I might go back in time and right so many of the wrongs history has allowed to happen."

"Can't do that," said King Edward. "Not every one of the Wise can!"

"It does take special training," Ada agreed.

In their chatting over ancient rights and wrongs, I was overlooked. I was becoming quite used to it. "*If* you don't mind, Donne, *might* I be informed what prevents these lads from using their doubtless high powers to waft themselves out of this hellhole?"

Donne can affect an incredibly irritating smile of the sort used with forward brats who have grown too big for caning. "Henry the Usurper was a wily man. Do you think his powers were strong enough to wrest the crown from young Edward in fair battle?"

"Not by half!" cried the King in his own defense.

"And not even little Diccon would be fool enough to accompany a known rogue like Henry into the purlieus of the Queen's Tower, which *is* guarded by magic. But if you were a little boy, and quite bored with all the rigmarole that royalty requires, would you not jump at the chance to go on a lark with a man you know you can turn into a toad *so*—?" Donne snapped his fingers.

"The old turd said he'd a present for us." Diccon, Duke of York, spoke up, his tears dabbed away under Ada's gentle hands. "Two weasels, white all over, but for a red saddle."

"He said he'd trained them to run at each other like destriers," Edward said. "Tie little straw men to their backs with wooden lances in their hands and let 'em run. He was hiding them in the Tower, because our Lady Mother didn't like us to get too interested in playing war."

"A lamentable weakness of many mothers." Donne stood up. "The box containing the promised weasels in truth contained a powerful spell. When opened by King Edward, Duke Richard at his side, Henry's enchantment struck them. From that moment on, any attempts on the part of the princes to use their own powers would trigger an aging spell. They would age rapidly; age to death, in fact."

"A monarch without full use of his powers cannot rule Britain," said Ada. I thought of Victoria and felt the blood leave my face.

"Why did they remain here, then? Even if they could not rule, why should they lurk in the Tower and let Henry steal the crown?"

"Ah, there's the perverse genius of old Henry, Weston! While an otherworld voice released likewise from the fatal box was informing them of the spell to which they had fallen victims, Henry was already outside the White Tower weaving a *second* spell."

"He summoned up a fiend," said Diccon, lower lip all atremble. "A fiend commanded to tear us to pieces as soon as we set foot out of this Tower."

"We couldn't use our powers to get out, 'cos we'd die of old age on the spot," said Edward. "And we couldn't use our powers to fight off the fiend. For all we know, it's still out there, waiting. He made it a special sort, the kind that feasts on children."

"In short, no way out of the Tower for the princes, by magic means or ordinary methods." Donne knelt and put his arms around the boys. "Henry's spell left them the use of only so much of their powers as needed for extending their lives and playing minor pranks such as the one you witnessed. A long life they have had, if not a merry one, and their youth is eternal."

"Unless they use their powers. I see," I said. "What a shame. I had hoped your young friends might be the means for your escape, but I would not have them buy your freedom with their deaths."

"Nor I, Weston, nor I."

"In Cernunnos' name, why not?" Ada leapt up from the bench as if struck by lightning.

"*Why not?*" I sputtered, taken aback at such unexpected ruthlessness in so lovely a vessel. "My dear lady, the boys would *die*, that is 'why not'!"

"Not at all! No, not necessarily, Dr. Weston." Now it was her turn to pace, and she exhibited a remarkable Donnesian flair for it. "My town house is not that far from the Tower. It would not require much mana to convey Donne there." She squatted on the floor with Donne and the princes and rattled off a stream of—to me—gibberish.

I, unlike Donne, never took a First in mathematics at Cambridge. Of course I had only his word for that.

"Yes," he said softly. Then louder, "Yes, that is so. If I recall your published calculations, such a small amount of sorcerous energy expended should not harm— But no, by my reckoning it would age the lad who cast the transporting spell to about seventy years. It is one thing to spend an endless captivity as a carefree boy, another entirely as a dotard."

"But Mr. Donne, I mean for *both* of the boys to cast the spell upon you."

"Both . . ."

"Refer to my calculations again when you have the opportunity. Magic may be either the work of an individual or a group. Bran himself needed the aid of his fellow Druids to create the Wall, and to this day it is maintained by a group of the Wise, not by one Master alone. One Druid might have power enough for such a task, but it would drain him utterly. He would die. Such concerted efforts require only a fraction of each member's power."

"Magnificent!" Donne sprang up and seized Ada's small hands, lifting her to her feet. "And as obvious as something hidden in plain sight. My dear Lady Lovelace, it seems that I have much yet to learn. I could not ask for a more charming teacher."

"Boys—Your Majesty, your grace—will you help us?" Ada was never so appealing. The King and his brother were mere striplings, but children of a lusty age when a man was scarcely out of swaddlings before he became aware of the gentler sex's attractions.

"Even if we die!" declared Edward the Outplayed.

"Oh, but you won't die," said Ada. "You will age—both of you—but only until you are about twenty-five or thirty years old."

"And what is more—oh, an excellent jest on dead Henry's bones!—you will be able to walk out of the White Tower free men," Donne gloated.

"Donne, how? The fiend—"

"The fiend, Weston, is looking for two *boys*. Not two young men. I rather doubt the fiend is able to stomach young men. Besides, fiends are all fury and no intelligence. Once free, Your Majesty, I suggest that you and your brother present yourselves to the Department of Living History at Cambridge. They will be happy to help you make any adjustments to your new lives."

"Well . . ." The former King took a deep breath. "Are you ready, Mr. Donne?" Donne nodded. "You ready, Diccon?"

"Let's do it." The boys clasped their hands together. Diccon closed his eyes and furrowed his brow. A faint glow began to emanate from the pair. A twin nimbus formed around Donne. As I watched, Donne's figure wavered, then flashed from sight.

" 'Where does the candle flame go?' " Ada quoted.

"Where? I wouldn't know," said a resonant voice only vaguely familiar. King Edward the Outplayed stood six feet tall and proportionately brawny, a fine-looking man with his warrior-father's roving eye. His brother was a lesser version of the same model.

"We touched your mind to find where you'd like him sent," the Duke of York told her. "Then we sent him there."

King Edward the Outplayed regarded his brother. "Well, old Hal Pinchpenny may have been the gods' first word in buggerarses, but at least we may thank him for some elegance in his spells." When Diccon looked puzzled, he added, "Our clothes, fool! They *did* grow with us. Not that I'd mind having you take a closer look at what I've to offer, my lady." He winked at Ada.

"Dr. Weston," said that imperturbable woman, "it is time for all visitors to leave the Tower." We retrieved our hampers and linked arms by common consent. "Wait a few minutes after we have gone before leaving, boys. It would not do to have four people exit a Tower cell which only two entered."

The grown King guffawed. "Hardly, my love! Diccon and I'll leave this cell the way we came, then walk out of our own as pretty as you please. They don't bother with guards on it—hardly ever did in the past and certainly not these days. But give us a kiss for luck, eh?" He tore Ada from my arm and bussed her with much enthusiasm and little style.

His whoop of pain could be heard all the way down the Strand. Ada smoothed her hair and prissily removed the small, very angry demon that had latched onto His Majesty's upper lip by the snapping claws it had in lieu of hands. She spat on it and it disappeared.

"Your first lesson, Your Majesty, is never to kiss a woman unless you are certain she will appreciate it." With that, we took our leave.

It was already growing dark when we rode from the Tower. "I wonder how the princes will adjust to present Britain?" I said as I helped Ada down from her coach at the steps of her town house. It was a modest specimen of Georgian architecture, complete with Classic pillars flanking the door and a marble Venus imported from the Continent ready to greet us in the foyer. Rome has never conquered Britain by might, but her culture has managed to seep through cracks in Bran's Wall. Our finer arts were the richer for it.

"They'll be fine, but I am glad I'm not a tavern wench in

Cambridge-town now. Imagine having one's puberty leap out at you all of a sudden, after four hundred some-odd years on the simmer!" She set down her hamper and blew a silver dove to life in her cupped hands. "Bring Merriwell, my sweet." The creation flew away. Ada's magic might have been dilute, but it was very pretty.

The little dove returned riding on the shoulder of a lean, deadpan retainer of the breed whose worth is always calculated in gold but whose wages seldom see silver.

"My lady called?"

"Merriwell, this is Dr. Weston. As the hour is late, he will be staying the night."

"I shall inform Cook, my lady. Shall I take up his luggage?" He meant the hamper.

"Take that to the kitchen along with mine and have Cook tidy them both. Oh, and as Dr. Weston has arrived somewhat on the spur of the moment, please find him suitable clothes for dinner and the night."

"Very good, my lady. I shall have to put him in the Unicorn Room, if that will be satisfactory. The Dragon is already occupied." He broke this news to me as if it were a national tragedy, but one which Merriwell would lay down his life to rectify, were he so commanded.

"Is it?" Ada's glance was mischievous. We both knew by whom the Dragon was taken.

"Yes, my lady. A gentleman arrived at the house some time ago. I should hazard to guess an hour. Maisie discovered him in the Dragon Room. It pains me to report that she made rather a to-do about it belowstairs. As the gentleman presented himself as one of your ladyship's acquaintance and asked to remain until you should return, I saw no harm in allowing him to stay. Since he was already in the Dragon Room, it seemed convenient to leave him there. Will he be staying the night as well?"

Ada turned a rising giggle into a sneeze. "Yes, Merriwell. Provide him with anything necessary. I will see Dr. Weston to his room myself."

"Very good, my lady." Merriwell shuffled off, toting our hampers. I had no doubt that were Donne to call for naked dancing girls, Merriwell would provide. Had his lady not said 'anything necessary'?

We ascended a curved staircase whose marble had the warm glow of polished alabaster. "The Unicorn Room is this one," she said as we passed the first door at the head of the stairs. Proceeding along a corridor softened by thick tobacco-colored carpet, she named each room. "This is my solar, and the next is the master suite. That has its own bath, but here is where you may bathe if you feel like more than a light wash-up, in which case your room has its own piped water and basin. The jakes is at the end of the hall nearest your room—this is such an old-fashioned house. And *here* we have the Dragon!"

She did not bother knocking. It was her own house, after all. Donne was seated before a fireplace carved from a rare striated green marble. It had the form of a dragon's maw, whence the name of the room. A meerschaum pipe was between his lips, a mulberry dressing gown was tied at his waist, and he appeared to be at peace with the world.

"Lady Lovelace, there is a special place in the afterlife reserved for your man Merriwell," he said by way of greeting.

Merriwell himself materialized in the doorway. "Begging your pardon, my lady, gentlemen, but there is a caller below asking to see Mr. Donne. A rather short party, if I may be permitted the liberty. Will this be the gentleman you sent for, sir?"

"Ha! He doesn't waste time. Excellent, excellent. By all means, Merriwell, show him up."

Minutes later, Friedrich Gutmann was planting a lingering Continental kiss on Ada's hand while Merriwell provided a decanter of sherry and closed the door.

To me he said, "So you finally found the stomach to get him out, eh?" Donne distracted him before I had to shame myself with a truthful reply.

"Friedrich, there has lately been a great turnover in personnel at the Palace. I want you to find employment there—in what capacity is unimportant."

"How do you know they'll hire me?" The dwarf leered and took a slim cigar from his waistcoat pocket. He clipped the end neatly and lit it, filling the room with nauseating smoke.

"I have faith in your powers of persuasion, Friedrich. You will get in. How long you will stay is another matter. Once hired, I would have you go to the Queen. Use any ruse needful to be near her. Report back to me when you are able on her actions, her state of mind, and above all on those nearest her. I would appreciate it were you to start at once."

Friedrich blew more smoke. "Just as you'd have it, my

friend. I shan't even pause to take a glass of this beautiful amontillado with you."

"Herr Gutmann," said Ada, "if you can help Mr. Donne in this, I shall send a full pipe of it to your house."

When Friedrich had gone, Donne called council. By unspoken consent, we made Ada privy to the entire case. "She has as much at stake as any of us," said Donne. "Perhaps more. Her father is deeply involved, albeit unwillingly. Trust her as you would myself."

We further agreed that it would be folly to return to 221B Baker Street for the nonce. Donne's escape from the Tower was discovered by now, and our flat would be the first place the Golden Brotherhood would look, then keep under surveillance. As for the possibility of an all-seeing dragnet spell being cast over London and turning Donne up at Ada's house, the lady herself set my mind at ease.

"For the Brotherhood to examine every nook and cranny of London is monumental. There are not enough Druids left free to undertake it properly. However, you never know with those old loves, so I've gone ahead and cast a shield-spell of my own. Any all-seeing spell of theirs lighting on this house will see all . . . except Mr. Brihtric Donne. He will blend in with the draperies."

"My lady, you continue to amaze me," said Donne.

We dined well that night. I found that the inimitable Merriwell had procured a set of evening clothes in my size, and when I retired for the night I had a silk nightshirt and cap awaiting me on a tenderly opened bed. Brandy heated in a balloon over a candle on the nightstand.

Merriwell would have pursed his lips to see his ministrations wasted on me. After a wearying day and all his efforts to lure sleep into my bedchamber, I remained awake. I was too worried about Victoria. What schemes was Kitchener pressing upon her even now? My arms ached for her, and the thought that perhaps we two should never see each other again tortured me.

Somewhere a bell chimed two. I sighed and touched my finger to the wick of my extinguished chamberstick. It kindled and I took it up, resolving to see whether Donne would let me pour out the burden of my heart to him. I did not like the idea of interrupting his first night's sleep in a really comfortable bed after the ordeal of the Tower, but I had to talk to someone. I padded down the corridor and knocked on the door of the Dragon Room.

I got no answer.

Donne was never a heavy sleeper. Like a high-strung hunting dog, he will often be set bolt awake by the softest noise. I knocked louder, with no results. To pound at the door was out of the question at that hour of the morning. I should have roused the entire household. Merriwell would have disapproved. Relying upon the strength of our friendship, I tried the doorknob. It turned, unlocked, and I slipped in.

His bed was untouched, unslept-in. A silk nightshirt and cap that were twins to my own lay lovingly folded on the pillow. I did not know what to make of this. Had Ada's spell been insufficient? Had the Iron Duke thirsted so mightily for Donne's blood that he had used his full powers to search out my friend and spirit him away? Whatever had happened, Ada had to be made aware of Donne's absence.

Merriwell stepped from the shadows as I was about to knock on the master bedroom door. "Please do not, sir."

"But I must, Merriwell," I whispered. "My friend is missing."

"I think not, sir."

"Eh? Have you seen him? The library! Is he there, by any chance?"

"We do not have a library, sir. I could find you some suitable reading material, if you so desire."

"Well, then—the kitchen?" Donne come over a bit peckish at two in the morning was a strange picture, but when you have eliminated the impossible . . .

"Mr. Donne is not below, sir, if that is what you wish to ascertain. And her ladyship's solar is locked."

I cast a quick glance at the door to the bath. No, there was neither the sound of running water nor splashing, and Merriwell confirmed my deduction with a gentle shake of his head. The jakes? And should I, wakeful and tense, not have heard his footsteps in the hall? There was only one place left to consider.

"No," I said to the master bedroom door. I walked back to the Unicorn Room in a daze, Merriwell as my discreet sheepdog. A glass of warm milk and honey materialized in his hands. He watched me drain it. I felt drowsy at once, and he assisted me to bed.

"Whatever remains, *however improbable*, must be the truth, sir," said Merriwell. "Good night, Dr. Weston. I do so enjoy reading your stories in the *Strand*."

CHAPTER ELEVEN

The Case of the Herringmonger

"You're chipper," I said to Donne when he came down to breakfast.

Donne investigated the covered dishes on the buffet, heaped his plate with eggs, hot rolls, kippers, and kidneys, then said, "You may enjoy your prudish self-righteousness for approximately five minutes longer. Then I shall be grateful if you will drop it."

"Hoity-toity," I mumbled. He ate his breakfast with relish and pushed the plate aside.

"Now, Weston, let us attack the problem at hand." He stretched his legs out under the table and pressed his palms together, tapping his chin lightly with the fingertips. "Thanks to your visits, I was not as cut off from news of the outer world as some might have desired. I know of the sorry state of Bran's Wall. I know of the blight on our fair country. I know what it will mean should the Queen not heal the land." He looked at me with sympathy. "I see that you know, too. The Rules Britannia are gone—the only instrument capable of restoring Britain—and the Queen is in Lord Kitchener's power. Daily he draws the noose tighter."

Donne leaned forward across the table, reminding me of a tiger about to spring. "I put it to you, Weston: Why does he hesitate?"

"Why—?"

"The man was one of Britain's ablest leaders before vanity led him to imagine himself King of Britain. Ambition drove him to the brink of frustration. What chance was there for a man lacking the blood of the Wise to become King? Magic had raised a wall as substantial as Bran's own to keep him from the crown. Thus began the years abroad, the years of study, the years it took Kitchener to sell his soul and master that most insidious body of foreign magics, the Oriental. Now afrits dance at his command—and kill. Steel weapons are in the hands of his mortal minions. It is through some fell sorcery that every Druid ship setting out to repair

Bran's Wall comes to grief. If you were a man with such powers, why would you waste your time courting the Lady of Britain when you might face her in open battle?"

I considered the matter well. "If I were a good military man like Kitchener, I should hesitate to launch an offensive until I was sure that all factors guaranteed me an easy victory. In the meantime, I should weaken my opponent's defenses. I suppose time is everything."

"Weston, you are not beyond hope after all. *Time*. The key to the stolen Rules lies hidden there, in a word. Kitchener bides his time. But now another question. You are most insightful today. Kitchener's hashashin carried cold steel, but only hand weapons. Kitchener is not the man to smuggle in a calf when he can steal an entire herd of cattle. You recall the marvels that our Continental friends showed us in the way of heavy artillery when we were last abroad. Why is Kitchener content with guns and knives? Why not cannon?"

"Well, Bran's Wall, don't y'know, and—ah—hum . . ." I frowned and sought answers in my teacup. Guns or cannon, what did it matter? No crumb of refined iron or steel could pass Bran's Wall. Even breached badly enough to admit foreign magics to British soil, the Wall would have to be fallen to nothingness before it would allow deathmetal to pass.

Donne affected a wry smile. "I read your conclusions in your silence. Tell me, Weston—you who were at my side while the entire process of steel-making was explained to us in detail by Monsieur Lapin of the Academy—how do you make steel?"

"Why, it's fairly simple, Donne. You just—you just—you simply—" I blinked and cudgelled my brains, but nothing came. I grew angry and snarled, "You tell me!"

"I cannot. I no longer know how."

"What! You twit me, Donne. Your mind is as retentive as a wronged woman's."

"A pretty figure of speech. Overdone, but pretty. I am being honest with you, my friend. Not only do the spells of Bran's Wall prevent any steel from coming into Britain, they also cancel all knowledge of the steel-making process. Moreover, Continental books on the subject are found to have select pages mysteriously reduced to rusty ash when they enter Britain. Alien metallurgists visiting these shores return home having to relearn the simplest tenets of steel refinery. Britain has some deposits of hematite—iron is the world's commonest metal. Any Briton with access to a forge may produce iron, but who would risk the wrath of the all-seeing Brotherhood? And iron is brittle—too brittle for the casting of really superior weapons."

I got up from the breakfast table and began to pace nervously while Donne looked on and had more tea. "Then it is impossible! Impossible! Where did Kitchener get those steel weapons, then? Did his afrits make them?"

"Even magic has boundaries. There is a balance in supernatural things as well as natural ones. The most horrific monsters of the underworld are the most ignorant. Nor can they create something out of nothing. They would need materials and a model if they were to fabricate arms for his lordship."

"By all the gods, Donne, you pose a riddle with no solution!"

"On the contrary. At times to arrive at the solution to a problem, one must be that solution."

I flung myself down in my chair in disgust. "More riddles."

"Patience, Weston. The natural world, as I said, has boundaries. Our senses and the sum of our beings exist in the two planes of space and time. Even Henry the Usurper gave thought to this. If the spatial menace of this obliging fiend did not do for the princes, then his temporal measure—the aging spell—would. Steel cannot get into Britain. Can it get out?"

"If it never gets in, how could it get out? You just told me there's no possibility of bringing it from the far side of the Wall or making it on this side."

He raised a cautionary finger. "Ah, but there was steel in Britain that was never brought in from abroad. Once upon a time, Weston, once upon a—"

"Bessemer!" I smacked my fist down on the table.

"Precisely. Bessemer the Heretic. Bessemer the Genius is more appropriate. He discovered the process of forging steel right here in London long before it needed be rediscovered on the Continent."

"But he died, Donne. The Brotherhood killed him."

"So it is said. Yet between the time of his discovery and the time of his death, steel existed in Britain. If Lord Kitchener cannot bring steel into this land through space, why not through time?"

Had a large bullfrog leapt from Donne's mouth at that point and begun to sing "A Wandering Minstrel," I should not have been less flabbergasted. "Through time? A mad idea!"

"No, Weston, a brilliant idea. Genius is often the twin of madness. I intend to try my theory. In the meantime, I would have you go tonight to the Café Royal. Lady Lovelace thinks her father will be there. He attends regularly, every fifth night."

"He's looking for us. But why doesn't she just send him a message to come here?"

"If that were possible, don't you think she would have done so? He refuses to implicate her in his troubles. She is a capable woman—quite capable."

I did not think it would be politic or within the limits of friendship to ask Donne to elaborate upon Ada's capabilities. A blanket of sunshine lay across the table, and a clear sky beckoned. "I think I will take a little stroll, Donne."

"Excellent, Weston. So long as you are at the Café Royal tonight."

Merriwell met me at the door, presenting a mahogany swagger stick on a velvet pillow. The day was fresh, the air full of the most wholesome of London's many smells: buns baking, seasoned wood burning, apples and violets piled high and fragrant in pedlars' baskets. As always, my steps took me down into the Strand. London's most genteel thoroughfare and I had a strange affinity. There was no street half so pleasant, to my mind, in all the town, nor any eatery to compare with the tender delights of Simpson's. Not Renfield's, Lug knows.

My stroll had begun as a purposeless ramble, but after a brief revel in the morning's sensual impressions, I found my mind ever returning to Donne's latest theory—that of steel coming into Britain through the portals of time.

If I had not feared the repercussions of using my powers, I could have scryed an answer for Donne on the spot. Crippled as I was by Deirdre's death-curse, I could do nothing. Then, where the Strand swerved closer to the Thames and the indescribable smell of that river touched my nostrils, I bethought myself of Old Jim, the mysterious fishmonger.

The man spoke riddles, but with the air of one who also had the answers. His accent I had long since placed as close cousin to that of the Picts dwelling in the far north of Britain. Did his folk share the old magics with mine? I strode towards Billingsgate Market yet again, determined to find him and find out. What was more, I had theories of my own about the case, and needed someone to hear me out. Donne always made a better actor than an audience.

The sun was climbing the sky as my route took me from the Strand into the Embankment. Several hours wanting of noon, and yet I already spied several London tarts, brazenly painted and heavily scented, plying the riverside. To my chagrin, one such sorry creature attached herself to me.

"Good day, guv," she chirruped. "Nice day for a little walk, now isn't it?" She threaded her arm through mine—a plump arm sheathed a sight too tightly in plum-colored bombazine. From top to toe she was a study in blaring purple, even to the smears of colored grease on her eyelids.

"Take yourself off, now, Miss. I've nothing for you."

"We'll see about that, won't we?" Her speech surprised me. There was nothing of the lower-class pronunciation or intonation. "I've got ways of persuading a gentleman to change his mind. When I was in service— Here, if you pay, I can tell you how I had it all my way with Lord Melbourne himself!"

"The only place a woman of your trade ever saw the likes of Lord Melbourne would be from the visitors' gallery of Council Hall."

The strumpet brayed with laughter. "That wasn't where we did it, sonny. *When I was in service,* I said. Before I quit pretending, and took to the job that pays better full-time. Here, do you know the crumbs they pay us girls in Buckingham Palace? Winnie and Sarah and Liza and me used to talk about nothing else. And now they've let Winnie and Liza go, and no one knows what's become of little Sarah, and I'm on the life. It's a queer world, guv."

Queer enough. My hand tightened involuntarily on her wrist. She looked down and leered. "Changing your mind already?"

"What—attractive gloves," I said, avoiding her eyes. They were sisters to the pair I had seen in two widely separate though equally horrible settings.

"Like them? Care to buy a pair for your wife?" She elbowed me in the ribs. "You won't find gloves like these just anywhere in this town. Last time Liza and Sarah and I were together, we found this awful little place, but my! —didn't that old geezer sell the prettiest things for the brass. I'd never've got these if we three hadn't been together. You won't catch me in a neighborhood like that alone! But you're here, aren't you? Come along, then. You can give me a bit of a tip when we get there if all you really want's a pair of gloves. And if not—" Her tongue darted in and out between her empurpled lips like an adder's.

"The gloves; just the gloves."

She had not exaggerated. It was a truly vile section of London to which she led me. I suppose I could have put her off, but I felt impelled to see this shop of which she spoke. Could he have been there to read my mind, Donne would have despaired. I was suddenly consumed by the fancy that were I to find this shop, the case would be as good as solved. Did the streetwalker not say she had worked formerly in Buckingham Palace? Had she not mentioned the name of Sarah? Was she not wearing lavender gloves whose appearance evoked fearful memories for me?

Threads, threads, threads! Only the wise detective knows which ones form the warp and woof of his case and which are merely hopeless tangles.

"That's the place," said the woman. It was a half-timbered hunchback of a building squeezed in between its betters. Above the blackened door a sign swung back and forth on brassy hinges: Ye Olde Curiosity Shoppe. "Well?"

I pressed a shilling on the wench and sent her on her way. She hooted at me for a spendthrift fool before slipping into one of the many strait paths webbing the area. I did not give her another thought as I entered the musty shop.

A bell's silver tongue announced me. The young man already in the shop jumped at the sound. I am afraid that I overreacted as well. He was clad in the snowy robe of a full Druid. I did not care for my last few encounters with the Golden Brotherhood.

"Oh I say! You did give me a start. I am all right now. Come in, do come in. You must see the marvelous things this old gentleman has to offer." I saw no old gentleman and said so. "He will be back in a moment," said the young Druid. "He is looking for something I requested."

"Something rare?"

"The gods alone know whether it's rare or common as dirt! I have forgotten what it was. I only asked for something I did not see displayed because I wanted to get him out of here. I wished to be alone, the better to impress the details of this wonderful shop upon my mind. I am making notes for a new book, you see." He gave me his hand, his blue eyes merry. "Master Dickens, sir; Charolis, to my friends. Whom have I the pleasure of addressing?"

"John H. Weston, M.D." His handshake was firm in spite of his narrow, ladyish hands.

"Not *that* Dr. Weston? Then we are fellow writers! I have read your enchanting stories in the *Strand* magazine. Are you perhaps familiar with my work? *An Imbolc Carol*? *A Tale of Two Scythes*? By next Beltaine I hope to finish my present novel as well as fleshing out the notes for *The Mystery of Edwin Druid*, but—"

His effulgences upon the writer's life were cut short by the reappearance of a hoary man from behind the greasy curtain separating the back room from the shop proper. He handed young Master Dickens a tarnished silver abortion whose use could not be guessed by a sane man. "That what y'meant, Master?" His voice grated and whistled like an organ with ruptured bellows.

"Yeeees. Quite. How much will you take for it?"

Three-and-six changed hands and the Druid departed. The old proprietor turned to serve me.

He must have been alive the day Bran's Wall went up. He was barely alive now. No part of his body was without wrinkles or curvatures, and his breath played flute sonatas as it heaved in and out of his lungs. "I understand you stock gloves," I said.

"Gloves? Gloves! Yes, gloves! Of course I stock gloves. All colors. All sizes. What length will y'have, sir? Hoh, but is it men's or ladies' y'want? We must be specific, sir, that's all." He bobbled back and forth behind the counter at amazing speed for a relic, and not a trace of age could I see in his upturned eyes.

"Ladies' gloves—ah, length doesn't matter. She would like lavender ones."

"Lavender?" His woolly eyebrows rose and fell several times. "Now isn't that strange! I had half a dozen of lavender in, and there's not many shops in London trouble to carry that color at this time o' year. Well, snick-snack, three of 'em fly out the door in one day."

"You don't say. The lady must have liked the—"

"Lady? Y'don't get many come in here can afford to buy more'n one pair at a time. Trey o' young chits come in to'gether, two of 'em buy a pair each, and then a furrin-lookin' woman. Handsome enough, in her way, but wrapped up like a bleedin' purple cocoon in some sort o' heathen dress. Had a big red blot right here, too." He stabbed the middle of his forehead. "Don't ask me why."

I was likely to swallow my tongue, I was that overwhelmed by my good luck. Could I ever forget the "furrin-lookin' woman" who had undergone such a repulsive transformation at Madame Marushka's seance? Whatever she was—ogress, monster, fiend of Kitchener's controlling—she had a penchant for violet. I imagined her entering Hope's bank, releasing the crimson leech from beneath her voluminous robes and casting the spell that would cause it to grow beyond the limits of nature, then destroy the unfortunate tellers. Meantime, she would feign private business with Hope, enter his inner office, and then show her true semblance. Men do die of fright. Hope had, and poor Harry at the seance.

"I'll take a pair."

"These do, sir?" He laid them out on the counter. I waxed enthusiastic over them and paid what he asked. "I'll just wrap 'em up for y', and if y'd be good enough to give me y'r name and address . . ."

"Whatever for?" I tried to keep my excitement from showing, but here was a lucky chance truly unlooked-for!

"Just the way I run my shop. I like to see who comes back, where the custom comes from." He took a dusty ledger from the shelf behind him and spread it open, then pulled his pince-nez down a bit to search for an errant pen. A shrill whistling came from the inner room. "The kettle!" He rubbed his twisted hands together merrily. "Just time for a nice spot of tea. I hope y'll join me, sir. I've seldom the chance to enjoy comp'ny over the cups."

Dreams of glory, what dreams! I would take tea with the man, find some excuse to send him from the room, and flip through the ledger. I would find the ogress' address, which in turn would betray Kitchener's hideaway—surely one does not keep peris and djinn in Pall Mall; there are zoning laws—and culminate with the finding of the Rules Britannia, all hail John H. Weston, M.D., and this time let Donne write up the bloody case for the *Strand* magazine!

All hail John H. Weston, idiot. The dotard could not have been more cooperative. He brought in two cups, I asked him for sugar, he went to get it, I found the proper entry in the ledger just before he returned, I dosed my tea with two lumps, sipped it, and fell to the floor in a dreamless black cloud. No more than I deserved. *Fool!*

When I came to, I was bound securely with thin, biting twine. The old man was leering down at me, one eyebrow off, one eyebrow on. Behind him stood a figure hooded in white, back turned towards us.

"He's awake, Master." Now he had the voice of a man in his prime. The second false eyebrow fluttered from his fingers. A huge handkerchief scrubbed the greasepaint of age from the fellow's high, domed brow and sharp features.

I was not at all surprised to see Lord Kitchener come to stand beside his minion, pausing but to draw away the hood. "So I see, Morganwg. You have let me down, Dr. Weston. The Queen clings so fervently to her memories of you that my courtship of Her Majesty does not go the way I would wish. I had hoped your attraction lay in mental prowess—no other solution to the mystery of what she sees in you is plausible. But you were laughably easy to entice here and capture. Like a gudgeon, you snap at any bait."

"Well, that's one down, eh, Master? Shall I make an end of him?"

"That," said Kitchener, "will be my pleasure. But you will be rewarded. As a glove-seller, you must know we have only the left hand here. I think you would prefer to eliminate the right."

Morganwg's feral eyes sparkled evilly. "*Donne.*"

"Yours, after all the years, all the humiliations, all the plans he has thwarted for you. I will even help you find him."

"Morganwg." The name escaped my lips in a marveling whisper. Kitchener smirked.

"You've heard of him, certainly. Do his looks surprise you? Napoleon himself was also a short man, but a man's true measure isn't found in his height—or his blood. Your Brotherhood will have many lessons to learn—those whom I allow to live long enough to learn them."

He raised his arms slowly from his sides until he looked like the half-moon blade of a Gaulish battle-axe. Words in a foreign tongue began to pour from his lips. I saw Morganwg quail and tug timidly at his master's gown. "You're not summoning *her*, are you?"

Without losing a syllable or a beat of the chant, Kitchener backhanded the man with vicious force. Morganwg staggered, the left half of his face aflame.

A circle of sickly yellow light began to whirl in the air between Kitchener and myself. Wings sprouted from it, wings that were all the colors of dawn. They were tiny at first, no bigger than sparrow-size, but as the circle glowed more brightly, they grew. Rags and tags of scarlet trailed from between each pair, then doll-like creatures hung there in the ever-growing circle of flight. Kitchener's calling was joined by a choir of faint, sweet voices emanating from the glowing ring. Louder they came, and louder still, until the room was filled with a swarm of the most painfully lovely winged women, each face a poem of ivory, black, and rose. Their circle shifted axis, turned to a spinning crown above Kitchener's head, then slowed. His chanting and their answering song both died. They hovered, waiting.

"Have you ever seen their like before, Dr. Weston?" Lord Kitchener made a casual sweep of his hand as if he were inviting me to comment on a bed of dahlias rather than a diadem of immortal beauty. "They are peris, purchased at some expense—not purely monetary—from their former owner, the Old Man of the Mountain. You may have heard legends of his followers: the guild of the hashashin?" He grinned, enjoying the joke. "The guild has, since my last visit to the Old Man, been dissolved. The hashashin and the peris alike now serve me. They are not the only ones."

At a sign from him, the peris appeared to transform themselves into living stars. A brilliance emanated from them, silvery and intoxicating. I was momentarily dazzled, but when the dark spots cleared from my eyes I was able to see the entire room clearly. We were no longer in Ye Olde Curiosity Shoppe.

I rolled over awkwardly, using my left shoulder to help myself into a sitting position, the better to see the wonders of the chamber. A shallow silver brazier, its ashes cold, held the sun's central place in that cosmos. Its planets were played by a multiplicity of odd and intriguing containers, their exotic shapes molded of every conceivable combination of metals found on earth—save only that no deathmetal formed any atom of their essence. His lordship strolled to the brazier and began a slow, outwardly spiralling circuit of his treasures, pausing here and there to hold up an especially striking item for my examination.

"Do you see this bottle, Dr. Weston? Within these simple confines is the demon Kezariah. His is the hunger and the ability to cleave the universe to the source of its power, then bestow what he thus gains as a free gift to man. What man may do with it—" Kitchener shrugged. "That is the beauty of demons. They never stop to think."

He proceeded until he came to another object that struck

his fancy. "As an officer in Her Majesty's overseas forces, I was granted more liberal travel privileges than most Britons. I took full advantage of them. Under the pretense of scouting out new territories for our childish cattle raids, I went far afield. There is magic in the world, Dr. Weston. The East is full of magic. It is ripe, like a summer-swollen melon, waiting only to be pierced and drained dry." I have seen cats with such smiles on their faces; so have many birds, just before they die.

Kitchener held up a bell then. He took particular care to muffle the clapper in his other hand. "Pretty, is it not? It comes from Nippon, where once an emperor commanded a temple bell be cast of all the precious metals in his realm. But the metals were all too proud to mix; the bell would crack in the mold. The bell-caster was shamed before his emperor. He would either succeed, or commit ritual suicide. The old man had a daughter who loved her father dearly. She went to a spirit-reader who told her that the one thing that would bind gold to silver and silver to copper was a maiden's blood. At the final attempt for the making of the great bell, this self-sacrificing girl threw herself into the cauldron's molten sea. There is no bell in all the world with a sweeter tongue, they say."

"The bell you hold, is it—?" It seemed so small!

"Heavens, no, Dr. Weston. You underestimate the pooled treasure of Nippon. That bell is many times the size of a man. But it is a charming story; inspirational. And so a wizard of that island thought to duplicate it on a smaller scale. His daughter, however, had inherited a fine measure of her father's evil craft and not a whit of filial piety. She resisted the very suggestion of self-immolation." He turned the bell slowly, so that it caught and cast back the peris' glow. But how fiercely the reflected candescence burned the eye! Even Kitchener had to lower his head.

"The young witch went uncooperatively to her death. Her father, rather wisely, decided not to experiment with the resultant bell. Perhaps someday I shall have the need to hear what this dead Nipponese sorceress has to say."

On and on he went, revelling in the occult wealth he had accumulated. Demons and djinn slept in those bottles, plagues and nightmares slumbered fitfully between gem-studded coverlets of carved sandalwood and malachite. His hands shimmered up and down the walls of the room, where row upon row of charms and talismans hung from linked chains of electrum, gold, and lead.

"If every soul ever sacrificed to gain the power of even *one* of these amulets might be assembled in this room, what a congregation of the damned it would make! And these, all these, are mine."

"I should think you'd be satisfied, then," I said. "You could carve yourself out quite a passable little kingdom on the Continent. If you dislike the laws of Britain so much—prejudicial against non-Druids and all that—why linger?"

I had no idea I was such a born humorist. Kitchener laughed loud and long. When he regained control of his emotions he said, "It is not my pleasure to run away. I have come to lay an iron blade across the throat of the Golden Brotherhood. I shall rule *here*, in this land and no other, in the land where I was born! I want the crown of Britain, and I will have it!"

He clapped his hands together sharply three times. The peris began to circle again, describing a closed arc perpendicular to the floor. They closed ranks without diminishing in size until their wings melted into a soft white blur in the center of the frame their bodies made. I could no longer see Lord Kitchener; he was on one side of the ring, Morganwg and I on the other. The wheel of wings rippled wildly, then bit by bit the dimpling surface began to solidify until I thought I could see my own face reflected on the peris' melded wings.

"The glass of far-seeing," said Lord Kitchener, and as he spoke the peris renewed their song. A vision formed.

The mirror showed a large and airy atelier. Prominent there was an outlandish metal contraption that stood on what looked like sleigh runners. Two men—one in the robes of the Wise, the other in a scholar's threadbare academic gown—were giving it a thorough examination. The peris' song rose and changed key; we could hear what the men were saying:

". . . sure it is safe. I have already tested it. All it does, basically, is offer me a focus for my own power of temporal matter-displacement. I can control it better through the machine, you see."

"Why, I never dreamed—that is, I had desperate hopes that tales of your phenomenal machine were not mere idle rumor. My work at Cambridge depends upon a fine point of British history that is not sufficiently documented—"

"Yes, yes, dear chap, so you told me. And I'll be more than happy to send you where you like; or should I say 'when'?"

The Druid's face radiated warm good humor. The starveling scholar seized his hand and pumped it violently, his myopic eyes glittering with the fever of too many books and too little fresh air. He was a poor, gaunt measure of a man, and I was mentally prescribing diet and exercise for him when he said:

"I can't thank you enough, Master Wells. So little is known about—well, you understand enough about my research to see why I prefer not to call him 'the Heretic,' the way everyone else does."

"Taranis shield you, boy! I'll be paid enough if you clear old Bessemer's name. I don't like to see any man falsely accused, least of all a fellow Druid. Just sit inside the machine and I'll send you on your way."

Which he did, just as I saw through the supposed Cambridge scholar's disguise. Donne! He threaded his way into the webwork of the machine, sat down, the whole structure vibrated around him, and *snap!* Donne was gone.

The mirror split into rushing wings. The peris darted up to the rafters, then settled down to float in the air behind Lord Kitchener, enthroning him with their glory.

"Well, Morganwg, your work will be easy. You have seen where your prey is going. Familiar terrain, for you. You may see to it." Morganwg ran off, not without a bow for his master. Kitchener raised his left hand, thumb and ring finger touching, and my bonds fell to the floor. He looked at me, then at the peris.

"I give him to you," he said, and faded from the talisman-hung room.

There were eleven of them, all told. Eleven perfect faces, eleven slender forms, and in all that beauty I could not see one spark of human emotion. Even doll faces have some trace of false feeling painted into the porcelain. Their faces were flat and lifeless. Then they smiled.

Their teeth were like double rows of thorn—black and clawed, fading to dull grey against scarlet gums. Their folded wings began to mark a dead-march beat. They moved in unison, and the air itself throbbed with each stroke of their pinions. One of them drifted closer to me, her sisters falling into ranks behind. Her pale hands touched the neckline of her gown, and it fell away to offer me white flesh, flawless, smooth as jade. Her movements in midair were unspeakably voluptuous and meant to entrance.

I was unable to take my eyes from her ravening mouth, no matter the final consolation she offered me.

I backed away without realizing I was moving. I did not have far to go. My hands touched one of the trinket-laden walls all too soon. The naked peri alit and folded back her wings. She closed on me, her hands reaching out for mine. The merest brush of her cool fingertips was enough to inflame me, in spite of myself. I responded instantly, my body struggling to free itself of the mind's restraint, wanting only to join with her, and to Annwn with the consequences! I found my hands trailing up her arms to touch her neck, tracing downwards to cup and press the breasts my mouth hungered for, breasts cool as glass, never made to nurse a child, breasts without nipples to mar their impossible perfection.

You are ours, we are yours. We can serve no other man but you. Every one of us is virgin, untouched. You will be the first, the only. Each of us will be the path and the substance of Paradise.

A thick, hot smell of greenhouse flowers clouded my head. I could hear their common breath softly rasping in and out, always together, always as one. I stepped away from the wall as if dreaming. The peris gathered inward, surrounding me, their eyes round and shining, rimmed with kohl. Skilled fingers peeled away the layers of my clothing one by one until I felt hairless skin clinging to the length of my body and heard an amorous moaning in my ear that came from the creature in my arms.

Does she please you more than I, me dearling?

The voice, thin and mocking, sounded inside my mind. My head pulled up with a jerk from the peri's inviting lips and my eyes swept the circle of patient watchers. There was one more among them than before. Deirdre's eyeless sockets peered from between two faultless faces, her skull whiter than their pearly skin.

Oh no. You have much more to suffer before I allow you to die, sweet Johnnie mine. That's my bride-price, and this bit of pretty shan't rob me of it! Look about you, love, before you take your pleasure. Sharp teeth, quick claws, and the hunger of deathless things surround you. One seduces the prey, but once you take her, they take you.

The spectre misted away, the peri ring closed up, but I

had shaken off their tender spell. Deirdre's hatred was like ice water thrown over me. I gave a hoarse shout, a man awakening from a nightmare, and pushed the naked peri from me. A loud, angry humming filled the room. The peris' wings vibrated like bowed violin strings, and their empty faces darkened. Only their leader still attempted to lure me back into her embrace, using every trick of light and shadow and subtle movement to tempt me. My flesh yearned towards her again, and again I had to conjure up the vision of dead Deirdre to maintain control. I screwed my eyes tight shut and wheeled, striking out at the peris behind me, bursting blindly from the circle. I ran but a few steps before hitting the wall.

There are other deaths we deal, mortal man. We only offered you the gentlest one.

I opened my eyes. They were ranged in a half-moon, their leader now indistinguishable from the rest. No; she was the one who held the dagger. Silver and smiling, the blade winked at me. It was small, a doll's blade.

Oh, but it draws blood! Very little blood, but it cuts. Cut by cut, we shall have you. Cut by slow cut, until you will beg us to offer you again the rending death, the devouring death. Foolish mortal man.

If Deirdre's spirit lingered close enough to hear the thoughts the peri projected to my mind, she must have laughed. Yes, and laughed harder, knowing that I had in my hands the ability to call up the powers of earth to aid me, but that I would not dare. How could I, with her curse upon me? She knew me too well, my Deirdre, and she knew I would sooner die than save myself at the cost of those I loved. *Foolish mortal man.* Oh yes, that I was, but I could not change. Not even now.

I felt something cold and knobbed pressing into the small of my back. The peris were swaying back and forth, the tips of their toes brushing the floor, the dagger dancing from hand to hand along their line and back again as each spirit laid her own tagline of cruel power on the metal. Each cut the blade would make would carry the wills of them all. Unthinking, I reached around to remove the thing keeping me from pressing my back flat against the wall—for all the good a wall at my back would do me when the dagger finally flew.

My hands tingled. I raised the object to my eyes and the tingling grew stronger. One of Kitchener's damned talismans, and swollen with magic. *Open me! Open me!* I thought I could even see its rounded sides throbbing like the red walls of a living heart. *Yours is the power, my lord! Oh, set me free!* The beating of it—shaped like a shell cast up by the waves—the heavy, hypnotic pulsing—the waves—the sea—

Your powers to tap the earthmagic are strong, my teacher said, his grey eyes mirroring the waves. *That is as it should be; a weak man cannot rule. You can set the magic free, focus it, control it, draw it up from the depths where rock flows like water and water seethes with life. Even before you could do this, your power was strong enough to open other magics than our own.*

Other magics. I cupped my hands in a second shell around the talisman and set the magic free.

Darkness blossomed from my palms. A black pillar of oily smoke shot up to the ceiling and ripped itself wide into the hulking, demonic presence of a monstrous djinni. The peris fell back in a confused flutter of wings.

What is your will, Master?

"Save me." Truly I could not manage to say more than that, and that much I said in a cracked, trembling voice.

Your will is served.

Ponderous fists like thunderheads reached down and enveloped the shuddering peris. If they screamed, the sound could not escape. I heard a frail, high chirring, like cricket-song, and then the djinni opened his hands and showed me them empty. A tuft of iridescent feathers drifted past my eyes. So much beauty, so much evil; I felt an incongruous pang of regret for the peris.

What will my master have now?

I picked up the orphaned feathers and contemplated them. How different from the afrit's sharp-edged plume! "Oh . . . I don't know." I waved my hand vaguely at the four walls. "Sink all these amulets in the sea—your own as well."

The djinni frowned. I could hear the wrinkles on his brow forming and smoothing with a sound like an old leather chair being sat upon. *My own? I have displeased?*

"Not at all. I free you from it, and I want you to sink it so that no one else can call himself your master. But first, destroy all the rest of these sorcerous playthings. That's my will, since you ask."

The djinni was broad-chested and coal-black from the waist up. From the waist down he was roiling smoke, so the bow he executed for my benefit was problematic. *My heart-*

less heart and soulless soul ache with regret, most beneficient one, but I am unable to fulfill your request.

"Devil you are."

Devil I am indeed, exalted benefactor. But only some of these trinkets may I destroy. The rest are under protective spells that place them beyond my humble powers. He was bald as an egg, but nonetheless he groped for a forelock to tug.

I scanned the walls and passed my hands over the amulets, then wandered through the room, touching bottles and caskets at random. "You're telling the truth. I can feel the repulsion spells. Lucky thing your amulet wasn't covered by one, eh?"

The djinni poured part of his smoky nethers back into the brass clam that he'd called home, the better to get to eye level with me. I saw my entire face neatly reflected in the pupil of one amber eye. *My master is my master truly. I am but the shell of power. You are its source. I abase myself humbly before my better. But—* again the leathery creaking— *why then did one of your mystic command need my miserable aid in dealing with those feathered vermin?*

"Djinni, old boy, it is a long story, and since it's far from done, why don't you do what you can to lighten the ballast in this room, then take yourself off. You're free, as I said."

Rearing up to his monumental height, the djinni touched forehead, lips, and heart in an Oriental obeisance. *I hear and obey.*

"You do that," I said, and started gathering up my scattered clothes. By the time I was fully dressed, the djinni had removed a good third of the talismans from Lord Kitchener's clutches and gone off to wherever retired djinn congregate.

I left the room by the same door Morganwg had used earlier and discovered it took me into a conventional cellar. A scraggly London rat sat atop a stove-in keg and wiggled its whiskers at me boldly. There was a flickering oil lamp set into a niche beside a flight of mossy wooden steps. Climbing these and pushing tentatively on the trapdoor above brought me up under a rag rug which, when wrestled aside, admitted me to the familiar outer room of Ye Olde Curiosity Shoppe.

Autumnal twilight made the streets of that foul neighborhood sinister. I hastened back to Ada's town house and found her wearing a track in the carpet of her salon.

"Epona's mane, where have you been?" she cried when she saw me.

I told her. She clenched her fists and looked as if she wished she might use them on me.

"Was he *so* right about you?" she demanded. (No need for me to ask who *he* was.) "Are you *that* hopeless? Sweet gods, to command the powers of a djinni and set him free? What were you thinking of?"

"I was thinking"—I spoke with measured calm—"that it's wrong to enslave anything, magic or no."

"Magic!" She snorted. "What would you know of magic? The djinni might have been commanded to fetch you the Rules Britannia easy as thinking. But no, thinking isn't easy for you, is it?"

I dislike overwrought women. They always tend to insult me, for some reason. "I believe that Donne would have been just as hesitant as I to recover the Rules through such means. Besides, Madam, if you'd been listening to what I just told you, you would see that the djinn was not all-powerful. If Kitchener thought to spell-shield most of his talisman collection, surely something so precious as the Rules lies under more layers of protection than we might count."

Ada collapsed into an embroidered chair. The inimitable Merriwell materialized with a brandy and soda for his mistress. She swallowed it at a gulp and raised her forlorn face to me. "Forgive me, Dr. Weston. It is only—I am so worried. Mr. Donne is gone, and I don't know where."

"Gone . . ." I recalled Kitchener's instructions to a delighted Morganwg, and I blanched. "Lady Lovelace—Ada—do you know any Druid named Wells?" I told her of what I had seen in the peris' mirror.

Ada shook her head. "The name is common enough, especially among the Brotherhood. There are whole branches of the Wise bearing that name, for they once were the keepers of the sacred wells of sacrifice."

"Yes, but this one is a specialist in time travel, and he must be in London proper, or else Donne would not have reached him so quickly. Who would know where to find such a man, though?" I pondered the question and voiced my thoughts. "Donne himself would set the Irregulars on the trail. Cuchulain and his lot should be back from their damnfool cattle raid by now. I'll go see Mildred—but that's Baker Street, and what if Wellington's still posted a watch on our lodgings? Ah, no, no, that won't do."

Ada clasped my hands. "If you tell me how one summons the Irregulars, I shall do it. But you must do me a favor in return. This is the night to find my father at the Café Royal. Go to him. Help him. Please."

Minutes later, while Ada readied herself to rouse the Irregulars, I sailed down the front steps and into the street, walking as fast as I was able to reach the Café Royal. The ominous evening fog was already sending tendrils of milky yellow mist down every street and byway, although the lamps were still holding the worst of it at bay. I doubled a corner smartly and collided with a solid bar of wood that rammed the breath from my body.

I gasped painfully and grasped the plank to steady myself while the spots cleared from my eyes. Something furry rubbed against my wrist and meowed.

"Weel met, lad." Old Jim's bristly face grinned out of the fog. His cat Tam gave me another friendly rub as I held on to the rim of his fish cart.

"Well met? I searched for you this morning! Damn, why is it that you always vanish when I want you and turn up when I don't?"

"Ye'r turn wi' the riddles this time, eh, lad?" He made a low sound in his throat that could have been mirth. "But ye're no the good wi' 'em yet. Maybc that's because ye dinna know what ye truly want yersel'. Now 'tis I have nae time fer ye, so fare ye weel."

"Wait!" I held fast to the barrow, but felt my fingers penetrate the wood like sand, closing on nothing. The ghost of a cat's cry trailed away in the night.

CHAPTER TWELVE

The Adventure of the Layman Mendicant Association

Like most good Britons, I had my favorite resorts of an evening. The bar at the "Cri' " was one such, and like many of my narrow-minded fellows I assumed that everyone in the city of London had a haunt more or less similar to my tastes. Not all would be as flash as the Cri', to be sure, but the general ambience—the *feeling* of the place, if you prefer—would be akin.

That was before the Café Royal.

From the outside, it looked much the same as its sister establishments. Once inside, however, more thresholds than one were crossed. A gleaming black bar ran the length of the main saloon, gilt-spattered mirrors behind it reflecting a wealth of bottled spirits—*not* of the kind I had just dealt with, but more pleasant and potable. The bar itself was ordinary enough, but its patrons were not. All of them were in some way connected with the arts.

Now why must the word "art" bring out the worst in a man, as if it were a license to assume the morals of a lizard and the grooming habits of a sick guinea pig? Donne at his most whimsical could not have come up with a fraction of the improbable fancy-dress outfits the Café Royalists affected. I stuck out like a crow among peacocks in my dull tweeds. Debauchées and soiled doves, decadents and those merely aspiring to depravity shrieked and chattered all around me.

I did not see Lord Byron anywhere. I would have to wait and see if he showed himself. A blear-eyed man at the marble-topped table nearest me was doing just that. His mate seemed unimpressed.

Someone touched me gently. "Dear sir, would you mind helping a lady in distress?" Golden-lashed cornflower eyes implored my protection adorably. The lone crow had found a suitable, if temporary, mate. My fair petitioner was clad nearly as conventionally as myself, in her case wearing fawn silk cut modestly ample.

"It will be an honor. How may I serve?"

A blush spread over her face. Her looks were not delicate or fine, but their very bluntness enhanced her pretty ways. "My sister—not *quite* the pride of the family, you understand— asked me to meet her here." She looked away from me and murmured, "She is an actress." It was clearly a painful confession. "I have only just arrived and—I would rather not wait alone. Will you forgive my forwardness?"

Forgive it? I welcomed it! We took a table and I ordered a passable Sauterne over which we might await our respective appointments. We were only halfway through the bottle when a raffish waiter came along with a second one.

"I did not order this, my good man," I said.

"Compliments o' the Layman Mendicant Association, sir!" He winked at me and pulled the cork. "His Majesty the President requests the honor o' your attending him at his table, when you've a mo'."

"There is some mistake."

"Over there, sir." He flourished a damp linen towel towards the largest table in the room. I looked and could not but recognize the thick features and thicker body of London's most notorious playwright, poet, and wit, Mr. Oscar Wilde. Only the week before Beltaine, Donne and I had attended the premiere of his scathing satire *Lady Windermere's Faun.*

Since Lord Byron still showed no signs of appearing, I thought it might be wise as well as courteous to go over to Mr. Wilde's table and thank him for the wine. He was the most conspicuous creature in a room full of formidable rivals. Once Byron did arrive, he could not fail to look in Wilde's direction and see me at once.

Wilde held court, as it were, but what a court! He did not bother to rise when I approached, my timid lady clinging to my arm and trying not to stare.

"Dr. Weston, I am thrilled to the soul!" His podgy hands still could exert a firm grip. "Join us." He waggled over to the left on the red plush banquette, discomfitting two of his retainers. What a menagerie! Of the eight young men with Wilde, half were of the thinnest aristocratic blood in Britain, the other half were obviously stableboys and guttersnipes stuffed into ludicrous evening dress.

"Dr. Weston," Wilde trolled in his rich tenor, "writes."

"Slop," said one of the aristos. He sat on Wilde's right, and as my lady and I were on the left I had to lean round the playwright's bulk to see this incisive critic. He had fine blond hair and a precise little nose that cried out to be broken for him.

"Don't be horrid, Alfred," said Wilde. "One of the chief tenets of the Layman Mendicant Association is to beg beauty of an ugly world, not add to the already existing ugliness."

Alfred snitted.

"Dr. Weston is the dear, close, irreplaceable companion of a truly admirable man," Wilde went on. "I mean, of course, Mr. Brihtric Donne. He is an inspiration, a living proof of the cornerstone of all true philosophy. The ancient Greeks did well when they sequestered their women—I mean you no offense, my dear," he added for my escort's benefit. "Women are simply not capable of sustaining thought without trivializing it. Only when two minds of equal potential commune can man hope to remove himself from barbarism. For this to be perfect, one mind must be the superior of the other—the beloved teacher; the trusted guide. Brihtric Donne, as Dr. Weston had written so charmingly in his dramatic vignettes for the *Strand* magazine, has relegated the fair sex to their proper niche. His reward has been the development of the highest intellectual prowess in all Britain and the unstinting devotion of a loyal friend."

He clapped me on the back, and I nearly leapt over the table.

"Bully for the loyal friend. Why don't you make him a Layman Mendicant too, Oscar?" Alfred yawned loudly and downed the sticky green liquid in his glass. He leaned into Wilde and showed me his teeth. "*Mendicant*, Dr. Weston. *Beggar*. After all, what's a letter or two wrong to Brihtric Donne's dear, darling, *devoted* friend?"

In the name of my friend Donne, Friedrich Gutmann's girls, and the Countess Lovelace, I bashed the brat's face.

"Alfred!" exclaimed Wilde. Alfred, sliding peacefully to the floor, did not answer. Wilde spat curses at me and fumbled for Alfred's witless form beneath the table. The gentle Celtic drawl was gone. Wilde was enraged. I tried to get my fair charge and myself away from him, but once he hoisted Alfred's blood-spattered face into view he bellowed, "Andy, there's a five-pound note for you if you get him!"

I knew he meant me, and not kindly. Andy was the beefiest of the stableboy crowd. He took the direct approach, launching himself across the table to tackle me by the shoulders. I lost my balance and went over backwards onto the marble. Glasses and bottles flew everywhere. Andy's pals got into the spirit of the thing without the incentive of Wilde's bounty. Among the four of them, I was spread-eagled on the table. Andy smashed the bottom from a wine bottle and swung it back to slash me. I struggled, threw off one of the youths holding me, but the others clung fast. The broken glass sliced air, crashed into the tabletop inches from my face. Green splinters narrowly missed my right eye.

"Hold the bastard better, Jimbo!" Andy had another bottle to hand. The lordlings were making chirping sounds of excitement. One of them grew bold enough to wrest the bottle from Andy's hand and replace it with a heavier one.

"Yes, that's it, love, teach him! Teach him!"

"That I'll do, don't worry." Up went the bottle. The little lords flung themselves upon me, to be in on the kill. "I'll teach 'im good," said Andy.

I never got that lesson. Behind Andy's back one of the plush gilt chairs described an arc that started gods know where and ended smack on Andy's thatchy skull. The stableboy folded up and joined Alfred in repose.

"Take that, you bleeding cowards!" roared my lady friend; roared it *basso profundo*, too.

"Tommy, you bitch! Back off!"

"In a pig's arse! I'm not standing by for this, and if Mr. Wilde's lapdog's down, it was a fair blow struck. A fair blow, and Dr. Weston's not going to have less than a fair fight!" The "lady" tore off his wide-brimmed hat, taking his flaxen coiffure with it, and stripped his kidskin gloves to bare impressively meaty knuckles. "Who's bloody next?"

The mulligan was on.

I acquitted myself rather well to begin with, until the fighting spread to other tables. Old grudges were settled and new ones begun before the Café Royal's *corps d'élite* of bouncers poured into the saloon and ejected as many of us as they could lay hands on. I was lofted out the front door in the third wave. The cool night air made my bruised and scratched face sting.

"That's London for you," I told the moon.

Picking myself up, I stepped gingerly over my guttermates. The brawl inside the Café Royal had subsided, and I did not know whether my reappearance would be welcomed, but I had to go back. Lord Byron was still—

"Dr. Weston." It was he. He hugged the shadows, but there was no mistaking that voice or, when the lightspill from the café's open doors touched him, that profile.

"Lord—Geordie. Geordie, you've no idea how glad I am to find—"

He cut off my protestations. "I have no time. I am watched, followed, the eyes are ever upon me, even now. You too must have a care; his servants also follow you. I no longer care about myself. I no longer matter. What must be said *will* be said. *Save the Queen!*" He dug his fingers into my hands. I felt a folded paper shoved between my fingers. He tried to go, but there was one thing I had to know.

"Geordie, wait. You're of the blood. I must find a Druid; a particular man. He is key to this case. How can I find him? His name—"

Byron's hand shot up. "No names. You want Berkeley; Little Queen Street, number 25." He left me without further word.

Well, I supposed I wanted Berkeley, then. I summoned a hireling chariot which deposited me before the designated address. The buildings in Little Queen Street were ancient, though with some air of respectability still. I called earthfire to my fingertips and read the note Lord Byron had given me before seeking out whoever Berkeley might turn out to be.

Gibberish. *Sole daughter of my house and heart, is your mind like your mother's? Nay, I'll not number you the reasons pro and con. I am quite capable of adding one and one and getting ten; but so are you. Boatswain was a nobler beast than I, but he is dead, and you know where he's buried. If not, 10, 1, 10011, 1011, 101, 10010, 10110, 1001, 1100, 1100, 101 will reveal much to the patient delver. Adieu.*

I crammed the paper back into my pocket. Here was a matter for Donne's mind, not mine. I rang the bell, rousing a very grumpy landlady who directed me to go up two flights if I wanted Berkeley and drop dead. After Lord Byron's conundrum, her remarks made sense.

"Who's there, this hour?" Berkeley was twice as disgruntled as his landlady, twice as fierce, and twice as tall. He scowled down at me, and I am of a good height. "What the devil do you want?"

"Mr. Berkeley, I apologize for the intrusion, but—"

"That's *Captain* Berkeley to you, mate. Aye, Captain, in

their teeth, the squirming maggots!" Like the djinni, he had to bow to look me in the eye. "Here, now! I've seen you. You were to the Palace. Who sent you here? If it's to give me back my job, you can tell 'em it was never theirs to take. Filthy bleeding foreign scum."

"Captain, I am afraid that I know nothing of your job."

He straightened up then and redoubled his hostile looks. Abruptly his face relaxed and a deep sigh shook his huge frame. "Come in, then. Come in. I knew it was precious too much to expect."

His flat consisted of one room, with a shallow fireplace for cooking and no washing-up facilities I could see. The place had the air of a dedicated bachelor's digs, a lot of jumble in awkward places but no real dirt to mention. The exception to the general disorder was a wooden clothes-stand beside the window where two immaculately polished boots stood rigid sentinels beneath a fastidiously kept Palace guardsman's uniform.

"So that is how you know me," I said. "You're one of the Queen's guards." He had the physique for it.

"Bleeding *was,*" rumbled Berkeley. "Gave me my notice, they did, weeks back. Now they've got one of Lord Kitchenstink's odd-toms in my place, and him as scrawny a piece as you'll ever see. Whole damned corps is overrun with the like. Gods, what asses they look, what a disgrace to the uniform!"

When he mentioned the uniform, he cast a look of love on his own. I saw the towering busby standing a bit to the left of the boots and imagined what a monolith this Berkeley would look when decked out in full regalia. I then thought back to my last visit to the Palace, and the peculiar faces now seen beneath the guardsmen's busbies. "It was a sorry day for Britain when they dismissed you and your fellows," I said, and I meant it.

Berkeley warmed to me at that. "You're not half a bad sort, Dr. Weston."

"How did you know my name?" I was not ready to admit the existence of another man with Donne's preternatural skills in deduction. I knew I had not introduced myself.

The forcibly retired guardsman guffawed. "Always takes 'em sudden, it does. I'm no Druid, sir, but I have my little ways. I figure as it's a good guardsman's duty to know who comes and goes at the Palace. I make it a point to make enquiries and latch a name to a face soon as a stranger enters the door. You I first saw come in on Beltaine eve, though you didn't see me."

"I was unconscious."

"That, and precious heavy for the boys toting you to the Queen. Gods save her. Oh, I've a gift for this sort of thing. Once it's in *here*"—he aimed a finger at his temple—"it's in for good. Dr. John H. Weston, M.D., 221B, Baker Street." He rattled off my particulars with a schoolboy's grin.

"Amazing, Captain!"

"Haw! That's nothing. Now, what can I help you with? You didn't come round to a stranger's house this time o' night just to hear who you are and where you live."

"I was referred to you by a friend who said you could help me find a Druid."

"Find one? They've been thinner of late, but it's no trouble finding one yet."

"A *specific* Druid; a man named Master Wells whose specialty is time transportation."

"Wells . . ." Berkeley laid two fingers to his lips. "Master Wells . . . You know, Dr. Weston, that name and what it conjures up in a man's mind—a thirsty man—one who hasn't had the price of a pint as often as he'd like, since being dismissed—"

Hints are never wasted on the desperate. I hustled the titanic Berkeley down the stairs and into the corner pub, where I proceeded to learn that it takes four pints of bitter to make the guardsman sing.

"There's more than one Master Wells on the rolls of the Brotherhood, Dr. Weston. Brian the Imagist made a book of all the Brotherhood's faces, names and all, at the Iron Duke's request, and we guards can check it out whenever we like. I took the chance to look it through, page for page, just so I'd have all the names and faces up here"—the temple again—"if it'd be needful. The image book also put their special talents down. Now there's more than one Master Wells left in London, even after that nasty business two years back with Master John Wellington of the same name, but the only one with time-travel skills lives at 40 Horns Way."

"Horns Way?" I had never heard of the street. Unlike Donne's, my mental map of London consisted of the larger thoroughfares, with great areas hatched off and inscribed *Here Be Demons*. "Where the gods is that?"

"Why, it's just—" Berkeley closed his mouth and looked annoyed. "You can't bloody get there from here. Wait.

Come back up to my flat and I'll lend you my *Morton's Fork and Knife Guide to London*. It's got a pretty good map up front, for all it's just a where-to-eat book." He smiled apologetically. "I'm a bear for names and faces, sir, but a baby when it comes to giving street directions."

I had no alternative but to return with Berkeley to his digs. Once in, he rummaged for the *Guide* under his tousled bed. The first object he fished up was not it.

"My topper-brush!" He was ecstatic. "The old busby's needed a good brush-up for days. Here, Dr. Weston, would you mind reaching round under here while I see to my topper? You're welcome to all found, as they say, and you won't come across anything that bites." He richly enjoyed the jest and left me to search under the bed while he reached for the shaggy black fur helmet.

The busby sprang!

I rolled from under the bed at Berkeley's scream. He beat at the ball of fur with his brush, to no avail. Four agile, clawed limbs uncurled themselves and dug into the front of his coat. A wicked, pointy snout and two ruby eyes likewise emerged, but worse was the naked red tail and the gaping double rows of needle teeth. The animal covered half of Berkeley's mighty chest, its tail lashing, and snapped at his wrist. Blood spurted from the wound; the brush dropped.

I scrambled upright and seized the beast by the tail. It turned its narrow head with a reptilian hiss and snapped at me too. "Oh you would, would you?" I clenched my teeth, gripped the base of the tail firmly, and tore the hideous rodent from Berkeley's chest. Its claws left huge rents in the guardsman's jacket, and I saw some blood beneath. Before it could fasten its teeth and claws onto me, I bashed out its brains against the wall.

Kneeling beside the still-heaving body, Berkeley said, "A rat. But the size!"

"Things grow out of all knowing in the tropics," I said. "I have read reports of such creatures being found on the island of Sumatra. Someone does not want me to reach Master Wells, Captain Berkeley; someone with access to monsters like this one. He must have had one of his servants replace your busby with that beast while we were at the pub." Lord Byron had told the truth, I reflected. I had the uncomfortable, unmistakable feeling of unseen eyes upon me. "I am sorry that his attempts should involve you, who are innocent."

"Well, I'm not!" Berkeley's hackles were up. "Not sorry a bit! You'll reach Master Wells, sir, and I'll see to that! Bloody foreign rats coming into decent British homes where they're not wanted . . ."

So it was that I was escorted to number 40, Horns Way, by one of Her Majesty's own Palace guards in nearly complete (*sans* busby) tenue. He left me at Master Wells' doorstep, saluted smartly, and marched away.

CHAPTER THIRTEEN

The Case of Vendee, the Wine Merchant

It was very late, nearly dawn, that doubtful hour when all hope seems to have fled the earth. The yellow fog trailed through the streets, but its time was done. A morning breeze already was scouring the London streets.

I pulled Master Wells' bell—his was a single-family dwelling. My mind prepared a fulsome speech of apology while I waited. One does not generally knock up Druids at such hours, not unless one fancies being turned into one of the lesser amphibia. As further precaution, I clasped the stick faithful Merriwell had presented me earlier; Master Wells might not be the one to answer the door.

He was. Moreover, he answered my ring cheerfully. "Hullo." Small and pixieish, plump as a summer sparrow, he urged me to step inside, sit down, and have a "small summat" to take off the morning chill, all before he bothered to ask my name.

"This is most kind of you, Master Wells."

"Kind? Piffle! The Golden Brotherhood are the servants of the British people, my friend."

"I have often been told so, but some of your brethren can be quite—"

He pushed away the hypothetical Brethren with short shoves of his chubby hands. "I am not responsible for how other Druids view their duties. I only have time to see to my own. Would you care for more?" He waggled the decanter at me. "No? Well, shall we see what I can do to help you, in that case?"

"Master Wells, just seeing you alive and in good health is enough for me at the moment."

"Is it? Extraordinary! I mean, it's always been enough for *me*, but— Who are you?"

"I am John H. Weston, M.D. You may have read my stories in the *Strand* magazine." Best get it over with, I thought.

"The *Strand*? Fancy that!" He helped himself to another

drink. "Forgive me, but I have no time to read anything more than my correspondence, and sometimes not even that." I felt a rush of warmth for the little Druid.

"Master Wells, earlier today you received a man clad as a Cambridge scholar."

"Padraic MacFinn, yes, a very amiable chap. Doing research on Bessemer the Heretic. I did what I could for him. If he's a friend of yours, you needn't worry. He's gone back in time, you see, to Bessemer's day, and because I haven't quite gotten the spells down *exactly*—even using my new device for focusing my displacement powers—he should be back to the present anytime from this very minute to a couple of days hence."

"You will bring him back?"

"Oh, I needn't be here, on the spot. After all, it would be awkward if he'd a mind to return the morning I'd gone out to do the marketing. He might think he'd been abandoned in time, lost in the past. I am sure it's a frightening feeling. I experienced it myself a number of times while still an acolyte, and sharpening my talents. Just popped back a year or two, for openers, but when you can't get back to *now*—well, how would you feel, running to catch a today you never could overtake because yesterday's wrapped around your ankles?"

"Then how will he get back?"

The Druid held his empty glass up to the coming daylight and swirled the dregs. "I am still the source of time-displacement power for your friend's return, but the machine is the means. If he but follows the instructions I gave him, the machine will pick up on his person, locate me anywhere within the walls of London, draw the power needed, and use it to pull him through."

I did not want to ask my next question. People do not care to hear it when buying life insurance from the Scryers' Guild, much less from a total stranger: "But Master Wells, what if something—the gods forbid!—were to happen to you?"

Master Wells stared. "To me? Oh dear. Yes, I see your point, Dr. Weston. No wonder you've come here so early, worried about your friend Padraic. If I had suffered an accident— Oh dear. Yes, he'd be stranded, then. Oh dear, I really must find a way to alter the machine so that it can store some of my power and bring folks back whether I'm about or not. Thanks ever so for bringing this to my attention!"

I bit my lower lip. "Can you bring him back now, then fix the machine?"

"That's out of the question. The time traveller alone selects the moment of his return. That is part of the law governing the displacement spells I embody. You can't kill a man who isn't meant to die, though you may slash at his throat with your sickle all you like. Likewise I can send whomever I choose backwards in time, but if he is not meant to return to *this* era again, then that is how his own threads are spun. It has something to do with action, influence, and outcome. I think the gods are mucked up in it somewhere, too."

An idea came to me. "You sent my friend. Can you send me to join him?"

"Certainly. To the very place I sent him, if not the very second. The machine will come close on both sets of coordinates; close, not dead on. I shan't ram you into any walls, of course." He thought that was funny. "Come back tomorrow. Or should I say later today? The sun's nearly up."

"Why can't you send me there now?"

"My dear Dr. Weston—" Master Wells rested his hands on his white robed knees. "I need little sleep, but I do require *some*. I must gather my strength for the spells you will need. By your looks, a nap would do you no harm either. Go home and come back later, well rested. You must have your wits about you when you go back in time. One of my clients must have been sleep-addled and said quite the wrong thing while witnessing the famous Purge of the Schismatics under King Canute. (That's what he went back for, though I don't know why; bloodthirsty young chap he was.) I never knew what became of him until they drained the old sacrificial bog in Mag Mell Park last April. He was recognizable, but not himself; not himself at all."

I decided to take Master Wells' advice. Before I left, I gave him a word of warning. I described Morganwg as best I could, then cautioned the little Druid against admitting anyone answering that description. "Considering his talent for dissembling and disguise, you'd do well to admit no one, Master," I added.

"But whyever would this Morganwg fellow ill-wish your friend Padraic enough to harm him through me?"

I could not confide the intricacies of the case in a Druid, no matter how genial. I leaned forward and lowered my voice. "University matters, Master. Faculty rivalries. They can wax ruthless, I fear." He appeared to understand.

"I lost a third cousin in the War of the Brazenose Levitation. He was sent down—rather precipitously. I shall pray for your friend."

Satisfied that Wells would protect himself until my return, I hied myself to Ada's. She was awake; she looked as if she had not yet been to sleep. I gave her the note from her father and told her of my adventures.

"I can make neither head nor tail of it. I suppose he means you are the 'sole daughter.' Can you interpret what he means?"

Ada read it through, then rubbed her eyes. "I am so tired right now that I very well could add one and one and get ten. We should both sleep and attack our tasks when rested."

Merriwell saw me to my room, waiting until I disrobed so that he might spruce up my clothes. From the way he held the garments, he seemed to be contemplating a mercy-killing for my shirt and smallclothes. I fell into an exhausted sleep.

I awoke I knew not how much later with the strong sense of being watched. I flew bolt upright in the bed, ready to face down the worst Lord Kitchener might send against me. No black-winged afrit or foam-mouthed giaour met my loud "Who's there?"—only the swarthy, happily cynical face of His late Majesty, Charles II.

"Odds fish, Dr. Weston, you keep whoremonger's hours."

"I have only just gone to bed, Your Majesty."

"*Quod erat demonstrandum*, as our ancient enemies might say. While you swive, my niece Victoria remains in peril. I have waited patiently for word from you, and, having received none, I have come to demand it."

I resented his allegations. "If Donne and I have not contacted you, sir, it is because our one contact has been summarily cut off. Hope is dead. As for your niece, I'd have you know that I love her more than as my ruler. Indeed, I hope that the passage of time since our last meeting has not cooled her affections for me. I have not swiven a goddam soul. Have not swived. Swoven. *Whatever* the bloody perfect is!"

This brought a glitter to King Charles' blackberry eye. "Don't you know the Queen's British, Dr. Weston? And you an educated man! So Hope is dead? I shall have to have a report. Will you be so kind, or shall we find Mr. Donne?"

I explained Donne's absence, then told the former King all I knew. I concluded with Donne's theory that Lord Kitchener was biding his time until he might be beyond doubt of immediate success. "He is courting the Queen. If she gives in, he will have what he desires: the British crown. If she does not yield, he shall have to make another move. What that move shall be . . . She is caught between the pincers of a nutcracker. Surely Victoria is aware of the afflictions of Britain—just as surely as Lord Kitchener's foreign sorceries are the cause."

King Charles grimaced. "Most worldly magics can blight crops and plague cattle, even the most primitive. Curing and cleansing spells are more demanding. Without the Rules, she can do little, and before long the Council will start thinking of the ages-old remedy for the ills of the land."

"The Queen's blood." My throat was bricky.

"Hers." His mouth was no longer loose and sensual, but tight and grim. "Kitchener knows, and he would seek to drive her into his arms with the threat of that sacrifice. Wed him and live or refuse him and die. He will bring her to the altar one way or the other."

The King had been sitting at the foot of my bed. Now he got up and prowled from the bed to the window and back. "I have spent too much of my magic on myself, Dr. Weston. I have lived the life of a libertine, filled with selfish, heady pleasures of the flesh. The time has come for me to remember that I am also of the blood, and that blood is worthy of more noble conduct. I shall spoil Lord Kitchener's pretty game. I shall go to the Archdruid himself and lay the case before him."

"Wellington? No, you can't! Victoria will be—"

"Peace, Dr. Weston. Victoria will be unharmed. I have husbanded my powers over the years, and though the Iron Duke may rage and champ, I have the magic in me strong enough to compel his obedience and help. He cannot stand against both Victoria and me. He will forgive her the loss of the Rules—the whole Council will unite behind him in this—or they shall have a King with whom to deal!"

Misgivings flooded me on hearing Charles' bold, forthright plan. "If that is the only way . . ."

"Dr. Weston, we have no time to consider any other ways. Get dressed. I will contact the Duke and have it out with him right now. You are to form part of the vision I send him, and your testimony may soften his initial wrath."

I, soften Wellington? The man hated me to the bone. I still remembered the look he had given me when he thought I was asleep in the Queen's bed. And what he would do once he learned that I was not the "common herbalist" he scorned, but one of the Dark Ones he feared? Ah, well! I decided to put aside my objections—they would come out soon enough once the Iron Duke saw my face—and go along with the King's wishes.

Charles rang for Merriwell, who appeared bearing my freshened clothes and a breakfast tray set for one: tea in a rose-patterned porcelain pot, toast in a silver rack, and a coddled egg. Merriwell rested his impassive gaze upon the King.

"Begging your pardon, sir, but was I present to admit you to the Lovelace residence?" he inquired blandly.

"No, my good man. I chose not to arrive through the front door. Any inconvenience?"

"None, sir. I apologize for the lack of preparation for your arrival. I shall bring another cup forthwith. Pray excuse the oversight."

Charles laughed heartily. "Ods fish, I'd have given a pretty for you to have been my servingman when I sat the British throne! If you were any more composed, I'd send for the undertaker. Do fellows blink in and out of the rooms here as a matter of course?"

Merriwell missed the humor. "Of late, yes, sir. When the master is at home, things are rather more settled."

"The master?" I asked.

"The Earl of Lovelace, sir," said Merriwell. "My lady's husband."

"I was under the impression that—that she was—a widow, perhaps."

"No, sir. She is not, to my knowledge. Will Assam tea be satisfactory, sir"—he turned back to the King—"or would you prefer a fresh pot of Keemun?"

"Just bring me a cup on a silver tray; silver, mark me."

"Silver, sir. Very good, sir." Merriwell blinked out of the room and back again with the cup and tray in an effortless way that put all such Druidical comings-and-goings to shame. His Majesty picked up the cup as soon as Merriwell was gone and concentrated his attention on the tray.

He had last performed a similar feat of conjuration across Mrs. Hendrik's samovar. Summoning visions of the past was harder than calling up living people, though you would never have guessed it from Charles' cavalier legerdemain. "I shall be first to speak to the Duke," he said, "but I want you standing right at my shoulder. He must see you from the first. One does not have eavesdroppers hidden out of sight during these spells; it's not done. So." He pulled a chair closer to the bedside table where he had rested the empty tray and made me lean over his left shoulder until I could see my face reflected clearly in the shining frame. "Now."

His hands passed airy patterns over the tray until, like opening a shuttered window, light split outward from the center. It was a dizzying light, grey and turbulent; the light of a storm-filled sky. The Duke of Wellington held himself defiantly upright at the rail of a pitching ship, his beard whipping out behind him, his white robes drenched with spume.

"Govannan! Govannon!" His shout reached my ears clearly, above the roar of the sea. A stripling who looked too young for the Master's robes he wore clawed his way along the railing to the Iron Duke's side.

"Master—Master, the captain says he can't get the helm to answer," the youth panted.

"Is that all you and the other pups have been doing? Calling for help from the captain? Why did I invest you with the white robes when you're not ready to leave your swaddlings? Ah!" He did not bother hiding his disgust. *"Must I wipe your noses for you before you die?"*

"Master, we have been doing more. The storm took us by surprise. We were readying the spells of strength for the Wall when we first felt the waters go wild. Culhwch and Erian broke free of the trance and tried to soothe the sea, but they say their powers would not come. Masters, the others are free of the trance now; they wait for us below. If you join your powers to ours, shall we not break the storm?"

I saw the Iron Duke's stern and imposing mien flow out of him like sand. He looked away from Govannon, looked out over the waves to where a rocky coast was looming beyond the breakers.

"No," he said. *"My powers are gone too. Whatever force rules the wind and tides that push this ship onto the rocks yonder will not let us go. It is as if we are fish drawn in towards that shore by an inexorable line. What has such power? What pulls us in, helpless? I do not know. I am old, Govannan. All my life I have labored for Britain's sake. I*

thought that perhaps I was too old, and that was why I could not save our ship alone; that young Druids with fresh magic might succeed where I have failed. But that is not the question now. We are the last of the Wise, and we are no match for this evil. Once we are gone, Bran's Wall must crumble even more, until no particle remains of its spell. Then Britain falls." He put his arm around Govannan's neck and leaned upon him, an old man. *"Weep for Britain, boy. Weep for Britain."*

The grey light flowed across the tray with a hiss of seafoam washing the pebbled shore.

"This is bad," said the King. "If the Archdruid himself is lost, this is monstrous."

"We never saw him *die*," I suggested.

"Dead or alive, where is he? Which coast shall we search? I am afraid, Dr. Weston, that we must look to this business ourselves."

"I had better fetch Donne, in that case."

"What? All the way back to Bessemer's time? Dr. Weston, we are damned short of our own time! Let Donne return when he will. We have much to attend to!"

"We *must* have Donne." Fear can make me very stubborn and insistent. The King fingered his thin black moustache.

"Some of us must; that much is clear. Very well, Dr. Weston; see to it."

Downstairs Merriwell was waiting to take the King into the salon to meet his unwitting hostess. I left Charles bowing over Ada's hand and assaying her charms with a connoisseur's practiced eye. For myself, I hastened around to the Lovelace stable, where I found a fat Shetland and a pony gig. I commandeered them both and drove back to Master Wells' address.

"Dr. Weston, you do look refreshed. Quite ready for your little jaunt? I have been scrupulous about your warnings. I have admitted no one and even paid five-and-six for a specially trained Acolyte of the Law to enchant my front door against hostile callers. Pray come up and we'll get you off to your friend in jig time."

We climbed three flights of stairs before reaching the atelier I remembered from Kitchener's peri-glass. I imitated Donne's cautious method of seating himself within the apparatus while the Druid made some last-minute inspections and adjustments. He handed me a small scrap of leather with several lines of characters burnt into the hide.

"Those are your instructions for coming back. Don't lose them, and follow them implicitly. The spells call for you to travel down to Salisbury Plain before you return—one taps auxiliary power wherever one can with enchantments of this magnitude. Don't worry. Even in Bessemer's day you could purchase space-displacement spells on every street corner."

"Purchase?"

"Oh my, yes, we mustn't overlook something like that." Master Wells pursed his lips. He scurried over to a rustic armoire in the corner and rummaged through the drawers until he withdrew a small chamois sack that chinked faintly. "Currency of the day, Dr. Weston. Your clothes won't matter—they were just as used to the fashionable excesses of the gentry then as now—but pay in modern coin and you'll end up in Newgate. We can't have that. I'm doing my best to have you come out close to your friend's coordinates, though not on top of them. That wouldn't do; trust me. Once you're there, you'll want to go to Vendee's, do you understand? Vendee's. He was a vintner, and Bessemer took rooms above his shop and cellars while working on his—his unfortunate studies. Ready? Off you go."

For want of anything like reins or other steering apparatus, I was holding on to two of the brass loops that belled out like a birdcage around the attached leather-covered stool at the heart of the machine. Master Wells went round the left side of his contraption and laid his hands on a panel of fine metal mesh level with my shoulder. At first I perceived nothing happening. Then I imagined I saw thin turquoise spirals radiating out towards me from the tiny grille. I wondered whether something had caught fire—conflagrations born of magic bring smoke and leave ashes in the most unearthly hues—and was about to warn Master Wells when the "smoke" touched me. It was not smoke, not by any means; nor was its touch gentle. It had all the solidity of human flesh, and just as I made this discovery the spiralling plasm drew back, formed a ball, and struck me so strongly square on the breastbone that blue-and-orange sparkles danced across my sight.

When these cleared, more than a century of time had peeled away.

London had not changed much, I was relieved to see that. The Druid Wells had been correct when he told me no one would remark upon my outlandish dress. One can never shock London. I might have been a refugee from the royal court, parading my new feathers for effect among the commons before trying them out with the *ton*, as they called it. I took only a few minutes to get my bearings and look about. The little Druid had served me well. Across the street a large sign with a fat bunch of grapes beckoned: *Vendee's Wines, Special App't. to His Majesty and Ye Gentry.*

Mr. Vendee himself manned the counter within. Row on row of aged oaken casks marched up the wall behind him. Crates of black bottles stood in neat array here and there in the shop, whether awaiting delivery or simply for effect I could not say. Two chairs beside the fireplace and a butler's table laid with a decanter and a pair of glasses added a warm note of domesticity, but Mr. Vendee was all business.

"Well, well, well, *do* come in, sir, *do* sit down! Stab me, but you *must* be Lord Pruett, ain't I right? Lord Marberry wrote that he was recommending my humble stock to your inspection, m'lud. Now, I have put by a pipe or two of the very *finest* Port wine that you could desire. A veritable symphony in grapes! Will it please you to have a seat, m'lud, and taste the offering?" His powdered wig bobbled with excitement.

I stopped him before he could herd me over to where the decanter waited. "Mr. Vendee, I am not Lord Pruett. I am here seeking a friend of mine. You may have seen him, a man dressed like me."

Vendee had the veiny look of a man addicted to sampling his own stocks, but now an even deeper shade of purple suffused his face. "Like *you*? You won't find many a buck in your turn-out, old boy, not this side of Vauxhall."

I made an annoyed sound. "I beg your pardon. I meant that I am seeking a Cambridge scholar." I had forgotten Donne's rig as the mythical "Padraic." It was a wise choice; scholars' robes have not changed in centuries. Nor, I'd venture, have scholars. "We are to meet your lodger, Master Bessemer."

"Hmph. Well, why didn't you say so in the first place? A gentleman turned out so went up to speak with the Master not ten minutes ago." Ah, the wonders of Master Wells' invention, to send me so close upon Donne's trail! "You've only to go through that archway and right. There's a flight going up to Master Bessemer's rooms." He shuddered convulsively, dislodging a shower of white powder from his artificial locks. Even in this century, the Golden Brotherhood made ordinary folk nervous. I wondered whether Master Bessemer bothered to pay Vendee more than a token rental for his lodgings.

I thanked Vendee for his help and went through the archway indicated. This took me into a narrow hall. A second archway stood directly across from me, and through it I saw Mr. Vendee's office. A plump little clerk scribbled busily away in a huge ledger. Two thick-thighed apprentices who had been lolling on a packing crate leapt up when they heard my step, but on seeing that I was not their master, they subsided into sloth again. Certainly the clerk was not going to try imposing any authority on a pair of brawny bully-boys like them.

The steps were where Vendee had told me, and just beyond them, at the end of the hall, was a thick nail-studded door that might have done the Queen's worst dungeon proud.

" 'Sthwine cellar, guv." One of Vendee's leather-aproned apprentices had come up behind me as I considered that awesome portal.

"Beg pardon?"

"Where 'e keeps th' bottles, 'at's wot Oy said, ain't it? Yew th' King's factor? Oy'm t' shaow yew round."

"I'm sorry, no. I am just going up to see Master Bessemer."

"Ow." The lad spat expressively. "Syve y'seff th' steps, guv. Yew daon't look much loike yew c'n tyke too bloody much hexercise wivout comin' t' grief. Master's not been in t'dye."

"My good chap, are you sure? A friend of mine went up to see him not ten minutes ago."

The apprentice rolled his tongue from cheek to cheek. "Skinny old bookworm sort? We sawr 'im go up, Bob an' me, roight enough. We see ever'one as goes up, we do. Sort o' keep things safe fer th'master's prop'ty. It don't do t' have some types runnin' about th' plyce too bloody free, naow do it?" Something in his eyes—hard and brown as coffee beans—told me that I was included in the class of "types" he did not like to have running about too bloody free.

" 'Ere! 'Few go up there anyway, yew just 'ave that friend o' yours come down smart-like. Oy'm not 'avin' Master Bessemer's rooms hinterfered wif. Then 'e complains t' aold Vendee and it's Bob an' me gets th' lash for't."

I stood at the foot of the steps and cocked my head. "I

hear voices. Master Bessemer *must* be there. Maybe you just missed seeing him come in. Perhaps, being one of the Wise, he transported himself abovestairs by magic."

"Wau-*ker*! Bob an' me, we've fetched Master Bessemer a bottle or two, compliments o' Vendee, and Oy made bold enough t' arsk 'im shy 'e trudged up th' stairs day in, day out, when a baby knaows th' Woise c'n flitter 'ere an' there like bloody birdies. 'Ow, that we can,' 'e says t' me. 'But magic leaves a tryal, it do, and Oy've not tyken these rooms t' 'ave moy brethren pick up a trial lyde plyne as that! Stairs'll do me quoit well whenever Oy come 'ere, me boys!' 'E said that, talked t' me just loike Oy was 'is equal, too. Naow, y' arsk me, Oy'd sigh yer bookworm friend's loike all th' rest o' them types. 'E's arf dotty an' a-talkin' t' 'isself. Yew march roight up there, smart, and get 'im down."

In a level voice I swore to the fellow that I would obey his directions with all haste. Inside, my heart was pounding and my stomach churning. I *had* heard voices above, I *had*! Donne was not talking to himself, and if Bessemer could not go up without the apprentices spying him—if he only used the stairs rather than leave a "trail laid plain" for other Druids to mark his spell-assisted comings and goings—then with whom was Donne speaking?

I had a terrible fear that I knew.

The stairs were thick and well laid. They did not creak too loudly as I ascended. About halfway up I saw a landing and a door left slightly ajar. Bessemer's lodgings would lie directly over the front room of Vendee's establishment. I glided across the landing and peeped cautiously at the crack.

Morganwg stood with his back to the mullioned windows. Their frosted glass admitted bright, rippling light that played prettily along the barrel of the gun he held on Donne. My friend had stripped off the Cambridge scholar's robes and was just letting his spectacles fall to the floor with the rest of his disguise. Morganwg smirked.

"Yes, that is how I prefer to have you, Donne; as yourself. Otherwise I should feel cheated of the pleasure of killing you."

"A pleasure no doubt heightened by the means you intend to use." Donne waved a hand languidly at the gun. This casual gesture made Morganwg jump. "Why are you so edgy, Morganwg? One would think I was the one holding the trigger."

Donne's archenemy was sullen. "I have come close to

finishing you a number of times; each time you evaded my schemes. I don't trust you. Even if you stood mother-naked before me, with no possibility of a weapon within your reach, I should not trust you. And if you were the one holding the gun, you would not trust me."

"No." Donne spoke evenly. Although I could not see his face, I was sure he was showing no fear, no matter what he might be feeling. "I would pull the trigger quickly, and so dispatch one of the lowest creatures ever to foul British soil."

Morganwg's chuckle sounded forced. "I'd think that in this instance, at least, you and I might be in sympathy. Under Lord Kitchener's reign, Britain will at last be free of the tyranny imposed upon the common man by the Golden Brotherhood. You should rejoice with us, Donne. You above all men despise them."

"You are imprecise, Morganwg. That has always been your undoing. I do not despise the Golden Brotherhood. That would be tantamount to despising wisdom itself. I have nothing but respect for the heritage they have preserved for my people over the centuries, and the peace they have given Britain. I only disapprove of their reluctance to allow the mass of British subjects to seek answers not given by magic. You speak of the common man, Morganwg. Like the Druids, you fail to realize there is nothing common about the British man, if you will but give him the chance to prove it. But your master Kitchener will shatter peace like an eggshell. Greed is his god, and ambition. He will seek to meet the Continental powers in war on their own terms. Steel and coal will blacken the land when he forces our people to arm for conquests they neither want nor comprehend. What was once the sweet, green isle of Britain will be little more than an endless valley of darkness."

"Enough!" Morganwg's high brow furrowed, making his prominent nose look all the more beaky. Seeing Donne and Morganwg together was like watching the squaring-off of two rival birds of prey, but Donne was the princely falcon and Morganwg little more than the carrion vulture.

"Enough." Donne remained calm. "You mean to shoot me now, I see."

"Shoot you?" A low laugh escaped the villain's thin lips. "Shoot you? Shall I bother with that? I have only to return to present London and kill Wells to leave you here forever. That would be amusing. You thought that only the Druid

Wells had the power to traverse time. That was before I surprised you here. It was easier for me to come here than it was for you. What is time to a supernatural spirit? What are centuries to an afrit or millennia to a djinn? Thanks to my master, these fiends have become my favorite steeds. Magical steeds, and worthy of me! You, who affect to scorn magic, should come to appreciate it before you die. Lord Kitchener could not have touched the Rules Britannia himself, but the daevas who serve him revelled in the altar flames before fetching him the book. I could not have travelled to this century save on the wings of demons."

A note of anger crept into Donne's words. "At least you keep fitting company these days, Morganwg. A fine preparation for the hell that awaits you."

"But you"—Morganwg raised the gun—"shall see it first."

I rammed my stick against the door and dived into the room, hoping to knock Donne out of range when Morganwg fired. The door flew wide and struck the wall with a report so loud that if the gun went off, both sounds merged to one. I landed flat on my stomach, never having touched Donne. Taking advantage of the momentary confusion my entrance had caused, he had flung himself upon Morganwg and now wrestled with him for possession of the gun. From the way the smaller man clung to it and tried to bring the barrel round, I realized that it had not yet been fired. I struggled up, eager to aid my friend, but felt my wounded leg double under me with a pain that made my eyes water. Fortunately, Donne was well able to fend for himself.

Risking a moment when Morganwg might have levelled his weapon and fired, Donne unexpectedly released his grip on the gun, sidestepped lightly left with the practiced footwork of an expert boxer, and struck the man a bare-knuckled jab to the jaw that sent him reeling. Donne followed this with what looked like a rugby tackle and Morganwg crashed down. My friend thereupon disarmed him and held him at bay with his own gun.

"We were speaking," Donne panted, "of what I would do were the situation reversed, eh, Morganwg?" To me he said cheerfully, "I am extraordinarily glad to see you, Weston. You are forever compelling me to revise my estimation of you." He sucked his left hand like a child, the right hand—which held the gun—never moving a hair. "The human jaw is a marvellously hard bone, Weston. You shall have to prescribe an herbal soak for my knuckles when we return."

"You'll never return alive," Morganwg croaked. I hoped his jaw was twice as sore as Donne's knuckles. From the look of the bruise starting there, I had my wish.

"Why won't we?" My leg still throbbed and made me short-tempered. "Is Master Bessemer so deep in Kitchener's pocket that he'll try to stop us when he gets here?"

Morganwg's laugh was shrill and unpleasant. "Bessemer's deep, all right, but not in his lordship's pocket. When my master first appeared to Bessemer, he promised the old fool protection even the Brotherhood couldn't pierce, and freedom to get on with his experiments. So Bessemer set to work and made us steel—not much, but enough. A wonderful creature, your djinn is. He can't bear the touch of deathmetal, being magic, but he can shift its shape without touching it. Bessemer made the steel and Kitchener's djinn made it into weapons. But Bessemer caught wise. Somehow he learned what my master's purpose was." An awful leer twisted Morganwg's face.

"So you murdered him," said Donne. "Not the Golden Brotherhood, but you."

"If you want to see Bessemer, go down to Vendee's cellars and crack that big tun of malmsey wine, Donne."

"Literary allusions from one of your ilk. Amazing, Morganwg." With the gun still aimed at the master criminal's heart, Donne haled him upright. "We have an appointment with justice, I think. We are about to right one of the wrongs of history."

"Here! What's all this racket been?" Mr. Vendee stood, plump hands on plumper hips, and glared at the three of us. I was only surprised that the sounds of the scuffle had not brought his clerk and apprentices as well.

"Mr. Vendee, help, for the gods' sake, help me! Here be two lunatics fresh escaped from Bedlam! Save me, on your life!" shrieked Morganwg, and jigged like an eel in Donne's grasp.

Little Vendee, to my horror, was a brave man. He attacked Donne fearlessly. While he would not have stood a chance of overcoming my friend, he did manage to get between Morganwg and the gun. Poor fellow, he had never seen one and had no idea of the danger he was in! But Donne knew, and was loath to risk firing if it meant the life of an innocent. I tried to drag the vintner away, and in the ensuing chaos, Morganwg managed his escape.

Worse followed. Seeing his foe making off, Donne allowed himself to become distracted, which brief inattention permitted Vendee, by a fluke, to seize the gun. Its weight gave him the idea that it was some sort of bludgeon. He swung it wildly, first at Donne, then at me. It was anyone's guess whether he would deliberately brain us before he accidentally shot us or vice versa. Luckily for us, the excitement of the struggle made Vendee careless, and I landed a lucky blow of my stick across his knuckles. The gun fell from his hands, discharged with a roar when it hit the floor, and shattered the front windows.

"Sink me," breathed Vendee, eyes goggling. A tremor began to shake his fat little body. I thought he would fall to his knees. "Sorcery. Oh, Masters, can you ever forgive me?" It was all too much for him. He *did* go to his knees.

"Mr. Vendee, do get up. We are not of the Golden Brotherhood." Donne sounded weary but resigned. He forced the vintner to stand. "If we were, we should not have touched this"—he retrieved the gun—"so willingly. Nor are we Bedlamites."

Vendee gaped at the gun, even daring to touch the still-warm barrel. "Deathmetal." He was shaking again. "I know the man who called you Bedlams. He's been here many a time before, to visit Master Bessemer. I thought he was one of the Wise, but if he was involved with *this* . . ." A thousand surmises flickered in and out of his eyes. "Oh Lady Epona, save me! *I'm* involved as well! What will become of me when the Brotherhood learn I've been a party to aught touching deathmetal?"

"They won't learn a breath from us," I said, hoping to calm the man enough to cease his piteous wailing. "We shall even take this with us when we go." Even as I spoke, Donne pocketed the gun. Vendee's gratitude was most affecting. We had to dissuade him from pressing every bit of coin on his person upon us. As we left, I politely suggested to Vendee than he check his supply of malmsey when convenient.

"You are a sly devil, Weston," said Donne when we were in the street again. "Not a word to him of what he may find in one of those barrels."

"I don't want to be nearby when he does make that discovery. I am sure that our able Mr. Vendee managed to dispose of Bessemer's remains secretly enough, or else why would the rumor persist that the Brotherhood caused his vanishment?"

"Weston, you continue to astound me!" It was wonderful to see his smile after a parting that might have been forever. There was never a soul on earth for whom I felt a deeper and more abiding admiration and affection than Brihtric Donne.

Alas, his face soon turned sombre. "We must try to return to our own time, my friend, although I wonder if the effort will be worth it. Morganwg can slip from age to age easily, using the powers of Kitchener's creatures. He must be back in the present by this."

I understood his gloom at once. "You think he has gone back and murdered Wells? I warned the old man . . ."

Donne snapped out of his dark mood. "We should not assume too much, Weston. We must make the effort. Wells is a Druid, and as you say, he has been forewarned about Morganwg. Let us never give up hope. There is a certain Lady who is depending upon us. For her sake, we will follow Wells' directions to effect our return."

It proved to be just as the little Druid had told me. Transportation spells were readily come by in Bessemer's London. Before long, Donne and I stood upon the wind-swept Salisbury Plain. The grey slabs of Stonehenge raised their lichened mass against the sky a spear's throw from where we stood.

"There's a mystery I'd like to solve, Weston. These heroic stones were standing even as we see them now when Bran himself was a boy. The Druids, for all their wisdom, don't know what to make of them. They speak of blood sacrifices performed on this site. But when a man stands in the presence of evidence that those who came before him were capable of greatness, he seeks to diminish that greatness. He finds some way to belittle the folk who had the impudence to worship other gods than his." He gave me a canny look. "I don't suppose your people had anything to do with these?"

"I'm afraid not, Donne. My old Teacher told me about Stonehenge, but he confessed himself just as puzzled."

"Well, it is a relief to hear that the Pictish wizards are not as omnipotent as Druid lore paints them. You may perform the mumbo-jumbo Wells prescribed with a clear conscience, Weston. As referred magic—Druidical at that—it will not violate your geas."

"Which you regard as *more* mumbo-jumbo."

Donne shook his head. "It is a very real source of sorrow to you, my friend. I do not trivialize that."

It was a cool day, but the threat of rain on the horizon had kept off the curious and given us full privacy among the stones. We recited the words and made the necessary motions, following exactly the directions we had on our leather strips. We went through this routine once, and again, and a third time before Donne finally let his arms drop to his sides.

"Wells is gone."

I had not wanted to be the one to voice that terrible certainty. Now that it was said, I asked, "What shall we do?"

"We might begin by returning to London. That will take some time, unless there is a modest country Druid dwelling in the nearest village who can send us back. In London itself I suppose we might search for another of the Wise with Wells' peculiar talent. That will take quite some time, I think."

Time. Yes, that it would. Time displacement was the rarest of all magics. Even were I to break the geas Deirdre had laid upon me, it would not help us. Time travel was no part of the earthspells. As I allowed despair to fill me, I saw a stooped figure come hobbling over the downs towards us.

"Donne, someone in coming. Hadn't we best hide? This isn't London, and they dress most conservatively in the country. Whoever this is may have us taken up by the authorities, and we'll be that much farther from getting back to town."

Donne took out a chamois purse of coins that was twin to the one Wells had given me. "So long as our money is not outlandish, we are safe. Only the poor become Jacks o' Bedlam. The rich are called eccentric."

At this moment our visitor came into view. She was an old hag whose face could be scarcely seen through her tangled grey tresses.

"Good day, Mother," Donne greeted her.

Her raggedy clothes were as out of date as our own, but in her case they harked to the previous century. "Good day t' ye also, boys. Here I be t' answer all yer wishes. They call me Moll Scryer in t' village. What'd ye care t' know? I'll summon up visions! Oh, I has ways o' seein', young gentlemen, as ye'd never dream on! Only a ha' penny fer all ye love, an' I shall ha' ye see t' ends o' t' earth, if ye're so minded."

Donne demurred, but the old beldam was insistent. He shot me a pleading look. I suppose that having the fair sex as my department included even those members *emeriti* thereof. I consented to have Moll Scryer conjure me a vision.

"We mun go into yon grove, good Master," she said, laying a startlingly strong hand on my arm. "There's a pool there. We mun have water fer t' scryin'."

The sooner I let the ancient witch have her say and collect her penny, the sooner we might get back to London and locate a Druid like Wells. I followed her into the small stand of trees a short distance from the monument. Here, as she said, we found a pool not much larger than Wellington's ceremonial cauldron. We sat on the verge where cress and bluebells grew and she thrust her thick hand under my nose, wriggling the fingers impatiently. "Ha'penny."

I fished into my purse and came up with a full copper. This largesse nearly undid her. "I'll scry ye pretty, Yer Highness, I will."

"Scry or don't scry, only get it over with. Save your flattery for other customers."

She spit dead-center into the pool. "I know what I see. Have a care ye do the same." Her arms swept out over the still water like bird's wings, and when she curved them inwards again to form a circle, hand touching hand, the vision came.

Victoria.

"Victoria!" I called her name. I could not help myself. This was no ordinary vision. I felt as if we were in the same room—the antechamber of her Palace suite. There was a huge fire laid on the grate and she was well dressed in cream velvet and lace, but she looked wan. A glow of desperation burned in her eyes. I thought she heard me. Her head came up suddenly, her eyes turned from the flames, but it was only in response to the door opening. Lady Byron came in.

"Your Majesty is well?" I wished I might have struck that look of false concern from her face.

"As well as I can be."

"You might be better. If you would come to your senses, all will be well for you. We are growing tired of your coy games. The time has come for you to make your decision, or it will be made for you."

" 'We'? Are you and Lord Kitchener joined at the navel, my lady? A likely pair you make! You should be the one to marry him, not I."

Lady Byron allowed this to pass without comment. *"It is nearly Sammain, Your Majesty."* She said this in a low, slow voice, relishing each syllable. I saw a shudder wrack the Queen. *"Your allies are gone. You have no one left to whom you might turn. Britain ails, and your blood will cure her. Are you so eager to shed it? What have you left but to marry my master?"*

Victoria rose from her chair with the stately grace of sacrificial smoke. *"I have married more than your master. I have chosen the man who will rule beside me, but even his love is nothing, for he is only the second to whom I have given my heart. I am the bride of Britain, and the land will not let you have me so easily."*

Her frivolous court dress ran like snow under the sun. The lace melted away, and the cloth itself shrank upwards until the Queen's arms were bare, one breast bare also, and Lady Bryon saw the short bronze sword she held. The Queen took advantage of her captor's surprise. She sprang forward and twisted the woman's arm behind her back, holding the sword blade just under Lady Byron's straining ribcage.

"Now we shall leave this place—once my Palace. When I return, it will be to drive Lord Kitchener and all his filthy servants into the sea. You are my passport, Lady Byron, should any of that alien crew seek to prevent me."

"Brave woman," I said softly, my breath rippling the water. "My gallant love." Victoria was herding Lady Byron for the door, but before she could touch the knob, it opened. Lord Kitchener was there, and with him a woman wearing the color of twilight.

"I did not think you had become so much the lamb, Victoria," he said. *"Although I would have liked it, I mistrusted your docility. This is more what I expected from the once Lady of Britain. Lay aside your sword. The time for such things is over."*

"I have more than a sword to help me," replied the Queen. The woman in purple turned towards the fire. I could not see her face.

"So do I," said Kitchener. He stretched out his hand towards the woman as if he meant to hand her into a chariot. *"I think it is time you made the acquaintance of one who is worth all of your pitiful little swords."*

He touched her lightly with his fingertips. "*Kali.*"

The fire roared up in a hungry yellow wave and seared the purple veils from her body. Spider limbs unfolded themselves in pairs from her shoulders, and her small, rouged feet began to stamp out a rhythmic beat upon the Queen's hearth while the brass bells bound to her ankles and the ridiculously tiny silver cymbals in her hands played exotic counterpoints.

"*Kali. Durga. The Black Mother. Kali, the goddess, drinker of blood.*"

Her mouth gaped and clashed shut, the bloodstained tusks champing. That ghoulish face recalled the horrors I had witnessed since the case began—the crimson leech and the poisonous lizard, Hope dead, and Master Caradoc, and little Sarah. There was an aura of obscene flirtatiousness in her dance. A girdle of skulls clocked out chalky cadences with each sway, each spin, each undulation. Blood dripped from a bowl she held, blood spattered the Queen's body, blood filmed the room with a scarlet haze so thick I felt the salty tang of it on my tongue and fought back the sickness in my throat. The Queen gave a smothered cry and flung Lady Byron aside. Her sword came up and across with the practiced slash of a battle-tried fighter. She severed one of the many writhing arms. It fell to the floor and wriggled like a snake while black blood wrapped itself in a cloak around the dancing goddess.

"*Kali, who drinks blood.*"

And the arm was gone from the floor, rejoined to the dancing body. Four swords flailed the air. In her sightless, gore-drunk ecstasy, the goddess threw back her head, and I saw that corpses dangled from her ears, shaking and jouncing with her gyrations. The four blades fell as one across Victoria's sword, shattering it past repair. Lady Byron seized the Queen from behind. She plucked a thin chain from her neck and used it to secure Victoria's hands. I could hear her gasp when it touched her flesh; an iron chainlet, it had to be. Lord Kitchener made a mocking salutation to the black goddess, and the dance stopped.

She was only a woman wrapped in purple robes.

"*It is almost Sammain, Your Majesty,*" he said to the captive Queen. "*I think you need some time away from the pressures of Palace life during which to give my proposal serious thought. The loyal staff I have provided to serve you here will see to it that no one, no one, bothers you from now until then."*

"At least if I die for Britain," said the Queen, *"I will have the satisfaction of knowing the Rules will remain beyond your power. You need my help to tap their magic, and I will never give it."*

"My dear Victoria," Kitchener replied. *"If you die on Sammain night, rest assured that it will not be for Britain. If I may not have the power of the Rules, than I will make sure that the manner of your death itself buys me back more sorcery than what the Rules deny me. Take her away."*

Lady Byron forced the Queen towards the fireplace. The woman in purple watched indifferently, from under hooded eyes, as a passageway opened beside the hearth and the two women entered. Lord Kitchener was about to follow them when the woman stayed him with an imperious touch. Her slim hands were sheathed in lavender gloves.

How much longer, mortal man? Her lips never moved. I heard her words as he did, in my mind. *Promises are poor sacrifices. I have not drunk my fill. You pledged much when you called upon Kali Ma to serve you. I do not serve for nothing. You are powerful, but you are no god. In the great dance, you and I watch each other. When you make the one step that must come, the false step, the step against the knives, then I will take what was promised. To me it does not matter whose blood I drink.*

Lord Kitchener stood his ground before her, his eyes like two stones, almost as cold as hers. I have never said that the man was not brave. *"You will have blood, Kali. My word is good. Until Sammain, remember. I am no god, as you say, but a man can bind the gods to his will, if he has the stomach for it. On Sammain night, you shall drink your fill; you shall drink the blood of Britain."*

The woman's mouth turned up at the corners. Yellow tusks showed, and a trickle of blackness.

"Victoria!" I thrust my arms out towards the secret door and only wet them to the elbow. A frog croaked indignantly and hopped from the bank between my knees into the center of the pool. The crone rocked back on her heels and cackled.

"That were a game fer me, sir, but now I trust 'tis plain that I've some powers worthy of yer attention. A scryer's paid t' see. There be no secrets. Yer black Pict's blood runs as clear t' my eyes as yer name and rank among the Dark

Ones. We can do better business than ha'penny scryings, Dr. Weston. Ye be a prince among yer little people, and a prince commands all the secrets of Pictish magic, even they that the Dark Ones kept back from Bran the Blessed. And ye love the Queen." She brought her gap-toothed mouth close to my ear.

"I can save her. The future's all I've shown ye. Ye owe nothing to them that sent ye into exile. And fer what? Fer a vain girl's death, fer a curse ye never deserved, fer a geas that I could help ye overcome! Nothing, nothing at all do ye owe the Dark Ones! Give me all their secrets and I'll serve ye faithfully. Teach me what even Bran never knew and ye and I shall make a different vision surface in the waters." Her voice dropped to a stertorous whisper. "Give me the Dark Ones' magic."

For a moment I stared at the now-clear surface of the pool. It had been no charlatan's trick, but a true seeing of the future; I could sense that. I was too much the son of a royal line of mages not to recognize real magic. She knew who and what I was also, and must realize she dared not lie to me or brag falsely about what she could accomplish. If I gave her the knowledge, she could be the one to wield my powers for me, and Deirdre's geas would be impotent to stop her.

But to do that, I must betray my own.

I refused. Victoria, whose heart knew me so well, would have understood.

"Double-damned fool!" the old crow shrieked, her grime-rimmed nails raking the air. "Then take my worst wi' ye!" She flew from the thicket and I never saw her more.

Donne was waiting for me by the outer ring of standing stones. At first I thought he was alone, then I saw that he was earnestly conversing with a person or persons just out of sight around one monolith.

"Ah, there you are, Weston! While you've been off chasing pixies, I have met a local gentleman who will see to it that we get back to London posthaste."

I felt something rub against my ankles. Tam looked up at me innocently and mewed. Old Jim the fishmonger slid round the stone, smoking a poisonous pipe. I began to speak, to let Donne know that this was no lucky meeting, that I knew this man from our own London. What in blazes was he doing here, and with that knowing cat?

My throat shuddered, producing silence. I could not speak, and Donne did not notice. Old Jim winked.

There was nothing for me to do but nod and go after them as the fishmonger set the pace over the chalk plain to a dusty cart track which in turn took us up and down the rolling countryside until we spied a trim village. The old man took us through the well-kept streets until he found a thatch-roofed cottage that satisfied him. He held the gate open for us and shepherded us up the walk.

"Go right in, gents, go right in," he said. There was not a hint of the Northern accent I'd always heard him use. "Master Gorbaduc's a reliable Druid, and one of the best for travel spells. Reasonable, too. Go right in."

Donne and I did so, but once within the humble cottage my friend stopped short. "Bare!" Just so, there was not a stick of furniture to be seen, nor was there even a fireplace. Four blank white walls held us in a box.

"A trap!" I cried, and even I regained the use of my tongue, the lone room began to fill with billows of thick smoke that drained all strength from my body. "A trap," I moaned, sinking into oblivion. The last thing I saw was Victoria's ghost, carried inexorably away from me into the clouds.

CHAPTER FOURTEEN

The Adventure of the Statesman, the Beacon Keeper, and the Tame Cormorant

I came to, much to my surprise, in the downy comfort of my bed at Ada's town house. I tumbled out, paused only long enough to ascertain that I was still fully clothed, and tore down the hall like a madman to Donne's room. My friend sat as before, feet to the empty fireplace, but this time with a look of deepest melancholy on his fine-drawn features.

"There you are," he said. It was impossible to tell whether he was surprised, disappointed, or totally indifferent to my presence.

"How did we get back here? What happened, Donne?" I demanded.

Donne shifted his thin body a bit in the chair. "That, Weston, is another thing I begrudge magic. It leaves one with either too many possible explanations for a single phenomenon, or else none." He leaned forward to gaze at the ashes on the hearth. I became aware of how chilly the room was.

"She is a married woman, Weston."

"Who is? Oh, Ada? I knew that." After Merriwell told me, I did. "Is that what's troubling you?"

"I think that as soon as we have resolved this case, especially Lord Byron's part in it, I shall terminate all further contacts with Lady Lovelace."

"In heaven's name, why? There being a Count of Lovelace in the offing doesn't seem to bother Ada a bit. She's a beautiful woman, Donne—beauty often sets its own rules—and one of the most highly intelligent—"

"I do not need you, Weston, to tell me what is so patently obvious. Lady Lovelace is a woman such as is seldom met with in this world. I regret nothing of what has passed between us. She has her code, I have mine. She will be dealt with from here on as a client, nothing more."

I did not like the idea of Donne's treating Ada with his cool, judicial attitude, the one he reserved for ordinary women. To my eyes, Ada was the second-least-ordinary woman in the world. "Don't tell me you only just discovered her husband's existence, Donne. Not you, who can recite a person's nastiest vices just from a cursory glance at his fingernails!"

Donne wore a grim smile. "You may imagine what a hard pill it is for my pride to swallow the fact that the poets—those least rational of men—are often right. Affection blinds the eye—and the mind. I have done well to avoid it. It is fortuitous that this discovery concerning Lady Lovelace has arisen. Now I can get back to my normal course of life."

It struck me then that but for my presence, what a fundamentally lonely course of life was Donne's.

My thoughts were interrupted by Lady Lovelace herself, who came in without knocking, as she had every right to do in her own home. She and Donne exchanged a look that all but told me that they had already sorted out their differences and returned to the purely businesslike footing of professional and client. Neither one gave any outward sign of longing or regret. I marvel at the British talent for preserving appearances.

"I have solved my portion of Father's code," she said, laying a paper across Donne's knee.

"That was quick," I remarked. She gave me a puzzled look.

"I had more than time enough and to spare. I never knew that Father was in any way mathematical. That made the solution all the more surprising. He worked hard over this. The clue is here." She pointed to the sentence where Byron mentioned adding one and one to get ten. "Binary. The numbers that follow are written in binary code."

This required some explanation for me. Donne filled and smoked a pipe while Ada tried to educate me to a system of counting not based on groups of ten. If, instead of counting on your fingers, you were to count on your elbows, you would see the underlying principle of it. Or so I guess; it was purest Attic Greek to me.

"You see, in our common decimal system a one in this column—the second over, reading right to left—stands for one group of ten. A one in the next column left stands for ten squared, or one hundred. The next column is for ten times ten times ten, ten cubed, or one thousand. But in binary we use only the numerals zero and one because each column handles groups of twos. One-zero means one group of two. One-zero-zero is two squared, or four, and so on. A binary numeral written as eleven would really mean one group of two plus one unit, or three, total. One hundred one would be two squared plus one, or five. Do you see?"

I damn well didn't, but she did, and she had solved her father's code, which was all we needed. "So what have we got, then?" I looked over Donne's shoulder. "Two, one, nineteen, eleven, five . . ." I read off the numbers and registered a blank. Donne was able to regain his old, wry smile.

"Not got the faintest idea of what he's saying yet, have you. And yet once taken out of binary, Byron's message is embarrassingly simple to decipher. It is a straightforward number-letter code, and the corresponding letters spell out 'Baskerville.' "

"Oh, they do?" I must have looked and sounded exactly like a sheep. Now he laughed.

(It may be underhanded of me, but there are times when I deliberately play the fool for Donne. I am nearly the sum of any close companionship he has in this wide world. There are brief touches of other people's lives against his own—just ask Friedrich's girls if my word isn't enough—but these are superficial at best. I had fleeting hopes that his encounter with Ada might ripen into something more like ordinary human entanglements. Since this was not to be, I wished to distract him, to draw his attention away from affairs of the heart, to make him think, "It is all right; good old Weston still needs me." Let those who read this think of me as the eternal bumbler, Weston the clown whose pitiful sallies make Donne's deductions all the more wonderful by comparison. I fancy myself more the politician, and the gods know how often politicians play the fool.)

Donne was on the point of making things plainer for my benefit when the inimitable Merriwell materialized with tea among us.

"Please excuse the intrusion, Madam, but the individual for whom Mr. Donne sent earlier has arrived."

Donne rubbed his hands together. "That will be Friedrich! Show him up, Merriwell."

"Very good, sir."

"You are just in time, Friedrich," said Donne when Merriwell showed the little pander in. "Lady Lovelace has succeeded in decrypting part of her father's message. Perhaps you will have something to contribute too, while we try to solve the rest of it."

Friedrich snickered. "As if you'd give anyone else a lick at solving a mystery! But I'm game. I'm at a loose end now. They gave me the sack at the Palace."

My eyebrows rose. "It didn't take them long to discharge you. Did you manage to learn anything in such a short time?"

"A short time? More than a fortnight. I worked as a page, and I was lucky to get the job. The Gaulish ambassador was making his yearly visit, and it wouldn't do to have the Continental powers notice anything amiss. You know, Her Majesty's court is nearly solidly packed with Orientals these days. There's no telling what the Gauls would do if their ambassador remarked on it, so the few British faces left were called upon to wait on the Queen and the Ambassador's suite for the duration of his visit. Once he was off, so was I. So were all remaining Britons."

"Did you say a fortnight?" Mentally I began counting days. It did not seem possible. No, it was quite impossible.

"I see by your expression that you are coming close to learning the disquieting truth about time travel, Weston," said Donne. "It is the least exact of all magics. When I found myself here, in the present, I wondered at the unseasonable chill in the room. Unseasonable for September, yes, but not for the end of October. We have travelled through time, and we have paid for our trip in the same coin."

"But then—what day is this? What has happened?"

Ada spoke up then, and I saw the lines of strain around her eyes. "After you set out to bring Mr. Donne back, I tried every means available to reach my father. His late Majesty, Charles II, placed his Druidical powers at my disposal, but even these were useless. My father has vanished from our ken. My father, and all but a handful of the Golden Brotherhood."

"That's true," said Friedrich, "and I never thought I'd say I miss seeing those white robes on every street corner. London isn't London without them. Britain's not Britain. The news coming down from the other countries is similar; the Druids have vanished, nearly to a man."

Your allies are gone. You have no one left to whom you might turn. Again I heard Lady Byron's harsh voice taunting Victoria. Victoria's allies, the vanished Wise. Moll Scryer's conjured vision reasserted itself in all its horror. A scryer can only read what the future holds; the present is closed to her. But at what point in the future would Victoria face that bloodthirsty goddess? Lady Byron and Lord Kitchener both had mentioned Sammain, which falls at October's end. But how long before Sammain were the events in my vision? Was it too late to reach my love and warn her, or had the moment already come and gone somewhere in the weeks Donne and I had lost? The Druids were gone. Was she?

"In mercy's name, what day is this?" I cried.

A tall shadow fell in our midst. King Charles had come. "What day, sir? Two days before Sammain! Od's fish, and why not two days before the crack of doom? It'll be all one." He edged closer to Ada, pretending great interest in the paper she had given Donne. She laughed and stepped a pace away from him.

"Your Majesty, *please.* You don't have to pinch me. I am vine-ripe."

He put on an innocent look. "Who's this Boatswain, sweetheart?" His long finger jabbed at the paper with Byron's note. "And all that scribbling just to say 'Baskerville'? The Baskervilles aren't more than catchpenny Devon nobility. Got a curse or two in the family history, but dull as dormice beyond that, I vow."

"Your Majesty is correct concerning the Baskervilles," said Donne. "And since they are so unimportant, why conceal their name so thoroughly, using a code only one person in Britain—Lady Lovelace—could begin to solve?"

Ada now addressed the former King. "Boatswain was a dog of whom my father was very fond, Your Majesty. He took great pains with the inscription raised above the beast's burial mound." For a moment her careworn look deserted her. She smiled fondly, thinking of her father. "I was only a child the first time he showed me Boatswain's mound, but I shall never forget what he said: 'Ada, there are many men who show less love and loyalty to their fellows than Boatswain ever showed me. Yet these same men repose beneath cairns of imposing size, and so it has always been throughout the history of Britain. The greater the mound, the less substance it conceals. That is why I have not given Boatswain the grave of an ordinary animal, but one to rival that of any noble British family.' "

"Get your coat, Weston," said Donne.

"What?" Charles demanded. "Where are you two off to

like that? You haven't answered my question! Or your own. *Why the Baskervilles?*"

"Lady Lovelace has answered all, as her father planned she should, Your Majesty." Donne was up and casting aside his dressing gown. "Only she would know the significance of the binary code. Only she would know the identity of Boatswain. Only she could bring up a childhood memory of words uttered over a dog's grave that would tie all this together. True, there was a great element of risk in such a personalized cypher, but desperate men often make the best gamblers. We are going to the Baskerville estate in Devon, Your Majesty, where we shall no doubt find a family burial mound of impressive proportions. The less important the family, the larger the mound; I have long noted this phenomenon and agree with Lord Byron."

"Donne, we can't—that is, I can't. I must go to the Queen! She is in terrible danger. If it wants only two days of Sammain—" Hurriedly, agitation making me falter, I told them all I had seen in that harmless pool on Salisbury Plain.

The former King sucked breath in through his teeth. "If that's a taste of the powers beyond Bran's Wall, thank all the gods that I'm a British man who serves a brighter rank of divinities. Gods who drink human blood, forsooth!"

"Your Majesty," Donne said quietly, "according to what the Druids teach, the gods themselves demand Victoria's blood as the price of healing Britain."

King Charles scowled. "Then the Druids shall have to speak to me about it first! And the gods shall have to change their tastes!"

"Donne, I must know if Victoria is still all right. If the events I saw have not yet come to pass—"

"Just so, Weston."

"She was all right when I left Palace service," Friedrich put in. "That was only yesterday."

"Much can happen in a little time, Friedrich," said Donne.

"Your Majesty—" I turned to the former King of Britain. "Could you summon a vision of the Queen?"

Charles looked a trifle hesitant. "In these last few months, Dr. Weston, I have used more of my powers than in nearly the past two centuries. I had hoped to conserve something of my magic to continue the very happy pursuits of my old age, but— Ah, welladay! Perhaps I truly have overstayed my welcome. Yes, by all means, I shall call up Victoria." He removed the tea things and once more used the empty silver tray for his instrument. Victoria appeared. She was in her office, conferring with Lord Melbourne, her Prime Minister. Lord Kitchener stood by the window, pretending disinterest in whatever they were discussing.

"We'd best not speak to her," Charles whispered. "The less that whoreson knows of our actions, the better."

Victoria wore the same gown I had seen in Moll Scryer's pool. Her hands were clenched, and as we watched she shot up from her chair and shouted at Lord Melbourne:

"Do fishermen's shallops ride out the worst of the North Sea storms, yet a sturdy coaster manned by Druids sinks without a trace?"

Lord Melbourne lowered his head before her anger. *"I only report the news that has come to me, Your Majesty. We must call an emergency session of Parliament. The common people must be warned. This Sammain will be the first in untold centuries that the Golden Brotherhood have not been present to stand between the living and the risen dead."*

"Not one? Is there not one Druid left in all my kingdom? It is impossible!"

"Your Majesty, many folk of the blood are left in your realm, but their powers are of the weakest. You know the difficult decisions we have had to make in Council these past weeks, ever since the Duke of Wellington vanished. You were there when we wrestled with the problem of priorities—whether to make further attempts at the repair of Bran's Wall or to forbid any more of the Brotherhood to venture onto the sea. Sammain seemed very far away to us all. Alas, that it is no longer so."

The Queen took up her pen and began to scrawl something on the paper before her. *"Lord Melbourne, I will convoke Parliament. How soon can the Commons assemble? Will it be in time to arrive at some solution to the Sammain question?"*

"That we must see. We won't have a full House, you understand. The North Country members will be hard put to it to find a Druid left who can transport them here on such short notice. What's more, I hope that I can find one able to send this proclamation to the full membership of the Commons."

The Queen finished writing and held up the paper. It turned to a merlin that perched on her wrist. She nodded, and the windows opened to allow it flight. *"The proclamation has been sent,"* she said. *"Enough of them will find a way here. I only hope that they may come up with some practical ideas concerning Sammain. I should think it would be enough to warn the populace to remain indoors if the dead ride."*

Lord Kitchener glided over to stand with one hand resting familiarly on the back of Victoria's chair. If she disliked this, she gave no sign. *"Your Majesty knows why simply hiding on Sammain will not be enough. Once, in the ancient days before King Bran, all a wise man needed to do was to keep to his home fire and let the spirits ride freely past. But when the might of the Golden Brotherhood grew, their patience with the British dead dwindled. Strength breeds arrogance."* He showed his teeth.

"My ancestors made many errors," Victoria admitted. *"But I do not think that their decision to mew up the British dead on Sammain—to prevent them from riding out of their graves and mounds and barrows—was done out of arrogance. They did it as a sign of their strength, yes, but a sign so that the common people might be reassured and feel always safe while the Golden Brotherhood watched over them, even on a night when the powers of evil are greatest."*

"Whatever the reason, they have denied the dead," said Lord Melbourne. *"I see his lordship's point. There are tales in the West of the occasional accident befalling a local Druid that prevented him from performing the proper Sammain rites. Horrors are then reported. The dead ride with a vengeance. The rage of long imprisonment drives them to brave even crossing doorsteps and coming to the hearthfire itself. I do not like to think what will happen if all the dead of Britain rise. We shall be undone."*

"I shall see to the dead of my line, as always," said Victoria. *"I shall make them the necessary sacrifices at Stonehenge. And the Commons may call upon me to protect London proper."*

"That's something, at least," said Lord Melbourne.

"Yes, that—" Lord Kitchener froze in midspeech. He looked here and there before his gaze came to rest.

"What are you staring at, man?" the Prime Minister demanded.

"Nothing."

But his eyes had been fixed on mine.

King Charles smeared his fingers over the tray, clearing away the vision. "Ods fish, did you see that? He sensed us! We'd best not risk another seeing."

"At least you know the Queen's still safe," said Friedrich.

"But for how long?" Donne was now ready to depart. "Weston, go to the Queen, since there may yet be a chance of saving her. As for me, I am off to Baskerville Hall, in Devonshire."

Friedrich opened the drapes an inch and looked out. "You won't get there before Sammain eve comes, Donne, not even if you get the fastest horse available, and I judge this isn't a good Sammain for being caught out of doors. At least the Queen herself said she'd protect London."

"Pox take Lord Kitchener and all his crew!" cried King Charles. "If I expend my last drop of magic to bring him down, it will be well spent! Dr. Weston, I am going with you to warn my niece. Do not try to prevent me! As for you, Mr. Donne—" He saluted my friend on both cheeks, then touched his middle finger to the spot between Donne's eyes, the ordinary gesture ending any transportation spell. Donne was at Baskerville Hall before Charles' arm was back at his side.

"I am coming with you too," said Ada. "I will only be a moment." She ran from the room before we had the chance to gainsay her.

"Well, not me," said Friedrich, likewise heading for the door. "I'm going to take care of my own housekeeping until this is over. I've done my part." To the former King he added, "Stop by our place again some time, Rowley. I've some new girls with some old ideas. Or is it the other way around?" He sang a Saxon song as he went down the stair. I have every faith that it was filthy.

Ada returned shortly, wearing the garb of the Daughters of Boudicca—short doeskin tunic, matching trews, an abbreviated traveller's cape, bronze shield and shortsword. On her feet were Roman sandals, carefully preserved with layer upon layer of woman's spells. When all the Romans on British soil were slain, it seemed a pity to waste such fine footgear.

"You're a cony done up in wolfskin," said the former King, trying to chuck her under the chin. A look was enough to deter him this time. "I can see I'll need to work this old chestnut on you two."

"What old chestnut?" I asked. Then I looked at Ada. Where the warrior lass had stood I now saw a light lady dressed in the style of King Charles' heyday. Clusters of lovelocks bunched at her ears, and kiss-curls swept across her brow. But who wasted much time looking at hairstyles when the low cut of her satin dress revealed Ada's breasts almost to the nipple? "Good heavens!"

Ada tittered—her shield had inexplicably become an indigo feathered fan. "You should see yourself, Dr. Weston! La, what adorable curls you have! And those scarlet-heeled boots—quite simply the last word in bravery. Your Majesty is an adept at seemings."

Her compliment pleased Charles, who preened his moustache. "Well—*harum*—I had practice enough in my youth when I had Wizard Cromwell to face. But now's not the time for tales. We shall have to ride to the Palace; I'd rather save my magic for more vital moments."

We rode as noisily as possible through the London streets, to all appearances a party of frivolous aristocrats out for one final lark before the grim Sammain season came upon us. I shall ever remember that ride. The streets were bleak and bare. The houses we passed stared at our cavalcade with windows so empty that it was easy to imagine London become a city of the dead. And so it might yet be, when Sammain eve came on.

We dismounted at the gate and allowed Charles to bully his way past the guards. The uniform fit them badly, dwarfed them, and a man ill clothed is easy to overrule. The guard Charles buttonholed forgot his guardsman's role so far as to open the doors for us and summon a porter. I took over and dismissed the little fellow out of hand.

"Be off, we know our way. Cernunnos curse you, you poxy whoreson beggar, don't you know us? What! Od's fish, not know the Queen's own blood relatives? Swive thy mother, you ballockless lackey, begone before I—"

I was spared having to make specific threats; the man fled. King Charles roared with laughter. "*Ballockless lackey?* Oh, a telling blow, sirrah; you are a wicked, wicked man. *Swive thy mother,* forsooth?"

"I was only trying to sound authentic."

"Well, don't. At least you rid us of him, although he has probably gone to summon help. We shall take the inner passage to Victoria's suite, in that case."

There was no need to hope for a finer guide than the erstwhile King. He opened a panel in the wall and led us through, closing it silently behind us. We joined hands—to strike any sort of light would have been foolhardy—and he conducted us through the maze within the wainscotting.

When he stopped, it was to lift a minuscule peephole and see whether the Queen was alone in her sitting room.

"We are in luck," he whispered to Ada, who passed it on to me. "She is alone. Poor girl, she is crying. I think that, in the circumstances, you should be the one to speak to her and announce us."

I did not argue. He lifted the seeming from me, making my appearance normal again, and showed me how to unlatch the hidden door from our side of the wall. I worked the catch as softly as I could and stepped out.

"Victoria?"

I spoke softly, nonetheless expecting her to jump up in surprise or fright. She did neither, but lifted her teary face from her hands by degrees, and by degrees also I saw a smile replace the tears.

"John." She said it warmly. "I knew you would come." She extended her hands to me in a regal gesture of welcome, and I knelt at her feet. She let her fingers wander through my hair until I seized them and held them to my heart. "Isn't it absurd?" she said. "I half imagine that you are a dream, and will vanish if I let you go."

"He's real enough," said Charles, taking this moment as best for his entrance, Ada behind him. "I hope you're not the sort of woman has to pack for every trip; we are all leaving the Palace at once."

"Leaving— Dear Uncle, I have wanted to escape for months! But my efforts are futile."

"Futile? Rubbish! You may not have the Rules, but you've your own stock of powers. What prevents you from whisking yourself to Land's End, if you've a mind to?"

"See for yourself. But you must go back into the passage and watch from there."

"Why?"

"Please. It will be plain."

Charles looked annoyed, but we all did as Victoria asked. Inside the panelling, he stationed Ada and me at twin peepholes near the one he had first used.

Once we were hidden, Victoria faced a small writing table and uttered a few words that caused a wooden bowl full of roses to appear; simple stuff. Ah, but what followed was not so simple, for the color left her skin and she glowed with a pale orange radiance. I was so overcome by this unforeseen consequence of workaday enchantment that it took Ada to point out:

"She isn't moving; not at all."

"*Taranis' bolt!*" I cried. That is, I tried to. Ada's soft hand muffled my mouth.

"Hush. Watch."

I had to. Within moments, the door to the Queen's rooms opened and Lady Byron came in. She wore a smug look as she studied the immobilized Queen, then raised the pendant gem she wore on a chain around her neck to Victoria's lips. The orange glow subsided and the Queen came back to life.

"What foolishness have you been dabbling in, Your Majesty?" She spoke with sickly-sweet concern.

Victoria touched the roses. "I wanted to see whether anything could cheer me now."

"Oh? Is Your Majesty melancholy? And with the festive season so close! Dear me, that won't do. I have pressing business elsewhere—there is some minor trouble in the kitchens—but I will be back directly, and then the two of us can have a nice long chat."

Charles, Ada, and I jostled each other rudely in the dark passage, struggling to be first out the secret door as soon as Lady Byron left the room. "Now do you understand?" said the Queen. "So long as I am within these walls, any use of magic alarms Lady Byron and roots me to the spot until she uses that countercharm to free me. It is only when Lord Kitchener has me directly under his eye that the spell is temporarily lifted."

Recalling the vision Charles and I had shared of Victoria turning a sheet of paper into a hawk, I saw the truth of what she told us. Kitchener had been present.

"Hum." King Charles rested his chin on his hand, contemplating the situation. "Can't use your magic to escape, eh? Bad, very bad. And I suppose Lord K's guards know enough to stop you on sight if you try walking out like an ordinary woman? Yes, certainly." He subsided into disconnected mumblings.

"Why don't *you* just use your magic to transport her out of here?" I asked.

"You're not of the blood, are you, Dr. Weston? No, or you wouldn't ask. *The lesser vessel cannot move the greater.* That's from Bran's studies, before he took on the kingship of the isle. As the reigning sovereign of Britain, there is no greater vessel than Victoria—she may transport me, but never I her. Oh, I can work superficial magic on her—even destructive spells, if I grow weary of life—but transportation? No."

"Donne said even magic had limits. I see he was right—again." Charles and I returned to examining the problem of the Queen's imperative escape.

"Your Majesty," said Ada, "might I suggest the little princes' gambit?" With me to back her, she related how the boy princes in the Tower had left their prison unmolested as grown men. "Your uncle can use his superficial magic on you unhampered; he has just said so. And what are face and form but the thinnest of superficialities? Let him exchange our looks. You will walk out of here a free woman, wearing a borrowed skin. I will take your place here."

"But how will you escape?" The Queen was not the sort of lady to permit another to assume perils meant for herself.

Lady Lovelace did not look worried in the least. "I shall manage."

Before there was time for Victoria to utter another objection, King Charles worked his spells and the two women changed forms and places. "Oh!" exclaimed Victoria, in Ada's voice as well as Ada's doxy disguise.

Charles gave me back my rakehell's turn-out, then he and I each linked an arm with the Queen while Ada took up the very place and pose of the distraught Victoria that I had seen in Moll Scryer's pool. The future is malleable stuff. Ada said that she would meet us at the entrance to Mag Mell Park, and she sounded as if she meant it. I wondered what sort of new ending the poolside scene would have now.

Rejoin us she did, and we did not have to wait long. Charles returned the ladies and me to our original looks and dress. Ada's fighting gear was a bit the worse for wear. When asked about this, she said, "Mother and I had a nice long chat. When this is over, I must explain to her the dangers of forming bad associations. Now, Your Majesty, we have business at Baskerville Hall in Devonshire. Will you accompany us?"

"With all my heart. It feels so wonderful to be able to use my powers freely again!" She flung her arms wide like a bird taking wing, and Mag Mell Park's dark palisade snapped into the gritty shingle of the north Devon shore.

"This is not Baskerville Hall," I said. (Even when I am not playing the politic clown for Donne's sake, I sometimes come up with independent inanities.)

Victoria only looked fondly at me. "It is not polite to materialize a party of this size unexpectedly in a Briton's home. Baskerville Hall is just up that slope, beyond that stand of oak. I was Sir Hugo's guest for a rout there once. There is a stair farther along the tideline."

The sun was setting on the waves. A lighthouse's lonely tower stood black and ominous against the dying light. So many ships lost at sea, and most of them off this very coast! It was a sobering thought. We rounded the point, still looking for the beach stairs. We found something else entirely.

A fat old gentleman in a striped jersey and sailcloth trousers, his uncapped head bald as an egg, squatted on the shingle. He held a long, flexible line in his hands, its other end in the water, but his pose belonged more properly to the lakeside fisherman than the ocean caster. He was waiting, idly waiting. Then the line went taut, and he shouted happily before straightening up and dragging it in. At the other end was a medium-sized black bird wearing a tiny collar on its slender neck and bearing a fat fish in to shore.

"*There's* a useful beast for ye, gentles!" He held the fish high for our inspection. We were more interested in the strange bird. "Cormorant, ladies; fine bird. Touch 'im if ye like. I've trained 'im not to snap at anything without fins. Ye're none of ye merrymaids, are ye?" He winked slyly and stared at their concealed nether limbs.

Victoria, looking completely alien to this wild shore in her velvet and lace, stooped to caress the cormorant's sleek head. The bird tilted his head back under her petting and nudged her for more, like a spoiled cat.

"He seems to like ye," said the bird's owner. "Be ye from the hall?"

"No, but we are just going there," said Victoria. "Are you from there?"

"Bless the lady, no!" The fat man's laughter made his paunch jiggle and creased the shiny red skin of his hairless pate. "See that lighthouse there? That's my charge, 'tis. And it's soon enough I must go back to mind the beacon. Ah, we've had terrible calamities on this shore, gentles, and not the fault of the light!"

"The Brotherhood's ships." I thought of all those lives, lost, and a deep sadness fell upon me.

"Not *them*?" The beacon keeper looked truly shocked. "I saw the ships come in hard against the rocks farther up this coast—come in hard and true as if the captains had all gone mad and were heading the ships for the rocks a-purpose. But the Wise? They'd never do such a thing! Oh, awful, awful! Why, you'd think there was a line made fast to each prow, or a leash like I've got on my pet here, for it never mattered how the wind and time were a-running, the ships all pulled in to shore on a hawser-straight line."

"Magic," said Charles so low that I heard him only because we stood together. The beacon keeper had keen ears as well.

"Gods love ye, sir, and that's my idea on the matter exactly! Why, often there'd be fair sky and sun shining when the ships rode in, but a storm from nowhere blew behind 'em and a black cloud swept over 'em when they met the rocks. Don't think I don't go up the strand to look for survivors, or send to the hall for aid. But never a soul we found alive, and never a corpse in the sea. Look out there. Look north, gentles. That's where the Dark Ones dwell, across that channel. This evil business is all their doing."

"What!" I exclaimed. "Are you mad?"

"Sane as ye be, sir." The fat man looked at me suspiciously. "It's sense I'm speaking. What do we know of the Dark Ones, hey? Good King Bran 'imself pried their wicked secrets from 'em, to keep 'em from using such spells against honest folk. Left the little black buggers with a handful of sand and a heartful of hate for decent Britishers. But they've been up to no good, and now they're out to pay us back by murdering innocent seafarers. Ha! But just ye wait until our good Queen hears of this! She'll know how to treat the bare-arsed bastards. She'll ride her armies into their mountains and burn 'em out like the vermin they be! Picts! I'd rather have dragons."

I made a titanic effort to control my emotions. What good would it do to tell this swine that his notions of Picts were as flaccid as his—? Well, there were ladies present. One of the ladies—Victoria—spoke up.

"I am afraid you are mistaken, my good fellow," she said mildly.

" 'Bout the Picts? Hardly!"

"Have you ever seen one? Spoken to one?"

He grew truculent. "No. But *I know*!"

"I'm sure you think you do. As for your Queen, I must tell you that invading the Picts' lands is the farthest thing from her mind. King Bran the Blessed did not come by the Dark Ones' magic in *quite* the way you imagine. It was a theft, and somewhat of a betrayal of hospitality. That is the sad historical truth that his descendants must live with always. If your Queen ever does enter the Dark Ones' mountains, it will be to ask forgiveness, not to make war."

"Why? She scared of their magickings? Because if she is, she's daft—meaning no disrespect. They *talk* a fair show, but what's it boil down to? Jugglers' antics and cardsharps' tricks; no real magic at all!"

My darling met his hysterical allegations with a disarming smile. "I hope, then, to have the opportunity to measure their magic at first hand. I should love to meet the Dark Ones. And if I ever do have that chance, I must take you and your adorable cormorant with me. If their magic is true, perhaps you've been wrong about them on other counts as well. And if it is false, as you say, we shall need your cormorant to get food for us while we visit them."

The beacon keeper scratched his head. "I don't know what to make of ye, m'lady, I don't. Here, will ye trust an old salt far enough to come with me to my post? I've something I'd like to show ye, but there's not room for yer friends abovestairs at the light."

"I trust you with my honor," said the Queen, giving him her hand. With that, they vanished.

"What will the poor man think, being whisked off like that?" Ada asked when she stopped laughing. "Maybe he'll mistake the Queen for a vengeful Pict!"

"We must go after them!" I said, starting for the lighthouse, but Ada held me back.

"Her Majesty is able to take care of herself. She doesn't need us. I'm sure she can reach Baskerville Hall on her own." There was no room for argument. Ada and Charles hustled me away.

I did not see much of the outside of Baskerville Hall upon our arrival, evening already making the facade indistinct. Nor did I pay much attention to its architectural details on the following morning, for we all had our minds otherwise occupied. Therefore I apologize to the reader who cares for such things and can only say by way of excuse that I hope to return there someday and fill in this unfortunate lacuna in my narrative.

Inside the Hall, we presented ourselves to Sir Hugo Baskerville's man, Brendan, who conducted us from the foyer to a largish room where we found Donne in earnest conversation with the master of the house.

"Weston! Your Late Majesty, Lady Lovelace, do come in. Sir Hugo was just showing me his collection."

"Ugh!" cried Charles, and fled the room.

"Oh my!" Ada clapped her hands to her mouth and followed him. I stood there like a fool until I took a closer look at the collection in question.

The walls of the room were hung with a startling assortment of iron—iron in weapon form. There were arms of obvious Continental origin and some of primitive British make, as well as Roman antiquities. A viciously spiked morningstar was bracketed next to a starburst of curved swords, and a hollowed elephant's foot sported a bouquet of spears and pikestaffs. There were others: maces, knives, iron-headed arrows, crossbows and quarrels, a deadly lot.

"Can't blame 'em for rabbitin' off like that," said Sir Hugo. A man as chinless and twitchy-nosed as he was a fine one to go calling others rabbits. Limp blond hair clung to his narrow head in a way that reminded me of an egg slightly cracked at one end and leaking yolk. "Odd lot, Druids."

"But liberal enough to allow you to maintain your collection as a sort of minor provincial museum. I admit myself impressed," said Donne.

"Oh, there's a deal of iron in this part of the country, Mr. Donne," said Sir Hugo, patting the morningstar affectionately. "The Brits round here mined it and used it in the days before Bran was king, don't y'know. The Golden Brotherhood ain't ashamed of what's history; they just don't fancy iron much is all. Now then, how many of you will we be having for supper?"

"We are four, Sir Hugo: myself, Dr. Weston, the Countess of Lovelace, His Late Majesty, and Her Majesty."

"Not Vickie! Epona's luck, but it'll be good to see her again! Fine figger of a woman, ain't she?"

I was so taken aback by Sir Hugo's impertinent manner that I did not bother to ask Donne how he knew Victoria was with us. And why bother, after all? He always knew, and damned if I'd give him the satisfaction of showing off his mental gymnastics before this backcountry booby. "A bit more respect when you speak of the Queen," I said frostily.

"Respect? Gods above, and don't I have enough to do with loving Her sweet Majesty? Respect her too? 'Course I do. That goes without sayin'."

"Sir Hugo . . ." Donne took him aside and had a word with him. His expression when he looked back at me changed radically; he was a man impressed.

"That so? Rhiannon's tits! Dr. Weston, allow me to shake you by the hand." He did so, gave me a head-to-heels stare, then added, "Son of a bloody drunken tinker's bitch."

What a thing it is to have a reputation.

Her Majesty joined us for an excellent supper in the formal dining room of Baskerville Hall. Donne fidgeted through the meal. Time, as he explained more than once, was of the essence. This did not matter to Sir Hugo, who flatly refused to guide us to his family's burial mound.

"It's after sundown, y'see. Won't do to go mucking about in a burial mound after sundown, especially not this time of year. They've an old scarecrow of a Druid down in the village to mumble through the Sammain-eve rites tomorrow night and make sure our local dead stay nice and snug, but it don't pay to risk stirring 'em up more'n the old gaffer can handle."

To Donne's dismay, Victoria, Charles, and Ada all agreed with Sir Hugo. He might have overridden the young noble's protests and sought out the mound himself, with me, by night. But in the face of such uniform opposition, even Donne thought twice. He had condemned much of what the Druids did as mumbo-jumbo, but never once had I heard him scorn the ceremonies for the placation of the dead. Donne had lived long and seen much.

We were given comfortable rooms for the night. Mine overlooked the moorlands that began where the kitchen gardens ended, behind the hall. The moon was a day away from her fullest, and the silvery light turned the wild, rolling lands to a second sea. I stood by the window, my thoughts empty of anything but the contemplation of beauty. When I heard the door behind me open I said, "Come in, Donne. You must see this. It is lovely."

A dainty hand slipped into mine. "Yes, very lovely," said the Queen. I felt my face flush with embarrassment at my error. Fortunately the room was too dark for her to see it. She kissed my lips lightly. "You may not have your friend's ability to identify an unexpected visitor by his tread, but you have other talents." She kissed me again, this time more meaningly. "It has been too long a time apart from you, John."

We made up for all the wasted days that night. Her loving was by turns demanding and languid, playful and full of unspoken regrets. I have known many women in my life, but none to touch Victoria. Lovers are made by more than the touch of skin to skin. For some, the act of love is enough to satisfy—it is an end in itself. But for us it was only a bridge, the best poor means by which we might each slip into the other's soul. *You are my other self,* I said wordlessly, and I heard her respond in the same way, *And you are mine.*

When we slept at last, it was not for long. An evil dream invaded my rest, and Victoria had to shake me awake. "John, what is it? You were screaming." I shuddered like a man with fever and clung to her. How to explain? How to explain? Deirdre's ghost hung in a fading tissue of translucent bones and sea-tossed rags on the air. *Tell her of me, John. Tell your love of me!*

Did Victoria hear the silent taunting? I will never know. I only can say that something impelled me to tell her everything that night. I told her who I was and what I was. I spoke of Deirdre's curse and my exile. I did not stop talking until I caught myself repeating something I had told her once already, and she never offered a look or a word that betrayed how she felt about my revelations.

I sighed, feeling lighter in my mind. "Well?"

"Well what, John?"

"Well—well, I'm a Pict."

"I know. And a Pictish prince, moreover. You have told me that more than once. I might believe you are bragging."

"Doesn't it—change anything? Do you—mind?"

"You are a very silly man." She commenced playing with my moustache. "I shall be very much distressed if you shave this off, you know. *That* is something I should mind. But as for you being a Pict, you have always been one, ever since I first knew you. That is what you are, and what you are is what I love. I shall marry you, John, if *you* don't mind."

"Yes, but the Brotherhood—"

"The Brotherhood. The gods know what has become of the Brotherhood. But I tell you this, my dear: Were all of them massed in this room tonight, armed with the most potent and fearsome spells, I should defy them all and take you for my consort. Yes, and bed you before their eyes!"

"Please not."

"Poor John. Such a prude. Does *that* go with being born Pictish, or is it a nasty habit you picked up in Britain?" Her eyes looked dreamy in the moonlight. "How I wish the Duke of Wellington were here. A prince—even if of the Picts—is not exactly a common herbalist. A crown royal is nothing to be sneezed at."

Of course, I sneezed. "Please leave my moustache alone, dear heart."

"As you like it, John." Her hands found other occupation.

She was not in my bed when the morning's first faint light woke me, but I found her at breakfast with the others. Donne was having none of the tasty spread Sir Hugo had laid on for his regal guests, but paced back and forth by the tall windows and did what he could to ensure that none of us enjoyed a bite.

"At last," he snarled when the last napkin was folded. Sir Hugo helped Victoria into one of his own capes while the grooms brought round six fine horses.

"The family mound's not too far off," said Sir Hugo as we rode out. "Don't know what use it'll be to you. We Baskervilles haven't used it for years. Why, not since the Regency, don't y'know. Fearsome waste of time and money to open the passage and close it again, replant the turf and all, just to send Great-uncle Whatzis off to his bloody rest eternal. We've a perfectly nice little mausoleum now. Sure you don't fancy seeing that?"

"The mound will do nicely," said Donne.

"Oh." Sir Hugo looked disappointed. "Well, there she is. Looks like an old beached whale, don't she?"

The Baskerville burial mound did indeed resemble that monster of the deep, although a real whale would not have looked any more conspicuous. While the surrounding moorlands and bogs were by and large featureless in that area, the mound itself reared up to artificial heights meant only to call attention to itself. Donne slid from the saddle and made a quick circuit of the mound, then clambered to the top and down again.

"Completely covered with grass and other natural vegetation of the region, although there are one or two wildflowers growing on it that are not common in Devonshire. The earth was moved from some other site, and dormant seeds came with it. Your ancestors were not the kindest of masters, Sir Hugo."

This slur on his forebears did not trouble the vacant-faced Sir Hugo. "Bunch of heartless bastards, every one. Old Gor Baskerville raised this mound. Went off to Gaul and took him a bride there—not that the lady was willin'. Then he takes her name—that's why we're Baskervilles, pure Gaulish tommyrot—and thinks to impress her by having his thralls toss up this little pimple. Ladies ain't changed much. When I want to woo 'em, I send flowers, not tombstones. Lady Yolande de Baskerville put a bit of Gaulish seasoning in his soup one night and old Gor got an early look at the mound from the inside. But he'd got her with child, and the estate was nothing to dislike, so Yolande stayed on."

"Open it," said Donne.

"What? The mound?" Sir Hugo shook his head. "Out of the question. You think I want old Gor himself poppin' by tonight for a stirrup cup?"

"If you do not do as I say, Sir Hugo, you will find more than old Gor on your doorstep tonight. Open the mound."

"Can't. Have to send back to the hall. The passage's been filled in for ages! Ain't you listening? It'll take four stout fellows with spade and pick to clear out the earth, and then—"

"*Permission* to open it, then," said Donne. He motioned for Charles, Victoria, and Ada to step forward. "I would say the buried entrance is . . . here."

"That's where it is, right enough," said Sir Hugo. "Oh, by all means. Druids can be deuced handy for the heavy work, can't they?" He smiled, showing excellent teeth and an idiot's natural charm.

Ada stepped up to the mound. "I haven't much power, but I shall try." She held her arms out straight before her, palms upward, and bent them to perfect right angles in the traditional gesture of opening. Nothing happened.

"Sweetheart, may I?" King Charles doffed his plumed hat to Lady Lovelace, then together they repeated the gesture, powers joined; to no avail. "By all the skulls of Wizard Cromwell! I've worked harder magics without thinking. What knavery is this?"

Victoria looked worried. "Uncle, do you feel well?"

"Well enough! I've still magic and more in me, if that's your worry, girl. But the damned stuff won't *work!*"

"Let me."

"No," said Ada. "Let us all." They stood in a row and joined hands, Victoria the heart of the line. Small as she was, I felt the strength of her inborn sorcery emanating from that slight frame. What could stand against her? What, against three of the blood?

The mound stood. It stood untouched, unmoved, the frailest blade of grass on its flanks untroubled by as great a concentration of power as our group could assemble and still leave my own curse-bound magics out of it. I saw Victoria and Charles grow grim, bending and bending all their energies against the mound until either the earth or they should crack. And they might have been the ones to succumb in that useless battle had not poor Ada given a little moan and fallen senseless.

"Stop, damn you! Stop!" shouted Donne. He knelt beside Ada and took her up in his arms. "Can't you see you're powerless here? Think! Think! What is the one thing that can impede your magic?"

Charles rounded angrily on Sir Hugo. "Your triple-poxed array of deathmetal's to blame, sirrah! Either sink it in the sea within the hour or I'll tie the whole filthy mess round your scrawny neck and send you both to Nodens' chambers!"

Sir Hugo quailed, but I said, "How can it be, Your Majesty? We're farther from Baskerville Hall now than when we arrived on the beach. The Queen used magic then, unimpeded."

"Excellent, Weston!" exclaimed Donne. Ada stirred in his arms and looked at all of us, bewildered. "Fear nothing, Lady Lovelace. Your blood is indeed dilute. You could not take the strain of long spell-casting against a wall of iron." He set her on her feet and supported her until she was able to stand unaided. "Well, Sir Hugo, it looks as if we shall need to send for those spades and picks after all."

"If Brendan can get Willard and Arden to pitch in, we should have the entrance cleared in a day or so," Sir Hugo said cheerfully.

"A day!"

"Rather. Most of the mound's pure earth. The burial chambers go deep under the surface, and the raised part's just to keep out robbers and the like. Perhaps I can get more men up from the village—"

"But that will be too late, man!" Donne strode furiously back and forth the length of the mound. "This night is Sammain eve! If Lord Byron's riddle reveals nothing important, at least we must try our best to unravel it. He directed us here for a purpose; it is all we have. We have no other hope! Britain has none! There must be an answer, there must!" He paced out the mound faster and faster.

There was an answer, but not one I was willing to give. I took Victoria aside and said, "You know, Pictish magic's not quite the same as yours. We—we're closer to the earth and her three sisters. Iron is only a part of her, for us. I suppose I could—" I found it difficult to continue.

She understood. "You could open the mound, couldn't you? But that would break the geas, and if Lord Byron's clue is nothing—Belinus knows, the man was flighty enough before this business—then you will have brought disaster on yourself for no good cause."

"Not on myself. On those dearest to me."

"Then your geas is even harder to bear. Dear John, we shall find another way to open this mound. I will not have you hurt for what may be a wild goose chase." She embraced me.

Something burned me through the velvet of her dress, the tweed of my coat and jacket. In surprise, I pulled away.

"John?"

"Victoria—what are you wearing?" She seemed puzzled at my words—rightly so, I should think—until I clarified: "What are you wearing *there*?" I pointed to a spot between her breasts.

She slipped a finger under the high collar of her dress and pulled up a strand of carefully knotted wool on which a pale blue stone disk hung. Reverently I brought my hand up to it and felt again the constant, mighty heat I had perceived so clearly when Victoria took me in her arms.

"Where did you get this?"

"This? The lighthouse keeper—the one with the trained bird—he gave this to me. That was why he asked me to come to his rooms. He claimed he'd found it on the shore and that the village Druid said it was—forgive me, John—'filthy Pictish magic.' He said he'd turned his nose up at such nonsense, but since I defended the Dark Ones so staunchly, perhaps I ought to have it. It was a pretty, ladyish thing, he said, and the Picts hadn't any more *real* magic charms to their name than a—ahem—than a sow has balls. He was a *most* vulgar man. I liked him. What is it, John? Is it truly a Pictish charm? You are staring at it so strangely!"

Only the Teachers among us may possess it. Only those men and women who may hone the skills of the highest-born magicians. It is called an Earth's-eye. It can unlock many riddles, many doors. I remembered my own Teacher wearing his proudly. I asked to hold it, and felt the warmth of it. *Do you like it?* he asked me. *Oh, yes!* I stared at it with all the healthy greed of youth. *Then I shall give it to you someday. Perhaps when you ascend the throne that you're meant to have. A king is also a Teacher of sorts.* I looked downcast. *I won't be king for years. And I'm not sure I want to be.* He smiled at me then, for my Teacher loved me very dearly. *In that case, maybe I shall have to give it to you earlier; when you have need of it.* And the small shape-shifting sprite that always clung to my Teacher's robes put on a cat's guise and rubbed against my ankles.

I have the power to draw the magic from talismans without applying any magic of my own. Lord Kitchener's captive djinn had given recent proof that I had not forgotten how to do so.

I seized the Earth's-eye and ran past Victoria, past the others, past Donne himself to lay the amulet on the mound's grass-grown side. A fissure snaked up the slope, radiated outwards, swallowed the small blue stone. The unbarred gate to the Baskerville's ancient dead stood waiting.

"I say! That was a fine bit of work," Sir Hugo said to me. "How'd you manage it, old man? You of the blood? Been holdin' out on us?"

"No."

"Oh. Just askin'." As I turned away I heard him mutter, "Barmy enough to be the bloody Archdruid of all Britain."

Sir Hugo had the right to be the first one in; Donne followed. The passage was too narrow for us to enter any way other than single-file. Somehow I found myself at the end of the line, for I had stopped to recover the Earth's-eye from the churned soil. "It widens out some farther in," Sir Hugo called back to encourage us. "Just keep on my trail and don't get off into any side halls. Bunch of dead ends and minor shrines, y'see. Path's going to slope down a bit before we come to 'em."

Victoria was just ahead of me. "John," she whispered. "John, when you opened the mound, you—you didn't use your powers . . . did you?"

"Only the stone's. I am still as useless as ever."

"Not to me." She gave my hand a warm squeeze, then stumbled.

"Keep both hands on the walls, Victoria. The going's not of the evenest." I could just make out the dark curve of her head bobbing once in agreement.

The terrain did slope downwards, as Sir Hugo had warned us, then began to take a right-hand spiral. We had long since left the sunshine behind. The darkness and the underground damp were absolute, yet I would not have thought my Victoria prone to a lesser human's fears of the dark. To my surprise, she hung back and hugged me unexpectedly.

"Take me out of this place, John! Oh please, take me back to the surface!"

The others heard her cry and likewise stopped. "What is the matter, child?" asked King Charles, who had preceded her into the tunnel. Behind him Ada, Donne, and Sir Hugo struggled to see what was going on.

"This is an evil place! A wretchedly evil place! Oh, don't you feel it? Can't you tell?"

"Dear little one." King Charles dwarfed his tiny niece, even though the tunnel forced him to stoop. "I confess that this mound does give me a nasty chill in the bones, but we must go on."

"Why? Why?" Victoria pressed against me, her voice rising. "Because Lord Byron sent a message telling us to come? Lord Byron was with Kitchener! How do you know he is not with him still? This is a trap, I say! He will close us in here, and we shall all die! Damn him for a traitor, we are as good as dead!"

Ada wriggled around King Charles and calmly slapped the Queen full in the face. Victoria gasped, and the glow of her astonishment and wrath lit up the passageway with a firefly's brevity. "How *dare* you!"

"In my father's name, I dare," responded Ada. "I think I may truthfully say that if he was ever in Lord Kitchener's service, it was all my mother's doing. My father is a man who ought to have stuck to his verses; he was an innocent where people's ignobler instincts were concerned. If he meant to trap you, or any of us, he might have done so by surer and more convenient means than a complicated code that I alone could decypher. Your Majesty, somewhere in this mound is a large quantity of the one substance strong enough to interfere with the magic of the greatest vessel in the land—yourself. And as you have been born with the magic a part of you—brain and blood and bone—is it any wonder that you feel so frightened when such a great part of yourself is nullified?"

Gradually Victoria released me. "I apologize, Lady Lovelace, both to you and to your father."

"To his memory," said Ada quietly. We continued into the mound.

Victoria and Charles, being the most powerful Druids

among us, felt the icy spell of the buried iron more severely. I sensed the effort they both put out to cover the still-growing urge to panic and retreat. We had come to that part of the tunnel where the side chapels began, and I was wondering whether I should take Victoria's hand to give her courage when my own hand was seized.

Seized from behind and tugged with such force that I fell into one of the little alcoves. A rough hand tasting of salt clapped over my mouth before I could shout for help, and a heavy weight pressed down on my chest. The stink of old fish blew hot in my face, and my free hand clawed at a thick, furry pelt. Eyes like green witch-fires held me.

Visions of forgotten British demons said to haunt ancient grave mounds assailed me. What business had I, an alien, among the dead of this land? Then a tenuous light began to bloom from a tiny niche high up on the alcove wall.

"Let 'im gae, Tam, let 'im be."

How had such a small cat managed to pin me down so heavily? He sprang off my chest and retreated to a corner of the shrine, where he commenced a long wash-and-brush. I rolled over and saw the well-known face of Old Jim, the fishmonger.

"I know you now," I said.

"Took ye lang enow, laddie." He sat on the edge of the offering table, a tray of smelts in his lap. He threw one to the cat, who changed into a cormorant, caught the fish easily, and returned to cat-shape to enjoy it. "So, ye've solved it at last. Yer friend would've kenned in a moment what I be."

I stood and brushed the dirt from my clothes. "But why? Why have you come after me now? Did the Meet send you?"

Before he could answer, Donne's voice echoed loudly up the tunnel. "Weston! Weston, come here!" I startled and made for the alcove archway.

"At *his* beck and call, are ye?" My Teacher made no effort to hide his mockery. I wheeled about to confront him, for the first time in my life feeling anger towards the man who had forged my powers, taught me their mastery, and followed me into exile—the gods knew why.

"Yes; and he is at mine! Do you think for a moment that he would not come to me in my need, if I called him? Count the years I have been cast out from my own people, count them! And for what? Did the Meet ever ask for my testimony? Did you ever think to question Deirdre's death more closely? No, all you had to see was that I was the cause—and never mind that the death itself was Deirdre's own doing? *Whosoever brings about the death of another, let him suffer for it, according as the Meet shall devise.* Oh, I recall our wonderful law! Well, I'll tell you this much: Donne would never condemn me with my side of things unheard. Donne would never cast me out as you have done. Donne would stand by me, as I would stand by him. If I have gained one worthwhile lesson from my exile, it is this: The bonds of friendship and loyalty are stronger than the bonds of blood."

Old Jim rubbed his grizzled chin, and his features ran like wax into the likeness of Moll Scryer. Tam purred, then croaked loudly, the frog who had jumped into the center of the forest pool. *"Ye owe nothing to them that sent ye into exile."* I heard those selfsame words come back again, in the old woman's voice. *"Nothing, nothing do ye owe the Dark Ones!"* Moll Scryer cackled and was Old Jim. "But ye kept faith wi' yer folk, lad. E'en when ye risked much t' do it. Ye ne'er betrayed us, though ye hated us e'er so. Gae ye t' yer friend, Johnnie—gin that's the name ye wish. If 'twas Donne as taught ye t' be leal an' true, he shanna be forgot when t' reckoning time comes."

Donne called me again, more urgently. I had no time to puzzle over my Teacher's words or presence. I ran as fast as possible, my hands guiding me, until a great light ahead illuminated my way and I emerged in the central room of the Baskervilles' barrow.

I shielded my eyes from the light until they might adjust themselves. While I stood half-blind, I heard Donne say, "Weston, I trust that you still have that blue gewgaw you used so effectively to open the mound?" I fumbled for it in my pocket and held it out. "Excellent." It was snatched from my grasp just as I was at last able to see my surroundings.

I stood as a man stunned. Donne and the others were massed at one end of an underground chamber that stretched away for an untold distance. Torches set beneath numerous air vents to the surface made it bright, but perhaps that brightness was in part due to the shining whiteness of the Druids' robes. Held to the granite walls by manacles of deathmetal, the Golden Brotherhood of Britain gazed in disbelieving silence at their rescuers.

Donne touched the Earth's-eye pendant to the fetters of the Druid nearest him and they fell away.

CHAPTER FIFTEEN

The Assistance Which May Perhaps Someday Be Described

Baskerville Hall was chaos and pandemonium. The corridors clattered with the running footsteps of servants, village folk, acolytes, Druids, and myself. From the moment Donne had freed the last of Lord Kitchener's captives, all had been madness. Who would know that the underground chambers of Sir Hugo's ancestral mound could hold so many of the Wise? Even discounting those few who had made unfortunate and stubborn attempts at resistance, and thus perished in captivity, the nearly full complement of Britain's Golden Brotherhood was a large number with which to conjure.

"You there! Weston! Where's that cauldron?"

I snapped to a halt, my arms weighed down with two osier baskets crammed with every bit of edged cutlery the Baskerville kitchens could provide. The garden sheds and greenhouses had been also plundered of anything resembling a sickle or usable for the slitting of a cow's throat. I was expected to relay my loads to the hastily cleared ceremonial site in the midst of Sir Hugo's small forest preserve, but one does not plead previous commitments when the Iron Duke calls. I dropped the baskets, spilling knives, and popped into the "best" parlor, which the Archdruid had taken over as his improvised headquarters. Two other high-ranking Druids flanked him where he stood, poring over a scribbled parchment sketch map of the immediate region. Blasphemous comparison or not, he reminded me of a painting of Julius Caesar and his generals planning a campaign, which I had seen when Donne and I toured Rome.

"Empty-handed?" He still did not like me very much, although his imprisonment and subsequent liberation had mellowed him somewhat on the subject of Donne.

"Sir Hugo's laundress says you're welcome to her boiling copper, but it's full of clothes right now. You can have it when she's done."

"Sucelus! And didn't you explain to her that this is Sammain eve? Where is the old crone? I'll send one of the acolytes to dump her blasted washing and fetch that copper now!"

"Pick a burly one for the job, your grace. It seldom does to anger a British washerwoman. The ladle she uses to stir the linens is rather formidable."

"Thank you for your counsel," said the Duke. And he went so far as to smile.

I gathered up the scattered knives and sprinted to the main door of the hall, where a line of Sir Hugo's grooms sat mounted on swift horses, each waiting only to be tossed some parcel or basket and be off to where the rest of the Wise had congregated. Earlier that day the distant grove had resounded with the chunking sound of axeblades felling venerable trees, then had been filled with the grunts of yoked oxen, uprooting the stumps, and the shouts of their harried drivers. Before this day was done, these same oxen would receive a strange reward for their labors, dying under the Druids' knives in sacrifice. Thick-armed yeomen from all the countryside around labored long to cut the trunks down to logs and kindling, laying a Sammain bonfire such as Britain had never seen. I passed the baskets of knives to the first groom in line and gave his steed a slap on the rump for luck. As he galloped off, I trailed back into the house.

From the kitchen end of the hall came the noise of argument and struggle. Most likely the Duke of Wellington had sent his acolyte after the copper-cum-cauldron, and that luckless fellow was learning firsthand much of the temper of honest laundresses when disturbed in midwash. While I stood there, privately pitying the unknown victim, I was almost trampled by three priestesses, going full tilt, their arms overflowing with herbs from the back gardens. One of them stumbled slightly over my foot.

"Stupid! Get out of our way!" she barked at me. So much for courtesy. So much for gratitude. So much for John H. Weston, M.D., lifting another finger to help that frantic crew.

How weary I was! I felt that I had done enough for the cause, running here and there, fetching and carrying like a booby. Donne had done nothing since the release of the Druids but stand aloof, dispassionately explaining our god-sent presence for Wellington's benefit. I wondered whether he was going to put in a word on my behalf—who had opened the mound, after all, and who had provided the device to unlock the Druids' fetters?—but I never got the chance to overhear. I was an able body, and all able bodies were drafted at once to race the declining sun, making sure all was ready for the Sammain-eve ritual.

"Weston! Hey, Johnnie! In here!"

I had slumped against the corridor wall, the better to sulk and reflect upon ingratitude. Now a familiar voice hailed me through a crack in the woodwork that tilted open unexpectedly behind me. I fell in upon Sir Hugo, who, with open arms and brimming glass, welcomed me into a cozy little hideaway study. Winking conspiratorially, he clicked the door closed and motioned me to take a chair. Booted feet up on Sir Hugo's escritoire, Lord Byron greeted me with a discreet huzzah.

"Johnnie! At last you're here. This is exquisite brandy Sir Hugo's laid on, exquisite. You look like all the shades of Annwn. Have a tot. Oh, and do accept my thanks. I have not had the chance to show my gratitude properly yet, but I shall do so once I recover my health."

If complexion were any gauge of health, Lord Byron was growing more robust by the sip. I had a taste myself, and felt remanned enough to play the censor. I wagged my finger at the refugees and said, "How long have you two been hiding in here?"

"How long has the Iron Duke been puttin' honest folk t' hard work?" giggled Sir Hugo.

"Disgraceful!"

"Balls." Sir Hugo finished his glass and poured another. "Good administration, that's what I'm cut out for. Got him the people for the work, didn't I? And who said, 'Go right ahead, your grace, and chop down that lovely little stand of trees that's the only fair huntin' for miles about'? Damned decent of me."

I had some more brandy and decided that any man possessed of such a cellar must indeed be of high moral character, damned decent, and favored of the gods. Always the proper guest, I considerately changed the subject. "It looks as if we shall be done in time, gentlemen."

"Well, that's a relief," said Sir Hugo. "More I hear of what might've happened this night, less I like it. It don't do t' have the dead runnin' about. Mollocks up things too much. I'm a peaceable man, Johnnie—don't mind if I call you Johnnie, eh? Call me Hugh—and I say there's a place for everything and everything in its place. Fancy having old Gor in the front parlor after all these years! No, that won't do. Have another pour."

I had another pour. As the brandy warmed my soul, the bliss of isolation from the brouhaha beyond the wall grew into a deep and enduring affection for Lord Byron and Sir Hugo—or Geordie and Hugh, staunch fellows, friends of my bosom forever, blood brothers, companions unto death! (Well, it was *very* good brandy.) In this amiable mood I said, "When Sammain's done, I want you all to come round to 221B, Baker Street, and we'll have a right old time. Bring the family, too. Someone's got to eat the scones. Bring all your lovely families."

"Can't," said Sir Hugo. "Haven't got one, beyond the spare nephew." This realization undid the poor man, and he began to snuffle loudly.

This was too much for dear, dear Geordie, a prince among men. He and I took turns patting Hugh on the back and refilling his glass—and our own, to save time. "Don't take on so, old man. Family's not all it's made to be. I've a wife I should let you have for cartage fees alone!"

I took umbrage. "Sir, your wife may be a bitch, but I will not stand here and let you insult the mother of that paragon among women, Lady Lovelace."

"Parawho? No, don't speak of her, Johnnie, pray don't! She has abandoned me, the heartless girl. Did you not see with what outbursts of affection she greeted me when you first discovered us all locked away in that mound? 'Oh Father, Father! Thank all the gods,' and so forth. You couldn't pry her off me. A dear child. But where is she now? Now, when a father needs the comforting presence of his daughter to smooth his brow and hold his hand after that terrible ordeal? Where, where is my darling Ada now? Bereft, I stand upon the shore where late the dancing waters gleamed. Mine eyes seek out the—the—Hmm. Got a pen about, Hugh? I think I'm on to something."

Lord Byron commenced rummaging through Sir Hugo's escritoire, but I asked, "Yes, where *is* she? I've been all over Baskerville Hall seven or eight times, and haven't seen a trace of her. Or the Queen."

"Gods save her!" cried Lord Byron, seizing his glass in an access of patriotism. We echoed, and drank.

"Or King Charles," said Sir Hugo, returning to the matter. "Won't see 'em, either. What the Wise are doing here is all well and good for the rest of Britain, but the royal dead of the isle can only be laid to rest this night by one of their own blood. The Queen's off to Stonehenge to perform the rites, as usual, and His Late Majesty's gone with her to help. Wouldn't be surprised if Lady Lovelace trailed along, and your friend Donne. Damned inconvenient. Could've used him. There's been a crime."

"A crime? A serious one? Of what sort?"

Sir Hugo stared at the dregs in his glass and uttered a muted belch. "Serious enough, I swear, what with that Kitchener fellow still on the loose. Bloody well storin' all that cursed deathmetal in *my* family mound—and gods alone know what he's done with the family! I've a mind t' offer my services t' the Iron Duke and run the bastard to ground like a plaguey fox, once Sammain's seen to. Aye, there's nothing like a nice ride t' the hounds near Baskerville Hall. It's an experience you won't soon forget."

"The crime, Hugh?" I suggested.

"Robbery!" he said, waving his empty glass aloft. Then he sank into an abrupt and noisy slumber.

"Can't hold his liquor. Typical squire type," Lord Byron remarked, up to his ankles in Sir Hugo's private papers as he continued his search for the elusive pen. "Never mind it, Johnnie. You're not the detective. We'll wait until Donne returns and put him on the scent."

"On *what* scent?"

"Here, no need to take that stuffy attitude, old man."

"Geordie, I am sick unto death of being thrust into Donne's shadow. I realize I have not his genius, but the more basic reaches of the art of detection are not beyond me. Now, what has been stolen? The silver? It's probably off at the grove, with every other knife in the house. Jewelry? I shall have the Archdruid himself locate it if one of the locals has turned lightfingered. What is missing?"

"Weapons," said Lord Byron. Before I could comment, he added, "And they're *not* on their way to the grove, that much I can guarantee. No Druid here would touch 'em. Part of Hugh's collection's gone wandering—not many pieces, true, but why? Who'd want all that deathmetal? None of the locals, I can vouch for that. Iron's borrowed trouble, especially with a man like the Iron Duke in the neighborhood. The old gent probably came by that delicate appellation because the other Druids'd as lief deal with deathmetal as with him!"

There come moments when the brain ought not function well, but does. A horrid thought came to me, which no amount of brandy could banish, and I felt bound to ask those few questions which would confirm or deny a conclusion I dearly hoped was wrong.

"And you say Donne is—not available?"

"I know for a fact he's not available. I am the cause of his absence. It does no good to go to ground when a fellow like Donne is about. He picked the catch to this little snuggery, surprised Hugo and me, and dragged me off several hours ago."

"Whatever for?"

Lord Byron folded his arms across his chest, and a puckish smile curved his lips. "To quote the man himself, 'You've served Britain handsomely by fathering a woman of Lady Lovelace's achievements, sir, but it is time you did something more. I require immediate transportation to Mabdown. No, don't cudgel your brains. It is a small, nondescript village in Wiltshire. Even your puny powers should be enough to accommodate me.' He doesn't mince words, your friend Donne."

"No, he's not known for diplomacy. Mabdown . . ." I frowned.

"I wager he'd advise you not to cudgel *your* brains about it either, Johnnie. He showed it to me on a map and asked to be transported to the downs just outside the village. Less chance of landing in someone's herb patch that way. I did as he asked, and no one was more surprised than I when my rusty mite of magic did indeed prove sufficient for the spell. At least I *think* it was enough. For all I know, poor Donne is floundering in the River Avon right now. I may have over-or undershot the mark."

Slowly I voiced a portion of my fears. "Stonehenge is in Wiltshire, on the downs. And I recall a small village within walking distance of the stones, although I never learned its name. If Donne asked to be sent anywhere this night, it must be for some vital reason. Could anything be more important than the Queen's rites?" I sought out the brandy decanter for moral support, and found it was empty. "But if he has gone to be with the Queen, why did he not depart Baskerville Hall when she did?"

Lord Byron made that Gallic gesture denoting that one does not know and furthermore does not care. "He might've said he wanted to be sent to Stonehenge proper, then. It would've been an easier target. Magic draws magic. And I have since learned, rather painfully, that countermagic will also attract great sources of power. The deathmetal Lord Kitchener buried in the mound pulled in the Druids' ships like a magnet. Power calls to power, either positive or negative. You constantly attribute portentous motives to Brihtric Donne. Maybe your friend simply wishes to surprise my daughter once the spells are done, and does not wish to intrude on the Queen's Sammain rites. He is a fine detective, but in matters of the heart, we poets can also make deductions to astound the layman."

"You know where Ada is? But earlier you said—"

"All that carrying on I was doing about Ada was for Hugh's benefit. He's always more generous with the best brandy when his sympathy's aroused. I saw my girl take off with Her Majesty and the former King hours and hours ago. Donne was right there, saying ta-ta to them all, polite as you please. Yes, a nice surprise to turn up later, when the rites are done and the need-fire's been lit; that's when the fun begins."

"I would not call laying the dead to rest *fun*."

"The dead," said Geordie, "are not the only ones who will be— Well, Sammain's not Beltaine, but more than a few pairs of lovers have declared one bonfire as good as another for keeping warm."

"The relations between Donne and your daughter are professional." I tried to sound righteous, on Donne's behalf. I did not do it well.

"So they are," said Lord Byron. "And I'm a virgin. Donne had me transport an outsize wicker hamper to Mabdown with him. How many consulting detectives go picnicking with their clients after dark?"

"Few enough. Geordie, you are a sporting man. I'll wager you whatever you like at your own odds that when we find Donne, we shall find that his hamper conceals the missing pieces from Hugh's collection."

"Is that so? A very tempting bet. Why on earth would he make off with that trash?"

"Because it is deathmetal, or mostly, and that is the one substance creatures of magic—even Eastern lore—cannot abide."

"Eastern— Kitchener?"

"The same. We have freed the Brotherhood, but they are more than occupied tonight, while the Queen herself will be poorly guarded. Yes, she has her power, and King Charles is no weakling—even your daughter has some strength of magic upon which to draw. But Kitchener commands more. He meant to have her tonight, and what is there to stop him in the attempt? We have thwarted him, but not defeated him."

Lord Byron's lips were pale. "Donne is only one man. Even armed, he has no magic. And I have seen what Kitchener can do! Gods, Johnnie, this is frightful! Ah, the Queen, the Queen!"

"All the more reason for us to reach her. Donne is only one man, as you say, but he has the determination of a dozen men, and he is a loyal Briton. He would die for Her Majesty. Alone against Kitchener's forces, he has little chance, but with us at his side—"

"How, Johnnie, *how?* The sun must be almost down by now. We cannot possibly reach Stonehenge in time."

"Why not? You transported Donne there—or as good as there. Why can't you transport us?"

Lord Byron sat heavily in the chair beside Hugh's escritoire, his eyes shut. "I wish that were so. I wish I had the powers of Bran himself tonight. Don't you see, Johnnie? I am a spent man. I never had much magic to begin with, and what I have, I use sparingly and clumsily. Even so, tonight the Iron Duke himself has need of every man with one touch of Druid's blood in his lineage. All the fires of Britain are extinguished on Sammain eve, and the need-fire we kindle in the clearing at moonrise must bear the magic to relight every hearth in the land. I sent Donne off as a favor, for I deeply owe him one in exchange for freeing me from the mound. More than that much magic I cannot spare."

"Damn you, and do you owe the Queen nothing? And your own child?" I yanked him roughly to his feet and worried him like a terrier with a rat's scruff in its jaws. "*I* opened the mound! *I* laid the Earth's-eye down! *I* loaned it to Donne, and with it he released you from your shackles. And stole the praise for it! It is *me* to whom you owe a debt, not Donne."

In my anger, I had forgotten that Byron was not a man to take such brusque handling kindly. Something white and hard flashed in on me from the left, and the world cracked open in a shower of spangles. I landed in Sir Hugo's lap before hitting the floor. He grunted and went back to sleep.

"Sorry," said Lord Byron, who was not. He helped me up and studied his handiwork. "That'll go all black and blue. Can't say you didn't earn it. Now look, I'll tell the Iron Duke what you suspect, but none of his crew'll be able to do anything about it until our own rites here are done. I can't help you, no matter what it turns out I owe you, and that's that. But Johnnie . . . whatever or whoever opened the mound and freed us was a source of power. If it was yours—if it was you—why can't you use it to reach Stonehenge as well?"

Why . . .

"Excuse me. There is something to which I must attend." If I sounded cold, I had good reason. The left side of my face was pulsing with pain, though I bore Byron no ill will for what he had done. He was right, I had deserved it, and his blow had sobered me in more ways than one. No, the formality in my voice was solely due to the sudden, urgent need to be alone. I slipped from the secret room and sought the solitude of the Baskerville Hall gardens.

The sun was down, but a few streaks of dying light still made the sky beautiful. An early star hung with quiet loveliness in the branches of a pear tree. In the hush of coming night, many ghosts glided through the softly whispering leaves. My thoughts turned to my friend.

"You are sad tonight, Weston." Words from years ago, when Donne and I had wandered through the magicless lands of the Continent, and borne witness to the wonders ordinary men might create. The abandoned temples of foreign gods sheltered a tribe of Roman cats, indifferent to the splendors of the Caesars. *"These ruins often make men introspective. You are thinking of your home."*

"I have no home."

He rested his hand on my shoulder. Only I could read more in his thin smile than another might perceive. *"There you are wrong. A man's true home is not the structure which shelters him from the elements, nor the land on which his house stands, nor even the limits of a kingdom. You have been unjustly cast out of your kingdom, but your home is here."* He touched his heart almost casually. *"And I assure you, no power of earth or heaven shall ever dispossess you of it, my good friend, not while I live."*

I knelt at the foot of the pear tree where a patch of wild heal-all grew. The deep purple flowers were like the mouths of tiny dragons. If I were to touch it, I knew that I would feel again the tides of earth and life flowing upwards from hungry root to stalk to blossom. Every growing thing on the world's surface was a channel to draw the deep magic up from darkness to light, living reins that bridled creation itself. For the right mage privy to Pictish magic it would only take the word and the will of a moment to harness more power than Bran and all his issue ever dreamed.

I am John H. Weston, M.D.: *Magister Demonii*, Master of Demons, as Donne himself once titled me; Donne, who had gone forth boldly to defend his Queen, and my beloved. Could I do any less, or was I truly only another man's feeble shadow? He had not even told me his intentions. Why should he? The Weston he knew was ever one to shy away from independent action. And what would happen to me if he were unable to say, *Weston, do this; do that*? He would not risk my life as easily as he ventured his own.

Was it Deirdre's geas I feared, or something more? Ordinary men as well as exiled princes have been known to take refuge from the great summons of life. Some die while in midflight. Some stop in time and recognize that there is a point when a man must cease to run away. With the silver evening star my only witness, I took up the reins of magic again, took them up by the roots of a humble heal-all plant.

My bones shook within me as all the old powers came rushing back into my body. The sky itself veered and sent the stars skidding. I gasped for breath, drowning in the fifth element to which I had been born and which I had denied for far too long. Then, abruptly, it was over. I was a part of the earthmagic that was, in turn, a part of me. Standing, my arms stretched a passing breeze into wings that lifted me high above the rooftree of Baskerville Hall. In the upper reaches of the night sky I took the wind as my horse and rode for Stonehenge.

Like Donne, I did not choose to arrive exactly on the site itself. There was the chance that all was well. My unexplained presence would only disrupt the most solemn rituals. The moon was not yet up. Dark slabs blotted over the snowy sweep of Caer Gwydion's stars when I alighted on the downs, and the glow of Victoria's need-fire was little more than a rushlight at that distance. I determined to approach as discreetly as possible, and so poured my substance into the chalky ground itself.

When my Teacher had first showed me how to swim through the layers of earth as easily as an otter dives into a mountain stream, I had been afraid. Then the wonder of seeing the world's secrets plain before my eyes—eyes that had become all of me—grew intoxicating. I would plunge into the ground on any pretext, sharpening my rough talents until there was no man of my race who could equal me.

For a master of Pictish magic, any one physical element can be made to assume the properties of any of the other three. For me, air might grow firm as earth beneath my feet, earth yield up the burning qualities of fire. To move through the Wiltshire earth was like walking through water. I made slow, graceful progress, coming up inside one of the standing stones. My eyes could see through the alien rock, though what I saw was slightly blurred and dimmed. I breathed with the stone sheathing me and waited.

Victoria was there, inside the circle, and King Charles, and Ada. I did not see Donne, but if Byron's transportation spell had worked, it might be that my friend was even now trudging up to the ring from Mabdown, or else quietly biding his time, watching and waiting in the dark, like me.

My love had kindled her small fire close to the foot of a block of stone sunk at its full length into the ground. A small, shabby cauldron was suspended above the flames by no means of visible support. King Charles had not put off his antiquated finery, but Victoria and Ada were both robed in white, golden fillets binding back their hair. Ada held a silver bowl from which Victoria took bits of vegetation with which she fed the seething pot. King Charles guarded a pile of kindling sticks, culled no doubt from the same stand of trees where "Moll Scryer" had given me a nightmare vision. He fed these one by one to the fire.

"Done," said Victoria. Her arms fell wearily to her sides.

"All but the moonwaters," said Charles.

"Here they are." Ada unstrapped a leather flask from her belt. "I will pour them out when necessary."

Victoria looked right at the slab in which I was hidden. Her eyes followed the line of the stone upwards, to the heavy lintel topping it and its neighbor, balanced there by unknown hands. "But that is all that needs doing. We have finished in plenty of time. See, the moon herself is not more than a span above the horizon. Oh, what a relief! Ada, scour the bowl and pour out the moonwaters." Ada knelt and filled the silver bowl from her flask. Victoria spoke next to Charles. "Uncle, will you begin our invocations?"

"*Uncle?*"

Even wrapped in stone, that voice made me tremble with rage and unwilling fear. Lord Kitchener stepped from the lee of a bluestone, and Morganwg came after. "I hope, sir, to have the pleasure of also being on such affectionately familiar terms with you, after the Queen and I are wed. You are one of the few British monarchs I ever sincerely admired."

"I take that as no compliment, you plague-faced son of a

whore!" The late King's hand lit on the hilt of his bronze sword. "Get you gone! You disturb our ceremonies."

Lord Kitchener cut a sharp, military bow. "At your pleasure, sir. I shall be off as soon as I have your niece's word of marriage. We are as good as betrothed."

"As good as damned!" Victoria's blue eyes sparkled. "You may go hang, and soon, and I'll provide the rope for it before I'll think of marrying you. Your plans are undone. The Wise are free, and now they know the face of their enemy. You had better flee Britain while you can. I would not care to be in your skin when the Golden Brotherhood hunt you down."

"And you will of course spearhead the chase? What do you think of such a wife, Morganwg? Shall I still accept her?"

Donne's nemesis chuckled at a private joke. His thin arms hugged a small casket tightly against his chest, and the firelight picked out flashes of gold from the catch and fittings as he shook with contained laughter.

"Who is that creature?" King Charles asked. "You'll need better allies than that, if you mean to escape with a whole skin. And it shan't be left unpierced if I've a say in the matter." He stepped forward, already drawing the sword.

Kitchener stood his ground and smiled. "You have no say. I mean to rule Britain, with or without the Queen's consent. But she would do better to submit to me. Far better. It is a poor strategist who reveals all his allies at the first sortie." He touched the bluestone which had sheltered him.

The black wings unfolded one by one, the unnatural feathers scraping protests from the neighboring stones. A countenance of sheerest evil leered at the three celebrants, and I understood how it was that poor old Isaacs had perished of fright when he saw the afrit's face before him.

King Charles' sword slid from its scabbard before Victoria or Ada—or I—could react. The bronze glowed with red-and-silver twists of energy that only sorcery could evoke. The afrit snarled murderously, livid lips curled back from ghastly fangs, and spread its wings to take the air, meaning a hawk's death-dive against the defiant King. Charles did not wait for that. He thrust himself right for the monster's belly, indifferent to the taloned paws and eagle's feet that scored and maimed his flesh. The ensorcelled blade flashed downwards. The afrit's shriek prickled across my brain until mercifully cut off by King Charles' second, fatal, slash.

He stood above the fallen nightmare, his own blood streaming, but he grinned. "You—" he began, addressing Kitchener. Whatever he meant to say, boast or threat, we never were to know. A fist of blackness hurled itself at him from the stars, crushing him to the earth. His sword flew from his hand and clattered to Kitchener's feet while the second afrit tore Charles open with a stroke of its claws and feasted.

"It does not do to kill their mates," said Lord Kitchener. "They pair, as we do, Your Majesty. See, even while they await my next command, they roost together." A wave of his hand caused the Queen's need-fire to flare up, its light filling the shadowy precinct of the monoliths. Every lintel stone hosted at least a brace of the winged horrors, some were the perches for more. "Nature and supranature both deplore your single state. Will you learn from this to accept my suit?" He indicated the pitiful remains of the former King. Morganwg laughed more coarsely. The afrit ceased its gorging and tried to take up the corpse, intending to fly off and finish its ungodly meal in privacy.

Like thought, Victoria hurled her priestess' dagger at the fiend. It lodged at the juncture of the black wings, then burst into white-hot energy that enveloped and consumed both afrit and prey. "There is my answer!" Victoria shouted. Her eyes were dry. If there was to be a later, that was when she would weep for her uncle. The obsidian dagger was back in her hand. Ada had hers likewise at the ready.

Now, I thought. I stepped from the stone.

I stepped into fire. All around me the rock burned, grey-and-black-and-cyan torment. I tried to move, and the smallest effort brought a pain beyond telling. I howled with it like a wild dog, howled until I thought my head would split from the echoes. Then I felt the touch of something cold across my lips, a soothing relief from that most dreadful agony, and my heart blessed the source.

Thank you, John. Did you ever dream to bless me? Deirdre's skull pressed sea-washed cool bone against my cheek. Her fleshless fingers still lay on my lips. I could not answer, I could not move, so great was the terror possessing me that I might bring back the anguish of the stone's unflaming fires.

You have brought this on yourself, sweet Johnnie. Like so many of the errors in your life. You have dared to take back your magic, and what could I do but let my curse come home? Oh, it's a strong ill-wishing, John! It took much from my spirit to bring it true. Alas, once it has run, I will be dispersed to void and nothingness. You will not see me again. But I shall have the satisfaction of knowing that one you deeply love shall suffer for your boldness. You shall not move from this stone until the curse has claimed its due. Then use your magic as it suits you, Johnnie, but every spell you cast will be an elf-shot in your heart, recalling the memory of one who dies tonight because of you!

The skull moved until I was staring into its empty eyesockets, and through these, through the stone holding me, until I could again see my beloved. My pain and Deirdre's taunting had taken place in a special part of time. Outside the stone, only moments had passed.

"Why will you be so stubborn?" Kitchener asked. "You are no match for my forces. My offer is not so bad as all that. You need the Rules again, or else it will be your blood the Wise will take to heal this land. But if you marry me, we shall use the Rules together, and never more will you be troubled by the Brotherhood. Your powers and mine united will breed a race of sorcerers who will extend the boundaries of Bran's enchantments beyond the sea, until first the Continent, then the East, and finally all the lands of the earth will answer to us and our descendants. Were you not born to rule, Victoria? I was born the same."

"You were born to devour, not to rule! If it takes my life to save Britain, then so be it. For I love this land, and I understand the demands of love. That is something you will never know," said the Queen. "That is why I know that even without the Rules, somehow I will find the strength to defeat you and your swarms of monsters. I will, for I must."

"And I," said Ada. She threw her dagger at Lord Kitchener's unprotected heart without warning.

Morganwg bounded into the dagger's path, the casket up to deflect the blade. When the two objects came together, there was a loud report and the casket fell. Its lid sprang open, releasing a being whose looks I had seen too often, but never like this. Never had the goddess Kali come forth in her full majesty and size, the all-devouring horror of annihilation incarnate: Kali the destroyer, the Black Mother, the drinker of blood, of life, of light. Even the afrits quailed and huddled together on their perches before her.

"You are hers from the moment you deny me again," said Kitchener. "With your blood, she will drink the blood of Britain, and grant me kingship of the land in return for this great sacrifice. But I had rather not have it so. To sacrifice one to Kali—and such a momentous one as the blood of a Queen!—means that I must be indebted to her forever. Give me dominion over the Rules, Victoria! Open their secrets to me."

Victoria stood straight-backed and proud. Not a trace of softness was left in her. She was sword-wielder, spell-maker, Lady of Britain. It would take more than a threat of death to make her back down now. Nonetheless, her hands tightened on her drawn dagger and shook ever so slightly. She did not want to die, nor bring the death of Britain with her blood. Kali's face, dark red and agape with blood-greed, loomed above the tiny need-fire, waiting for the Queen to reply.

She shook her head.

"Then you shall see your precious Rules once before you die," said Kitchener. "And you will go to your death knowing how near your hands they were." A sphere of purple light rose from the palm of his left hand and floated like a soap bubble to alight on the sunken slab—the so-called stone of sacrifice. The rock heaved upwards, sending dust and clods of earth flying. In the blackness revealed beneath, a white fire glowed. In the heart of the blaze the Rules Britannia waited, untouched by Kitchener, and untouchable without the aid of one born to use them.

Victoria gave a high-pitched cry of surprise and joy before flinging herself at the pit's treasure. Kali's huge foot stamped down, cold golden bangles clashing, barring the tiny Queen. Victoria fell back, but Ada caught and steadied her.

"You had your creatures steal them, but you can never use them!" It was Ada who flung the taunt in Kitchener's face. "Even if I die tonight, I will have that much satisfaction."

"Oh no, Lady Lovelace," said Morganwg, sidling nearer to his grim master. "You will find very little satisfaction in death. You see, you are reserved for me."

Lord Kitchener's gaze rose lazily to the ranks of afrits clawing the lintel stones. "Take them."

Helpless! Helpless! There is no despair to match what I felt as I watched the abominable creatures unfurl their glittering wings and ascend the night sky, ready to swoop down on the women and hold them fast. What hope had they left, once the afrits had them pinioned? What hope but that death might come swiftly? But it would not. I could read that much in every line of Kitchener's face, of Morganwg's.

Not Kali herself looked half so monstrous as that unholy pair. She would kill and drink blood because that was the essence of her godhead, but they were men. They were supposed to be men.

The afrits circled above, then their leader dived.

Victoria leaped to meet his plunge with the point of her dagger, Ada shielding her back. She managed to score the creature's ebon flesh, and the afrit soared up, thick blood dripping, to make another attack. But as his birdlike call directed another to dive while he recovered, they were cut off in a blood-curdling screech. The razored wings crumpled and he fell.

There was no time to measure the confusion that ensued. Bereft of their leader, the remaining afrits attacked the women without plan or direction. And one by one, as the air filled with the discord of their harsh cries and thrashing wings, their leader's fate overtook them. One by one they shrieked and plummeted to earth, clawed legs curled tight against their bellies, the shafts of arrows protruding from their breasts.

Arrows! The circle of Stonehenge was thick with their flight. Lord Kitchener clapped a shielding spell around himself as soon as he saw what was happening. Kali herself was grazed by a dart, and her howl made the rock around me creak and splinter. She stamped her feet in frenzy, dodging the bolts. Morganwg was not so favored as to share his master's shelter. An arrow lodged in the fleshy part of his left arm. He pulled it free with a grunt of pain and stared at the bloodstained head. "Deathmetal."

"No better death than you deserve, Morganwg." Donne leaped into the light. He dropped his stout English longbow as he came, the empty quiver slapping against his back. Two bronze blades were jammed into his belt, and the thick iron handle of the Teuton morningstar. Its chain hung about his neck like a tame serpent. He tossed the swords to the Queen and Ada, then made his stand between them, swinging the morningstar in great sweeping arcs over their heads. One of the surviving afrits came too close and had its sloping forehead smashed in.

"Kali!" Kitchener made a gesture of sharp command. The goddess obeyed, but the iron ball scraped her flesh and she jumped back out of range, tusks champing in yellow froth. She would not brave the touch of iron again soon. The dead afrits were testimony enough to its power over seemingly deathless creatures. Blows that would ordinarily only wound had killed, struck with deathmetal.

"You can't keep her off forever, Donne," Morganwg snarled, binding up his wound with a strip of cloth torn from his own shirt. He looked harassed. It was entirely possible that Kitchener would order him to the attack, and he had always been one to prefer assassination to single combat. "The goddess will take you and the Queen at a mouthful!"

Donne lowered the morningstar. The afrits had gone back to their perches, where they shifted from paw to paw and gibbered uneasily among themselves. Kali stood apart, her ornamental skulls gleaming warm ivory in the firelight, biding her time. This lull allowed Donne to answer his archenemy. "I do not require much time. When the rising moon tops that lintel stone there, the Sammain rites all over Britain must be done. The Druids will seek the Queen then, and when she does not reply, they will come. If all your pet horrors were strong enough to face the full strength of the Golden Brotherhood, Kitchener, I doubt you would have waited so long as this to act."

A bold afrit made a sortie, and the morningstar lashed out, ripping one wing back at a crazy angle. Ada finished the beast with two quick cuts of her sword, the blade shining with new-laid spells of destruction.

Lord Kitchener loosed an unintelligible oath. Donne smiled, the morningstar again describing graceful circles overhead as easily as if it had been made of string and paper instead of iron. The weight of it and the strength needed to keep it circling must have been considerable, but Donne never betrayed a hint of weariness. There were huge, unguessed reserves of stamina in the man. "A half hour; less," he said.

"I have not yet tapped all my resources, Donne," Lord Kitchener replied.

"An expert tactician like you? I expected as much." The iron ball held its orbit firm. "Neither have I." I was the only one who knew it for a bluff. The women gained confidence from it, however, and Kitchener lost somewhat of his.

"Why wouldn't you bring the amulet of the djinn?" Morganwg was strident. "They might have shifted the shape of that iron weapon to lumps and nuggets!"

"I came prepared to face the Queen—more than well prepared. Be silent, Morganwg."

"Not by half." The villain mumbled it just loudly enough

to guarantee his master hearing it, then covered his scorn with an unctuous smile.

"Redouble the attack!" shouted Kitchener. His fists shot up to seize the stars.

The afrits could no nothing but obey. They attacked in a wedge of claws and cutting wings. Other beings also sprang from the starry skies. What hells did the Continent hold to spawn such monsters? What sinister paths had Kitchener walked to gather them into his power? Creatures I had no names for, creatures with heads of beasts, the distorted bodies of men, hurled themselves upon Donne, Lady Lovelace, and the Queen. The morningstar whined and sang, smashing bone. The women's ensorcelled bronze swords darted out to sever parts that never should have been joined.

My friends fought hard. Were it an ordinary battle, they would have garnered honorable deaths. There was no way they might stand off Lord Kitchener's minions forever. But—as Donne had said and Kitchener knew—it was not a matter of forever. "Take them! Take them!" the dark man shrilled. I saw his apprehensive eyes mark the rising moon.

"Summon more, Master," Morganwg cried. He stared at Donne. There was a great lust consuming him, a lust to see Donne die. "You have others at your command. Call them!"

"Fool! Would you have me expend everything?"

"If you don't, much good your strategy'll do us once the moon's up."

"Shut your mouth, you coward. You stand here doing nothing, and nothing will be your reward when this battle is done."

"You promised me—!" His hands scrabbled for Lord Kitchener's sleeve and slid from the shielding-spell.

"Get away. You are a slinking wretch, Morganwg, useful once, but now . . . now I wish that Donne had your backbone and you his. He is ten times the man you will ever be!"

Morganwg stared, his gaunt face working. Then he uttered a wordless roar, seized a small rock from the ground, and flung it with all his might. And a simple stone from a madman's hand did what all Kitchener's evil court could not do. The missile struck Donne sharply in the side of the head. He staggered, losing his grip on the morningstar, which flew from his hand on its own momentum and was lost in the outer darkness. He collapsed, and though Ada and Victoria took several more of the monsters, without the iron to protect them it was not long before two braces of afrits separated them, twisted their wrists to make them drop their swords, and held them defenseless.

They bound Ada to one of the upright stones. Kitchener's magic lowered the upended sacrificial slab to earth again, and Victoria was stretched upon it. Donne recovered consciousness in the clutch of two afrits. What remained of his lordship's corps of demons stood in silent attendance. They gave the two swords, abandoned on the grass, a wide berth. Kitchener nudged one with his toe and chuckled.

"Well done, Morganwg. I knew that precious ego of yours would serve me better than yourself."

"That makes no difference to me. Your schemes would have come to nothing but for me. The great Kitchener, ruler of fiends extraordinary, unable to disarm a mortal man! As an officer and man of honor, I trust you'll settle your debt to me handsomely once you come to rule this island."

Kitchener gave Morganwg a surprisingly mild look. "I prefer to pay off my debts more promptly than that—when I acquire them, in fact. I dislike having obligations hanging over my head. Don't I . . . Kali Ma?"

His hand was a flicker of fire-streaked brown, scarcely to be noticed. But it was enough. The goddess gave a howl of exultation and tore the luckless Morganwg open like a chicken. She drank his blood with loud, terrible sounds of relish, then let the shriveled heap of bones and skin fall. A hyena-headed thing crept from the ranks and gnawed the sorry remainder.

Donne himself uttered an exclamation of disgust and pity. Victoria gasped, and Ada looked quickly away. Kitchener appeared amused. "Does it bother you to have your life's work ended so cavalierly, Donne? I'd imagine you would be grateful. You were often reported as saying you wanted Morganwg dead. He would have rejoiced in your death."

"He was my enemy, Kitchener, and Britain is better without him. But by all the gods, he was a human being, and even he was owed some human dignity in death!"

"Don't waste your sympathies on him. He knew how deeply I hated to be reminded of my debts. Now he has served me as partial payment to what I owe this charming divinity." He indicated Kali. "She is an insatiable creditor, which is why I would prefer to master Britain without her aid. Well, Your Majesty? You have seen what it is to die by the Black Mother's hand. You may think you can face it. Perhaps you can. But first you shall see your companions go to her—slowly."

He retrieved one of the stone daggers—like the bronze swords, these had fallen to the ground in the aftermath of the battle. Ada's arms and legs were starfished against the rock. He laid the sharpened blade to her cheek. "Now that Kali has dined so well on Morganwg, perhaps we must pique her appetite again. Will you aid me, Lady Lovelace? I have heard what a perfect hostess you are. I could do this with my bare hands. I may change my mind and use them after all. It will not be as neat—as this." He sliced the dagger down. Ada screamed.

Donne broke free of the afrits and snatched up the other dagger without breaking stride. He was upon Kitchener before the wizard knew it, and the short black blade slashed for his throat. Donne could not miss. He did not.

Kitchener laughed.

The shielding-spell was still protecting him, but nothing armored Donne. My friend was still immobilized, dumbfounded, gazing at the shattered knife in his hand, when Kitchener's own dagger found his heart.

"How could I . . . forget?" He grasped the hilt protruding from his chest and pitched forward.

It is done. Deirdre's voice in my ear had the dying fall of the ebbing sea. The moon darkened.

"Now, my lady—" Kitchener turned again to Ada.

"No! Oh no!" cried the Queen. She strained against the creatures holding her down.

Lord Kitchener came round slowly to look down at her. "Is it surrender? Wise."

"No!" I burst from the stone, released with the completion of Deirdre's geas, freed by the blood of one I had loved now seeping into the earth. "Face me, now. Turn and face me! There is no power on this earth or beyond it that will save you!"

I called on him to aid me, the root of my house, the servant of one master alone. The ground buckled, birthing him, bright red and brilliant with the earthfire, the molten heart of the world, the Red Dragon. He rose up in majesty beneath me, his back my saddle, and from his jaws I took the sunsword of the royal Pictish house, the blade forged when heaven and earth lay together and bred the races of man.

Fire met fire. The Red Dragon roared and leapt into the air. I leaned across his neck, guiding him with my will, until his breath melded with the sunsword's blade. Kali Ma bellowed a challenge, death and bloodspill against us. Death met with fire, and burned. I stabbed for her eyes. The flames shot up as they pierced her skull. Fire boiled the blood she had drunk, and crisped her uncanny flesh to ashes. Where these blew, the gods may surmise.

Kali was destroyed, but Kitchener still had his legions. They swarmed like maggots, and like maggots we crushed them. I blocked Donne's death from my mind, aglow with the reconquered joy of mastering my powers, of cutting down my foes. But my joy was short-lived. There were too many of them. Kitchener no longer directed their attack, but bent himself to calling up more and still more horrors. The circle of Stonehenge grew a ghastly crop of serpent-bodied men, many-limbed and horned demons. The Red Dragon's fire ravaged their ranks, and the sunsword scythed them down, but it was not enough.

I saw the final being Kitchener summoned. It was a bull, white and gold and red, with the grave face of a bearded man, a jewelled diadem, and eagle's wings. With the one afrit he had spared from combat, Kitchener dragged the Queen across the bull's back. He was shouting foreign words above the din. What could they be but the evocation of some power still more dire than Kali Ma? And how would he buy its service but with Victoria's life? We were surrounded, weighed down by the numbers of his creatures. They clawed at me, biting and tearing wherever they could get a purchase. I did butcher's work with the sunsword, hacking them away. We would not be able to fight a way through them in time. Moonlight shone on the dagger Kitchener held poised in the air above Victoria's breast. It was steel.

A human shout filled the night. The moon, resting on the upper edge of the lintel stone, cast phantom light. And the phantoms rode to meet her.

Their steeds were clattering bone, but their pale faces were plain enough to see, and the clothyard shafts their frontriders loosed were real enough to wound and kill. One struck the man-bull in the flank. He bawled and lurched aside. A second shaft pierced his temple. He toppled against one of the standing stones, and his death throe rooted it over. The lintel it had helped uphold crashed down, obliterating a knot of Kitchener's beasts. Victoria rolled in the opposite direction and seized her abandoned sword.

The riders came on, like storm clouds racing across an August sky. Boudicca was there, hair flying, calling the wrath of all the gods down on her foes. William and Canute rode after her, Lord Caradoc and Arthur in the van. They were the royal dead of Britain, denied completion of the rites that would make them rest this night. They had risen, as they must, and they rode against the man who had marred the Queen's rituals. Charles himself rode last of all, and I could see the blood still fresh on his face, the grim purpose as he spurred his skeletal steed.

They annihilated all the monsters that Kitchener had ever commanded. The confines of Stonehenge became a charnel house of unnatural corpses. It was a slaughter in the truest sense of the word. The sunsword in my hand illuminated those few creatures who tried to fight back—and failed. One cannot kill the dead.

Kitchener tried aping Donne's maneuver, using his steel dagger to keep the noble dead at bay. His shielding-spell glowed palely with the strength he was expending to maintain it. A red-haired warrior woman reined in her mount just out of his range and sprang from the saddle. I knew her from her court portraits as Great Elizabeth, Britain's Queen. Even in fighting garb, without jewels, lace, or satin trappings, she was formidable.

"Llew's death! I am heartily sick of your toys, fellow!" Hands on hips she contemplated him. The others made an end to their massacre and one by one joined a growing circle of ghosts ringing him in.

"Stay back! Back, all of you!" A dew of poorly mastered panic was on his brow. "This blade is deathmetal!"

"Deathmetal!" Elizabeth's laughter was echoed hollowly by the rest. "What is that, to the dead?" She unbound a golden sickle from her waist and sliced open his shielding-spell like a wineskin. Before he could speak another word, Victoria leapt in front of him and with a single deadly stroke severed his head from his shoulders.

"Deathmetal," said Victoria. She picked up Kitchener's head by the hair and held it high, to the cheers of the assembled ghosts of her bloodline. "It bought him his." The dead gave another battle cry and beat with sword and spear-butt on their shields in thunderous triumph.

I cut Ada free of the standing stone and stroked her wounded cheek. Flesh—which is after all only earth in a warmer guise—became the seamless whole of water under my fingers. I left not a scar. She never thanked me. We looked at each other wordlessly for a breath or two, then tears flooded her eyes, spilled down her cheeks, and she ran to throw herself on Donne's corpse. The sound of her keening would have frightened a *bean sidhe*.

Victoria knotted Kitchener's head to her belt, the proper place for that grisly trophy. I never expected her to faint into my arms or praise the gods for bringing me to the rescue. She had shown some weakness before, but in the final confrontation there was no denying her inner strength and depthless courage. She was as great a master of spell and sword as I, and I would not have had her as anything less. She sheathed her blade and slipped her arm round my waist.

"I am glad you are here, John," she said. Her voice choked off to a half-uttered sob. She too was crying, and so was I. We did not look at each other; only Donne, and poor, unhappy Ada. Death could not cheat him of his nobility, nor take any pride in this conquest. Ada removed the stone dagger from his deathwound, composed his limbs and closed his eyes between her sobs. He seemed to be taking his ease upon the divan at home, lost in contemplation of the final, insoluble mystery.

A flurry of sound riffled through the lines of the British royal dead. It grew louder, until it demanded our attention. The mustered ghosts and their skeleton steeds thinned and parted. Between their two foggy wings came an old man in shimmering robes of green and blue and gold. These fell to either side of the huge, catlike beast he straddled. Silver antlers sprang from its brow, and translucent dragonfly wings from its shoulders.

He dismounted and knelt at my feet. "Please," I said, compelling him to rise. "You are my Teacher. I should be the one to kneel."

"I do not kneel to your rank, but to your valor." He beckoned his fabulous mount to draw near. It rubbed its heavy head against his arm and purred like any common kit. "You have never seen Tam's true shape before, have you? And it's been long since you saw me in my Teacher's robe." He looked around the stone-girt circle. Wherever his glance fell, the bodies of the slain monsters vanished like sun-touched dew. The British royal dead murmured among themselves.

My Teacher looked at them long, then said, "Yes, we are Pictish men, this warrior-mage and I. We sleep with the five elements of this world forever in our blood. I sense you fear us. Why? We have never had any quarrel with you."

A second time the ranks parted. A white bearded titan of a man stepped through, his robes white also, and a king's gemmed circlet in his flowing hair. "We fear you, Pictish men. We fear you for the wrong we did you so long ago. The wrong *I* did you." He leaned forward on his Druid's staff. "When we rose from our grave mounds this night, the rites undone, we might have wandered aimlessly over British soil forever. But it was you who called to us; you who told us of the peril; you who sent us flying, armed and mounted, to this place in the hour of danger and need. Why? Why have you saved our land and our line? Have you forgot the ancient betrayal? I have not. I am Bran, falsely called the Blessed, and I do not understand."

I answered for my Teacher; for my people. "Britain is ours as well as yours, Lord Bran. You took the help we might have given you freely, if you had only asked for it. Your folk and mine have been outcasts from each other for too long. I can tell you from my own experience of the outcast's lot, never to know rest, or true contentment. I always felt as if some part of me were missing. The living have too short a time to waste over the quarrels of the dead. Let your children open your cities to us, and we will open our mountains to you again. One land, one people, and one tie of magic to bind us."

The dead raised a lusty cheer.

Victoria embraced me. "It shall be as you say, John. This island will be one. What more can content you, my love?" I did not answer. My eyes were on Donne.

"You cared for him, then, so deeply?"

I kissed her with all the tenderness I had in me. "You question that because it disturbs you, my beloved? I did love him."

"No." Her words were grave and simple. "I ask because I feel the same. I loved him too, as did she." She indicated Ada. "As did many. You above us all have some right to that love."

"I wish it were my blood that spilled here tonight rather than his." I slashed the sunsword impotently at shadows. "I am master of all Pictish magics, but death—ah, death is a natural part of the world, and my magic can never step across the bounds of what is natural."

The Red Dragon pawed the earth nervously, for I had mentioned the one veil past which our most learned wizards had never penetrated. He took refuge from his fears by flowing back into the hidden places that were his home. Our powers took the qualities of the elements and shifted them subtly. Death was not subtle. Death, and what came after, lay beyond our teachings.

I felt Victoria take my free hand in hers. "Mine can." She raised her bronze sword until its blade twinned the sunsword. The twisting lines of power jumped from her weapon to mine, lashing them together. "Annwn!" she shouted, raising our united swords to the heavens.

And the dead answered, *"Annwn!"*

I tried to pull away from her and could not. My sword held me. She released the binding of our swords and stepped away from me, her other hand dipping into the bosom of her white robes to pluck out a spectrally shining branch of mistletoe. This was the holy plant the Druids only gathered with the golden sickle, at the proper hour, to be caught before it fell to earth in priestess-woven webs.

"I will bring your friend back to you, John," she said. The parasite plant cast its own peculiar luminescence on her face. "I must walk in Annwn some day; this night is only a foretaste."

She laid the mistletoe on the slab of sacrifice. The rock parted like the petals of a rose. The Rules Britannia levitated through the irised opening. She sheathed her sword and took the carved box from the fire, which vanished as soon as its guarding work was no longer needed. She had described the box precisely to Donne, and we had both seen it in visions. It was like welcoming an old friend home after a long and wearying war.

"Victoria, I cannot see you risk yourself. The Golden Brotherhood will be coming. Do you think they'll allow you to do what you intend for Donne's sake?"

"No." She answered quite calmly. The Rules were hugged to her bosom. I could imagine her holding our first child that way. "They will say I am working sacrilege. After death, the soul must be reborn, but not to the same shell it abandoned. There is a silly child's tale of a magic cauldron that could restore dead warriors to fighting life, but they never spoke. An animate corpse is not the same thing as a living man. I will bring back his soul from Annwn, or I will leave mine there. The Brotherhood will do what they dare to stop me. Kiss me now, John. The dead are going home, and I must follow."

I kissed her, but I did not let her go. "I'm coming with

you." I sheathed the sunsword and placed my hands around the Rules. "I swear it by my magic and yours. Annwn will gain two new souls or lose one."

Her face was regal, composed, unreadable. "We must hurry," was all she said.

So we left Stonehenge together, my love and I. She took up the holy mistletoe again and used it to light our way as we trailed behind the departing dead. We rode in a slow, pale cavalcade, up and down the rolling, moonlit land. They kept to no human pathways I could see. But then, the moon soon was gone and left us virtually blind. High walls of earth towered above us. We had entered a black gorge of some kind. A few stars could still be seen in the ever-narrowing strip of sky overhead, but all too quickly the walls of the chasm met and blocked these from sight.

I drew the sunsword, and added its light to the mistletoe's tremulous gleam. There was little to see. Underfoot I felt the dry crackle of sere grass, here and there made sadder by small white specks of alien wildflowers. The path grew tighter, and Victoria took the lead.

"How can you see where we are going?" I asked.

"I follow the ghosts."

I strained my eyes and craned my neck, but could see nothing beyond the branch of mistletoe which she held like a traveller's lantern. I said as much.

"I don't see the phantoms either," she admitted. "I can just make out the shine of their horses' bones. That is what we follow."

From far ahead, I thought I detected the sound that horses' hooves make when wading across a shallow stream. The empty splashing sound grew louder, and a smell of weedy lakewater came with it. The way widened for us. The surrounding dark grew less totally black. We could see the difference of shade between rock walls and overhanging sky once more, although it was not a sky made to hold moon or stars. Mists swirled and streaked its curving upturned bowl. The smell and sound of lakewater were unmistakable.

"We are alone, John."

We were. A monumental pile of disjointed horses' bones lay heaped at our feet. The dead had taken flight from our company, returning to their homeland eagerly. It was the diffused light of their winged souls that lit the night of Annwn. By their glow, we saw the black barge waiting for us.

Why do the living, who have the earth, seek Annwn? asked

one of the four veiled and crowned women who knelt in the sombre vessel.

Victoria bowed with reverence. "Dark Queen, passage is not forbidden. We come peacefully."

No. You will only disturb the peace of Annwn. But come. Passage is never forbidden into our land.

We stepped into the barge, which tilted under our weight like any ordinary ship. I did my best not to gaze too long or too closely at the four mourning Queens, but I had no choice but to look at the stiff, white, fully armed body of a tall, fair man stretched at length on a pallet in the center of the barge.

Make your passage silently. Arthur sleeps. His soul has ridden and fought hard this night. Now he must rest, if ever he means to wake again.

We crossed the ghostly lake and came to the other side. No sooner were we ashore than Victoria turned to the four Queens and said, "I am Victoria, Lady of Britain. I hold the Rules." She let them all see the carven box in her keeping. "By their spells and powers, I conjure you to keep to this bank of the holy lake until we return. Another will be with us."

Another? Flesh or soul?

"Soul." She picked a berry from the mistletoe and placed it at the feet of the first Dark Queen. "Returning to flesh."

It holds. We will wait only as long as the light lasts to keep us. The mistletoe berry sent out a pathetically weak spark, but a steady one.

I have heard them give many shapes to Annwn. Some say it is an island, some say it lies deep beneath the earth, and some that it can only be found above the stars. I cannot answer. There may be other ways to reach that dismal land than the one we chose. I will be content if I never discover any of them. All I can say is that it is a land as much like and unlike our sweet earth as any place existent can be, and still be understood by mortals.

Everything was very still. A great, boundless peace reigned. I saw trees and grass, the shy shapes of animals and birds, but heard nothing of their comings or goings or calls. Our feet passed noiselessly. I snapped off a twig, hoping for some sound to convince me that I had not lost my hearing. The wood made a reassuring crack, but the twig itself thinned to mist in my fingers.

"Where are they?" I asked Victoria. "Where are the dead? Is Annwn such a large place?"

"Annwn is written to be the size of a skin," said Victoria. "What sort of skin, or whether it was first cut in strips, I really don't know. It doesn't matter, John. We would never find Donne's spirit in the time allotted us if we had to locate him physically. This place looks as good as any for what I have to do."

We had come out from among the trees into what looked like a meadow. My eyes were entirely used to the gloom, capable of seeing various shades of blackness and distinguishing shapes and distances as if I were still on daylit earth. Victoria knelt in the short, brushy grass and opened the box containing the Rules Britannia. She leafed through the carefully lettered pages, then began a sweet song in a low, low voice. In that quiet land it sounded loud and brazen as a fire alarm. I almost clapped my hand across her mouth. Human noises here seemed dangerous, or defiling.

By the time she ended the song, my teeth were on edge. I took a deep breath of relief. "Is he here?"

"Some of them are."

A block of grey smoke belled and rippled between us and the trees. I thought I could just perceive the smudged outlines of human faces. "Donne?" I called tentatively.

"These are the newly dead. They still know enough to come when called. We must thin their ranks further." She reached up her arms. "Love me, John."

The uncanniness of place and circumstance would have certainly put all thought or inclination for lovemaking straight out of my head, had I been expecting it. Victoria's request was too sudden for me to protest in any way, and she followed up on the advantage of surprise with all the arts she had garnered over the years. I could not resist, or even reflect on the spectacle we gave the dead. When we had finished, the trees were visible through the shifting bits of fog.

"You see how quickly they forget? What we did meant nothing to many of them, and so they went away. The ones left still remember pleasure. This is what we must do now, John. We must go through all the ties of earth—conjure up food and drink, laughter, dance, even grief—until we can find the one shade new enough to Annwn to identify with all we show."

"But that will take— How long have we?" I looked at the branch of mistletoe. The moon berries were not so bright. Victoria saw this as well, and her face darkened.

"Not . . . as long as I'd hoped. This branch was not

harvested as fresh as might be. The calls of separation will take too long." She was silent for a time, then said, "John, go back to the barge. Go back to earth. I will discover Donne's soul and send it after you."

"I'm not leaving you here. How will you get back?"

"Go, I said!" She struck the ground with her fists. She was plainly afraid of the decision she had made, but she was not going to back down; not she. "I am the one responsible for Donne's death! If I had been more of a true Queen and less of a pleasure-giddy girl, the Rules would never have been taken from me!" She tore Kitchener's severed head from her belt and glared at the blank eyes, forcing her fear into hate, the better to hide it from me. "It is my fault that your treachery got so far," she growled at the awful trophy in her hands. "Go! Follow your lost soul to whatever foreign hell it's found!" She heaved the head far away. The gathered ghosts scattered in panic from the gruesome ball.

All but one. It stooped, and put on the lines of a human body, the better to investigate this unexpected find.

"*Donne!*" I shouted, and the blazes with the peace of Annwn. The spirit paused and regarded me. It was his; I had no doubts of it. "We have found him! Now we can go," I said to Victoria.

"Not yet. He must want to come with us."

"Want to—? Who wouldn't want to leave this place?" Her objection struck me as absurd; nonetheless, she clung to it. She was not without justification. In the course of our very short exchange, the spirit was already drifting off. It had lost interest in Kitchener's head too quickly.

"Donne! Donne, come back!" The spirit might have heard me, but did not respond. I sought to stop it by more direct means, causing the grey soil to rise up in a stout wall, obstructing its path. The ghost did not pass through this, but calmly floated alongside to reach the point where the wall ended. Extending the wall did not discourage it. It had all the time in creation; we did not.

"Summon him, Victoria!" I cried, still building up the earthen wall. "Bind him!"

"John, that's impossible. Ghosts are only summoned and bound when the sorcerer stands in the living world and the ghost in Annwn. We are in Annwn too. It's hopeless. We shall lose him after all. Go back to the barge, my dearest; please, go back!"

"Not alone. Not alone, after all this." I added to the wall

and made it flame. I set a ring of earthfire around Donne's spirit. Fire was too close kin to his own ethereal substance to contain him; he ignored it. I fell back upon hemming him in with the wall. I would die in the grey realm of Annwn, building an unending wall to keep in a dead man. I wondered how long I would labor at it before it drove me out of my mind.

Then I thought I must be going mad. Ada was beside me. She wore the gown she had chosen when she first visited Donne in the Tower, and she was smiling. I heard her speak, saying, "I have always enjoyed the works Scarlatti composed for the violin, Mr. Donne. Is this your instrument? Oh! A Stradivarius. You are a very fortunate man. Will you favor me with a sample of your playing?"

She looked as real as Victoria or I.

I dreamed I heard the sweet, plaintive strains of the familiar old instrument weaving a thread of yearning sorrow through the lifeless realm of Annwn.

The spirit paused to listen.

The Stradivarius itself took shape in the air between us, until I could see the mellow, aged glow of the pampered wood. Thin, sensitive fingers bowed a haunting melody. The ghost came nearer, fitting misty strands of his substance into the playing hands like gloves.

"Victoria—" I began. She stilled me with a gesture. Her expression of concentration was absolute. Inside my head I heard her say, *We Britons did not steal your Pictish magic because we had none of our own. There were Druidic spells that were old when Blessed Bran's soul was still many bodies' distance away. We may have neglected these ancient sorceries, but they can never be forgotten. They are illusion, and superb, unmatched command of illusion. They are in our blood. They are the dreams of the British soul.*

Scenes formed against the backdrop of the earthen wall I had erected: our comfortable digs in Baker Street, a fire in the hearth, the pungent smell of shag, a murky tobacco-smoke haze, the inviting sparkle of the tantalus. I felt something soft and cushiony bump into my elbow. "I do beg your pardon, Dr. Weston, I'm sure," Mrs. Hendrik exclaimed. I had nudged her bosom, and she looked as if she hadn't minded it a bit. "Is Mr. Donne—? Oh, *there* you are, sir. Come and have your nice tea before it gets cold." She set the painted tray down on our table and poured two steaming cups.

She was no sooner gone than the door flew open and a young man in rumpled clothes stumbled in, full of the desperate look of a drunken sot or a hopeless madman. "Thank all the gods I've found you in time, Mr. Donne! I am at my wits' end! Only you can help. There has been a crime, a crime most unspeakable. I have witnessed it, I know all, but no one will believe me. If you will only— Ah, but what is the use? Why should you be any different from the others? The problem is too great, those involved are too highly placed, the risk I run in coming to you is unthinkable. And for what? For what? To be laughed at by you in turn, and your friend Dr. Weston there? No, no, it is better that I go. Forget my face! For your own sake, forget you ever saw me!"

The distraught man lunged for the door, but the spirit was there before him. The hands holding the Stradivarius were completely opaque and real, a quality which spread like a blush up the arms, down the torso to the legs and feet, and lastly back up again until the face was cleanly etched and formed, though colorless. This solidified apparition forced our caller to sit down, then laid aside its violin and picked up a full teacup. Victoria's illusion was perfect, but it was illusion. The spectre drank impalpable tea from a cup that was not truly there. As he drank, Annwn's grey filtered from him the way the nebulous mists of dawn give way to sunlight. The more life flowed into him, the greater contrast he made with the conjured irreality of teacup, violin, harried client, and Baker Street flat. These departed gradually, softly, and I was left—smiling like an idiot, weeping like a child—to face my dear friend, Mr. Brihtric Donne.

He smiled too when he saw he was sipping nothing out of nothing. His grip on my shoulders when he embraced me was warm. Strong. Alive.

"Good old Weston. The final curtain is not yet to fall."

EPILOGUE

The Adventure of the Tired Player

We stood at the railing of London Bridge, Donne and I. Beneath us, the Thames flowed with unhurried majesty, the rainbow waters swirling around the ancient stone pilings. Spindly houses that must have stood on this bridge from oldest times tilted inwards, giving us grudging shelter from the late winter winds.

I pulled up the lambskin collar of my greatcoat and tried not to give in to the cold. Donne had summoned me to this meeting, giving no reason for his choice of such an uncomfortable rendezvous. I was still a frequent visitor to 221B, and Donne had been told a score of times to treat the Palace as his second home. Something was troubling my friend. He would tell me of it when he liked.

To pass the time until he might decide to speak, I said, "The Queen's Act of Toleration became law today, Donne. We were just celebrating the event when your message arrived."

Donne rested his knotted hands on the bridge railing. A gull dipped with the wind and he followed its flight. "Your lawmakers have a peculiar sense of humor, Weston. Toleration is a lukewarm word, and the people may embrace the letter of the Queen's Act lukewarmly."

"I fail to see what is wrong with it. What *were* we to do about all those folk Kitchener brought into the country with him? Send 'em back where they came from? That would take years to accomplish, and not a man jack of them wants to go! They're human beings, Donne. They did Kitchener's bidding because they hadn't a choice—all save the hashashin, and the Queen's guards handled *them* all right."

He tilted his head a bit to one side and smiled ever so slightly. "You don't follow me, Weston. My objections have nothing to do with those the late Lord Kitchener forced to enter Britain, to take over the roles of Victoria's Palace staff. I have gone among them, and learned how it really was that our recent foe coerced their allegiance. The stories

I was on the point of losing him, the man who had seemingly stepped into my life from out of my own imagination. When first I wrote of Brihtric Donne, I had no idea that such a person truly could exist, yet a part of me insisted that he must. He was the product of my own lonely musings, my desire for a brave and noble friend whose very strengths of mind and character might heal my own lacks. I had never questioned the circumstances of his arrival too closely. I command magic, but I cherish miracle. When a miracle lies cupped within your own two hands, you hardly dare to breathe for fear of startling it to flight.

The miracle was not that Brihtric Donne was real, but that his reality fulfilled the sum of all my yearnings, all my dreams. More: His were the penetrating eyes that saw through my excuses, the keen mind that analyzed and drew sense out of my confusion, and the fond heart that knew and taught me that I must be the source of my own salvation.

And for him, I was the final problem. It was as if now that my spirit no longer needed him to lend me his aid, he would depart. I felt as if somewhere a great curtain were slowly descending between us.

"Where will you go? And why? Say what you like, I can't help feeling that I am somehow to blame for this. Is it so?"

"You?" He laughed. "Still the romancer, Weston. You impute all sorts of dark, secret motivations to what is really a very simple affair. I wish to travel abroad again. I want to tour the Continent, perhaps travel beyond, to the lands that Kitchener explored. We have learned how perilous it is to ignore the outer world. Britain was surprised by foreign magics once, yet survived; she may not be as lucky the next time. Don't fret; I will be coming back. There is also a great deal I mean to explore on these shores. Do you remember Master Wells? He came out of Sir Hugo's family mound unharmed and went right back to work on his time machine. Think of all the mysteries there are in Britain's past! I think I shall enjoy solving one or two of them before I retire to Sussex and keep bees. However, I shall never again be able to read my own monograph *On the Isolation of the Queen* without thinking of your wife."

I thought that my emotions must overwhelm me. "Donne, the debt that we—that I owe you—"

He clasped my hand firmly. "—is as nothing next to that which I owe you. You gave me life, Weston. All else pales in comparison. More than you know, you gave me life."

Evening had turned to night. We saw the lights of London come on all up and down the Thames, like the grand processions of the *sidhe* when they ride out of the hollow mountains. A thin dusting of snow began to fall.

We said our goodbyes there, on London Bridge, in the midst of a snowfall. We passed between the houses sheltering us and came to the street that went over the bridge. Lanterns were lit, snowflakes dancing in their light like moths. We walked some distance together along the bridgeway, until we came to the Axe and Singer, a rustic public house and inn. I could not bear the thought of drawing out our leavetaking, so pounced at this opportunity for Donne and me to part ways. And yet, as he ambled on, I could not resist standing beneath the swinging sign to well-wish him with my eyes until he was out of sight.

He had only gone a few houses farther when a hooded figure stepped into his path. He stopped, and I saw the two of them apparently in earnest conversation. The other carried a small travelling bag, which was set down at Donne's feet. Donne shook his head several times in the course of their exchange—slowly and gently at first, then more and more emphatically.

I played the spy. Keeping from the lantern light I slipped from housefront to housefront, the better to observe this strange meeting. I might have spared myself the pains of secrecy. By the time I had inched up on them, the discussion was over. The other bent to take up the travelling bag. In standing upright, her hood fell back. Ada's dark eyes showed no tears, not even when she asked him one last time to take her with him. His mouth barely moved as he denied her. He remained where he was when she finally turned from him and departed into the whirling whiteness.

Surely what I saw on his face was only melted snow.

I went back to the inn.

About the Author

Esther Friesner was born in Brooklyn, NY. She received her B.A. from Vassar and her M.A. and Ph.D. from Yale, where she taught for several years. Now a full-time science fiction and fantasy author, she has published short stories and poems in *Asimov's, Amazing,* and *Fantasy Book,* and is the author of four fantasy novels. She currently resides in Connecticut with her husband and two children.